BAGHLAN BOY

Michael Crowley

The Book Guild Ltd

First published in Great Britain in 2020 by
The Book Guild Ltd
9 Priory Business Park
Wistow Road, Kibworth
Leicestershire, LE8 0RX
Freephone: 0800 999 2982
www.bookguild.co.uk
Email: info@bookguild.co.uk
Twitter: @bookguild

Typeset in 12pt Minion Pro

Printed and bound by CPI Group (UK) Ltd, Croydon, CR0 4YY

ISBN 978 1913551 049

British Library Cataloguing in Publication Data.
A catalogue record for this book is available from the British Library.

For Polly

'...tears he wept for his foiled journey home.'

The Odyssey

PROLOGUE

Baghlan Province, Afghanistan, September 2002

Eleven-year-old Farood squatted by a stream, his eyes fixed on a green warbler. He delved into a pocket for the crumbs he'd been saving for the bird. One rock closer and the bird would be in diving reach of the boy. It called – a warning rippling through the air – and the wind began to brush off the foothills behind him, dusting his eyelids, but he refused to blink. His right eye was lazy after an accident with a stick whilst playing with his older brother when he was five. He tasted the dust on his tongue, glanced at his father striding from the edge of the village below him. The warbler had vanished.

A blessing was said over handfuls of rice, three eggs and two small flatbreads. The last of the smoke loitered inside the main chamber of the four-room earthen house.

'He's been talking to the birds again.' His elder brother teased him.

'I'm going to catch that bird and then mother will make a jar for it.'

'You're too slow, Spider. You couldn't catch a hen.' Karam offered his palm as a target for his younger brother.

Their mother tugged at Farood's shoulder. 'Eat your meals.'

Turn the globe either way and you were having a light snack

on the go. Here it was a meal, a meal for five people. Hunger in Baghlan was like the wind, the dryness and the invasions.

'Karam loves a girl.' Farood's presence alone was a provocation to the eighteen-year-old.

'Shut up, Spider.'

'He wants to marry her.'

The woodpile in the next room was almost gone. Winter was moving down the valley behind September dust storms. Fuel for hot meals could not be paid for. A wedding could never be talked about.

'We had a thousand sheep when I was a boy. Across two hills. We would round them up on horses. The house was full of people and food.'

Before the Russians. Their father is tall, even for a Pashtun. Farood gazed at the sweep of his god-like arms as he gave most of the food to his sons. They believed his strength came from some elixir within him, from his race. They ask him to tell them about when he rode in the buzkashi, of the horses tearing at each other's necks. Two-year-old Yashfa tried to touch the griddle, but her mother seized her back to her lap. Outside from within the dust whorls, faint snaps of Taliban rifle fire were heard in the village. It was autumn and the Taliban were making their way to the foothills. War was a background sound, like radio on a city street; it varied with the seasons, came and went with the movement of birds and the appearance of tulips. The family talked about other villagers, of the behaviour of their children, of the possibility of rain. The wind fluttered the red curtain entrance and Farood suddenly noticed the fern green warbler again, turning its bill like a key. He crept towards it, taking some bread from his mouth and flicking it across the dirt. His father called to him, but he stood his ground. *We'll see how slow I am.* The bird and the boy froze. A man appeared alongside the sheep pen. Older than his father and taller, enveloped by a deep blue khet. Across his chest hung an ammunition belt, on his shoulder he carried a PK variant machine gun. Farood and his bird were invisible to him. He disappeared through the village. Then a second younger man carrying an AK47 assault rifle, pitted and weathered, behind him a third, no more than eighteen. He carried a Lee Enfield rifle date-stamped '1915'.

'Have you seen the Americans?'

Farood shook his head at the fighter, whose eyes targeted his father.

'Who is in there?' the fighter demanded.

'My wife, my child – a small girl,' answered Farood's father.

'Soon he will have to come with us. Allahu Akbar.'

He strode off to catch up with his comrades. The bird had gone once more. Farood closed his lips around a boiled egg as the softened cracks of rifles salvaged from old invaders began to pierce the wind once more. There were more fighters on the slopes, but no sound of the return – the impossible rapidity of American gunfire. The fat-tailed sheep would have to remain penned until tomorrow, or the day after.

Their mother washed her husband's winter shalwar in a trough on the street; Farood poured water into another trough for the sheep whilst Karam herded strays with a staff and their father sang to Yashfa, his Russian-made sniper rifle across his knees. He used sheep fat for gun oil, but it was as true as the day his brother took it from a Russian prisoner. When the Taliban move on, they will shoot a bird for the pot. Yashfa ambled from the house to watch her younger brother.

*

Twenty-five thousand feet above, a drone was circling. It had been hovering in the area for nearly an hour, its presence requested by marines who hadn't fired a round all morning. Now the sandstorm had left them looking for ghosts. The sands of Nevada were still; it was early morning and the sun had been up for an hour. The drone's operator was Major Catherine Lake. Lake used to be a fighter pilot, the second female Afro-American fighter pilot in history. Now she was a drone jockey. The pilot of an MQ-1 Predator unmanned aircraft system from a desk seven miles outside Las Vegas at Nellis Air Force Base. Her husband was pleased she'd been grounded, as was her new co-pilot, sensor operator Ryan Marshall, but she wasn't. Her maternal instincts hadn't registered yet and she missed being airborne. Of course, g-force, ejector seats and a host of other technical reasons prevented her from flying, but she didn't feel pregnant. She wondered if those instincts would ever make a show, whether the military had drilled them away. Less than four months in a cockpit, but a termination was out of the question so here she was, at a desk in a camouflaged trailer approaching the end of a seven-hour night shift, pretending to fly something on a television screen whose journey had already been programmed for her. Lake watched the drone's nose roll across the biscuit-coloured folds of the earth. *Where are they?* The enemy hid inside creases and crevices of brown paper, occasionally glowing on her flat-screen microscope. Lake and Marshall were being dry cleaned from every angle by revolving fans. A marine captain yapped at Lake out of the silo speakers.

'Well, there must be *some* fucker down there because someone is *fucking* shooting at us.'

The drone's synthetic aperture radar, handy for looking through haze, had been removed last month to preserve fuel – or, as Lake saw it, to lengthen her shift. Marshall switched to infra-red.

'I found them for you, Captain.'

'That's excellent, Major. Now would you mind fucking *shooting* them for me?'

Lake pressed a button and, after a two-second satellite delay, her last 114 Hellfire missile made its way to Farood's house, fusing it with the sandstorm. The little red glows on her screen were stubbed out and her shift was almost over. She began to return her drone to Forward Operating Base Delaram and halfway through its journey she was relieved by the day shift.

At home in her quarters her husband was still asleep, until the sound of her keys landing on the hall table woke him. She stood at the end of the bed in the semi-darkness; he offered his hand. Lake moved closer and he gently placed the flat of his hand on her belly.

'Has she moved today?' he asked.

PART ONE

PART ONE

ONE

Senior Officer Robertson was sitting in his wing office looking down the fifty-metre length of D wing. The office was at the top of a hexagon from where he could see every cell door. It was quiet time: that long-awaited mid-morning pause after cleaning and before feeding time. The half dozen lads privileged to be cleaners were lounging under the light and sound of the wing television, watching a music channel and working their way through a loaf of toast. A new lad, not yet assimilated to the group and its hierarchy, was standing alone at a window, gazing out across the grassed concourse at the centre of the prison, his mop and bucket idle. Robertson was into his fifties but still very much in shape. He had strong, weathered features, was barrel-chested and, with his white sleeves always rolled, bore the appearance of a naval captain as much as a prison officer. He was never anything else other than calm, which annoyed everyone, especially other officers. Beside him sat Scully, a relatively new officer who fitted in well with his colleagues, having started in the job burned out. He was balding, youthful and glum, and within weeks began to say how the job was *affecting his relationship*. Not to be accused of too much world-weariness, Scully was now defiantly growing a moustache for charity.

Robertson took the briefest of phone calls before responding to Scully's beseeching glance. 'C wing are moving four lads over here,' announced Robertson.

'Why do they always send the shite to us?' asked Scully.

'They can't leave them on reception wing. The place is filling up with rioters, some of them from London, most of whom won't cope.'

'Maybe they'll learn something, sir.'

'Isn't that why we're all here?'

That was Robertson all over, thought Scully. He liked to take lads on, straighten them out, never tired of it. If it meant talking to them in the middle of the night, spinning their pads three times a week or even rolling around on the floor with them. Robertson made the job harder than it needed to be. Prisoners didn't want officers in their face, asking them to think about their past, their future; they were taking a break right now and wanted to be left alone. The given logic among officers was that prisoners have a season when they will change and if this wasn't it, there was nothing you could do. Most of the cons knew how to run a wing as well as, if not better than, a lot of officers, and people like Robertson always wanted to disturb the natural order, like by giving the Afghan a cleaning job when he'd only been here five minutes.

Scully looked down the wing and shook his head. 'You let the fucker have a slice of toast and he gives it to the ducks.'

It was forbidden to feed the birds; the scraps only brought the rats. Birds came to the prison grounds in numbers. Gulls scavenged and fought with jackdaws, oystercatchers guarded the flower beds where they nested, ducks sidled up to arrow loop windows and gates. Some smaller birds strayed into the glass-domed wings. Soon they were beating their backs against the roof for the skies and not all of them made it to the Out. Prisoners would whip them with rigid wet towels twisted into staves, leave them on the landing for cleaners to sweep up.

Farood was trying to get some crust to a pied wagtail dipping behind the ducks. It was too slow.

Scully dropped a file from an exaggerated height. 'Do you know what I was thinking, sir?'

'I doubt it.'

'Maybe we should get the lads to update their own files.'

'Might be easier to read. Lock up the cleaners, shall we?'

Robertson marched out of the office with authority, like a referee onto a playing field, like the former soldier he was. The huddle under the television stood up and swallowed as he passed them.

'Behind your doors now, lads.'

Farood smiled blithely at Robertson. He smiled, the senior officer thought, whilst other prisoners grinned, usually because they had got away with something. The Afghan lad was tall, sinuous, his features sharp, always pointing at those that spoke to him.

'Farood, don't feed the birds. There's no need to.'

'Sorry. I didn't give them much.'

'How are you finding the wing?'

'Okay, boss.'

And all the time smiling. *How could anyone wear that expression in his situation*, wondered Robertson. Maybe he didn't have the words. Who would have the words after being sentenced to thirty years at the age of nineteen? Robertson tried to recall another lad who'd been sentenced to that. He couldn't.

'Farood, I want you to go to the kitchens and fetch the dinner trolley.'

'You'll have to show me.'

'It's alright, Barker will go with you.'

'Okay, thank you, boss.'

His courtesy was unsettling. It felt antiquated. Robertson wondered if the lad really was nineteen; he looked older. Not just taller and fuller than most others, but more cognisant of something.

Lads drifted back leisurely from education or other regime activities. Movement was an opportunity to catch up with other prisoners in one way or another, to get some air time. The sun was making a valiant last effort in north Lancashire and a few officers had responded by sporting dark glasses. Prisoners walked in small groups, hands down the front of their burgundy jogging bottoms. No one's hair was longer than a number one razor. Robertson studied the D wing traffic; Miss Nichols (Officer Nipples to Scully) ticked down a list as they passed the gate. Prisoners in cells on the balcony went to their doors; downstairs lads positioned themselves in the dinner queue.

Michael Atherton made his entrance into the wing without announcement, lingering outside the wing office, surveying the amphitheatre. He had the hardest of ivory and grey eyes, and they sought nothing in particular, merely the starting pistol of a reciprocal glance. Atherton was twenty. In a few months, he would be graduating from the young offender institution to a less frenetic adult establishment where he was sure to make an impression. He wasn't big, but he was solid, rigid and ready to snap. His north Manchester stare found two new lads moving into a double pad, unloading a plastic bag each of photos, letters and shower gels. SO Robertson was busy exchanging pleasantries at the dinner counter as Atherton got into range of their voices. They were not Scousers, so there would be no comeback from elsewhere. Walking straight into their pad, he picked up a shower gel.

'Got any burn?'

It was on. They had to crack him now or hand over the Golden Virginia. Atherton awarded them the dignity of handing the packet over rather than just picking it up, but he left with no promises in his wake.

It was feeding time. Mooching behind the counter in

whites were Scully on apples and sweetcorn; Barker, replete with appetising tattoos, on shepherd's pie; Kelly, who had been sacked more than once from every job in every young offender institution in England, on beans; and Farood, poised over the critical basin of oven chips. The queue staggered by without dialogue. Nobody attempted to ingratiate themselves with the dinner lads. That wasn't how anyone got what they wanted here, inmate or staff. Farood had learned early on that people were your enemy before anything else. When someone did utter something, usually about not wanting an apple or preferring white to brown bread, it was Kelly who switched on his rage.

'The next fucker who says anything, is getting these beans over their wig.'

Kelly wasn't a fighter, really. He didn't like fighting in the way Atherton did – 'straighteners' in the showers – he didn't do that. But he was violent and he went to extremes. The police believed he was insane, and up until moving onto D wing he'd been on twenty-four bang-up, eating in his pad. Robertson's solution was to let him loose in the kitchen.

A heavyweight Asian lad with a braided skullcap moved belligerently up the queue. Officer Scully attempted to lighten the atmosphere a little. 'Eh, what do you call an Asian lad on basic? A Tellyban!'

Robertson suppressed a sigh. What could he do about Scully? He was the one person on the wing it was pointless reprimanding. Some of the lads were worth the effort, but not Officer Scully. Atherton thrust his tray at Farood. The Afghan made no eye contact, put on a portion and smiled. Atherton left the tray where it was. Portions were broadly in keeping with wing hierarchy. The bullied got less than the brawlers and Atherton wanted more, but he wasn't saying *please*. He wasn't a Victorian urchin; he was from Collyhurst.

'What's this?'

'It's a portion,' answered Farood.

'It's takin' the living piss.'

'I have to give everyone the same.'

The Afghan had to learn something else. He'd just offered Atherton a fight, a straightener. It was on. It had to be.

Officers kept their distance when lads were eating; thirty-five at a time in groups of three or four, segregated by race and by urban area. The prison had a diversity officer on a governor's salary and two dedicated and derided officers, but integration was present only in one respect: the vulnerable and marginalised found each other, no matter where they were from. First-time prisoners sat together until they had permission to do otherwise. Farood was with Barker, who had 'made in Preston' tattooed on the back of his neck below a bar code. Although not in view, he had his girlfriend's name on his wrist. It seemed Barker had everything but a return address; which might have been handy since he had a crippling stammer. His eyes said a great deal about him and they spoke of defeat. Barker found Farood good company. The Afghan spoke slowly and carefully, at a pace that he could at least aspire to, and although he didn't always wait for Barker to catch up, unlike most people, Farood was usually still there when Barker finished.

'What jobs are there away from the wing?' asked Farood.

'B-B-est.'

'Where?'

There was a drawn-out pause as the words surrendered to Barker without a fight. 'The chapel.'

'Why don't you do that?' asked Farood.

Barker shrugged. From across the central aisle of the wing Atherton was sizing up Farood. He was jumpy; his boys were all anticipation, all in imagined dress rehearsal, all awaiting a cue. Atherton himself wasn't sure when it would be, or what it would be.

'Already... g-gotta job.'

'As what?'

'Inter… pre… ter for you.'

Farood laughed; Atherton squeezed his white slice into a ball inside his fist. His audience was waiting. Scully was nodding vacantly at something Robertson was saying; Atherton got to his feet and began overacting on the nonchalant stroll. Violence in the jail was eternal, but episodes were regrettably brief: officers would fall on top of lads before a round was out. You had to strike early and firmly, and you might want to employ some furniture or appliances from your pad: a tap wrapped in one of your socks, the other sock holding part of your sink shaped into a Palaeolithic dagger. Chances were, you would only get one or two digs in. Atherton wasn't averse to weaponry, but being tooled up implied fear, implied unfavourable odds. He leaned on the table as if he wanted to borrow the ketchup.

'You didn't give me enough chips, paki.'

'I'm not from Pakistan,' said Farood, not looking in Atherton's direction.

A clever bastard. He grabbed a handful of Farood's chips and threw them over his shoulder; then he flicked the arm forward and crashed his knuckles against Farood's eye. The Pashtun shrank back and looked ahead. He'd been hit before, a hundred times, a thousand times more than Atherton. Atherton's boys sprang into combat stance; the officers switched over to control and restraint mode as Farood's right heel immediately swung in an arc at Atherton's face, punching out one of his bottom teeth. Scully belly-flopped onto Farood, crumpling him to the floor. He pressed a knee into his lower back as he twisted and cuffed his arms. Robertson led Atherton off to healthcare.

TWO

rocuses were peering through the grass at last. The snow had gone and the mists had thinned out to a silvery film. All of a sudden, the river was in a hurry, and the faster it flowed, the more it became the colour of the sky. The rain in Baghlan province came seldom and heavily. After a four-day visit in May, the river could not carry all the water and some of it carved rivulets beyond its banks through the village and into houses, gradually dissolving earthen walls as it did. Even so the rain was welcome; it brought hope. What could the rain give? Wheat by the ton for the people in the stone houses who owned land, goats' milk and lambs' meat for the families in mud houses who dreamed of owning land. Every day new grass grew, more and more of desert ground was covered, more of it grazed as soon as it greened. Vegetable shoots appeared here and there on the crumbling terraces along the hillsides; on the alluvium flood plain below sunlight dripped off the thickening skins of melons. If given a chance the land could give trees for wood and fruit, and it could give wives for husbands.

On this day in the village of Khosh there was a wedding. A teacher was marrying a farmer's daughter. He'd paid the bride price many years ago when he was a government teacher and the time had come for her father to honour the contract. This was despite much better prices offered since for fourteen-year-old Gulnar; the teacher knew he was an indebted man. For the last ten years his living, his life, had been precarious. The Mujahidin had destroyed the school soon after the war broke out, leaving only the madrassa. He lived off root crops and by turning his house into a covert primary classroom for those that wanted it and were prepared to pay. One morning the Taliban's religious police came to his house and told him to stop teaching, informed by those that were not prepared to pay or to see the word of God disputed. He thought about leaving but planted potatoes instead. Then the Americans came and drove out the Taliban. There was hope now of a new school, of an irrigation canal parallel to the river and of much else. There were two families in the village that were willing to pay for their daughters to be taught, but he knew that sooner or later he would be killed for that. The Taliban had been driven out of government – out of the village, even – but they were in the mountains to the south, in Samangan. They went there once before, when the Russians came, before they defeated them first, and then the other tribes. So, the teacher was content to teach only his wife.

The bride sat by her husband at the head of the wedding table. She held a small, decorative mirror in her painted hand, smiling coyly behind her wedding veil. The guests had eaten and within the outer courtyard some of the other villagers had gathered. They stood, mostly apart from one another, in silence, in bare feet. All their eyes were upon the door. The husband told his brother they should move outside before the evening set in and what was left of the food – the apricots and almonds in breadcrumbs, rice, a few beef mince patties, the last of the belly from the goat slaughtered the day before – was placed on a rug in the yard. The teacher was not wealthy; he could not do what the wheat farmers did, but he wanted others to share in his joy. Twenty-five or so were stood around; many of them he had taught when they were children. They were there now with their own children, waiting for the teacher. Farood, his brother and father stood at the back, his father the tallest man there towering above the crowd in his white turban. Farood was nine years old. Birthdays weren't observed, but he knew he was nine; he had been told and his eyes were above his father's waist. The onlookers from the village were invited to sit and eat. Some did, but most kept their distance and did not talk to the wedding guests unless they were spoken to. The guests, some but not all wearing clothes for the occasion, formed an aisle: men and boys on one side, women and children on the other. They clapped in time as the bride and groom emerged from the teacher's house, and the other villagers cheered and wailed. Saucepans were beaten; a man began to play a tola. He played quietly, the music sounding as if it was coming from elsewhere. Someone fetched a *zerbaghali* drum from inside the house and began to play behind the flute. A few years ago, the Taliban had tied a musician to a tree, shaved his head and made him sign a contract saying he would make a living another way. Many at the wedding now feared the potency of music. But then the bride began to dance, discreetly at first, turning her henna-painted hands along the flow of the flute, then skipping to the rolls and slow beats of the drum. Her husband led the clapping in time and his bride took off her wedding veil and tied it around her waist. Farood watched all this conscious of the delight.

A boy not much older than Farood, a rough, long-haired goatherd boy, invited himself into the courtyard, carrying a bundle over his shoulder. He laid it on the ground, revealing three small, imperfect, urn-shaped mud jars. Holding one aloft, he shouted at everyone, 'Watch. Watch with your eyes – you won't believe what you see!'

The groom's brother told him to leave, but the boy tossed the homemade jar into the air, kicked it like a leather ball. From amongst the shards a tiny robin fell to the ground; it lay stunned for a moment until it disappeared over the courtyard wall. There were cheers and laughter – a wall within the wedding party had been broken. A smile stretched across the dirty face of the goatherd boy. He held aloft another jar and held his other hand out for money. 'Who'll pay to have a go? Who'll pay?'

Farood tugged at his father's trousers and Karam swept his arm away, but Farood continued to plead.

'You do it, then, see if you can do it!'

A young man in wedding finery gave the goatherd boy an Afghani note and demanded the crowd clear a space for them.

'Ready? Are you ready?' cried the young man.

The goatherd boy with broken teeth and matted hair commanded the wedding guest to his position, making him wait as he bid the party clap in unison. The jar was thrown high, very high – the clapping stopped at its summit; it dropped and met a rising scissor kick. A bird, desert-coloured, was gone before the shattered mud reached the ground. Farood leaped off the ground and rehearsed his own kicking style, but the goatherd boy didn't harry the poor. He went to the groom, the teacher, who gave him two notes. Everyone clapped.

The teacher walked over to Farood and placed his hand on his head. 'Okay, see if you can do this. Kick it very hard now.'

Farood smiled up at his father, who nodded in gratitude and agreement.

The jar was thrown gently towards Farood, but he only kicked it back to the urchin to catch, falling as he did.

'Throw it higher for me,' pleaded Farood.

It dropped from the skies, but his scissor kick was too slow – the jar broke apart into the dust. A bird, a green warbler shaped like an English wren, staggered a few steps, reaching out one wing, trying to extend another, but half fell into the dust instead. It jumped, flapped violently along the ground under the laughter of the wedding. The goatherd boy picked it up, then broke its skull with a stone. The bride buried her face into the groom, Karam kicked his little brother and the other children laughed.

Ten years on, the memory humiliated him. His hands held the bars of the cell window as he stooped to locate the sun or a shadow. In England you had to have good eyesight to read the time. But the view from the segregation block wasn't the worst in the jail. He had the woods and some low hills with strolling cattle, even though his gaze had to make its way through a helix of razor wire decorated with rotting plastic, and beyond that the main gate where the sweatbox came and went from four times a day. Farood noticed a thrush hopping to and fro on a branch. He realised this was the furthest north he'd been. He'd seen fields and hills from the edge of his small town, but in the four years he'd been in England, he'd never stepped foot in what remained of the countryside. His foster parents had taken him to Blackpool once, to see the sea. Something he'd already seen plenty of during the many months at Calais. But they avoided his early life, wary of churning something up that they wouldn't know what to do with. They concentrated on providing comfort and were affluent enough to shop for a pastime; a middle-class British couple with the disappointment of one child offering hope to someone else. Grateful as he was for the substantial meals and the luxurious car journeys, he turned his back on it for a hostel when he was sixteen. A big mistake, he considered, that he could draw a line from to the ocean of time ahead of him.

Behind him, he heard the door flap squeak open, the turn of a key and the slide of a bolt, a variation on a sound he had heard in many rooms across two continents since leaving his village. An officer stood at the threshold of the cell holding a mat and a book. He held out his arms but didn't enter. 'Mecca's that way,' he said, pointing to the window.

The officer smiled warmly and handed Farood a Qur'an and prayer mat. The prison was keener on his devotions than he was. Consigned to the punishment block, he would miss Friday prayers whilst he was there, which was a relief to him as it absolved him of any insincerity. He was beginning to reconcile himself that God would reward him and punish others only in another life. There wasn't much he could do about how he lived, except wait. There was also the Iranian who went to prayers; a nice lad, happy, friendly, yet he hated him as he hated all Iranians now. He had become accustomed to speaking to God alone, in a darkened, filthy corner in a prison camp near Tehran. He wasn't sure what an imam could tell him anymore. He put down the mat and Qur'an and lay on his bed.

Prison is the art of passing time. Anything to break up the routine always helps: visits, the attention of a counsellor or a psychologist, conflict. Atherton knew how to make an afternoon vanish with a well-organised incident. Time was the enemy and, like everyone else in the jail, it would mess with you if you didn't stand up to it. As long as you were out of your pad you had an even chance of handling time. Unfortunately, officers much preferred you on the wrong side of an iron door, leaving you at its mercy. They too were on the receiving end of it. Whatever prisoners did outside of their pads they did as slowly as they could get away with. So, officers stood and watched as lads were overtaken by waddling ducks to and from the education block, and picked litter around the grounds like octogenarians. Farood considered how hard people worked not to get along. He'd never been able to adjust to the nexus of sarcasm at school, on the street or where he was now.

Atherton called from the next window, 'Yo, mate. Have you been down to the governor yet?'

Farood was confused at the absence of hostility in the voice. 'No.' He paused for two beats. He didn't want to fight every day. 'Have you?'

'No, mate.'

Periodically the flap of his door squeaked open and an officer's face loomed large in the deep oblong of glass. The Afghan had been placed on suicide watch with nothing to go on but the length of his sentence. It was standard practice when a lad had just become a lifer. Farood wasn't thinking about killing himself, though, he was thinking about justice, about revenge on the man who had put him in prison. God would administer his justice in the end, for sure, but he also needed his own. He had been so easily betrayed, naïve in the face of the police, the lawyer and architect of it all, Khalid. His last chance was his appeal. The right lawyer would make a judge see misdeeds at every stage of his case. But he didn't have the right lawyer.

The door opened. 'Show time, Farood.' The officer was standing to attention this time. He then marched his prisoner down the gleaming corridor to the adjudication room. Adjudications were somewhere between a visit to the headmaster's office and a magistrates' court. The governor sat behind his desk flanked by two dutiful civilians. The charge was read out, an answer requested. It was difficult to plead innocent to fighting if fighting was all you could have done.

'What reason did you have for fighting?'

'No reason.'

The governor looked to his desk for answers. What could he give him? It wasn't extra days. Everything said, someone should keep any eye on him.

'You've had a fight every week you've been here. So, you can spend a week here, where you won't be able to fight. That'll be all.'

Atherton was doing his pad workout in the next cell: press-ups with his feet on the bed, arms wide apart to maximise the tension, knuckles pushing up all his weight.

'Yo, mate! What did you get?'

'I have to stay here a week.'

'So will I, then.'

THREE

Baghlan Province, Afghanistan

He had been gone longer than he'd said. It had been hours. The glassy afternoon was dying; a colder night than the last was coming. *Maybe he'd been robbed*, thought Farood. Now that the Taliban had gone into hiding there were bandits again in Baghlan. Maybe he'd sold the sheep to Kochi people, which was as good as being robbed. When the sky declared it was time for evening prayers he began to wonder if his brother had just left the rest of his family to cope by themselves. If he had, then Farood knew what to do. He would herd his cousin's sheep and he would use his father's rifle. No one would starve. And he would stay.

Farood was squatting on a track, an hour into the hills to the south of his village. Behind him his mother and sister lay in the cave they had part-found and part-dug. A day-long fire had been lit to bake the earth and rid the four-metre square hole of the yellow spiders that would feed on you in the night. Straw lined the ground under their carpets. The boys had helped an old man cut his cave as well. In all, three families had made homes from crevices. They were out of the wind and Farood's family had a donkey to carry water from the village. They could boil water, keep a torch lit from sheep dung and mustard seed;

they could lie down and they could pray and sleep on sheep hides. By spring the rains would return what remained of their house to the earth and they could think about building again, if the Americans were gone by then. Even people whose houses and compounds hadn't been destroyed were leaving the village, selling what they had and leaving for Pakistan. Some would return wearing the black turban of the Taliban. Farood watched an American helicopter circle the plain below. In their wake would come the snipers, the bombs planted beside the road, in the wall and the river crossing, the questions about collusion, the executions, and then more rockets on houses. The village would drain away.

Behind him his mother lay with his sister Yashfa, who fluctuated between sleep and screams. He protested to his mother with his back turned. 'I have to look after Yashfa. Who will look after her if I leave?'

There was nothing his mother could say to console him, to explain or excuse herself. Karam came into view, leaning into the track, edging closer. The younger brother tried to read his face for clues. Karam stood drinking from a flask between his younger brother and his mother's eyes. Farood knew a deal had been reached. Two deals. A price for the sheep and a price for the agent.

'The agent is coming tomorrow to meet you. He has room for two more. For the price I can get for the sheep you could go a long way. To Europe.'

'How can I? I can't speak the language.'

'You'll have to learn, Spider.'

Karam looked in on his sister and then summoned Farood down the track. He walked like his father had, striding from the hips. He laid his arm on his younger brother's head. 'This is your chance, Spider. I wish I was going. When you come back, years from now, I want you to drive through the village in a silver car. You understand?'

The following morning the sheep were herded to the teacher's house. They were another wedding gift from the bride's father and the work that would go with them was a gift from the teacher to Karam and his bereaved family. A price of four thousand American dollars was settled on. For the number of sheep involved it was a lot of money, more per head than you'd get elsewhere. But in Baghlan sheep are more valuable than land because they are easier to live off. Half of the money would go to the agent to pay for Farood to get to the West; the rest would be spent by the family to eke out a living for as long as they could manage. The donkey was loaded with bags of flour, salt, okra and steel pans.

'Take this to your mother. Stay there, help her. I'm going to wait for the agent.'

'I'm not going today. I'm not ready to go.'

'You're not going today. He just wants to meet you. Tell you about the journey.'

Farood looked at the sheep they had just sold becoming accustomed to a new pen.

'And stop looking so miserable. It's going to be an adventure.'

He led the donkey up the hill but kept looking over his shoulder to his brother who had walked to the edge of the village where the road entered and left. A mile or so before Farood reached the cave, Karam was out of sight. The higher he climbed, the more difficult, the rockier the track became, before it ended abruptly and he had to scramble to the cave. He left the donkey at the end of the track and made two trips with the supplies. His mother had hardly spoken since the drone attack, only whispering into Yashfa's ear. All the same, for the last few weeks, Farood had continued speaking to his mother as if she did reply. He put the bag of salt in a corner and headed outside again.

'He's bringing the agent here.'

'When?' his mother called.

The boy turned in surprise. 'Soon. He's down there waiting for him.'

'Then get some more wood to burn.'

'We're not cooking for him. We're already giving him half the money for the sheep. Why do we need to give him our food?'

His mother was already opening the flour and reaching for a bowl. 'Do as I say.'

He went up above the cave to see what he could find, wondering why he had to be shouted at on his last day at home. Then he realised he didn't mind because it made it seem like any other day, which was how he wanted to remember it. There was precious little to burn. Not much you could call firewood. The cave was approaching the end of the treeline, except there were only shrubs, hence there were only twigs to burn and not enough. He had a bundle of sticks and grass which the flames would consume within a few minutes; he would need a lot more to ignite the dried-out powdery dung that was stacked up in the corner of the cave. The makeshift shelter was gradually inching towards becoming a place to live. Karam had bought some posts and plastic sheeting to catch the water trickling off the walls. He's also joined with another family in enlarging a second cave for their donkeys. They had agreed to share fuel and, if necessary, ground space, since at a thousand feet higher winter was bound to be more treacherous. Yashfa was on her feet exploring her new surroundings but was still to venture into the starkness of the daylight. They still had the chickens, who took their chances on the mountain and on the track. They were scurrying around Farood's feet when he spotted the pall of dust moving through the village. He watched the Land Rover materialise from the squall at the bottom of the track and felt its urgency. It had come from a long way, from further than he could see or know, and it had come for him.

Behind a tinted windscreen, an agent in a leather jacket was telling Karam in Dari that he had never taken anyone so young out of the country before. As the car crackled up the track towards him, he could see the driver with his brother beside him; he could even see behind them, where he would sit. Without even knowing, perhaps, he began to feel differently about what might lie ahead. Beneath the jacket, the agent wore a royal blue sports shirt; he wore dark glasses, a closely trimmed beard and long black boots. To Karam he looked like a man on an advertising board. The agent walked past Farood, twirling his keys, and looked up at the cave.

Farood ran to his brother and scowled. 'What are you doing in his car?'

'What do you want me to do, walk behind it? I need to find out how this works. Make sure everything's okay for you.'

'He's a Tajik. You can't trust them.'

'He's a businessman, Spider. He's taken a lot of people places, he explained everything to me. He has connections.'

'How it works is that he's about to take everything we have left. All the money from father's sheep. The family will never have sheep again.'

'We'll find other ways to live.'

'What other ways? There aren't any,' shouted Farood.

'Look, after you've made your money you come back and buy some more.'

The agent was now sitting at the front of the cave eating warm flatbread and okra as the two brothers approached. 'You're Farood? You like the look of the car? Go and sit in it. The front seat, if you like.'

Farood looked to his brother and retreated. He opened the driver's door, looked inside. *Does the Tajik believe that his luxury will make me trust him?* He didn't know what his father had always said: *You can't buy a Pashtun.*

In the wing mirror he could see the agent counting the money whilst his mother nursed Yashfa. The agent slapped the notes on his own palm. 'This will take him to Europe.' His voice contained enough cast-iron confidence to make someone doubt him. He spoke in a Tajik dialect of Dari that people in Baghlan grew up with, along with the Urdu and the Arabic of the madrassa.

'Where in Europe?' asked Karam.

'I can get him to Greece.'

'I hope so. I don't have any more to give you.'

The agent nodded on the contract. 'Have him ready for tomorrow. Early. And get him something for his feet.'

Farood's mother turned away to face the charred wall of the cave.

'You are buying something wonderful for your son, something he can't have here – a future.'

The agent walked briskly to the car.

Farood opened the door and decided to smile for him. 'I'm eleven now.'

'Don't bring much, you don't want to be carrying things.'

The boy nodded and returned to his mother. The car vanished into a cloud.

Yashfa was standing for the first time since the rocket attack. She lifted her arms; Farood kneeled and held them around his neck. His mother's hand was there by his cheek, holding a small roll of money. 'Take this. And hide it from the Tajik.'

'How much is it?'

'Two hundred American dollars.'

'What should I buy with it?'

She lifted her veil and her brown eyes possessed her son. 'You buy food with it, but only if you are starving; shoes for your feet if they become bare. That's all. Keep it until you get to Greece.'

Karam flung his little brother into a headlock and wrapped his fist around the notes. 'A spider doesn't wear shoes and I need some boots of my own.'

'Farood,' his mother insisted, 'I want you to go to the mosque to say goodbye.'

With his father dead and the sheep sold, there was no other

22

purpose to his day. Since they had moved to the cave, he had had too much time on his hands. Other children his age were clearing stones and rocks from the mountain road and asking drivers for money. Some vehicles stopped and some boys didn't come home. Without a father Farood was bait for the Taliban. Had he been older the family would have kept the sheep and he would have taken them out on his own, watched by all the other boys, carrying his father's rifle.

The mullah was a solemn yet temperate man beneath a greying trimmed beard and plain sack-coloured shalwar and *pakol*. He was handsome yet seldom smiled and was impossible to read. His eyes had the habit of settling on people and demanding answers. He had heard that Farood was about to begin the journey, but he was only one of many since the Taliban had taken up arms. The mullah remembered them all and he knew their spiritual cleanliness was in jeopardy beyond the frontiers, beyond the village, even.

'What have you learned here?' he asked Farood.

'Verses from the Qur'an, as many as I can.'

'But what have you learned from them?'

Farood looked past his teacher at the two children lying asleep on a washed-out blue mattress beneath the wall of the madrassa. There was always a different kind of light in there and today, even though it was still morning, it was shredded and dying.

'What it is to be a good Muslim.'

'You think you know? Tell me just one thing you must remember?'

He had been attending the school for five years, so he ought to have known something by now, but he didn't want to seem boastful, for the mullah didn't like immodest children.

'Allah will be with me wherever I go. East and west, wherever I turn.'

'Of course. But can you remember your Al-Ankabut?'

'Those who believe and work righteous deeds—'

'No. Do you think that your life will be easy by saying *we believe*? Your heart and soul will be tested, Farood. Things will happen to you that you do not deserve, but they will have a purpose. Anyone for whom Allah intends good he makes them suffer – no more than you can bear, though.'

A thought hurried the mullah away to his room at the back of the hall. The two children continued to lie motionless, dusty and slight; the slumber of hunger. He returned, and from behind his back showed Farood a grey woollen hat decorated with white stitching of circles and diamonds. He placed it on his pupil's head and smiled. '*As-Salaamu 'Alaykum.*'

*

'He's late. Are you sure he's coming?'

Karam didn't answer.

They had been standing at the edge of the village since the agreed time of 10am and it was nearly eleven.

'Maybe he's not coming. Not today.'

'He's coming, Spider, and you are going.'

'I don't mind going. I want to go. I'm going to be wealthy.'

'That's right you are.'

He was wearing a plain grey shalwar kameez, his new hat and a pair of brown desert boots that he couldn't stop looking at. They were indisputable evidence that he was leaving. Most footwear had been circulated around the village, more than once, but these were from a market trader's box. His mother had tied them for him as he stood in the cave. He took the few steps he could. She pulled his hat forward and he laughed.

'When shall I come back?'

'When you are a man.'

He knew he would be gone for years, but he didn't know how many, how long it would be before he stood on his own ground again. His mother reached up to his shoulders. Her hands shook and her eyes closed on him. Then she withdrew and ran her palms over Yashfa's wavy hair.

His brother squatted beside him. 'You are going a long way and you'll be gone a long time. Work as hard as you can for a few years, return when you can buy us the sheep back.'

Farood closed his eyes; his brother turned him around and led him away. He was ready. Everything else he would carry as a memory. The place he was from would be an ancestral map on which he would place all that was to follow. His mind was Pashtun no matter where he went and however others tried to shape it.

They were facing south, away from the village into the haze of the flood plain. The thought began to enter Karam that the agent would keep the money but not his side of the bargain. But then, if he did, he knew where to track him down. Finally, from the road through the village, from the north, a dirty silver Datsun clattered towards them. There was a driver and a front passenger. It pulled up beside them. The driver smiled. A small, slim Pashtun man in his late twenties, dressed in a dirty tan-coloured shalwar and blue waistcoat, got out. He had no beard and his hair was short with long sideburns.

'Farood? Come with me. I'm your driver for the first part of the journey.'

'Where's the Tajik with the big car?' demanded Karam.

'He just arranges things, others drive.'

The boy in the front seat took off his sunglasses. He was in his mid-teens, dressed in Western clothes and a grin. With the engine still running, the driver held open the rear door and beckoned Farood. Karam tapped his little brother on the back and he ran to the car. The car jolted off. He glanced around the inside of the vehicle, then turned to look for his brother. He saw the outline of Karam through a thickening screen of dust. He turned to face the back of the driver's seat, determined not to allow a single tear blur the road that lay ahead.

FOUR

Atherton was right. He and Farood spent the same amount of time down the block. Block time was straightforward. You were either behind the door or you were in an exercise cage. Your own individual cage, adjacent to the next one, which meant prisoners could only get at each other verbally. Initially Atherton and Farood were exercised at different times but then at the same time, deliberately so. When Atherton was let into his cage, Farood chose to look in the other direction. But the Manchester lad was surprisingly affable, as far as people like Atherton could be. He asked about the war in Afghanistan – or 'Afghan', as he called it. He said he knew a man on his street that had done a tour. He even asked Farood – or 'Roodie', as he had started to call him – where in Afghan he was from.

'From the north, near Tajikistan.'

Atherton nodded, but his geography didn't stretch that far. On the seventh morning their doors opened one after the other, Atherton waiting outside Farood's, next to an officer.

'Right, off you go then, you two.'

Atherton put on his bewildered expression.

The hefty officer made for the gate, swung it into the sunshine and looked to the sky. 'Hey, it's gonna be nice. But don't dawdle.'

'Yes, boss,' acknowledged Farood.

The two lads made their way back down the concourse to D wing. Officer Scully was holding a scratchy radio to his face at the other end. Prisoners were already working on the flowerbeds in the centre of the concourse. Someone straightened up from a wheelbarrow. 'Atherton, yer grass!' Atherton laughed. All the way back lads came to their windows, pushing their faces above the signs that said 'shouting out of windows will result in adjudication' and were surprised to see Atherton walking alongside the lad he'd been sent to the block for fighting with. Scully ticked them off on his clipboard at the gate and mumbled into his radio.

Atherton headed straight for the laundry. 'Boss, got my old cleaning job back, haven't I?'

'Behind the door – both of you.'

'No way. Who's taken my job?' Atherton looked around him. Someone desperate to get out of their cell would now be happily folding bedding and jogging bottoms. But Atherton would point out to them that they were trespassing.

Scully pointed his thumb to the balcony. 'You go to the block – you get sacked.'

Atherton and Farood sat in their respective pads. Atherton's south-facing cell was methodically organised: cereal boxes, empty and new, were stacked in fragile raked rows; his faithful toiletries and symmetrically piled *Top Gear* magazines; the poster of Paul Scholes. This was home; a home he controlled. In Farood's pad there wasn't much to order. He'd never had his own room in Baghlan and if he had, there wouldn't have been anything to put in it; neither had he collected many possessions during his time in foster care or the subsequent bedsit. Although he was going to be spending longer than anyone else there in prison, he hadn't yet come to terms with making this home. There was only one photo, next to the mirror, of a young woman. She was wearing a work suit, behind her the high-street opticians. He'd met her a few months before he was sent to jail. They'd met at a restaurant in town, where he worked for the owner, Khalid. Her sister had a business meeting with Khalid and the young woman in the photo, Sabana, had come along.

It was, he recalled, a Sunday, sometime between lunch and dinner, and the newly black-and-white-tiled room of fifty tables was empty except for the visitors, the owner and his willing worker, Farood. The accountant was unapproachably demure, high cheekbones and long eyelashes, dressed in white and pink, in bracelets and make-up. She made notes in a leather-bound book with an expensive ballpoint. Sitting next to her, Sabana's boredom was obvious. She was taking in the surroundings and watching Farood as he nervously made coffee and plated sweets from the cold cabinet. Cautiously he brought the tray over, bowing involuntarily and inelegantly before lowering it to the table. Sabana looked directly up at him, laughing with her eyes, absorbing him. Then Khalid looked at Farood, his eyes warning him away. Farood was wiping the coffee machine when she walked over in a blue sweater and jeans.

'Got any sugar?' she asked, as if they had met before.

'Of course, I'm sorry.' He produced a sugar bowl and made to move from behind the counter.

'It's alright, wait there.' She went back to her table and brought her cup over. 'Just one for me, please.'

He spooned in some sugar, carefully.

'It's good coffee. What do you do here?'

'I'm a waiter.' He wasn't; he washed dishes. 'One day, I'm going to have a restaurant like this.'

It seemed to be the done-thing in England – to talk big, to possess aspirations. But he didn't want to own a restaurant; he didn't know what he wanted to do. It had taken him almost a year to get into a school in England, by which time it was almost time to leave. He had revered the school: the uniform, the classrooms, the teachers and the library. He was astonished it was totally free, but the rudeness and the lack of interest of other pupils dismayed him. He still liked to read, to learn about British history. He loved Elizabeth I – she was never off the television in England. He had learned that this was the third time the British had invaded Afghanistan. He had hopes of continuing his education, but he would have to check with Khalid first. He always had to check with Khalid first.

Farood knew this was not what a Pakistani girl was interested in, so he began to describe his plans to make money. She worked in an opticians, was older than him by two years, though he cut that in half with a recognisable lie. She asked him if he liked working there and he nodded. Then she began to make fun of her sister, who was performing what she said was her 'accountant act', in serious expressions and feigned interest in the man opposite – Khalid with his 'businessman act', with those hand gestures that flaunted his gold cufflinks. Why did people act their lives?

'Why is your sister working on a Sunday?' he asked her.

'She's not really working, is she? What's Khalid like?'

'He works hard.' He could tell she wasn't convinced.

'This restaurant must be doing well.'

'It's busy.'

'The car he drives, the house he lives in. It's not that big a restaurant.'

He was flummoxed. 'How have you seen his house?' he asked.

Sabana looked across at her sister and Khalid, who was now holding his accountant's hand. 'He's married, isn't he?' she said.

Farood felt forced to nod.

'And I bet he's got kids,' she added.

She took out her phone to text her sister. There was a bleep across the room. Sabana looked straight at Farood, noticing how the pupil in his right eye had gone astray, and offered him her best smile. At that moment he sensed danger, for Khalid was watching him too.

That afternoon seemed much further away than it was. He wondered at Sabana's face at that exact moment, the expression she was wearing. He tore himself away from the photo and considered that even though life in prison in the UK was better, was safer, than the life he had known in Afghanistan, he would never make a home in a cell. That was for others, with all their rivalries, their out-the-window screams and promises of death come tomorrow. Suddenly an envelope slid between the door and its frame – Scully was doing the mail round. Farood sprang towards the wafer-thin column of light.

'Boss! Boss!'

It wasn't easy to get Scully to open a door, but he did at least return to yell through them at prisoners. 'What?!'

'I need you to get me in education.'

Scully relented and unlocked the door. 'To do what?' he asked.

'I don't know yet.'

Farood had already opened the official-looking letter. It was the worst of news. He was sitting on his bed with it in his hand.

'To do what?' repeated Scully.

'Oh no, boss.'

'What?'

'My appeal is going to be heard.'

'*That* is a good thing, Farood.'

'No, it's not good. You got to help me, boss.'

The door slammed and Scully was gone. He looked at the letter again. 'The Court of Appeal', its coat of arms. Then he looked at the legal firm representing him. Except they were not representing him; they were representing the cousin of a senior partner, Khalid.

He took the letter down to evening association and sat opposite Barker, who had his back to the rest of the wing. He smiled at Farood; he had missed him.

'You okay?' Barker nodded. 'What you been up to?'

Barker shrugged. 'C-c-clean-n.'

Farood put his letter from the Court of Appeal under his nose. 'Do you know anything about this?'

Barker did. Barker always put in an appeal. Barker always pleaded not guilty even when legally advised otherwise. He didn't consider it his job to do the prosecution's job for them. Barker took out a pen and wrote across the letter: *Last chanse, dont fuck up.* He could tell that Farood wasn't optimistic. He also knew that for the prisoner with the longest sentence in the jail, the stakes couldn't be higher.

'I don't want the appeal to go ahead.' Barker looked confused. 'Not yet,' added Farood.

'But the lawyer wan-wants the...'

Farood folded the letter just as Atherton swaggered over to their table.

'What's that?' snapped Atherton, but Farood just shook his head. Atherton held out his fist for Farood to touch.

'Roodie, come, sit with us.'

Atherton began swaggering back across the wing without glancing over his shoulder. Farood followed, if only to cement the end of the conflict, but also out of curiosity. It was time he learned more about the craft of being a prisoner.

Whilst Barker returned to his cell, Farood sat at a window table with Atherton and two of his boys: small, blank-faced, forgettable boys with hardened eyes. One of them asked him about his week in the block. 'He soldiered it,' Atherton told them. The three Manchester lads talked about how much time they had done in segregation and how to cope with the isolation and the slow passing of hours. One of them asked him, 'Did you get thirty years, yeah? How long they saying you're gonna have to serve?'

'Fifteen years.'

Even they could not think of a consolatory reply.

Officers Scully and Robertson were supposed to be in

the centre of the wing, surveying around forty prisoners. According to memorandums they should have been on watch for lads exerting 'undue influence' on other lads, or 'evidence of gang activity', which wasn't hard to miss. Instead they stood with a group of Asian lads near the wing office. Senior Officer Robertson had recently taken to mingling with this group of lads to discuss Islam and religion in general; he was continually explaining how similar their faith was to his. Only the other day there was something said at church that reminded him of the Qur'an, except the congregation he was in discussion with on the wing weren't that familiar with the text. For most Muslims in the jail, Friday prayers and Muslim study group on a Tuesday was down time out of pads and an opportunity to firm up the sense of unity with co-religionists. It bolstered protection and power as much as faith. Their top man was a heavyweight lad with the braided skullcap. His name was Atif and he was centre stage with strong arms and expansive gestures, pointing between Robertson and himself.

Atherton stared over at them, studying the group, the way that Robertson was supposed to. 'Hey, Roodie, see that lot over there. They're very cosy with the officers. Always wording them up, aren't they? And they got all the wing jobs. They got ours.'

'Who?'

'That one pointing at the SO – Atif. He's got your cleaning job, he has.'

Farood gazed across impassively as the stocky lad clapped his hands and pointed both index fingers at Robertson to explain something.

'You know him, Roodie?'

'Atif?'

'What's he like?'

'Thinks he's the main Muslim in this jail. Wants to tell everyone what to do,' explained Farood.

Atherton could see hostility and the embryo of an allegiance.

'I know for a fact they've got phones, Rood. And they're getting stuff brought in. Loads of gear.'

'How do you know?'

'He offered to rent one out to this guy I know. For some stupid amount of money. So, the guy rents the dog off him. Two days later he has his pad spun. He's a fucking grass as well.'

'Yeah?'

'Yeah.'

One of Atherton's boys with a C-shaped scar on his cheek summarised. 'He can afford to lose the phone and he keeps the screws looking the other way.'

Then Atherton turned to Farood and stated the objectives. 'So, what I wanna know is, how's he getting stuff in?'

'Why don't you ask him yourself?' replied Farood.

'He only helps his own kind. You get me? You go to the mosque with him? And an extra shower on a Friday's not enough for me to become a Muslim. Half the time they're speaking to each other in another language – I bet you can speak bits and pieces of it.'

'I speak four languages.'

Atherton grinned as this. 'You learned a lot on the road, didn't you?'

'But I don't want to be involved in trouble here,' added Farood. 'I've already been to the block.'

'For a week, mate. You're gonna be here a while, aren't yer? You can do your time the hard way – no phone, no weed, no contact with anyone outside except a couple of visits a month – or you can have some comforts and a little bit of respect on the wing. People who'll look after yer, Rood. Or do you wanna be like Barker. A victim?'

Farood wandered off slowly, heading for the stairs. Turning, he looked back at Atherton and his boys and made a detour to Barker's pad.

Barker was sitting on his bed in a gloom of cigarette smoke

next to a pile of documents. He held out a slip of prison-issue writing paper for Farood. On it was the phone and fax numbers of the Court of Appeal and the address of the legal ombudsman.

'What's this?'

'Legal ombudsman. Where you… com… plain…'

'About my lawyer?'

Barker nodded, smiled.

FIVE

nglish teacher Julian Burgess didn't do tough with the lads. He was serious and kind, grammar school Lancashire, and he sniffed when his learners annoyed him. His clothes were an expression of his humility – he wasn't the kind of forty-three-year-old that prisoners knew or wanted to be, or could ever be frightened of. Instead he found himself relying on their unpredictable curiosity, plus his ability to bend each lesson towards their lives. He didn't try to persuade them to find jobs when they left the jail; neither was he offering advice on committing more lucrative offences more effectively – though after more than a decade in the industry he was capable of running a reoffending surgery. He believed that the worst kind of poverty was to be preoccupied with money and had embarked on a quest to free prisoners from their cultural deprivation – knowing in his bones that if he could equip only a handful, just one, even, they would be able to find their own way out of the mayhem that enveloped them. His subject was English and he taught it in whatever way he felt like on the day. Today's text was *Macbeth*, a classic for any ambitious gang member with pretensions towards the arts.

The carpeted classroom hummed with the sound of the computer server standing in the corner and from each wall shiny, neonate faces of conjoined computer screens stared in on everyone. At the far end of the room two prisoners were plugged into black towers, nodding rhythmically between earphones whilst at the other, Julian stood impassioning about Act One Scene Six to Farood, Atherton, Atif and Kelly. Four lads out of six was good going. Atherton had claimed the role of Duncan since he had himself once received near-fatal stab wounds. Kelly played his sidekick Banquo, as he did on the wing. Farood and Atif were sharing the lead as a theatrical device and to lighten the load. Julian himself played Lady Macbeth. Julian had shown his cast Polanski's film version up to Duncan's murder. They knew that Macbeth's beef with Duncan was universal in nature: having to take shit. Duncan strutted down the IT suite and into the castle courtyard, his eyes locked on to Farood. Behind him, Banquo did a convincing job of surveying a world that was completely new to him; nodding to his king he snarled, 'This castle hath a pleasant seat; the air nimbly and sweetly recommends itself unto our gentle senses.'

Kelly's voice was as high as the ramparts and his rasping Scouse overspill accent a delight to Julian's ears. 'This guest of summer, the temple haunting martlet does approve, by his love'd mansionry, that the heaven's breath smells wooingly here... Boss, what's a martlet?'

'It's a bird.'

Kelly continued, 'No jutty, frieze, buttress, nor coign of vantage, but this bird hath made his pendant bed...'

Kelly was all conviction, like he was reciting an alibi with certitude. He loved acting – knew it was what he should have done all along. He was the most distracted and explosive of repeat offenders but had recently declared himself a Buddhist, which had given him a certain amount of cache in the jail. He told other lads that he was sleeping much better since taking up meditation, not to mention the relaxed-looking woman he spent an afternoon a fortnight with.

Atherton asserted his authority over his subjects in the only way he knew – giving Macbeth the eye.

Atif, who was technically still offstage, could tell it was on. 'Why are you staring at me like that, Atherton?'

'Cos, I know what you're fuckin' up to, that's why.'

'No, you don't, how do you? He doesn't know, does he boss?'

'I can fuckin' tell you wanna be on top,' explained Atherton.

'You can't tell nothing mate.'

Atif was equipped with all the violent recklessness of Macbeth and none of the prevarication.

'Guys, let's play that with irony, shall we? …Would you like to live in Macbeth's castle as seen in the film?'

'It's a shithole boss,' said Kelly.

'Sooner live here.'

'So, say it like—'

'We're taking the piss?' said Atherton.

'Exactly,' confirmed Julian. 'Shouldn't find that too hard.'

'Want me to walk up here again, boss?'

'Yes, Atherton. Then I want to go to our two Macbeths on the next page and their struggle over his conscience. Atif, you're the part that wants to kill Duncan; Farood, you're the part that says *no*.'

Farood scanned the words. Where did it say that? He could see 'pity', 'angels', 'knife', 'heaven', even, but not 'kill'. He knew how to work at language. Growing up as he did close by unheeded borders, by eleven he had made his way into three languages as well as the Arabic of the madrassa. Hiding, scavenging and travelling across two continents, he had absorbed some Greek and French, and lastly, he had learned to operate in English. But the words in front of him were a game that the writer was playing with him. The story though, felt familiar.

'Boss, what happens to this Macbeth in the end? Does he get away with it?'

'He gets killed, Farood.'

'Who by?'

'The man whose family he murders.'

'What's his name, this man?'

'Macduff.'

The Afghan thumbed his way forward in search of a reckoning and then it was Atif's moment. He squeezed his abdominals, flexed his pectorals, and plodded through and past the words as if they were his own creed. Atherton turned his back and Kelly adopted a more reflective pose with one foot upon a chair, his elbow on his knee. Julian let out a director's sigh.

Atif closed his book. 'Boss, I shouldn't be doing this.'

'You're dead right,' pitched Atherton.

'Why?'

'Boss, it's forbidden to me. In my religion, it's haram.'

Atherton began laughing whilst Kelly offered an opinion on direction. 'Boss, I think you should let Atif go and get someone else in.'

Farood raised his hand. 'Boss, when someone kills a person, they don't do this much thinking about it. The other person, their life, is nothing to them.'

'I wouldn't be so sure about that.'

'They would kill you and never think about you again.'

A woman entered the room without knocking and an appraisal of her began before she had closed the door behind her. Whilst Kelly was engrossed by the sight of her thighs, Atif placed himself alongside her pearly skin; none were as thorough as Atherton. His gaze consumed the tied-back hair, the flushed neck, the stretched silk shoulders pushing apart her cardigan.

He was just at the small of her back when Kelly walked right across him. 'Miss, is that Truth… Your perfume?'

She'd had years of it and knew how to survive this eternal turnover in boyish interrogation.

Kelly persisted. 'No, hang on, it's Jo Malone, isn't it?'

Atherton laughed at the clever bastard. Kelly took a step in towards her. She swung a look at him and then coldly announced to Julian she had come for Farood. As she left the room with him, Julian gave way to a look himself.

Kelly put his hands down his jogging bottoms and whispered into his teacher's ear, 'Like a piece of that, would you, boss? You *dirty* bastard.'

She led Farood down the corridor to an open area in the education block where two officers were slumped at the far end. She took him to a desk, dropped a file and sat down opposite.

'I'm Harriet, your probation officer here. I want to talk to you about your sentence.' Her abrupt expression was matched by her tone.

'My sentence? Why, miss?'

'You have a lot of time ahead of you. Have you thought about courses, qualifications?'

The question confronted him like another impossible journey, one that he was yet resigned to making. He wondered if she'd thought how she would fill the next fifteen years. He imagined her face at the end of it all.

'You were at college, weren't you?'

'In Burnley. I was doing engineering.'

'Well, you can do almost anything here through the virtual campus – how about doing a degree?'

'How can you do engineering in here?'

'There are other courses you need to think about. Offending behaviour courses, victim awareness. Have a look at this list.'

He didn't. Instead, Farood pulled out a folded piece of paper from his sock and opened it out on the table. 'Miss, I got this letter today about my appeal. It's next week.'

Harriet read it impatiently. 'What are your grounds for appeal?'

'I didn't do it. I was there, that's all.'

'Sometimes that's enough.' She didn't lift her eyes from the page.

'Miss, the lawyer's no good. I want another lawyer. I didn't even ask for this.'

'You need to get this postponed?'

'Can you do that for me?'

'You need to speak to your lawyer. That's their job, not mine.'

'But the lawyer is not on my side.'

Harriet pushed the letter back and shut Farood's file. She got to her feet.

'Miss, do you think thirty-three is old?'

*

He didn't go back to Macbeth. It was Friday – half-day bang up; everybody had to be back from work by half eleven, dinner was at a quarter to, then behind the door until association at seven. By quarter past noon the lights were out on all the wings, lads were sleeping and the morning shift officers were on starting blocks. As always there was one more obligation before it was over – Friday prayers. There were forty or so Muslims in the jail, scattered across the eight wings. They were not a tight group – a firm, a gang, nowhere near as belligerently cohesive as the Liverpool lads, but on Fridays before and after prayers, if someone had reported an insult, they would come back to wings carrying their Qur'ans and indignation that simmered until evening association. From everyone else's point of view, they had no right to complain at all since they all got an extra shower and another ninety minutes out of their pads each week. Farood didn't care much for the congregational prayers in the jail, since the congregation didn't exactly pay attention. The imam was a small Lancashire man, soft in features and accent, who struggled up and down the hill to the jail on a bicycle.

In the pre-prayer showers Atif spoke about giving up education, unless there were separate classes for Muslims. He told the others that we should all raise this with the imam. It held the attention of some, but Farood turned his back and left the showers. En-route to the chapel, Atif touched fists with his brothers, and introduced himself to new arrivals and new Muslims from other wings. A Polish lad, who had recently converted, walked by his side, taking in advice about Jews controlling the media. Everyone walked at the same pace as Atif. He took pole position in the prayer room, placing his mat centre stage then pressing his nose to the floor, with his Qur'an wrapped in a towel beside him. Today's sermon from the imam was about the importance of humility, the dangers of avarice and the sin of theft, *the taking of wealth from others.* He spoke about the enormous shame of those Muslims involved in the recent riots in London and Birmingham. A good Muslim, he said, understood that being was more important than having. *Adornments of gold, this was nothing but enjoyment of the present life: The Hereafter, in the sight of thy Lord, is for the righteous.*

There was always a queue after prayers to speak to the imam. Many of the questions were sincere, concerned – about visits, officers, about being picked on, but many were about avoiding going back to the cell until 7pm.

Official letters were part of the asking and Farood had his in his hand. 'Sir, see this. It's my appeal. It's going ahead, but I need to stop it.' Farood handed over the letter.

'Then you need to tell the lawyer, and they will cancel it.'

'They won't, sir – see, the lawyers are criminals, sir.'

The imam shrugged. 'What do you want me to do?'

'If you could explain to the Court of Appeal, they'd believe you.'

'No, they wouldn't. Ask the SO on your wing to let you make a phone call from the wing office.' He handed the letter back.

Farood left the chapel building and his co-religious behind and headed back to the wing. He considered praying in his own cell in future. Ahead of him Robertson unlocked the wing gate and looked in his direction. Occasionally he would ask about the service, so Farood tried to think of something to say before asking about making the phone call.

Just then, Atif jogged up behind him, placing his hand on his shoulder. 'What did you think?'

'About what?'

'The sermon. You know what I think? Who is this imam to say what the Qur'an means? We can read what's in there for ourselves. You must have had some good imams in Afghan.'

'They were all Hafiz.'

'Of course. You know, you could bring a lot to our group, Farood.'

At this, Farood looked sideways at Atif.

'You're from the heart of the struggle,' said Atif, putting an arm round him.

'Yeah, a war zone.'

'People in here would look to you.'

'For what?'

'For leadership, brother. Muslims here are straying from the path.'

'We find our own path.'

At which Atif jogged ahead and stood blocking his way. 'You have a responsibility a duty to take up the fight, man. You know the Qur'an, you know that much.'

Farood tried to brush past him; Atif side-stepped, blocking his path. 'Didn't you fight? Didn't your family fight?'

'You don't know anything about me.'

'I got you wrong, didn't I? You're not even an Afghan, are you, mate?'

They were not that far from Robertson, who hadn't quite heard what had been said, but the moment started Atif rocking on his heels, shrugging his shoulders, a stride away from Farood, he left his post. Farood took a breath, tensed his shoulders, then skipped forward for a scissor kick at Atif's right eye. Officers from other gates ran over to assist Robertson in *control and restraint*.

Farood held out his arms behind his back for Robertson to cuff. 'Boss, I need to make a phone call.'

'When you come back from meeting the governor,' replied Robertson.

'I need to make it today. About my appeal.'

'First things first.' Robertson took Farood down the block and filled in the familiar paperwork.

SIX

Mazar Highway, Afghanistan, 2002

It was a few hours to the highway. An asphalt road that rested quietly on the valley floor. As soon as they reached the tarmac, the rattling inside the car died. Only then did the driver point at his front passenger, announcing, 'This is Misha, he's from Mazar.'

Farood leaned forward and shook his hand.

The road was clear as it crossed a plain where the wind scattered dust onto the grey camber. To their left the Surkhab river gradually spread itself up against the exhausted rice fields. On the other side yellow stubble interspersed among coarsely ploughed clods of earth. Misha pulled out some chewing gum and offered a strip to Farood, who shook his head, then Misha declared, 'We're picking up someone else. At Pol-e-Khomri.'

The driver, who was their first guide in a chain across two continents, pushed in a cassette and began to sing along to the crescendos of a falsetto voice. There was an autumn sunset on their shoulders and Farood realised that he had never before spent a night away from his family. He was already a long way from home on a journey that didn't have a conceivable end. He looked out of the back window and considered how so much empty land gave so little. He knew he was poor. There were some families in the village with cars and radios and larger houses, with land of their own, which meant they would never be hungry. They were the wealthy. No cars were rushing in the opposite direction to Baghlan, only a few American helicopter gunships cutting through the mottled sky. He was leaving an empty place – he had been told to go, but he felt guilty all the same. The song bled away under cheers and hand-clapping as the driver turned down the cassette player.

'She sang at my wedding. Beautiful. Tonight, you'll stay at a house in Kabul then tomorrow, Quetta, Pakistan. It's going to be a good journey.' His grin flashed in the mirror.

Farood had been on this road before with his father to visit an uncle who was a coalminer in Pol-e-Khomri. His father had told him how his brother had ridden in the buzkashi in Kandahar, that he played the *tola*, that he was an old Afghan before he had gone to work in the mine. Farood suspected he had meant old in another sense, but the man also looked ancient: his face was so drawn on by labour and coal it was impossible to tell where his beard ended and his flesh began. The Russians had built the mine, but since they had gone conditions had deteriorated, now almost unmechanised with the showers dying off to an intermittent trickle. It was a dangerous place for a wage of a hundred Afghanis a day, and he had been awarded with a severe limp from a tunnel collapse. He was his father's last brother. Three others had been killed in the same day fighting the Russians. Many times, he was asked to come and live with them in the village, but always he wanted to stay in the miners' compound with the other men, digging by day, smoking by night. He would not know that he was the last brother.

Low hills closed in as they got nearer Pol-e-Khomri. The river quickened and the rice fields became smaller. Pylons steadied themselves on foothills. Round one last bluff and they were in the outskirts of a small place. It was a haphazard vista.

Farood could see that some of it had been destroyed, yet some of it was also being rebuilt. Once they were in the main street they could see right out to where houses clambered up hills as if the town was trying to escape from itself.

Inexplicably to Farood, Misha put on his dark glasses, wound down the window and leaned out. 'Do you know this guy?' he shouted at the driver.

The driver smiled and nodded. Cars clung to the centre of the road, chaotically fringed by burned out or abandoned vehicles on either side. The driver leaned forwards, pressing his chest on the steering wheel, muttering to himself.

'Where do you want to go?' asked Farood.

'This guy knows everywhere round here,' counselled Misha.

Producing a packet of cigarettes, he began to smoke. Just beyond a clay-coloured mosque was a small roundabout, and on it was sitting a vacant-looking man.

'Is that him?' suggested Farood.

They circled the roundabout, but it didn't register with the tall, bushy-haired man, unshaven rather than bearded, dressed in jeans and a tee shirt and short jacket. *Like an American,* thought Farood.

Misha shouted from the window as the car circled the roundabout for a third time. 'Hey, you, looking for a ride to London? Hey, we're stopping for a few days in Paris, you can come if you want.'

The man arose from his daze and ran to the car. Laughing at full volume, the driver steered the Datsun away from the roundabout, letting him make chase before allowing him to clamber in alongside Farood.

'My name's Farood,' he said, offering his hand.

He ignored the boy and shouted at the driver. 'What happened to the other car?'

'My brother's borrowing it. This car is better. No one suspects.'

'Suspects what? We're not doing anything except leaving this shitty country of ours.'

'I'm from Khosh. My village,' said Farood, glancing to his right; again, he was ignored.

Once they were out of the town, Misha took off his dark glasses, introducing himself to the new backseat passenger. His name was Jamal and he looked out of the window from under his hair. Very soon they were on the Khenjan Highway south of Pol-e-Khomri heading towards the Salang Pass. The further south they drove, the more the rain set in and the more snow there was on the peaks. Suddenly the river to their left widened, leaving small islands in its midst, then slowed so much it forked, with their road curling away to their right in a long, blind bend. Then unexpectedly there was a place – dwellings and stalls of corrugated iron, canopies and never-ending mud – a place that existed for the road. They slowed but had no thought of stopping.

Jamal turned to Farood and finally volunteered something. 'I never thought I would leave. That I'd get around to it.'

'Why are you leaving?'

His heavy eyes lifted up to Farood; they didn't seem to know. They were still searching for an answer when the car suddenly braked and the backseat passengers surged at one another.

'Taliban,' the driver exclaimed.

In front of the Datsun appeared a stripped-down Japanese pick-up truck turned war waggon, replete with four fighters clambering out the back.

'Relax. Let me talk,' said the driver.

A man in a black turban and a muddied beige mac was waving his rifle in wide sweeps. He had a long nose, dark eyes and large hands. Several others behind him had already fanned out across the road. Taliban checkpoints were not uncommon along mountain passes; nearer towns they laid mines for the Americans and the British. They didn't wait around to be seen enforcing a passing caliphate.

'Allahu Akbar.' The driver saluted everyone.

No one said anything. The fighter in the black turban walked slowly around the Datsun. Farood had seen a checkpoint once before; the village teacher had been dragged out of his car, the books in the boot burned, the teacher beaten, his car taken away so he could carry no more books. Most likely this too would end with a warning.

'Everyone out of the car!' commanded the long-nosed Talib.

No one moved. A mid-teens fighter lumbered his AK47 towards the car and stabbed the butt down onto the bonnet. The driver was out now, waving his arms as if this was a disagreement amongst friends. The three passengers reluctantly lined up on the road. Jamal looked into the sun with his heavy eyes and then spat. He didn't seem scared. But Misha the Turkmen was. Everyone else there was a Pashtun. Had he been a Hazara they would have shot him immediately.

The Taliban commander glanced at Misha, then his eyes bored into the driver. 'Where is your beard? Eh? All of you.'

'They're too young,' said the driver. 'And it's very dusty where these guys live. I had a long beard once. Longer than yours. But I could never keep it clean. It was a blasphemy.'

'I will tell you what blasphemy is,' snarled the commander. He shouted an instruction to the young fighter, who ran back to the truck.

Nervously, Misha began to say how late they would be getting into Kabul when a rifle butt put out two of his teeth. Falling to his knees, he tried to capture his own blood with his hands, amazed at the pool forming around his knees. The Taliban teenager returned with a cane taller than himself; the commander grabbed it and lashed at the Turkmen on the ground. Another Talib rummaged in the car and triumphantly held the driver's music cassette aloft. The commander was struggling to lash Misha; he gave his rifle to his young lieutenant so his stroke was unencumbered.

'You must have a beard. This is decreed!' His lash was continuous.

The lieutenant, now struggling under the weight of two automatic rifles, sought to feed his courage. He questioned Jamal. 'Have you prayed today? We will take you and imprison you until your beard has grown. And you will have to pay a barber to cut your American hair.'

Jamal looked straight back at the Talib, who was younger and smaller than himself. 'Why don't you go and find some Americans to punish? That wouldn't be so easy now, would it?'

'We killed some Americans this morning.'

Jamal laughed at this and Farood knew he needed to help himself. 'Good. Praise be. You are martyrs,' he said.

The fighter shouldered one of the rifles and pulled at Jamal's pockets. He found a photo of a woman in a pocket and threw it to the ground. 'We have to rescue the dignity of women from people like you.'

Jamal looked down at the photo and knew that the Talib was waiting for him to pick it up.

'Where are you going to?' demanded the Talib.

'Kabul. Then, who knows.'

'You're running away.' The Talib walked over to his commander and shed a rifle. 'They're running away, to the West. They're dogs.'

The four Taliban were now bunched around their truck; the one that had remained there seemed anxious about something – the captives could see him imploring the commander. Misha had climbed to his knees. His bloodied face was lowered to his chest, his bloodied back bowed. With his hands on his hips, he took three deep breaths and then ran across the pebbles and into the muddy river. The water was low, and in less than a dozen strides he was out the other side. The Taliban didn't notice at first, then the lieutenant brought his rifle to his shoulder, but there was nothing to aim at. Misha was behind an ice age-sized boulder. The lieutenant took a few steps but wasn't keen on wading into the river.

Farood shouted at the commander. 'Sir, sir, we're off to Kabul to build a madrassa.'

'Stop lying,' shouted the lieutenant, repositioning himself downstream.

Misha broke cover along the opposite bank. He sprinted straight, and then dived before the crack had ridden the airwaves. The young Talib lowered his rifle, surprised at his accomplishment.

'He might not be dead, go see,' ordered the commander.

His lieutenant stepped to the edge of the river and went no further. 'I don't want to bring mud into the car.'

The commander returned to the truck and climbed into the driver's seat, the lieutenant onto the back. The commander brought a walkie-talkie to his lips. They zoomed away to the sound of their own gunfire.

Misha was drenched head to foot from lying down under the run of the river. The bullet had missed him. They used a scarf to help bathe his face and back. No one said much in the Datsun on the road to Kabul.

When they drove through Charikar, Misha, who had been spitting blood out of the window, turned to the other passengers. 'Where's my beard? I've been trying to grow a moustache and I can't.'

'That's why they knocked your teeth out.'

Misha laughed at the truth of Jamal's statement.

Jamal turned to Farood. 'You still want to know why I'm leaving this country of mine?'

Not long after Charikar, dusk began to fall upon them.

Farood leaned forward. 'I need to pray.'

'We're not stopping until my house,' snapped the driver.

'We have to pray before it's too late.'

'Too late for what? It's already too late.'

Farood persisted until Misha took his side and he pulled over. Farood prayed on the narrow beach of a stream and was soon joined by Misha. The driver smoked, and Jamal lay down and closed his eyes. He took the photograph of the woman from his pocket and looked up at it against the darkening sky.

Then Farood stood in what light there was. 'You should pray,' he said to Jamal.

'The Taliban pray.'

'They're not Muslims. Not all of them.'

'That's not what they say,' replied Jamal, eyes fixed on the photograph.

SEVEN

Kabul, October 2002

The evening sky was bedding down over Kabul and the frost was preparing to settle on the earth. On the edge of the city, north of the Sherpur district, fires were kindling in the warped mud houses, under the fraught tarpaulins and amongst the rubbish mounds. And then there were the families of six, eight, bunched in the shadows with nothing other than a blanket between themselves and the coming frost. The week before the price of wood had doubled to a dollar for one *maan* or four kilos. This was more than the men, who spent their days breaking rocks in the mountains for others to build houses with, could earn in a week. The only comfort for those with nothing to burn was that they were invisible when night came. A group of five young boys were jostling amidst a pall of thickening smoke rising from a heap of rubbish. Sporadically illuminated by flashes from the fire's edge, Farood could just make out their profiles and Western clothes. They looked wild.

He was standing on the lower balcony of the agent's house in Kabul looking north. From the inside the house felt more like a series of houses; from the outside it looked like a garrison. Farood became disorientated as he and the other were led through a courtyard, corridors, up staircases, empty rooms and shown to one large bare room with mattresses on the floor where they were told to wash before a promise of an evening meal. The driver had broken into silence on arrival.

Their host, a fat, middle-aged Tajik man named Rastin, laid down the rules. 'There's plenty of room for you here. But don't leave this area unless I come for you. And stay off the balcony. There'll be a meal soon. I have a good cook.'

The room smelt fusty. The mattresses cradled the imprints of heads and hips, the door off to the balcony had broken slats, there was some handwriting here and there on the walls. The passengers looked nervous, disenchanted.

Rastin saw the blood upon Misha's shirt, put a hand on Misha's shoulder and left it there. 'Whatever happened today, try and forget about it. It's in the past for you. For all of you. I will find you a shirt.'

Misha looked back at him with glassy eyes, rolling his tongue around his mouth. Rastin looked to his other two passengers for some confirmation, but there was none. Why weren't they grateful to be in his house? People never were. They were brought from hovels and caves and hopelessness. They were brought into his home and cared for. His servants waited on them; he let them meet his family, stroke his dog. He was a smuggler not a jailer, but nobody seemed to acknowledge that. He set people free, took risks and he deserved what he had. But Afghans never change. They can't be helped; they all believe they are above it. They imagine themselves to be proud.

'I have some painkillers I can give you.'

'That would be good. But you know what would be better? If I could help prepare the meal.'

'Sure? You don't want to rest?'

'No. If I can't eat then I'd like to cook.' Misha stood his ground against his host's pity.

'Okay. Come with me. I'll get you that clean shirt.'

Farood watched as Misha followed Rastin, wishing he could

follow. He realised that his brother, mother and sister would have already eaten by now, but they would not eat as well as him. They would be lying down together in the cave, unable to sleep because of the cold. He shivered with shame as he had done when chasing Karam once; he knocked over a pot of boiling water, scalding his mother. She had hidden her face from him, muffling her cries whilst he stood, craving for his father to beat him. Instead he was forgotten about – he felt forgotten now. He switched on the light in the room, then switched it off again.

Jamal was outside on the balcony, trying to make out the structure on a hill in the distance.

'He told us not to go out there.' Farood was invisible and unheard. He sat on the floor and wondered who had written the message on the wall. He stroked his finger over the words: 'I will never forget you'. Where were they now? Perhaps they had left the person they loved back in the mountains somewhere.

Jamal spat into the wind and returned to the room. He lay down, his back to Farood. The eleven-year-old realised there would be more of this to come: waiting in rooms, looking at walls amidst strangers who would not speak to him. *How*, he wondered, *will I know when I've arrived at my destination? The place where I'm supposed to be?* As yet no one had said how long the journey would take. Surely there would be someone to tell him. He would ask the Rastin tomorrow. Maybe that Tajik with the big car, who had met his brother and taken the money, could be trusted after all. He ran his finger over the writing on the wall and crossed the dimness to the balcony.

In the shadows below two of the five boys were pushing and shoving a smaller boy in rolled-up tracksuit bottoms. They prodded him like a goat that refused to move. They kicked tufts of burning paper at him, some of which clung to him. Farood shouted at them and to his amazement, the tallest among them swept the embers off the youngest and saluted an apology. They seemed to confer for a moment. Then the oldest strode along into his own shadow until he was under the balcony, shouting up in a snappish voice. 'Where are you going?'

The question confused him. 'I don't know.'

A sudden squall extinguished the fire and smothered another question hurled from below. The boy held up his cupped hands to beg.

Behind him Jamal switched on the light and joined him on the balcony. 'He thinks you're rich.' Jamal motioned the beggar away, but he stayed, joined by the others, who picked up stones as they approached, running and throwing them at the balcony. The wooden lattice doors behind Farood and Jamal splintered under the barrage. All five boys were now throwing in increasing competition, stones echoing into the room. Farood and Jamal ducked down, crawling back into the room as a rock chipped off the plaster.

Just then, Rastin entered the room. 'What did I say to you?'

He walked straight towards the volley, stepping over Jamal, and withdrew a Glock 17 pistol that snapped angrily three times. There was a pause in the proceedings before he retreated from the balcony and grabbed Farood by the throat. 'Always do what we tell you to.'

Jamal would not be ranked alongside a boy like Farood. 'I went on to the balcony. It was my fault,' he said.

'It's all your fault. You and your people. Clear up this room.'

*

Misha placed the plate of meatballs and pilau onto the rug before they were halfway through the noodle soup. He was wearing an apron and had been giving orders to servants about more cream for the soup. He seemed reluctant to leave the kitchen as he fluffed the rice in front of the other three.

'Tajik pilau,' he complained. 'They put too much butter in everything.'

Farood watched Misha as he sucked mouthfuls of rice, watched Rastin throw meat to his dog – even the servants threw food away. He couldn't eat anymore.

'Tajiks eat horses,' whispered Farood, lowering his eyes in disgust.

'You know what, little man?' Jamal broke off to pick his teeth, 'When you decided to make this journey, you also decided to eat whatever you were given along the way.'

Misha held a grain of rice up to the light. 'Maybe you should've brought your own food.'

'All I'm saying is that it might have been a sick horse.'

Somewhere along the way, Jamal hoped this boy would be discarded. In the meantime, he would bestow some obvious advice. 'Just because there are people living in caves with nothing to eat, doesn't mean you have to starve as well. You left to become rich, didn't you?'

'I'm not a cave person,' said Farood, his eyes narrowing.

Rastin gave further instructions. 'Farood, there's some clothes in your room, change into them.'

Farood protested. 'What's wrong with these?'

'They're for going the other way. Once you cross the border, you're an illegal. All of you. You won't be long in Pakistan – you'll need to blend in in Iran.'

He put on the baggy tee shirt and jeans, rolled up the legs and tied the sleeves of the jacket around his waist. There were other people in the room now – Hazaras – two men, and a boy and his mother. Three generations who would not be changing into anything. The boy was a year or two younger than Farood. He had lost eyes. Farood remembered his father saying that Pashtuns should drink the blood of the Hazaras for what they had done to their women. He never said what that was, but it made them terrifying. He looked again at the clothes he'd been given, the same as the boys outside were wearing. The two Hazara men, father and son, talked amongst themselves into the night. *They would have stolen the money to pay the agent, slit someone's throat for it*, he thought. *They would've followed someone home, tied them up, cut off their nose so they told them where the money was. And that boy with them, the one with the blank face, would have watched it all.*

Men moved and breathed, prayed and whispered in the darkness. Farood was too anxious to sleep; he began to envisage his brother's wedding, a wedding where there was too much food, all prepared by Misha. He was moving through the wedding party, the air filled with the warmth of food, looking for his father when Rastin arrived to awake the room. He gave them all soft-boiled eggs and bread and ten minutes to report to the courtyard.

The younger of the two Hazara men opened the doors to the balcony. He had sunken eyes and a pencil moustache. He looked at Jamal and pointed to the hill in the distance. 'We call it Bibi Mahru. For some reason the Russians built a swimming pool on the top, but they could never get enough water up there.'

'Another useless hole in the ground,' muttered Jamal.

'The Taliban used it. They liked to execute people from the diving board,' said the Hazara.

'Hazara, why are you telling me this? Get away from me,' replied Jamal.

The man withdrew to sit with his son. Daylight soon flooded the terrain beyond the balcony, granting a clear view of the land at the city's end, beyond the houses and the fortresses that were edging north like breeze-block glaciers. The fires had all but gone. A man submerged under a grey shawl stared in their direction. A woman strode the uneven ground with a bucket. Looking down from the balcony, Jamal saw the plots and broken slabs of graves that the agent had built his house on.

*

In Farood's village a dozen men were crowded into a low house. At the front of the room sat three Taliban fighters boasting of their victories in Helmand far to the south. They described how they had fought the British, driving them out of villages and into their fortified compounds. They said the fight in the north wasn't going as well because the people there seemed happy to live alongside the invaders. There were too many Tajiks and Turkmen there who worked for the infidels. It was up to the Pashtun, people with pride, people who had seen off the Russians and the British twice before. The speaker wanted to know, who would stand up in Baghlan? From the front row Farood's elder brother, Karam, got to his feet and nodded.

EIGHT

The Bush Highway, Afghanistan

They were on the highway before the sun had dissolved the morning mist. The day would be dry and it would warm, a little. The mountains would waste into a desert; the river that flowed from them would slow to a tarry then widen itself across the plain along with the wind. Before long – before they had reached Registan – there would be killing on the highway. The carcasses of supply vehicles, of civilian cars, Taliban jeeps and charred flesh would soon be accompanied by others. The dead of the valley congregated there, beckoning travellers to join them on the 'Bush Highway', as it was known. America had laid out 190 million dollars to build a road halving the journey time between Kabul and Kandahar. Now everyone came to the highway: to invade the country, to kill those who had invaded and to flee the country; a stream of prey either way, day and night. The Bush Highway was galvanising the enemy more than any offhand US atrocity. It had given Taliban fighters a shooting gallery and a routine: lay mines at night, followed by checkpoints and executions at dawn, and then on to sniping and the detonation of roadside bombs by mid-morning. Soon after the opening of the highway there were grumbles within Taliban ranks about the longer hours imposed upon fighters. And as they waited for the agent and his passengers in the rolling hills and in the irrigation ditches, they cursed the Americans for building it.

They were in the agent's minibus now, the Baghlan boys with God's eternal foreigners, the Hazaras, at the rear cloaked in a ragged assortment of European and traditional clothes: frayed and patterned turbans and sunglasses, dusty shalwar and waistcoats. Farood was in the seat in front of them. He listened nervously and closely to their quietly spoken Dari, sensing their Mongol eyes sizing up his neck. When they came to his village it had been to sell untamed horses with sores on their backs, and he had been quickly ushered inside with his mother. His brother told him how his father and other Pashtuns confronted them, daring them to draw their daggers, threatening to flay them if they ever came back. Jamal looked across at them and considered they would only go as far as Quetta. They might think they were descended from Genghis Khan, but they hadn't inherited his sense of adventure. He looked ahead down the highway. He could see the expanse of plain between the two mountain ranges. The same plain that the armies of Alexander the Great and the British Empire had crossed on their way to Kabul. Though the desert was creeping towards them, there were still outbursts of green beside the wadis where almonds, dates and grapes grew; tiny villages hiding behind golden wheat fields, flocks of sheep and goats. Jamal considered he would miss the sight of roaming camels and wondered what else he would remember about his home once he was in the West. He would recall, he suddenly realised, that he was a stranger to everyone.

For the agent the scenery either side was only camouflage for the Taliban. He wasn't armed. A pistol or any other weapon short of a tank would create more trouble than it would solve. And the agent had good reason to fear an ambush. He had been stopped at a checkpoint last month, outside Ghazni, warned about profiteering by taking Afghan people into the arms of infidels. They had taken a boy from him – boys rarely made it all the way to Europe. He was forever hearing other agents talking about 'smaller packages' being lost along the way. If families persisted with enquiries they were usually repaid after a year or so; but only the balance after the agents had taken their cut for as far as they'd made it. Misha sat in the front next to the agent, his back stinging more than it did yesterday.

The agent looked into his rear-view mirror. 'If anyone asks, you are going to work for me in my factory in Kandahar.'

Some passengers nodded.

'What do they do there?' asked Misha.

'Where?'

'At this factory?'

'They pack food. Almonds.'

'Bit early for almonds. We should say fruit.'

There was a moment's muddled silence then Jamal said, 'Because Taliban never shoot the fruit packers.'

Two hundred kilometres down the same highway, Corporal Sean Hanlon of Alpha Company was chewing dust at the outskirts of a checkpoint. He had pulled down his goggles and raised his scarf over his mouth, but still the desert filtered up his nostrils and on to his palate. He spat. His sergeant and two privates were seventy metres behind him, never less; for if a car or a man was going to explode beside them, Hanlon wanted seventy metres of clearance and a split second to hug the highway. So they ambled back and forth in tandem like a well-disciplined offside trap. Hanlon's job was to decide which vehicles were suspect enough to warrant a search and direct them to park up next to his sergeant. Of course, the problem was, insurgents weren't afraid of being discovered, and assigning them to within an arm's length of three or four American soldiers, when they were attired in high-explosive shrapnel-embroidered underwear, only served to help the enemy. Therefore, the vehicles that Hanlon directed to his sergeant were the ones he believed carried no danger at all.

Anything the least suspicious, anyone faintly ominous even by Afghan standards, he waved through towards the British waiting in Kandahar. Otherwise every twenty minutes or so he ushered one, maybe two subjects towards his sergeant, who would point a gun in the faces of children, whilst a private waved a detector wand over mules and old men on bicycles. As a tactic it had backfired, literally. Those Taliban Hanlon ordered to float past in their Toyota Land Cruisers had eventually turned off to lay down in the hills and riverbed with their rifles, labelling this part of the Bush Highway as 'Ambush Alley'. Hanlon had been shot at many times; only once had a bullet found him, scattering his clavicle like a rack of pool balls. Six months later he was back on the hot asphalt. He could have been posted elsewhere, but he declined. Hanlon expected to be shot at, and at least he could return fire, he could fight; he couldn't do that if a boy on a motorbike burst into flames and blew his arms off. Being blown up was for civilians. Hanlon looked up the highway through his scope. The people from the mountains, from the remote north, from Baghlan, were closing in.

The minibus climbed to a plateau and was now in Ghazni City – an Afghan city stranded like the Ark, muddled to the outsider, hiding an unspoken order. It was market day in the old town and the agent's bus slowed between the stalls and carts and the choleric camels slouching gracelessly in the road. Men were soon herding around the bus. Many were armed; they were not all Taliban, but everyone looked like they were prepared for battle. Teenagers heaved RPGs, old men carried rifles like umbrellas, cradled them in the shade of ancient walls besieged by Queen Victoria's army. There were no American soldiers here. Not yet. They had entered fleetingly and then left, ranks depleted, returning to fire rockets from Apache helicopters into the same buildings that the British had shelled in 1839.

It was mid-morning and dry, as it would be most of the

year. An eagle spread its wings out beneath the sun, circling a minaret. The wind swirled. Farood looked up at the tower. It was higher than any building he'd seen before. There were many minarets here in this small, walled place. The agent pushed his bus forward from behind the steering wheel. Why were all these men streaming past them? The smell of warm flatbread and tea filled the bus. Farood could see children selling cherries and asked the agent to stop.

'You're not in a taxi. Get in a taxi if you want. Ask them how much it costs to Quetta.'

The agent tossed a cellophaned sandwich over his shoulder. Between the fig and spice stalls was a gun stall. Handmade weapons mostly. A blacksmith smoked whilst auctioning a long-nosed pistol. More spectators blocked their path. Misha anxiously lit up a cigarette. A crowd murmured in the distance, then spilled into sudden uproar. Heads turned in the minibus.

Misha leaned over and rammed the horn. 'Come on, let's go, let's go,' he ranted.

The agent's elbow dug into him. 'This is not your bus. Be calm, Turkmen.'

A vapour of fear entered the bus; Farood was immune. Guns and gunfire he knew. The only slaughter he had seen up to now were animals and the work of invisible drones on his village and his father. 'I've never been here.' He stood up.

'And you're never coming back.' The agent was sweating. 'This isn't a place to stop. We get through. Eat further down the road. There's nothing to see here.'

Yet Jamal could tell there was something to see. He glimpsed a group of men around a strewn blue shroud – a motionless, blood-stained, sodden heap. A man wanted to know who would bury her, wanted the body taken away.

'What was that?' asked Farood.

The agent knew what it was. Last month it was a pool of an agent's blood in the town square. Beheaded – and not in a single blow. Taliban decapitations were not executions for Tudor monarchs, not intended to be. The story had run the agent's route by mobile phone and bumped up fees. Ghazni was a Taliban town.

Leaving the highway was even more perilous. People began to desert the road and the bus sprinted through the market and out the other side. A small boy selling pipes took note of its urgency. Farood was standing in the bus, peering out of windows.

Jamal asked him, 'Haven't you had enough excitement for one day?'

'I want to look at things on the way.'

'It's not that kind of journey, believe me,' said Jamal.

Farood looked straight back at him. 'What do you know about what kind of journey it is?'

'You have no idea of what's ahead, do you?'

'And you're the expert, are you? You've never been to the West. So, go on then, tell me.'

Jamal turned back to the window. Ghazni thinned out like a diminishing sand spit. The agent drove fast; the highway flooded over the bonnet. The agent considered how he had to take all the risks of the refugee but then always returned from the border, living off others craving to cross it. The uninterrupted motion of the vehicle sent people to sleep.

Farood watched them and knew they wanted to awaken in a distant future. He would rather pray. Lately whilst sleeping, he had found himself behind a screen of dust, hearing the muffled screams of his mother. Then as the screen began to clear he would see the outline of his brother, digging beside him. Karam would stop digging and Farood kneel the other side of a crater, his father sucked into the grey earth and ash beneath him. His father's head, tilted up to the sky, his beard coated with dust, his mouth open in a question. There was a line across his midriff, as if it has been painted there. Below it the body was a haze of black and red. The boy stared wondering what was left of the man beneath. His brother shouted through the haze. 'Farood, leave him.'

He was woken by an awareness of the vehicle braking. There were cars and lorries all around the bus. They were in a queue yet nowhere near Kandahar. Off the road in the distance he could see the tents of Kochi people. People, his father had told him, who spend their whole lives without a house, who live almost entirely off sheep, every part of the animal consumed, exploited, traded. Unlike him they would never leave Afghanistan. Maybe what he was doing was wrong; maybe his mother had made a terrible mistake. But if she had, she had done so for his sake. He remembered the promise he had made to her that he would return, wealthy, successful, and to stay; and he would make that promise again this evening – to God.

Corporal Hanlon looked into the glimmer and then looked at his watch – a slate black cobra tactical watch. Back in Oklahoma it was still only 4am. He was always impatient for it to be light back home, counting down the hours in Payne County whilst patrolling traffic on the Bush Highway. When was the last time he had seen 4am back home?

His sergeant spoke directly into his ear through a radio. 'Hanlon, any chance of looking for some insurgents today?'

Last year of high school. The woods in early fall. That was when. He and his friends had camped there and stayed up all night. That was the morning he had decided to join the army, but for his own sake and not because of his old man. Back home fall was a long, slow season of colour. Hanlon hadn't read Keats, but he would have shared his awe.

'Copy that. Don't they usually come looking for us? …Sir.'

At home, the trees were getting ready to put on a month-long pageant. He wouldn't mind standing by the Cimarron River for five hours at a stretch, but here, here in Zabal, fall only brought Aladdin-like dust devils and a flat, thinning sky that was preparing to dump snow. Hanlon's earpiece crackled; he spun round and showed his palms to his sergeant.

'Hanlon, use your fuckin' radio!'

A semaphore-sized shrug from Hanlon.

'Bravo one to bravo three, state your position, Corporal.'

'I'm about eighty metres away from you, Sarge. That's me with the gun.'

'Bravo three... use the correct fuckin' call sign, over.'

'Bravo one – do you still want me to direct people to you who look like they have explosives?'

'That's exactly the kind of people I want, Hanlon. Not fuckin' children selling figs.'

'Bravo, bravo one.'

Fifty metres off the road stood an indiscreet two-man steel compound with a sniper and another pair of eyes. The sniper had *slotted* six civilians and a borderline hostile in the last month, though it was hard to be certain of the occupation or the intent of casualties after an average headshot. Yesterday the grandson's story that his grandfather was only comparing his gun to the sergeant's wasn't believed. Still, what can you do when your interpreters keep getting assassinated? You can't wait for Hanlon to yell 'don't shoot' down the radio, that's for sure.

Hanlon swung his arm to the right in a slow, wide arc and the minibus pulled over.

The agent checked his watch. It was doubtful whether they'd make the border by dark now. There was an agreed rate to cross into Pakistan, but it was one that the night border guards didn't always agree with.

Hanlon lowered his scarf at the driver side window. 'I want you to drive over to that soldier down there. Slowly. Understand?'

'I understand. Speak English.'

Misha nodded in respect. 'Where did you learn English?' he asked as they rolled forwards.

'An agent has to speak many languages.'

At last Corporal Hanlon was giving his sergeant some traffic – traffic that could well kill him and the private next to him – but that was what the sergeant had asked for. The minibus was definitely borderline. But then the borders of insurgency in this country were wide and just about every Afghan of whatever tribe walked the line.

'Hanlon, if you're going to send me truckloads, you need to pull your weight.'

'I am. I'm doing what you asked. Sir.'

'Shift your Okie ass down here.'

Hanlon turned and mimed 'fuck' at his superior and jogged the seventy metres to join the afternoon's target on Highway One. He ironically stomped to attention before his commanding officer.

'Okay. Let's get them off the bus,' ordered the sergeant.

'Why we doing that, sir?'

'So, we can fucking interrogate them, Hanlon. Christ.'

'Sir, we don't have an interpreter anymore.'

'Well then, search them, search the bus, goddammit.'

Hanlon waved his arm in an arc. 'Let's go, people, everyone out. *Ausgang*, you guys.'

The agent began to recite his story. 'They're packing almonds for me in Kandahar.'

Hanlon lined them up against the bus and stood a baseball pitcher's throw away. Across the road the sniper was watching it all in close up. The sergeant, a particularly tall man, legs almost longer than Farood, marched over and examined them from behind his wrap-around dark glasses.

'Take off your jackets and shirts, take them off,' shouted the sergeant whilst Hanlon performed a mime act. Jamal began to laugh.

'No – it's not a joke, my friends,' said the sergeant.

Jamal laughed even more.

'What's so fuckin' funny?' asked Hanlon.

'Is it true, soldier, you can buy anything in America? Even your wife. Did you rent her out whilst you're here? Maybe she rented herself out.'

Had there been an interpreter present he would've lied in translation and the outcome might have been different.

'Get on with it, Corporal.'

Hanlon grabbed the gawky Afghan by his long hair and dragged him to his knees. He tugged at his jacket. 'Take that fucking thing off.'

Jamal spat at Hanlon, a heavy spit that stuck like frost on his goggles.

'Jesus.'

Through the scope the sniper was scanning the scope's crosshairs, moving from Jamal to the driver to the weird-looking Chinese guys and back again. From the edge of the circle, someone suddenly moved. He swung past him, then found him, the boy, walking past Hanlon and the sergeant into the desert. The soldiers kept their eyes front.

'What's he doing? Speak to me,' demanded the sergeant into his radio mic.

'He's praying, Sergeant. Over,' the sniper replied coolly.

'Are we running a mosque here? Hanlon, search them for weapons. Sniper, be ready.'

Jamal had taken several digs from Hanlon and lay heaped at his feet. In response Misha and the agent continued to undress, but the Hazaras, wrapped in dusty reds and greens, were not moving and Hanlon was unsure what to do.

The father shouted at Jamal in Farsi. 'Hey, big man! Why don't you tell the Americans to shoot me?'

Jamal made it to his knees. 'If I could speak American, I would tell them to shoot you all.'

The sniper's circle fluttered from captive to captive.

The sergeant conveyed instructions. 'Why is he praying?

Take a circuit. What do you make of the driver? Keep moving. Could be any of them. Or the bus.'

A feeble crack sounded from across the road and one of the Hazara men folded towards the back wheel. No one seemed to notice at first with the traffic fizzing down the highway. Hanlon and his comrades watched for a response from the others.

The agent looked down the line of men and then to the heavens. He had lost passengers on this route before and there would be implications for him. He began to shout, 'God have mercy! Why have they done this?'

The sergeant was confused at this because he didn't look related to the casualty. The dead man's son pulled at his father's foot to wake him and the dead man's father cradled his son's head in his arms. The wife was screaming; the sergeant was calm. 'Move away from the body, sir. Please move away from the body.'

After a delay of some remonstrating, the Americans explained to the agent that they needed to keep the body. They gave the grandfather a card with a phone number on and explained through the agent that compensation would be paid. The remaining passengers climbed back into the minibus and headed for the border.

NINE

Lancashire, 2011

Farood lay on his bed, picturing an optician's front door in Burnley. He had watched the shop for over an hour from across the road on a spring day. It was a week after he had met Sabana in Khalid's restaurant and he didn't want the people she worked with to see him. High-street pedestrians obscured his view of the door. There was a break in the shoppers and she was there, standing in a pale blue business suit, pressing her lips together. He came forwards; she saw him, smiled and waved. They came together and headed down the high street as an older woman watched from through the optician's window.

After no more than a dozen paces, he pointed at a coffee outlet. 'I thought we'd go here,' he suggested.

'I need to stretch my legs for a bit.'

Sabana walked on; they walked towards the bottom of the precinct. He told her that Khalid had promised to train him up as a waiter, that Khalid felt he had the makings of a head waiter.

'Do they have head waiters at his restaurants?' She led him into a café and asked him about his journey to the UK.

'It was fine. Sometimes it was hard, but mostly fine for me.'

'How long did it take?'

'Few years.'

He talked about Khalid again: Khalid's car, how Khalid found him a bedsit.

'Where were you living before?'

'With a family.'

He had been fostered, but he never used that word. He had lived with people who hardly spoke to him, who he believed were motivated only by money. He burped and raised his hand in apology. Sabana hadn't touched her lemonade.

'What do you know about Khalid?' she asked.

He shrugged and asked her about her work. She told him about a man who came in with so much hair oil on that they had to clean every pair of glasses he tried on, as well as everything he touched.

'Nothing happens in opticians. That's why my family like it. Some guys come in a lot with excuses to talk to me. They look at themselves in dark glasses.'

He felt the jealousy rise in him.

'You can't trust a man who wears dark glasses. Not in England,' she added.

'No, you're right. Do you want to go to dinner?' The question had fallen out of him.

'I've got a sandwich back at work,' she said.

'After work, I meant.'

'Oh, okay.'

'Khalid will look after us.'

'I'd rather go somewhere else.'

'We won't have to pay there.'

Farood swung his legs off his bed and stood at the cell window. He had been guilty of the one thing his father had said he should never do. He had been bought, and bought cheaply. He was back in the block again, this time for kicking Atif. He had last seen Atif from the block window, the same day he'd swung his heel against his face, sitting in the back of a taxi next to a white-shirted officer. At the time he guessed he was being taken to the police station to press charges against him. He thought about his mother. For years now he had imagined her in a home that Karam had built after he'd left Baghlan. A house that was painted white, even on the inside, and there were carpets in each room, curtains, mattresses, jars and a bird in a cage. There had been no letters, no phone calls between mother and son for six years now. He hadn't been able to, hadn't tried, to tell her he was still alive.

Keys clanged and the bolt shifted, the door opened. It was Robertson. He half smiled at the prisoner. 'Farood.'

'Boss.'

'Sorry to say your appeal wasn't successful. The lawyer rang the wing.'

'The lawyer?' Farood sat back down on his bed and bowed his head.

Robertson walked away, leaving the door open.

Is that it now? For fifteen years? Maybe there's some other way, legally. 'Boss!' he called from the doorway. 'That lawyer. He doesn't want me out. To win the appeal. I need a new lawyer?' Farood's voice could not deny the desperation.

Robertson halted. 'It's not my job, but I can do it. Come back to the wing with me.'

Robertson told Farood to go straight to the dinner queue while it was short. Next to officer Scully, behind the server, dressed in whites, was Atif. He'd been given the critical job of dispensing chips. It was Robertson's idea, his way of diffusing tension. He didn't keep rivals apart; he brought them together and wouldn't entertain gang segregation on his wing. Inevitably there was violence, but usually there was a truce soon after. Atif's right eyebrow was stitched and covered by a white plaster. The eye itself was beginning to open to a slit. Farood presented his plate to the good eye whilst Robertson calmly looked on from some distance.

Scully savoured the tension. 'Gonna give him a portion, Atif?' he said helpfully.

Farood looked away and the chips skidded onto his plate.

Across the dining area Atherton half nodded. Farood sat at a table alone. He ate slowly, watched Atif throw down his whites and head for a table of Asian lads.

'Atif!' Farood was on his feet. His body and voice were apologetic.

The Asian lads were wondering which way Atif would turn; he went to Farood.

'How's your eye?' asked Farood.

Atif shrugged. 'How was the block?'

'It was a rest from here. I saw you from there.'

'Where?'

'In a car. Leaving the jail.'

'Oh. I was going to the hospital, man. Having stitches put in my face. Some fucking Afghan burst my eye.'

'What was that like?'

'I was chained to an officer.'

'The whole time?'

'Not when I was having my stitches put in. I was with a nurse. She was nice. Yeah. I wouldn't mind a week in hospital.'

'I'll try harder next time.'

Farood told him about his failed appeal, about Khalid and Sabana. Atif already knew about his sentence, as did most people in the jail. He told Farood what he was in for and what he was going to do to the people who had put him there when he got out. Atif said he owned property in Pakistan and his plan was to own a lot more. Swapping stories was customary on the wing. Prisoners began where they liked and fictionalised in the middle, redrafting as they were moved from prison to prison. Atif knew someone who knew a good lawyer, knew someone who would lend him a phone. He wanted to know why he ate with Atherton.

'He's a kaffir, Farood. White garbage.'

'Have you spoken to him?'

'I don't need to. You can't trust him.'

'He can't trust me, but he doesn't know that yet,' confided Farood.

Atif smiled, holding his fist out for Farood to press his against. 'You coming to prayers?' he asked.

'Of course.'

Except he wasn't. Scully turned Farood around at the wing gate, telling him the imam wasn't prepared to have him back for a while. Farood wondered if Atif had played the devout victim. As a consolation for missing prayers Robertson granted him the extra Friday shower.

When he got back to his pad Atherton was manoeuvring an unruly floor-buffer along the balcony. 'What yer sayin', Roodie?'

'How's it going, Atherton?'

'I'm a cleaner, man. I'll put in a word for yer. What you doing, banging out Atif?'

'We're okay now. We're friends.'

'I heard your appeal got knocked back.'

'When are you out, Atherton?'

Atherton didn't know when he was out. He was waiting on a new court date for another armed robbery, 'an armed', that the CPS had found evidence for. He had a daughter who he'd seen for a grand total of six days: he didn't do visits.

Farood switched on the television and turned the volume down. 'You're right about Atif. He can get hold of a phone.'

Atherton nodded and followed his buffer along the balcony.

TEN

Lancashire

Sabana was making the already-overfamiliar train journey north. She enjoyed visiting him, the solitude of the journey. The visits were important to him, though he'd never complained when she'd been unable to come. She already knew about the appeal and expected a difficult visit. Khalid had pretended to break the news to her sister. He was adept at giving people bad news. She remembered when Farood had rung her to say that Khalid had just given him some bad news, he'd have to work that evening, and they were supposed to be going out to dinner. She promised to wait, until Khalid had decided his shift was over. By then it was too late to eat, so they went to his flat. A room and a bathroom. The furniture was a bed and a wardrobe. She'd never seen such a narrow bed before. She could feel the floorboards beneath the carpet. The room was darkened and when he opened the curtains it was barely lighter. It wasn't a place she felt comfortable in. But it was his home and he wanted to show it to her. He knew what it was.

'Coffee?' he asked.

'Sure.'

He told her to take a seat, but there wasn't one to take. She

75

sat on the corner of the bed, which dipped beneath her. Below them a television reverberated up the wall. Her palms cradled the coffee mug. 'Are you cold?' She shook her head, smiling; he pulled out an electric heater from under the bed.

'Please don't put that on. You'll have to work for another twelve hours if we have it on for ten minutes.'

'Khalid pays the bills for me.'

She could tell he had no experience of girls. He only had experience of talk from the likes of men around Khalid, men who talked about women like they talked about cars, who would say that someone who washes dishes doesn't deserve to have a woman. He leaned into the heat. She placed her coffee on the floor and put both hands on his right hand. To him her unblemished hands were too slight; they made him feel ashamed. She folded her head onto his shoulder.

Sabana was often the only Asian girlfriend in the waiting room at the prison's main gate. There were plenty of Asian mothers and brothers, and brothers in the sense of gang members, by the looks of it. There were a lot of children, even though the people inside were yet to grow up. She smiled at a prisoner's mother holding a baby. She looked back at Sabana, uneasy and angry. Farood stood up as soon as she entered the visits hall. There was a moderate embrace across the table. When he got on to the subject of the appeal, he could tell she already knew.

Then she had some news for him. 'Someone's shot Khalid.'

'Is he dead?'

'No. He's okay,' she said. 'It was only in the shoulder.'

'Who shot him?'

'He won't say. But my sister heard him shouting down the phone that he'd already paid compensation. Which means—'

'It's the guy who he shot.'

'Sounds like it,' she concluded.

'This proves I'm innocent.' His voice was climbing the

decibels. 'Why else would Khalid pay compensation, unless he'd shot someone?'

'Maybe.'

'What do you mean, *maybe*?'

His voice was raised and angry now; he was leaning across the table. Sabana clutched her bag defensively and one of the officers on a platform locked his eyes on them.

'All it proves,' she replied, 'is he paid someone some money. Doesn't mean it was compensation, doesn't follow that he shot him.' Her voice too was angry.

He clenched both fists. 'Your sister's got to go to the police.'

'She can't.'

His head was in his hands. Sabana reached across the table and held on to his arm. It wasn't even her or her sister he was angry with. He brought both fists down on the table hard enough to stop conversations around him. An officer was standing next to him before they'd started again. Farood stood to meet him. 'What?'

He was taken back to the wing. Atherton was slouched under the wing television watching *The Jeremy Kyle Show*.

'Back early, Rood.'

'You're gonna have to get me out of here,' announced Farood. Atherton laughed. 'Who do you think I am?'

'First thing is, I'll get you a phone, then I'll tell you the rest.'

Atherton muted Jeremy Kyle, looked hard at Farood. It was on.

ELEVEN

Quetta, Pakistan, 2002

No wider than a corridor, the room was full again. It would have overflowed if those inside had been able to open the door, or force the one tiny, barred window. They were in a long purpose-built outhouse, at the rear of a Baloch family home which served as a terminus for people being smuggled into Iran. The agents were two Baloch brothers, for this was Baluchistan as much as it was Pakistan. The three from Baghlan were waiting – waiting with other Afghans, Pakistanis, Bangladeshis. Farood had lost count and lost sight of the people that had come and gone. Only when the door opened was there light enough to see his own feet. He had memorised the different tribes and as many names as he could; he had also tried to count the days – so far there had been twenty-three. They had been told they would only be there a night – two at the most – then back into another Mercedes bus for a day's drive to the border.

Farood, Misha and Jamal sat by the door to catch the occasional rush of air. It would open a few times each day for one of three reasons: to bring food and water, to bring or take people away, to bring or remove the slop buckets. Occasionally there was a fourth reason. They had been delivered into Pakistan at the border town of Chaman late at night. As expected, the driver paid over the odds to the border guards. Rastin, the chief agent in Kabul, wasn't pleased when the driver returned with the news of the dead Hazara. If passengers went astray in Turkey or further west it took time for families to find out and expect their refund. He could bank the money for a year or so. But this time, they hadn't got as far as Kandahar. It was bad for business and for his reputation. The Hazaras were within their rights to ask for compensation. Other agents would seek to step in, to cash in on his failure. So Rastin withheld the driver's cut for two people. Then he had the driver beaten and told him he wouldn't be used again. He would find another driver that was more persuasive, more belligerent or just luckier.

The two Baloch brothers had adopted a policy of maximising economies of scale any way they could. At Chaman they had put all seven into one Toyota Avensis, making good use of the generous boot. Farood almost passed out en-route to a trailer park near the railway station. When the boot was eventually opened, the air was thick with diesel supplies for NATO forces. They were unloaded into the trailer and left with the fumes and a bucket of warm water. They were warned to be silent, which no one found hard. After two days of dizziness and vomiting, a steel wall gave way to an avalanche of light. Crawling back into the car, they were taken to the concrete container at the back of the Baloch house, on the outskirts of Quetta. At least the room wasn't an oven at night. Some prayed with their backs against the shafts that silhouetted mosquitos – no one kneeled or scarcely bowed because of the pools of urine. After a few days no one spoke except for Misha, who, despite his torn gums and dryness of mouth, was a voice that could be counted on in the darkness.

'I don't think America will stay as long as Russia.'

The room was hushed while he waited for a response. Someone from the far end of the room: 'Why do you say that?'

'They can't afford it.'

Two or three people laughed.

'Whether they can or they can't, the Taliban will hide and wait until they've left. And when they come back, they will be worse.'

Jamal elbowed Misha. 'How do you know what America can afford?'

'I don't mean money. They can't afford to have their soldiers killed just to save miserable Afghans.'

'I like the way they saved us on the way to Kabul,' replied Jamal.

'That only proves my point. They're scared,' insisted Misha.

Farood wasn't listening; he was still watching the Hazaras. They were huddled opposite, holding their grief and shock. He could just make out some of their Farsi.

You are too old to fight.

Who will look after your grandson?

The Americans have my son. They won't give him a burial and I have run away.

Farood closed his eyes, remembering a room in his village mosque. He was outside, peeking around the door, watching his mother and brother wash his father's body. He could see his father's face, mouth agape beneath the beard. His father's right arm was gently raised; his brother sponged his side. His father's torso was as white as stone. Farood had rarely seen his father's unclothed body: after he had dug a well once and his arms were coated in mud, the first time they had gone into the mountains to graze the sheep together and he watched the giant of a man standing underneath a waterfall. The arm descended, limp and lifeless.

Farood breathed; Karam turned around. 'Get out of here, Spider.'

Farood stared at the wooden table behind his brother, the place where part of his father was missing.

In the concrete room the unspoken consensus was that

Afghanistan would always be at war because that was the one thing it was good at. Jamal reminded Misha that he was a Turkmen and therefore excluded from passing comment on the country. He had already been warned by the agents for talking too loudly. For the first few days, while there was space, Misha had paced about in the darkness. He didn't seem to tire. Despite everything that had occurred so far, he persisted with a propaganda level of optimism.

'This is the hard part. Once we get out of here, the easier it will get. This is a poor country, that's all. Turkey will be a lot more comfortable. I promise.'

As new people entered, he greeted them like a concierge, introducing himself and others in the room, explaining about the rations, telling them about his plans. When a Baloch brought in a crate of tomatoes, he said something in Brahui that Misha didn't understand before kicking Misha to the ground. He kept kicking him and pointed to the slop bucket, and Misha finally understood that he should be quiet and take out the bucket when told to.

The numbers were getting serious now; if they were heard and found by soldiers or police, people would want paid off, and paid off every month. Misha's eyes stung with the contents of the slop bucket and with the daylight as he carried it the short distance to the open sewer. The water situation became critical, and when people heard the padlock click or the bolt slide, they began to rush and jostle round the door, pulling Farood out of the way by the collar. This was a Pashtun room and Pashtun order was soon established.

The padlock was set free; the bolt slid and Farood looked to his left at Jamal. He was asleep, finally, in a position only the dead would find comfortable. He moaned and Farood decided to ask for a little water to give him. The water was wheeled in in a steel drum with a lid and steel cup on a chain. The water boss made sure no one took more than one cupful and was always the last to drink. Everyone understood their place now and waited for the Pashtuns to take their turn ahead of them. At the back of everyone was the Hazara woman with her father in front of her. The son – the orphaned Hazara boy – stood where his grandfather told him, in front of Farood, the top of his head under Farood's chin. Everyone's lips and tongues felt tacky, their eyes fixed on the water. The grandfather studied Farood, who didn't speak to the Hazara boy but did accept him. Misha was first in line behind the Pashtuns. Some Bengalis had made it to the water and were loitering. They drank slowly but knew they daren't drink more. The last of them dropped the cup into the emptying steel drum.

'Always there are more people but never more water,' said one.

'Go tell the Baloch,' said Jamal.

The Bengali put his finger in the face of the Hazara boy. 'He needs less water.'

When it was the boy's turn the water boss pulled him out of the queue and beckoned Farood forward. Farood drank.

The Hazara grandfather raised his palms. 'He was next. Get your hands off him. Don't touch him.'

Farood emptied the cup, looked up at the water boss. 'The Americans killed his father. I was there,' pleaded Farood.

'One less Hazara,' said the water boss.

'They also killed mine. Can I have some more? Please?'

The boss refilled the cup and Farood handed it to the Hazara boy.

'Oh, you're in charge now, are you? Where are you from?' asked the water boss.

'From Baghlan. So's Jamal too, but he's sick. Save him some water, please.'

'What's wrong with him?' asked the water boss.

'The Taliban beat him. Then the Americans.'

'Why does everyone like him so much?'

'He likes to argue.'

'He won't get much further if he keeps on like that.'

The bolt slid again, and a Baloch man heaved in a crate of tomatoes and flatbread.

Before his back straightened, the Bengali was digging a finger into his shoulder and shouting in broken Urdu. 'This is not enough water,' he said. 'This is the same amount of water as last week. Now look at all these people. You want me to start banging on the door? I paid you. I paid for this water. I want more.'

He swore in Bengali. The Baloch said nothing and left the room.

'Leave it!' was the instruction from the water boss.

Once everyone had drunk the water, the drum was carried over to Jamal. He was given two cupfuls and only then did the boss drink. People murmured their prayers: Surah Fatiha, hands cupped to their breasts, the Hazara Shi'a's hands left by their side.

Allah is praised, the Lord of all worlds. The Owner and Giver of Mercy, the King of the Day of Repayment. We serve only You and ask only You for help, guide us the straight path, the path of those You have favoured, not those deserving anger, nor of those who lose their way.

The bolt slid once more and this time three Baloch men came, one not seen before with tattoos on his face: a moon and stars inside barbed wire. He held a butcher's knife. The Bengali man's arms were held and the butcher's knife was thrust into his side. He froze like a manikin, then slumped and finally cried out. They left without saying anything to anyone. The blood began seeping from him. In the darkness it looked like oil or soup, and for once people were glad they couldn't see. But they could hear. The man cried out loudly at first, then long and low and continuous, telling the room, '*I am still alive.*' The Pashtun water boss tore the sleeves from his shalwar to pack the wound, but the Indian cotton was saturated in seconds. He stayed alive for three days. People stood in his blood as they prayed.

TWELVE

Pakistan-Iran Border

They had been walking for half the morning, or so it seemed. Farood didn't have a watch, nor had he been taught how to use one; he read the time in brightness and dimness, the length of shadows. Time, his time, was now in the hands of whatever agent they were to be with on each part of the journey. But that didn't stop everyone wondering how much longer this was going to go on for. They were in the foothills of Iran's eastern mountains, the Makran: a Martian-like landscape of ash and reddish rubble, its highest peak a dormant volcano. They were straddling the edge of Persia, the ground sinking beneath them as they walked. Below them ran the highway from Pakistan into Iran – the so-called 'London Road' – a drug and human smuggling route into the West. Heroin left Pakistan in the lining of seats and boots and bags and behind headlights. For those who were caught, like the man who has only a piece of bread to his name, or whose family will be murdered if he doesn't drive the car, the dusty little border town of Taftan is often the last they see of the outside world.

This particular day the road on the Iranian side was busy with police patrol cars, driving back and forth from the horizon to the town, as if they had repeatedly forgotten then remembered something. Ordered out of cars a kilometre east of the town, Farood and the others had been handed over to an Iranian agent who had then led them into the hills on foot. The agent was a short, barrel-chested, swarthy-faced man, who carried a stick and a Bulgarian-made Arcus pistol. Following and watching him attentively was an unpredictable Rottweiler dog. The agent had met the two cars where they had run out of road, handed over three cartons of water to the occupants without saying a word and made for the mountains. They had been in his company for the best part of a morning, but he was yet to speak a word to the eight illegals he was dragging towards a better life. Before the overnight car journey from Quetta, anyone not in Western clothes had been made to change, all except the Hazaras.

The Makran was an ocean of crevices, crags and caves. Although it was winter, by noon the pinkish rocks were warm to the touch. Prickly ash and grit scratched at their ankles. There was no wind, even at altitude. They progressed in a ragged single file with Farood in front, close behind the agent. Behind him was Misha, then Jamal, then the Hazara woman, striding ahead of her son, who was running to catch her but afraid of leaving his grandfather too far behind. Next were the two Bengalis whose companion had died beside them in the room in Quetta. They had been rickshaw cyclists and the taller one, like a lot of rickshaw men, carried a pronounced limp. His name was Padman and he had been towing people round Chittagong since the age of twelve, stricken by osteoarthritis by the time he was twenty-five. By mid-morning his limp had become a swing and the swelling around his knee could be seen bulging underneath the denim. He was at the back of the line and the agent's dog ran up and down, herding him along.

Misha delved into his chewing gum supply and wiped his sunglasses on his baggy white tee shirt. There was snow on the peaks above them, but the sun in the foothills had them trekking in twenty degrees.

'So, where will you live, Turkmen?' Jamal asked Misha.

'In Athens. Eventually I'll run a restaurant.'

'You have a restaurant in mind?'

'The first one I see, I walk in, I offer to wash dishes, take out the rubbish, whatever they want. Then I offer to cook, whatever they want, whenever they want. They make me their chef, I make a name for the restaurant, for myself, for my food. One day I open my own place.'

Jamal conceded with a few nods of his head.

Misha halted. 'What about you?'

'Me, I don't have any dreams.'

Misha shook a forefinger by way of correction. 'Dreams are no use; they always stay dreams. Ambitions is what I have. And I'm going to achieve them.'

The dog trotted up to them with a look of disapproval. They carried on. Water provision was tribal and thus uneven: Jamal carried a carton for the three from Baghlan, the Hazaras had their own, as did the two Bengalis. The Iranian agent had his own flask; what the others did was not his concern. It was up to people to keep themselves alive. Farood believed that if he kept close to the agent, he would win his respect, so he walked in competition with the dog. He wanted to show the agent he was not like the Bengalis or the Hazaras; he was tough and he could walk in his sleep. In the family treks to pasture the sheep, his father had praised his son's growing stamina whilst Karam shouted, 'You're sure you don't want me to carry you?' The family would walk for three days, beyond the temple ruins of Sorkh Kowtal, as far as Kondoz, with four to five hundred sheep, until they found enough grass for a month. They slept under Russian tents, impregnable to the wind on the plain.

His father once showed him the ruins of a Shia warlord's house, destroyed by the Taliban. 'Afghans kings are always killed in the end.'

The Iranian had walked many Afghans through the Makran,

admittedly never one so young as Farood before, but the boy's spirit just reinforced the agent's view of the Sunnis to the east; they were *mal*, animals. Even the Shia Hazaras were unworthy of respect, and when the grandfather halted for his noon prayers, the dog barked and the Iranian waved his stick at the grandfather. 'Move, *mal!*'

'Leave him!' exclaimed his daughter in Farsi the agent understood.

So, he did. He stepped up his pace. Losing one or two in the mountains was inevitable.

It was noon and yet there was no sign of the car below that would take these people to Shiraz. There were, however, police vehicles on the highway. The agent whipped his stick against his leg, then against the rocks and then the dog. From a side pocket halfway down his combat trousers, he took out a paperback book, a novel; opening it midway his eyes traced the right-hand page until they reached a point he marked with his thumb. He then sat down and shut himself in. The Rottweiler also rested.

Presently all the illegals arrived and stood in front of him awaiting instructions, too frightened to sit. 'Wait here!' he said, brushing out his hand, eyes to his book.

Every few minutes he would cup his hands around his eyes and scan the highway below. Once or twice he sprang to his feet, believing this might be the car. Misha and Farood looked with him. Misha offered the agent his sunglasses. The agent examined them and put them on.

'You get a bit of glare,' volunteered Misha.

'You think so?' said the agent.

He raised them on to his forehead and returned to his book.

'May I have them back, please?'

The agent's lips silently traced the prose on the page.

'I'm going to need them in Athens.'

'Shush,' commanded the agent.

The Hazara boy was searching for breath and holding back

his tears. 'Why won't you wait for me?' he asked his mother, standing beneath her unsure eyes until his grandfather swept him up with his arm and kissed the back of his head. Once he would've laughed, as would Farood, remembering how his father's long arm had pulled him out of a river when he had waded in to his waist to save a lamb.

The Hazaras' two-pint water carton was nearly empty. The Bengalis were sweating more than the rest and looked exhausted. The younger one asked Padman about his leg; he nodded, stood on the other leg and slowly revolved his knee before taking out a jar of liniment which he began pressing in, breathing slowly as he did. Farood was leaning under an outcrop opposite the Hazara boy, who was sheltered by his grandfather. He was tucked inside the old man's arm, his eyes shut tight, shaking a little in silence, tears held behind his eyelids.

'I'm called Farood.'

'His name is Hassan,' his mother shouted.

'Hassan, walk at the front with me. You walk the same distance as everyone else, but you feel less tired because no one is in front of you.'

A muffled reply came from inside his grandfather's embrace. 'I can't walk that fast.'

His mother walked over and dried his eyes. 'Why don't you do that, Hassan? Walk in front of me?'

He nodded.

'We will be the leaders,' Farood told him.

Farood lay down, folding an arm around himself like a cat's tail. Hours passed. Shadows distended. The agent watched every plume of dust on the road below, but it was never the right one.

He had almost finished his paperback when Jamal walked up to him. 'Be sure to let us know what happens in the end.'

'In the end, either the agent from Shiraz comes or you die up here.'

He folded the page, closed his book; the dog stirred and they began walking again.

For a while the terrain made it barely possible; crevices aspired to be gorges and everything underfoot was hostile, cut by ice and wind. Nowhere was flat; people were scrambling, climbing, sometimes falling. The Bengalis took it slow; Padman lowering himself down the jumps and dragging himself up the rises, pushing everything off his right leg. They lost sight of the others, Jamal glancing back impassively for the last time. He understood how people could decide to lie down and give up. Hassan's mother was close by her son now.

As dusk began to emerge, they finally reached a gap in the hills, the land dipping away in all directions to smaller hills and eventually to the open plain. Beneath them to their right, a shallow, dried-up river valley meandered towards the highway. The Iranian halted. His dog turned to do a head count and half a dozen desert larks burst free from the rocks at their feet.

He sipped from his hip flask and then pointed to the ground, confiding in Farood. 'We will stay here tonight.'

Farood brought the news to the others as they arrived. They questioned him.

'Where? Stay where?'

'Sleep on a mountain?'

The younger Bengali grabbed him by the shirt. 'Go tell the Iranian, we didn't pay to walk to London.'

But the agent wasn't taking questions; he was talking to Farood and only Farood.

An inky blue wash was bleeding through the remains of an orange light. More buoyant than the rest, Farood found Hassan in the twilight and put an arm on his shoulder. 'Hassan, come with me; we will find a place to sleep.'

Farood led him away from the group and eventually levered himself up onto a smooth platform. Lying on his front, he lowered his arm for Hassan. They were about twenty feet above the others and a breeze fell onto their faces.

'I have slept in mountains lots of times. Have you?'

Hassan shook his head, guiltily, but he could also tell there was no cover on this tabletop of stone and wondered if this Pashtun was even more of a fool than the rest of his tribe. Farood was peeking between boulders, pushing his nose into shadows. *Doesn't he know a cave when he sees one? Does he think I'm a lizard?* Suddenly Farood, who had been no more than a yard away, had disappeared.

'Farood! Farood!'

Hassan was surprised to find himself in a panic and then amazed to find himself peering into cracks to see the source of the cries from below.

'Hassan, Hassan… underneath!'

Farood had slid down a three-foot-wide, thirty-degree slot into a hole with a sandy basin and a skylight. It was the most perfect of cave-cum-traps. Better, even, than anything he had been in with his father or brother on their summer months in Kondoz.

'Hassan, come down here. We can sleep here.'

Farood crawled back up to show Hassan he would not be trapped.

'It's dry and with plenty of room.'

Hassan was suddenly sucked the other way. Peering over the rim of the hollow, Farood looked into the face of Hassan's mother, who was squatting with both hands firmly on Hassan's tunic. 'Leave him alone, he's not going into any hole with you.'

'It will be safer and warmer down here.'

'Safer than what? He's not some rat.'

'My father was killed too.'

But they were gone and he had no idea why he had said that. Alone, he lay down in the basin, looking up to the crescent moon. *They will be cold out there tonight*, he thought, *and then they will wish they are in my cave.* If they asked, he wouldn't let them in. This was the first time he had slept in a cave alone; before he had been with his father, lying next to him on a sheepskin. With a skylight like this Father would have lit a fire. And his mother would've made flatbread as Father told him how he fought the Russians and reminded him once more that three of his brothers, three of the boy's uncles, had been killed in one day. This is what his family had given up for his land; now he had left it behind – perhaps he deserved to be hidden away in a hole.

The sky in the skylight became a shroud of darkness. Farood dug out the stones from the sand to make a profile for his body as the warmth of the day evaporated. He slept, and as he did, he felt his father's fingers envelop his hand – they were icy and he awoke wondering why there was no fire. Alone, he brought his knees up to his chest.

Dawn arrived with gunfire: a drawn-out stutter, like the slow closing of a corrugated shutter over a distant shop. Then a whole street of shutters. In between the gunfire the revving of a jeep could be heard. He climbed up the spout and crawled across the rocks, wet with dew. There were soldiers on both banks of a gulley – Iranian commandos dressed from head to foot in black, the noses of their assault rifles jerking as they advanced, tarantula-like, downhill. Under their fire a bronze jeep began to sway and slow, and a man riding in the back toppled and spilled out as if he had fallen asleep. Another man jumped out from the front and immediately fell to his knees with his hands above his head. He faced up the bank towards his captors; the commandoes raced down towards him. Three of them circled him, then their nozzles flicked up and the brisk crackles reached Farood as the man sank to the dust. The commandoes had come through the mountains and, like illegals, had probably slept the night there awaiting the drug traffickers.

Whilst Farood and the others watched on, the Iranian agent

searched the road below to the west, ignoring the gunfire. There at last was the car, the white VW Estate, winking its headlights at him. He waved back, but the light continued to flash recklessly up the mountain.

Padman felt obliged to point something out. 'He hasn't seen you.' Padman hoisted himself onto a boulder above the agent and waved in long semaphore swings.

'Get down, you idiot. You want to let the soldiers know we're here?'

Padman could not decode the warning and began to yell. The dog pounced onto the boulder to enforce his master's command.

'I've done enough mountain-climbing in Iran for now,' continued Padman.

The agent dragged Padman off his pedestal. The dog remained until a rifle crack jolted its hindquarters sideways. It yelled for its master, tried to grip the rock with its front legs, but the dead weight of it rear-dragged the rest of it down the precipice towards the road below. The agent and Padman ducked down. The agent knew the commandoes would have spotted the car by now and would be deciding whether to radio in their corpses or advance on the illegals. The agent pointed his pistol at Padman's head then pointed it at the distance behind him. The agent strode off, back in the direction of Taftan, where they had started from the day before.

The walk back down took less than half the time. That was the only mercy. It was only a four-hour walk without any water. Around noon they arrived at a barn about two kilometres east of the border town. They were in Pakistan once more. Inside the barn the air was thin, as after a fire; there were some dusty foam mattresses and army-issue rough blankets. Jamal and Farood shared a mattress, Misha lay on the stone ground, Hassan slept in his mother's lap. The two Bengalis were slumped in the corner, Padman holding his knee with his eyes shut. The Iranian agent was outside, making a telephone call. His routine had been disrupted and he had lost his dog, a companion and a workmate, so he was phoning in a contingency. This was by no means a difficult part of the overall journey to Milan, or to Athens or to London, but Iran was working hard to make it more difficult. They were building a wall, miles long, either side of Taftan. And since bandits had acquired fleets of 4x4s to cart heroin through the Makran, Iran had sent commandoes to ambush them.

The agent's contingency arrived within the hour: a jeep with water, flatbreads and eggs, driven by a man in a leather jacket with a rifle. Farood guessed he was the agent's son. His face was sullener than his father's, angry at being summoned, but he obeyed his father all the same. He had brought with him enough water for people not to squabble over and while some gulped and others drank slowly, father and son conferred in a corner.

'Up! Up!' The agent flicked his finger. 'Get up!'

Padman, the rickshaw man, couldn't make it; his friend walked over to the Iranian and pointed to his own knee, shaking his head.

The son advanced and thrust his rifle barrel into his chest. 'Don't speak to me.'

The Bengali understood.

The passengers were bunched like prisoners as the agent began his address, whether it was understood by all or not. 'I should be rid of you by now. I should be moving other illegals. Now I have to do the journey all over again. Double my time. So, you have to pay more. All of you. Hand over your money.'

The Bengalis were confused, disturbed. They knew something about their situation had worsened. They shouted at the others in Bengali to no avail.

'We have already paid,' Hassan's mother protested.

'Money!'

The agent's son whipped a plastic bag open. The agent withdrew a hunting knife from his boot and stared at the woman.

Hassan gripped her arm with both fists. His grandfather stepped forward. 'I have the money.'

He delved into his midriff for a small roll of notes. They seemed satisfied with this, but then insisted Farood and the other men undress. The agent explored the piles of clothes, shaking every sleeve and trouser leg. He found nothing worth keeping. Misha made to collect his clothes.

'Stay there!'

The agent's son gathered some accessories: Jamal's watch, even the younger Bengali's glasses. Then he pointed to Farood's feet. 'He has new boots.'

Farood protested, 'They're too small, not worth anything.'

The agent's son slapped him about the head hard and laughed when he fell with his feet in the air. He grabbed a leg and pulled off the boy's boots. The roll of two hundred American dollars fell to the ground. They laughed even louder. The agent threw Farood a pair of canvas slippers. The next morning the agent insisted that Padman stayed behind with his son, because he needed to rest his leg.

THIRTEEN

Shiraz, Iran

arood came to with a jolt, startling Jamal. Jamal watched as the boy's light frame raised itself, headily, to a sitting position. Misha felt his brow. They waited for him to say something, Lazarus-like. Instead he jerked then vomited on his pillow – Jamal's jacket.

Farood had spent over six hours in the boot of a car between the Makran and Shiraz, lodged next to Hassan. What air there was had been infiltrated by fuel and it was Farood's head that faced tank side. People generally survived these journeys. It took them a while to recover and some heavy breathers did die, often somewhere further on in their journey; the seed of a brain haemorrhage germinating, or a seizure finally taking them by surprise in some smuggler's cellar in Turkey. Before that there would be difficulties with coordination, depression or just an anxiety about the taste that wouldn't leave their lips. But small boys inhale less. Farood supposed his dizziness to be the result of his head bouncing off the wall of the boot as the driver swung the car violently round bends. He had been unconscious when the boot finally opened. Hassan offered up his arms, shocked and squinting like an earthquake survivor, towards his tormented mother. She had screamed at the driver to stop hours before.

Eventually he did, but only to put a gun to her head so she would stop screaming.

The next time the driver spoke was when they passed two airport towers and a sign that said 'Shiraz'. Within minutes they passed through two high wooden gates and stopped in a courtyard.

'This is where you will stay.'

They saw a three-storey pale-yellow house, once a mid-sized hotel. Jamal and Misha carried unconscious Farood in with them. Hassan peered at him from over his grandfather's shoulder. Jumping down beside his mother, the family made their way upstairs to see if there were other Hazaras. The Bengali found some other Bengalis. There were between forty and fifty men in the building; in every room along the balcony, on every passageway people were camped on thin blue mattresses gathered in small groups. People came out of rooms, leaning on the balcony rail to stare. The driver went to meet a tall, wiry Iranian with an Alsatian by his side. He pointed out the new arrivals and they retreated to an office to do some accounting.

Jamal wiped his jacket. 'Go and find some water,' he said.

Who was he to give him orders? A Pashtun. A Turkmen was an outsider in Baghlan, even more so elsewhere. A bond would form between the three as they made their way together, but Misha knew it would be broken any time they chose.

Climbing the stairs, Jamal shouted after him, 'And see what you can find out about the food. Who's in charge and when we can get out of here.'

Looking back at the spectators, Jamal searched for any signs of seniority. A man with the build of a wrestler saluted from the balcony in his direction, but Jamal presented a stony face. Crowded though it was, it was not like Quetta. The converted hotel had high windows and white walls, men circulating, negotiating; a boy was selling cigarettes from a tray. There was weariness, fear and bustle. It was captivity, certainly, but at this moment it looked like sanctuary. They laid the slender, strong-boned boy down into the shadows beneath the stairs. Shiraz was cool and sunny in early November. Shafts of sunlight toyed with airborne dust. Misha returned with a bucket of water and a flannel. Jamal cupped his hands and poured it into Farood's insensate mouth, then again onto his face. Semi-conscious and coughing, the world still sounded like it was locked in the boot of a car.

'We thought you were dead, little man. But you're not. If you can survive that, you can survive anything.'

Farood lifted an arm towards Jamal where it swayed like a branch in the wind.

'I need water,' whispered Farood, his words drifting away.

He formed them perfectly again in his mind, but between his lips and Jamal's ears they got strangled and slowed. '*Waball... wabott...*'

'You've just had some water,' said Jamal, 'and I'm not washing your feet for you. Who do you think you are – a holy man?'

Farood managed a fist around his collar. Jamal tipped a sip-full onto his lips. The patient swilled and spat. He looked at his feet – they were alarming; they looked like someone else's feet, like something you might want to put in a clay oven. He remembered standing in the blood of a slaughtered lamb at a wedding and then walking blood-stained for days, imagining he was an ancient warrior after a battle. He slumped back.

'What's wrong with the water?' asked Jamal.

It tasted of diesel. Everything smelled of diesel. Farood's head was a vessel of pain. It felt enormous and the pain went to its frontiers and beyond.

Misha's eyes traced a gash across the arch of his right foot. 'Do your feet hurt?'

Farood shook his head and it continued to spin on the inside. 'I can't feel them.'

Misha pulled the sleeve of his tracksuit over his hand and

pushed the sole of Farood's foot. Blood seeped onto the cuff, but the boy didn't stir. 'Can you smell them, Farood?'

The patient closed his eyes, tilting his head side to side.

The second hike through the Makran had been shorter, but halfway through the canvas slippers were torn to pieces by the volcanic rock. Then there was nothing left to tear but his flesh. During the final descent he had crawled over the rocks on all fours like a crab. He could still feel the reddish rocks on his palms, but his feet were numb. A vein in his calf burned blue. Examining Farood's feet, Jamal hesitated with the dampened flannel in his hand. He couldn't decide where or how to start.

'Did you find out how this place works?' he asked Misha.

'This place is like a bazaar. You're thirsty, someone will sell you water. Sell you food if you're hungry. You want to wash? Some Punjabi will charge you to use his sink. The agent has four or five people working for him and they all look more vicious than that dog from Taftan.'

'Is there a doctor?'

'I didn't ask.'

'You should have. People look like they're living here. Maybe there's something to be said for not having any money and maybe when they realise we have none they'll move us on.'

Misha wondered who Jamal meant by 'us'. 'Then we need to get him some new shoes,' he said.

'How? We can't buy them,' snapped Jamal. 'They'll need to provide.'

'Then you go and ask,' replied Misha.

But Jamal was the eldest by five years; he presumed seniority.

Evening settled in. Prayers were over; everyone was awake, coming and going from rooms on the balcony, with towels, with handshakes. A queue was forming outside a door on the ground floor, presumably for food.

A boy selling cigarettes from a tray plodded down the stairs and approached them. 'Cigarettes, please, cigarettes. The best.'

He was a penguin-shaped early-teens boy who ought to have been taller for his age. 'Cigarettes will take the pain away.'

'He'll be fine,' said Jamal.

The cigarette boy swung himself away.

'They might hide the smell,' Misha offered.

Jamal and Misha joined the queue across the hall. The house was busy. Moving through Iran wasn't straightforward: even if you had money the Iranian police could not be bribed. If you were caught you would be deported, but not before you had been taught a lesson in a police station, then in a prison or a labour camp. As far north as Baghlan there were stories about illegals being thrown down wells or hanged in barns.

Hassan called down from the balcony wearing the smile of the recovered child. 'Farood! Farood! How are your feet? Are they okay? Are they still bleeding?'

'A little.'

Farood turned the sole of a foot. It was still wet, but the wound had stopped bleeding.

'Can I get you a towel?'

Farood accepted, sensing the comfort of his own age.

A few minutes later, the younger boy ran down the stairs. 'Paper towels is all I could find.'

Hassan must have emptied a dispenser. He placed them in a pile at the bottom of Farood's dusty blue mattress and sat down.

'Thanks. I need to wash these feet. Where are you sleeping?'

'Mother has found a room. A man has given us his bed. She's sleeping.'

'How is the old man?'

'My grandfather? He is having some tea. He says he doesn't want to go any further. He is talking about going back now.'

'Going back?'

'He's tired. And he wants to bury my father.'

Hassan looked at Farood's feet.

'How was your father killed?' asked the younger boy.

'A bomb landed on our house. Will you go back with your grandfather?'

'He won't go back. My mother won't allow it. We're going to a farm in Turkey. What about you?'

'I'm going to Greece. If they catch you in Greece, they don't send you back. They let you stay. But I'm going back to Baghlan, after I've made a lot of money.'

'How will you do that?' asked Hassan.

'I don't know. I have to find out.'

Hassan's mother leaned over the balcony, summoning her son. Farood watched him scale the stairs, his arm stretched up above him on the bannister. *I would be racing ahead of him now*, he thought. Instead he had to sit like a cripple while groups of men stared.

Jamal had now left the queue; he knocked on the office door in the corner. A wiry man swung open the door as his panting Alsatian got to its feet.

'A boy that came in with me, he needs new shoes,' said Jamal.

'You give me some dollars – I'll get you some.'

'His feet are a mess. Is there a doctor here?'

The dog barked; the wiry man laughed and patted the dog's head. 'He just needs to rest,' he said.

'When do we move on?' asked Jamal.

'There's a waiting list. I can move you up for some dollars. But your boy can't even walk, so how can you leave?'

Later the three ate flatbread with oil and string beans. Farood finally tasted something beyond diesel.

Then Jamal fetched a bucket of water and commanded Farood. 'Stand in it.'

Farood crawled out from under the stairs, put all his weight on Misha's arms and pushed until he was upright. He took a moment to adjust; he swayed like a man on stilts, shutting his eyes to the pain. Jamal reached under the boy's arms and lifted him into the bucket. Farood smiled at the sensation. He couldn't quite tell if the water was hot or cold. People watched, leaning over the balcony rail. In the days to come, the metallic taste in his mouth would turn to ash and the feeling in his lower legs would completely return and he would be sorry that it had. He turned his head down to the bucket; he saw the water had become brownish, like ditch water. He looked to Jamal for reassurance.

'Misha, go see if you can get some disinfectant to put in the water,' ordered Jamal.

'They don't have a doctor.'

'They'll have first aid. That office over there.'

'Stop giving me orders.'

Misha hurried off all the same. Jamal lifted Farood out and stood him on a mat of paper towels. They changed colour like wet sand. Behind him the man built for wrestling came down the stairs. He handed Jamal a dog-eared towel.

'Are you sure?' asked Jamal.

'Of course.' He gave Farood the towel; they shook hands. 'Afghans?'

'Pashtuns,' interrupted Farood.

'What happened to the boy?'

'They took his shoes at Taftan.'

'I have something for him.'

'Oh? What's that?'

'Something that will take away the pain.'

Jamal was about to spread the towel on the floor, but he hesitated at such a loose medical term from a man with a match in his mouth.

'And what about me?' he asked. 'Will it take away my pain too?'

'If you want. What pain do you have?'

'I'm an Afghan, aren't I?'

The big Punjabi man recognised the sentiment – *the more he endures, the greater the reward.*

'We'll live with our pain, thank you,' said Jamal. 'Here's your towel.'

'Keep it.'

The big man moved on to another group. Smiles, handshakes, a sympathetic tilt of the head.

Farood didn't want Jamal to feel he was under obligation to explain. 'I'm not in much pain,' he said.

'Don't worry, it will come.'

Misha returned with a bottle of tea-coloured liquid. They put some in the bucket, refilling it twice more, finally with hot water. Few words were spoken between the three of them. Farood had little experience of expressing gratitude, and although the warm water made his feet bleed, he didn't panic or complain. He remembered bleeding like this once before. He had been building a wall with his brother and dipped his arm into a belly of mud, gashing his palm on the rusty remnants of a magazine case. His father washed it, cut part of his turban for a bandage and told him to hold his arm above his head. Farood smiled – he couldn't very well keep his feet in the air.

'They won't heal until you start walking on them again,' was Jamal's considered medical advice.

The light which had been captured in the centre of the foyer had almost gone, replaced by an electric glow leaking from the balcony rooms. The cigarette boy started his rounds again; somebody was already reading with a torch. Farood slept.

Misha whispered to Jamal, 'If they won't ship us out of here until they've had some money out of us, and we don't have any, then, we need to tell them that.'

'You really think they'll believe you?'

'It can't hurt. I reckon we need to get out of here as soon as we can.'

Jamal pulled some green bean stuck between his teeth then flicked it away. 'We can't, though, can we?'

'Why?'

Jamal lowered his voice. '*He* can't walk.'

'Are we *walking* to Turkey?' Misha stood and walked towards the entrance door but met the driver blocking his exit.

'I want to go outside.'

'You can't. Not at this time. Against the rules.'

Misha wandered back to their place under the staircase. He looked around the foyer and up at the balcony opposite. Everyone was part of a group. He knew he had to be as well. He lay on his mattress. 'Then we need to get him some medication, some bandages, and shoes for him.' Misha made it sound straightforward.

Farood opened his eyes and whispered, 'Jamal, I think the water helped.'

*

Misha was out in the yard smoking a scrounged cigarette. Only one or two people at a time were allowed out during daylight hours. Some pink rose petals still clung to a crumbling bud against the high yellow perimeter wall. The stone ground was waiting to be swept. Towards the corner on the right was an unwanted fountain. Thousands of mynah birds were roosting somewhere close, their mass clicking sounds like a voice tutting from the heavens. Misha weighed up the perimeter. The wall above the gates was clad with steel spikes and the wall either side was so high that only the very top of the building opposite could be seen. He went over to the empty fountain and sat on its brim. Above the door was a veranda, a table and chair, a used ashtray. They had a view of the street. The spikes on the wall, he realised, were not about keeping people out – the drop down to the other was surely too great to scale – they were about keeping people in.

They had been there for ten days, less than the hellhole in Quetta, but somehow this place felt more ominous. There were far more people here, and they were always being watched. Misha realised that he hadn't seen anyone leave the building yet. The Afghan agent had told him that agents along the route were only paid once they moved people to the next agent and it was costing these people to keep them here, so what was the hold-up? Surely they were losing money?

He was standing on the fountain brim facing the wall when he felt something tug at his jeans. It was a black Alsatian. His owner, the man from the office, waved the dog back and ordered Misha. 'You. Inside. Now,' he ordered in English.

Farood was hobbling back and forth from a Persian window in his bare feet. Jamal sat with his legs up on the seat-wide sill, looking outside at the fig tree overhanging the wall, and the rotten figs on the ground. Farood grinned at Misha.

'He's making progress, don't you think? Soon he'll be running past Buckingham Palace,' said Jamal.

'Any news on some shoes for him?' asked Misha.

Jamal shook his head. 'Why don't you see what you can do?'

Farood could put his left foot flat on the floor but avoided putting any weight on his right. He picked up the pace.

Jamal responded with an encouraging nod. He addressed Misha whilst looking out of the window. 'What does your family do in Mazar?'

'They pray for rain. Farming okra mostly. For as long as I can remember, I've worked on two farms. My father's and the next farm. My father's farm is dying and the other doesn't pay enough, so I said goodbye.'

'You're a farmer boy,' emphasised Jamal.

'And I'd sell at the markets too.'

'You know, I think I bought your okra once. It was rotten.'

Farood laughed; Misha didn't.

'How did you make money in Baghlan?' asked Misha.

'Textile factory.'

'That's a good job.'

'Yeah, it was a good job, for Baghlan.'

Farood came to a halt. 'I have an idea. You both give me one shoe each, then I'll have two. After a while we can swap.'

Misha made his way over to the office, asked the question about footwear again, returned and said nothing.

FOURTEEN

Shiraz, Iran

As the nights became shorter Farood regained his strength. When darkness fell, he would close his eyes because everyone else did, but hunger always nudged him awake to watch the business of the building after dark. At home in their house and then the cave, he would lie awake gazing at embers or his brother. He remembered how Karam pushed him away one winter's night when he tried to huddle up to him. *You're too old now, Spider.* It was for men to huddle with women and children, not with each other. In a corner of the landing above, lighters were burning under foil and men were entering dream worlds. Farood had seen this before in Pol-e-Khomi, where old miners ravaged by labour and loneliness found peace with opium pipes. He noticed how one from the group moved back and forth to the Punjabi wrestler's room. Silently, a shadow rose from the mattress nearby, and he watched as Misha tiptoed across the floor and climbed onto a window ledge, opened the smaller window at the top and rested his midriff over the frame.

Farood sat up. 'Misha… Misha.'

Misha dropped head first, arms ahead of him, shadow crumpling into shadow. He returned to the fountain and stood on its edge, facing the wall. He was barely a foot off the ground, with another fifteen or so to go to the top of the wall. A demanding and risky standing jump. He squatted, took a breath, looked up. It couldn't be done. He got down and paced the wall. Starlings were gathered on the high wire. There was no light on in the room behind the veranda above him. If he was going to get over the wall, he would have to do it in silence. He squeezed his hands, then his feet, into the crack between the gate and the wall, and began to climb, gripping the gate, one hand over the other. He felt his toes crushing one another inside his shoes, but, taking his time, he reached the top of the gate, where he stretched for the wall. There was only a slim margin, five centimetres or so, between the steel spikes, on top of the gate, enough for fingers but not a hand. The wall along the side was without spikes. He pushed down with his left arm so hard he thought his forearm would snap. It wouldn't hold up the rest of him. He fell back into the yard.

He scaled the gates to the top wall for the second time. He took two deep breaths and swung his feet to the right. Both insteps made it on the sidewall. Releasing his arms, he hung upside down, walking his palms upwards. He stood on the sidewall, the spikes of the front wall before him. He went to the spikes and peered beyond them. There was a car on his side of the street, but the pavement was wide. He could do this. It was only like jumping a ditch, with a harder fall. He pulled back his shoulders, pushed out his chest, held his arms out straight in front of him, then jumped over the spikes, the pavement and onto the roof of the white Paykan taxi which boomed like a drum as he bounced off it into the road. He lay there, face down, listening to the Alsatian barking behind the balcony doors.

Sunrise. Greetings and prayers. The dog was in the yard taking a crap. The opium-takers were prostrate; Hassan was running along the balcony while his grandfather argued with his mother. Farood was walking back and forth across his mattress.

'Where's Misha?' wondered Jamal out loud.

'He's gone. I saw him climbing out the window.'

Jamal looked into the yard, then back at blasé Farood.

'Maybe he'll be back in a bit,' ventured Farood.

'Oh, really? Like he'll just knock on the door. I've heard stories about illegals in Iran. He'll be lucky if they don't kill him out there.'

'I called to him last night, but he didn't answer.'

'You should've woken me.'

'You're not his father.'

'What do you think these agents will do to us when they find out he's gone?'

Farood shrugged. The agent and his dog were back. The Alsatian returned to Farood's feet, trying to lick them as the boy tiptoed away.

'Fifty dollars for new shoes,' announced the agent.

'We already told you, we had our money taken in Taftan.'

'That's bad. I will punish the thief. In the meantime, you can use the phone in my office. Get your family to put the money into my account.'

Farood puddled on the spot. 'Fifty dollars is too much,' he said, shaking his head.

*

The winter sun climbed behind Misha. He had counted the turnings he passed from the jump and was already regretting making that decision. He should have fixed a landmark into his memory. He stopped and looked around him. Most of the buildings bore enormous pictures of a severe-looking Ayatollah Khomeini or a smiling Mahmoud Ahmadinejad. Noticing a fenced-off football pitch between two apartment blocks in the middle distance, he made straight for it. The pitch was deserted but still he stared. He had played some football, in the shreds of evenings after work, on a scrub field next to where he picked pistachios, but never on a football pitch. This, he decided, was something he would do whenever he reached where he was going. He would be there in the centre of the pitch, unpassable to opposition players.

He returned to the main road feeling unnerved but also excited. He was soon walking along a boulevard of birch trees, sopping with golden leaves. The buildings had vanished and between the tightly packed trees were glimpses of a dewy field. This was his landmark. Traffic was building from a trickle to a heavy stream, most going in Misha's direction. He decided that they, like him, must be heading for the city centre. He turned to walk backwards, threw out his thumb in the hope of free ride into town. The cars, far more modern and cleaner than anything he'd seen back home, ignored his appeal. Some drivers waved their refusal from behind their windscreens or out the window. So many empty seats he could be sitting on. At home, the first or second car would have stopped and taken him into Mazar. Hitching was how people got to work, but back home the people that stopped were also Turkmen, on their way to the Turkmen quarter to set up shop. It had been nearly a month since he'd left home. He knew himself that he smelled. And his clothes not fine or fashionable when he left, had been replaced by something shabbier. He turned his back on the unkind traffic but left his left arm hanging out like a scarecrow. He told himself that when he was driving to work, in a years' time or so, if he ever came across anyone hitching, he would give them a lift. He would fill up his car if he had to.

Ahead of him, he could see the avenue of trees discontinue to be replaced by shop fronts and workshops. Then the rear of a white car with rust on the wheel arches pulled over in front of him. Misha walked to the passenger window.

A young man with fine features stooped out, shouting above the engine's rattle in Dari. 'Where are you going?' he asked.

An obvious question but one that he couldn't properly answer. 'I have to buy some shoes for someone.'

'Get in.'

The car roared into a painfully slow momentum, other vehicles overtaking and hooting their annoyance.

'I'm Misha.' He held out his hand, but the driver didn't take it. All his concentration was on the steering wheel.

He flicked a glance at his passenger. 'Where are you from?'

'From Afghanistan.'

'A long way from home.'

'I'm going to make a new home.'

'There's plenty of opportunities here in Iran.'

'You think?'

'Of course.'

They pulled up and both stared at the red traffic light.

'If you like, I could meet you later, show you round Shiraz. I know some people taking on workers.'

Misha looked away from the driver, at the much newer, cleaner car next to them, at the brightening sky.

'I'm going to Greece,' he said. 'I'll be leaving this evening. Are you on your way to work?'

'To college. I'm a medical student.'

He told the driver about Farood's feet. But before he could ask about changing his American dollars, the driver bluntly recommended a brand of antiseptic cream and let him out opposite a shopping centre. In Mazar shopping centres were little more than a collection of small units and stalls selling carpets and food, but here was an air-conditioned palace. Not much was open yet, only the odd kiosk, so he window-shopped, loitering outside a jewellers for a while. At the head of the arcade, he came across a closed bank and sat down on the floor outside. He took off his left shoe and reached into the insole, pulling it up at the heel. Tucked into the hollow heel was a plastic wrap of American dollars. He unfolded two notes and put the rest back. He was still sitting on the ground when the staff arrived to unlock.

The bank staff's assumption was that he had been there all night and they seemed surprised, if not a little worried, when he followed them in. He went straight to the counter, but no one came to the other side to serve him. He was mindful of the time and imagined the morning food queue in the agent's house. He wondered whether the agent, or the agent's driver, would notice he wasn't there. What would happen when they realised he wasn't? He could see the bank staff talking to one another, probably about something they had watched on television.

He banged the counter with his fist. 'Miss! Miss! I'm in a hurry.'

Still they didn't come to him. He waved his money at them. The older of the two women came out. She looked at him briefly.

He slid his American dollars under the glass. 'Change, please.'

She didn't look at the money. 'Passport.'

There was a pause as Misha looked into the clerk's stern eyes. 'What?'

She took a breath and said the word again, slowly and more loudly. 'Passport.'

'I just want money.'

She shrugged her shoulders and returned to the back office.

'Hey! Hey!' Misha thumped the counter harder.

He knew that the Iranians and Americans didn't exactly get on, but he wasn't American and not to take their money seemed stupid.

He headed out of the shopping centre to the market stalls on a street that was gathering a cast: vendors constructing stalls, unloading vans full to the brim. He walked up and down, acquiring suspicion here and there. He remembered his uncle's stall in Mazar, the times he and his father had delivered baskets of okra, nuts and mulberries from the farm. The two brothers argued every time they met, about the prices and about the produce, and every time his father would curse his uncle all the way back home. Once, his father had called his uncle a thief, and he and his father ended up coming back home with all the stock, with the baskets full. After that, his father rented his own stall at the market, and Misha began work there.

Shiraz's market was slow to assemble, but around a corner he could already see a stall that would eclipse all others. A man was building tier upon tier of shoes, watches, biscuits, lighters, textiles; everything the shopping arcade had. The stall was still under construction, the man still adding things with a pole on a pair of steps. It was a mystery how the thing didn't collapse under the weight. Misha called up to him, pointing to a pair of trainers that would fit Farood, more or less. Misha gave the man the ten-dollar bill, and just as he was tucking the trainers into his jacket pockets, someone's grip clamped his arm above the elbow.

'Show me some ID.' It was a policeman, short and stocky, testing the seams of a black uniform.

'I don't have any.'

'But you have American dollars.'

The officer nodded to a second taller policeman behind him who reached into a pouch for handcuffs. Misha knew that what happened in the next few seconds would make all the difference to the rest of his life. He looked at the cuffs, then at the face of the shorter policeman and swung his forehead into it. He felt the policeman's front teeth on the frontal bone of his head and was on his toes sprinting between stalls before the policeman's backside was on the pavement. A whistle blew behind him and someone shouted, 'Stop that illegal!' Misha made turn after turn until the crowds were gone and his lungs were empty. He was bent double, facing the ground. He was lost, but he didn't feel like asking anyone the way. He straightened up and faced the high rise in front of him; he leaned back and fixed his eyes on the very top.

From the foyer of the top floor, he could see the market and beyond, the boulevard of birch trees leading out of the south of the city, a police car circling a roundabout. Back on the ground, he stayed clear of the boulevard – walking in the scrubby fields the other side of the trees. Within an hour he was looking at the gates to the agent's house from the outside. He could climb them for sure, but again, there were the spikes to deal with. He recalled the fig tree in the yard next door. If he could get to that, he could get back into the yard. He decided to wait for the cover of darkness or the arrival of a better idea.

Inside the compound Jamal watched Farood limp his way upstairs, barefoot, to the waiting Hassan.

The agent, on the way to the front door with his dog, paused at the scene. 'You can move on tomorrow. Leave him here with us. I'll look after him.'

Hassan and Farood played draughts in the Hazara's room. The mother was darning the grandfather's socks while the old man lay on a mattress facing the ceiling, his eyes half closed.

Outside Misha was sitting on the kerb thinking about his father. He would have been working in his poly-tunnels today, harvesting late peppers. If there was cotton left to pick on his neighbour's farm, then he would most probably be helping him. He envied the people driving past him, people who didn't have to look in an irrigation ditch to see if they could get through the winter, envied and despised them. There was still no sign of activity at the house next door. It too had gates, but they may as well have been climbing frames.

Then a chocolate brown people carrier with darkened windows sped around the corner and stopped at the gates of the agent's house. It was the same vehicle that had brought him here two days ago. The gates began to slowly part. Misha got to his feet, took a few steps into the road. He couldn't very well walk in beside the car without saying something to the driver, and anyway, what would he say? The driver would be bound to report him to the agent in charge. The car wheeled in. The gates paused – its arms wide open. Misha recognised the driver as he got out of the car, hitching up his trousers and shouting at his passengers to stay where they were. He then turned towards the door and Misha made for the narrowing gap, turning himself sideways, stooping down and crawling under the car. When the new arrivals were let out, he tagged along at the rear, peeling off to the Baghlan boys' corner as soon as he was in the building.

He enjoyed the telling of his story: the death-defying leap out of the yard, the journey into town with the doctor who offered him a job, stealing the trainers, fighting two policemen with his bare hands – and his narrow escape. As Misha reached into his jacket pockets, he found just one solitary trainer. Farood laughed.

Jamal broke in. 'Is this true?'

'Of course. Aren't you listening to me?'

'I'm listening and I can't believe it.'

'It's all true.'

'I mean, I can't believe you were followed by the police. Did they follow you here?'

'I lost them a long time ago.'

The story was ruined.

'Misha, Shiraz, what's it like?' asked Farood.

'Rich,' said Misha, slapping his knee. 'Very rich. The richest man in Shiraz could buy the whole of Baghlan.'

Farood smiled, holding his one shoe. He put it on and soon after ran to the front of the food queue.

Jamal told Misha what the agent had said about leaving the next day. 'I'm not going, though. They'll turn him into a slave if we leave him here. You go on ahead if you want. We'll probably catch up with you somewhere else.'

'I don't want to go on ahead. Why would I want to do that?

I've just been out there risking my neck to get him shoes. All we need now is one shoe.'

Whilst eating, Farood observed the cigarette boy on his rounds again. He had watched him emerging from the office each day, then returning after the round for a talk with the agent. and every day he came to their corner under the stairs.

'You want cigarettes?'

'If I had any money, I'd be wearing two shoes. But I know who does,' said Farood.

'Who?' asked the cigarette boy.

'I'll tell you if you get me some shoes to wear.'

'How do you know who has money here?' The cigarette boy sat down, laid his tray by his side.

'Because I saw this man take money from someone last night,' explained Farood.

'Who? Who is he?'

'Look at my feet. Look at what size they are. I want shoes that will fit me.'

The cigarette boy looked around for signs, looked for men wearing jewellery, anything he had missed on his rounds. For a moment the bigger boy, looking down on a captive that could barely walk, was in the weaker position. He recovered his sureness. 'You show me the man – I'll get you the shoes.'

They shook hands; Farood pointed. 'That big Punjabi above us. But you must search his room, his friends. He will have a lot of money somewhere.'

In the centre of the room, Misha was doing press-ups with his feet elevated onto the chair. He had taken off his shirt, and his forearms were lashed with scars, so much that no one cared to ask. The cigarette boy lugged his tray along the balcony and met the eyes of the Punjabi.

That night, the agent, his Alsatian, the driver and an Uzbek man in a woollen hat carrying a machete made their way into the

Punjabi's room and the rooms either side. They closed the door on each occasion but only twice were there raised voices and only once barking. The next morning, before he began his round and while the other two were asleep, the cigarette boy walked over to Farood in a new pair of Adidas trainers and gave him his old shoes.

FIFTEEN

Central Iran, December 2002

Farood was resting his head against the scented upholstery of the car, rubbing his face on it like a cat. The smell reminded him of pears. The world beyond the tinted window looked grey. They were heading west to Tehran. He pulled down the armrest and looked to Jamal and Misha, who appeared confused by the comfort, the luxury afforded to them. The driver's stare was frozen on the road ahead. It was the same fat-headed man who had picked them up at the border and put Farood and Hassan in the boot, but this was a brand-new car; this was the journey he had been promised outside his cave. He wasn't just being taken to a better life – he was already living one. Quetta and the mountains were behind him.

In the rear-view mirror, the driver's eyes found him. 'Put the window down if you want.'

Misha zipped his window up and down until he had just enough air rushing in to the back. A gazelle dashed through a lozenge of light. The driver was taking them to an overnight stay in Tehran. From there, the following day, they would be in Turkey – one step away from the West.

The driver tapped his fingers on the steering wheel to a song in his head. 'So, what's everyone's plans when you get to the

West?' His eyes found Jamal.

'I don't mind what I do, as long as I get there.'

The driver laughed. 'Of course you'll get there. People always get through. I've never known anyone fail to get to the West, one way or another.'

Jamal noticed something through the tea-coloured window to his left. It was a man selling apples from a roadside stall. They had to be last year's apples. Even as they flashed by Jamal could see how stale they were. For once, he volunteered something. 'I was a student when I left Baghlan. I'd like to finish my studies.'

'You didn't work?' The driver disapproved.

'I worked in a clothing factory half the week. With my wife.'

Farood asked him privately, 'Where is your wife?'

Jamal explained to the whole car. 'The Taliban bombed the factory, killed a lot of people.'

Farood's voice was softer still. 'What were you studying?'

'Engineering. I like machines. Prefer them to people.'

Farood smiled up at him. 'If the car breaks, then you can fix it.'

By mid-afternoon they had arrived in Isfahan. The windows of the people carrier were down. The passengers adjusted their eyes to the brightness and the palatial mosques. Parking off the central square, the driver led them to a café facing a horseshoe of raised rose beds. Small birds were feeding beneath the bushes. Despite the sunshine they felt December's coolness as they waited for food. The agent smiled and raised his coffee cup to everyone.

Misha told him how his sunglasses had been taken in the mountains. 'That agent, he wasn't like you. He didn't look after us.'

Jamal grinned at Misha's naivety. The agent lit a cigarette and strolled inside to the counter. A few minutes later, the lamb salad arrived and the waiter also placed a pair of sunglasses on the table. The driver handed them to Misha. Though they tried not to, they ate fast, Farood sucking dribbled yoghurt off his tee shirt.

'How are your feet, little one? Clever of you to get those shoes.'

Farood nodded, eyes on a plateful of meat.

Jamal wondered about the fate of the drug dealer – the Punjabi wrestler – in Shiraz. He guessed that would now be the cigarette boy's job. He thought about the factory: sitting over a machine, struggling to concentrate, gazing down the aisle at his wife. His work was sloppy; the supervisor reprimanded him daily. His wife tried to teach him, but he didn't concentrate, and in the end, they had sacked him. If they hadn't, the bomb blast would have taken him as well. Many times he had envisaged making this journey with his wife, but had never mentioned it to her.

He turned to the driver. 'How will we get across the border?'

'There will be no walking.'

The driver's phone rang. He slipped it from his outside pocket, his eyes on his passengers, his smile wide. 'They are with me now. See you very soon. That was the owner of the house. Everyone had enough to eat?'

The driver switched on the fan to warm the car. The sun was dipping. Thousands of geese, low in the sky, crossed the horizon ahead of them. Misha and Farood turned to one another, smiling at the spectacle.

'Sleep if you want. When you awake, you'll be in Tehran,' said the agent.

Farood and Misha slept peacefully, Jamal fitfully, and he awoke when he heard the driver's door slam shut and the locks bolt down. He leaned forward, shaking Misha's head from his shoulder. The driver was walking towards a white and green police car parked ahead of them. Behind – dirty white houses, chickens on the pavement. They were in a small town, maybe a suburb of somewhere else. A policeman was leaning on the front of the van, arms folded, yawning. He greeted the driver, who went to the passenger side window, where an envelope was handed over. *Surely it should be the other way around*, thought Jamal. Maybe it wasn't money in the envelope. But then two policemen headed for the people carrier.

They were taken to a police station on the outskirts of Tehran, to the underground car park for the three-storey complex of cells and offices, where two more police officers were waiting with a van. Before the three were loaded in, they were pushed up against a wall with the four officers facing them. One of them drew a baton. Misha cowered; the officer laughed. Then, one by one, each of the four policemen kicked the three illegals hard in the shins. After the second policeman had finished, Farood and Jamal fell to the ground and had to be held up for the other two to take their turn. With their wrists tied behind their backs with plastic ties, they were thrown into the darkness of the van. They felt every undulation of the road on their faces until they swivelled onto their backs and leaned against the sides of the cage.

Nothing was said between them for the first hour; finally Misha asked, 'Where are they taking us? Across the border?'

'You better hope so,' cautioned Jamal.

Jamal had heard of a camp, Tal-e Seeya, close to the border with Afghanistan. There were always lots of Afghans in Iran, and Jamal had met men who had been sent back who had been kept in Tal-e Seeya. They all said the same thing – Afghans were killed there. Another hour, then they were vaulted off the floor of the van as it drove down an unmade road before jerking to a halt. The back doors parted to an avalanche of light, from where they were beckoned out by the two police officers.

Farood's legs buckled under him and he fell face down. Jamal took a few steps away from the van and looked around. They were in a compound on a desert plain; in one direction he could make out a road. Behind him, soldiers were being drilled. He looked to the nearest policeman. 'Tal-e Seeya?'

He shook his head and got back in the van, which jolted away. The three were left, hands tied behind the backs, with Farood on his knees. He raised his head. 'Jamal. Where are we?'

'Still in Iran.'

Jamal looked about, expecting someone to come and strong-arm them somewhere, but they remained unnoticed.

A hundred metres away a group of men were working the other side of a fence, the chip of pickaxes echoing towards them. Misha walked over and tried to talk to the men, but he was ignored. He limped back, shaking his head. 'That driver was a bastard.'

'I thought you liked him,' said Jamal. 'He bought you a pair of sunglasses, a nice salad.'

'The lamb was coated in lemon juice. I didn't like that.'

'You know what?' said Jamal. 'The thing I didn't like about him most was that he sold us like slaves. Farood, can you stand? Get up.'

Farood hobbled towards Jamal. 'This journey is crippling me.'

'Something tells me you'll have plenty of time to get better.'

The door of an adjacent building opened and out came a soldier in uniform with a moustache and sunglasses. 'In here!' he ordered.

The guard led them upstairs to a balcony of barred cells, all empty. Their hands were cut free, then they were locked up: Jamal in one cell, Misha and Farood in another. There was a thin layer of straw on the floor and one arrow-slit window.

'Hey, Jamal, you're lucky, you have a cell of your own,' shouted Farood.

Towards the end of the afternoon, they heard the main door downstairs open and a crowd entering. Farood awoke and shuffled over to the bars. The guard led a group of nine men trudging up the stairs. They were nearly all Afghans, in bare feet, coated in peach-coloured dust. None of them even noticed the new captives. One was pushed into the cell with Misha and Farood. He was breathing deeply and slowly, and his right arm hung limp by his side. He slumped into a corner and closed his eyes. Farood studied his face and picked out the small scraps that had survived free of dirt. He reminded Farood of the miners at Pol-e-Khomri.

'What have you been doing?'

'Digging. Digging and shovelling all day.'

'What for?'

The man opened his eyes and gave Farood his full attention. 'That's why I'm here. It's why you're here.' He spat. 'We're here to work for them until they've finished with us.'

Flatbread was shoved through the bars by an Iranian boy. Farood had to wake his cellmate to eat, but the following morning the two Baghlan boys were still asleep when the cell door opened and their cellmate nudged them with his foot.

'Time to go, you two.'

Misha and Farood joined the slow procession down the wooden stairs and into the open compound. Farood looked up the line and called out to Jamal, who didn't respond. It was drizzling and the sun was camouflaged. The party headed a few hundred metres across the camp between blocks of soldiers exercising in unison on one side and crawling under barbed wire with rifles on the other. Whistles were being blown and targets shot at. The work party picked up tools and carried on from the day before. Misha, Farood and their cellmate were pointed over to a head-height pile of hard core, Jamal to a trench. They were given a shovel each.

The cellmate shovelled with one arm, scooping hard core into a wheelbarrow. 'Half full,' said the cellmate.

'What happened to your arm?' asked Farood.

'Lifted too much.'

When the barrow was half full, Misha hoisted the handles up to his chest and forced it into motion all the way over to Jamal's trench. He hurried back.

'They're not going to let you out of here if you work any faster,' said his cellmate.

'What happens if we just refuse to work?' asked Misha.

'You won't stay alive for long.'

'What are we building?' asked Farood.

'Barracks for soldiers.'

Farood attempted the next wheelbarrow load, but he could not raise the back off the ground. Misha took one handle, Farood the other. They faced each other and spoke in unison. 'One, two, three.'

They walked a few paces on the spot before grinding their way forward.

The guard watched from his office. He considered the Afghans. They spend all night sleeping on straw, get up like dogs and go straight to work without food or coffee. He could work them all day and still they wouldn't ask for food. They'd rather fall over, or steal or kill you. He watched Farood hobbling back and forth, a near cripple who would've been left to the wolves in his own country. He went and spoke to the soldier watching over the work party with his baton drawn.

Misha noted their attention.

'Heads down, keep working.'

The guard made his way over and pointed at Farood. 'You, come with me.'

Misha threw down his shovel. 'Hey, mister guard. We need him here. I can't carry this on my own.'

'Yes, you can. You're a tough little animal. You're going to build for us; he's coming with me.'

Farood smiled back at Misha as he was led to the guardroom.

The guard sat down behind his desk and took off his cap, brushed what hair there was back, and shuffled some papers into a tray. 'Sit.'

The armrests of the leather upholstery were frayed; the boy's heels were off the ground. On the wall behind the guard was a photograph of a general. Rain was pelting the window.

'You know how to make tea?'

'Yes. Good tea.'

'Heat bread, cook eggs, rice?'

'Cook everything, anything.'

'Good. Much better to be in here, than out there in the dirt and the rain.'

The boy's spirits lifted. He was shown into the kitchen, told about the boiler and the oven. 'You just press a switch, no flames.' He would need to carry the urn using a tea towel. 'A little tea will go a long way.' The cups, though plastic, could be washed.

'Your legs – what happened to you?'

Cautiously he told the guard what the police did to him in the car park and the mountain journey.

The guard shook his head in dismay. 'You know some police officers, they are cowards. We soldiers here, we think it's a disgrace to beat someone your age.'

They prepared the food and tea together. Farood swept the wooden floor. The guard told him how he had lost two brothers in the war with Iraq and that he had no children of his own. The guard allowed the boy to eat an egg whilst the tea was brewing. 'You need to build up your strength for this.'

By the time Farood carried out the tea urn, Jamal was standing ankle-deep in water. Farood beckoned people towards him, seizing his status as an orderly.

Misha marched straight to the front of the queue. 'Farood, what are you doing?'

'I've got this job now.'

'You're working for the guard?'

'He says I'm too young to work outside and I don't want to be locked up all day.'

'You think he doesn't know how to boil an egg?'

The cellmate laughed. Misha remonstrated with Jamal, who was lying flat on this back with fatigue. 'The sky has nothing but rain for us.'

When the work party returned to their cells, Farood wasn't there. The guard brought him up later and Farood was carrying a blanket.

'Guard looking after you, is he?' said Misha.

'I've been helping him.'

'Helping him do what? Beat some prisoners?'

'Make tea for soldiers.'

'I bet the guard is real nice to you, isn't he?'

'He told me about his family.'

'I'd love to hear about them. Farood, we need to get out of here. You need to watch the guard.'

'You know what I think. I think you're just jealous because I have a better job than you.'

'Yeah, and you have a blanket too.'

The next morning the guard came to collect Farood before sending the work party out. Wooden posts were being driven into the trenches – Misha and his cellmate were mixing cement.

When the tea arrived Farood acted like a veteran of his round. 'One cup each, take it easy now, take your turn.'

People jostled; the bigger men stood at the urn taking their time, more than their share, smiling at the new tea boy. Jamal, Misha and his cellmate waited at the back. It was the same when he returned with the food. The soldier had gone to eat somewhere else.

Still swallowing what was left for him, Misha strode into

the guard's office. 'The tea boy is no good. I know him. He's too young.'

'You want to take his place?' asked the guard.

'No. He needs my help.'

'Why does he need your help?'

'I'm a good cook,' insisted Misha. 'I could make everyone happy.'

'This is a labour camp, we don't want people to be happy, and Afghans don't know how to be happy – the shock would kill them. Go back to work and be miserable.'

It was dark by the time Farood was returned to his cell. The guard walked ahead of him, twisting his key into the lock. Farood reached the top of the stairs, halted, looked at no one in particular, gripped the bannister and began walking again, very slowly. Misha raised himself to his feet and made for the open gate. The guard's eyes transfixed Misha, then directed Farood into his cell. He walked with the tiniest of steps, moving one leg at a time. The cellmate handed him his blanket. Farood walked over to a far corner and stood there clenching it.

Misha could see dried blood around one of his ankles. 'You can't stand there all night.'

Only after Farood was sure all around him were asleep and silent did he lie down.

When the guard unlocked in the morning, Misha stood in front of Farood until the guard moved on. They headed out across the compound to what was now a building site. The outline of the barracks was defined now, with posts lined up in a long L shape. A wind had toughened the surface of the ground. *If it took nearly a month to accomplish this*, thought Misha, *then how long will it take to build the floor, the walls and a roof?*

'Farood, just stand by the cement mixer. Just pour in some water, now and again.'

But then he emptied the whole bucket, reducing the mixture to a slop that would never set. Misha delivered some to Jamal's trench, shrugging at his disbelief.

The guard emerged from the guardroom accompanied by an obvious superior, a colonel, in a long, grey coat, carrying a cane. His cap was pushed down over his eyes, his back was straight and his shoulders rigid. The guard walked him around the foundations while a soldier pretended to supervise the work party.

Misha filled up his wheelbarrow, launched it in motion, trundling towards the guard and the colonel. He was within a few yards of the colonel when the man raised his head to display a patch over one eye. Misha pulled up short, spilling the watery cement on the side of the trench when it would've been easier to pour it in. The guard tried to draw the colonel's attention elsewhere.

Misha refilled his wheelbarrow; his cellmate sensed the coming calamity. 'You want to get all three of us killed? Your friend said he liked the guard.'

But Misha set off and, from behind, casually dumped the cement about the boots of the guard and the colonel. They looked at their feet and then at Misha, who was waiting for a reaction, a resolution. The guard and the colonel walked on, shaking their boots; the colonel raising his voice at the guard.

For the rest of the day Misha was even less productive. Other workers protested and then gave up, throwing their shovels down.

No one in Misha's cell was unlocked for three days and nobody ate either. Jamal looked in as he walked past but said nothing. Misha banged the cell bars for the first two days, but the guard never came. On the third night – when Farood was muttering and snivelling and the cellmate lay with his limp arm draped across his chest – the gate was opened.

Before he could fully wake, Misha's legs were dragged on to the balcony. He tried clinging to some straw, then a cell bar, but the guard pulled too hard. His palms cushioned his descent down the stairs before he was swallowed into the guard's office.

Farood thought he would hear Misha cry out, but he didn't. He heard furniture being moved, something thrown at the door, the guard's raised voice and then Misha making his way up the stairs. He had blood pouring from his mouth and nose and one of his ears. The cell had been left open and it remained that way all night. By mid-afternoon the next day, Misha and Farood were in the back of a police van. The following day they were delivered to Herat, back across the border in Afghanistan.

SIXTEEN

Istanbul, September 2003

Farood leaned heavily to one side as he walked through the deserted dance floor collecting glasses and looking for scraps of food. He hadn't eaten much in the last few days – some pitta crusts, an orange and a peach he shared with Misha. This morning there was little left out on the tables – a few nuts and an olive or two. Farood carried the glasses over to Misha at the sink, wincing as he lifted the basket onto the draining board.

'Other side. This is where the clean ones go,' instructed Misha.

Farood shook his head and held his side.

Misha emptied the basket for him and dispensed some more advice. 'You see your ribs. They'll get worse before they get better. The best thing is to keep moving, even though it hurts like hell.'

Misha had a working knowledge about ribcage injuries. It had been over two months since they had arrived in Istanbul, and on day one they had both taken a beating from the club owner, Berzan. Particular attention had been given to the younger, smaller Farood, using a wooden rounders bat in short bursts. Before this they had spent more than six months making their way back through Afghanistan from Herat, through Quetta, over the Makran again, across Iran and into Turkey, where they spent two days in the luggage hold of a bus to the Anatolian side of Istanbul. They had to try again. Their families had paid for them to get to Greece and the agent in Baghlan would keep his word. If they went home his reputation would be smeared.

The second attempt might have taken less time had they not insisted on travelling together. Every day for a week they had argued which of them had been the last to speak to Jamal, and whether he would ever make it to the West, or even out of the camp. It wasn't easy to find a bus driver in Lake Van who would take two in the luggage hold. They were told there might not be enough air for them both, but they insisted all the same.

This time they had no trouble crossing from Iran into Turkey. They were sent north, handed over to agents in the Kurdish Workers' Party. There was no hiding, secrecy or rush. They stayed with a family on a smallholding close to the border. The husband taught them how to prune a cherry tree. When they crossed into Turkey it was on horseback; whenever they asked if they were in Turkey yet, the agent would always say, 'We're still in Kurdistan.' The bus from Lake Van stopped every four hours or so; during the stopover they were allowed to sleep inside on the backseats. They were dropped off at Berzan's club in the Scutari district of Istanbul.

Potbellied Berzan smiled from the door when they arrived at his club. The bus driver regularly brought him luggage-hold passengers. Farood and Misha were taken to the cellar where there were others, mainly from Bangladesh and Pakistan. Nine weeks later they were still there. There was no possibility of them going anywhere. Everyone who came through Berzan's club had to pay extra. It was the last stop before Schengen Europe, so no one was going to turn back. After the next border, they would eventually be free to roam and work throughout most of Europe with little or no border checks, so Berzan kept people until they, or someone they could phone, had transferred money into his account. On top of that, he took his cut from the agent of origin. If you didn't pay, he didn't feed you. He stood over people as they made calls to family members explaining what would happen if money wasn't transferred to his account. The amount of money he asked for depended entirely on his impressions, on where people had come from. Iranians he believed always had access to money.

On their second day Farood and Misha were led out of the cellar to his office and asked for a hundred dollars each.

Farood spoke to Berzan as he spoke to an imam. 'My mother gave everything she had to the agent in Baghlan.'

A reply very familiar to Berzan. 'Then I want to speak to this agent in Baghlan. I want a bigger cut, I've too many to feed here.'

Farood called out the numbers as they were pressed into the phone.

'This is Berzan. I've got two of yours here. A Turkmen called Misha and a kid from Baghlan. If I'm going to move them over to Greece, I need some money up front. The boatmen are putting up prices every day.' Berzan performed an 'Are you joking?' double take to the reply before pocketing his phone. 'He says he's never heard of you.'

Taking his bat from a desk drawer as if fetching a set of keys, he led them back to the cellar. Berzan always carried out punishment in front of others. Since their first day a lot of people had come and gone in groups of three or four, moved up the coast towards Greece.

Once a cultured-looking man had advanced across the cellar, his finger pointed at Berzan. 'I've already paid for my trip. Paid plenty. You get a share of that, I know. You'll get no money out of me.'

Berzan was methodical about violence; it was a routine task. He carried a silver flick knife in his boot but on this occasion, he went to the kitchen and returned with a carving knife. Farood counted fifteen incisions in the man's torso. Berzan was still stabbing the man after he was still and silent, the only sound the blade squelching through his flesh. The man was rolled up in a carpet and taken away; the two boys had to mop out the cellar. Sometimes, to save him the trouble, Berzan would show people a short film on his laptop. It began with a close-up of a man's face in a chair, the sound of Berzan's voice, slow and clear. 'You come to my club, expecting me to look after you. And you refuse to pay anything. Everything for nothing. For how long?' The camera jerked down to the man's hand, strapped to the arm of the chair with a belt. Another hand came into view, holding the wrist tightly. Then a third hand, holding a pair of pliers, slowly and clumsily snipped the smallest finger in half at the knuckle. The screaming caused the sound on the film to cut out for a few seconds. Then Berzan's voice was heard again. 'If you leave here without paying, you have to leave something behind.' Berzan had a number of short films, one involving a woman and six men. And if anyone was still in doubt, he had a living model to show people waiting in another subterranean lock up – a boy he would send for, whose age was difficult to tell, a boy with no nose and no ears. The first time Farood saw him, he wept in front of him. His own weeping haunted him.

'What's wrong?' called Misha one night.

'That's what will happen to us. We will have our ears cut off. And it might not bother you, but I don't want it happening to me.'

'You think I don't want my ears?'

Farood hesitated under the weight of what he was about to say. 'You could get your father to pay. He has money. He has a business. And you know his number.'

'He wouldn't pay. Berzan could cut off my head and he wouldn't pay.'

'You said he wanted you to run a shop.'

'I lied. He didn't want me to run anything. He wanted me to leave and never come back.'

Farood sat up on his sleeping mat. There was only Misha to hear, but he whispered all the same. 'Then we have to escape.'

'How? He'll find us and cut us for sure. Go to sleep.'

Farood lay down, reached into a corner for his tin and gently shook it. He would have to wait until it was heavier. The tin held their treasure – coins, a few notes, the odd earring, whatever they found when they cleaned the disco each morning. Most Saturdays there was a wedding, and weddings were good for leftover food and for treasure. There was one tomorrow, and they would clean before and after.

The disco area above the cellar was a long, narrow room with a sunken dance area surrounded by mirrors and seating. Misha struggled to control an electric floor polisher whilst Farood wiped the bar. At the top of the cellar stairs that led to the disco was a side door. Every morning Farood tried the handle, put his ear to the door and looked through the keyhole. That night they listened to the dancing above them, imagining the frantic movements of couples, of men pursuing women across the polished surface.

In the morning Berzan opened the cellar, yawning. He had fed them once in six weeks, but they barely looked any different. He shrugged and trudged upstairs; they followed. At the top he turned down the corridor to his office and they went the other way into the disco. It was a mess. There was wine, beer and broken glass on the floor, and what looked like blood and a broken tooth. But there were also the remains of a meal – rice meatballs, asparagus. There were shreds of flatbread on most tables. They made up two plates and two drinks – their first meal for three days. Then they ran their hands down the back of every seat. They found a handkerchief, a photograph and something that was jammed between the back and a seat cushion. Farood turned and drove his arm down to the elbow and tugged free a silver-grey bracelet watch.

He stood on the seat, holding it aloft. 'Look!'

'Show me,' demanded Misha.

'I found it, it's mine.'

Misha took a breath before explaining. 'Something like that, people come back and say to Berzan, "I left my watch here." When he finds you have it, I wonder what he'll do?'

Farood jumped from the seat and ran to the cellar. He put it in the peanut tin and found a new hiding place for it on an overhead beam.

When he got back upstairs Misha threw him a bottle of cleaning cream. 'We're out. Go tell Berzan we need some more.'

Farood looked behind down the corridor. Neither of them had been to his office since they arrived. Illegals didn't do that; they waited in the cellar until Berzan told them otherwise.

'Farood, he's not going to cut off your ears just because you need more cleaner to do your job.'

Farood stood at the side door at the top of the stairs and called down the corridor. There was no answer. He advanced a few paces. 'Berzan! Hallo. Mister Berzan.'

Berzan came around the corner, pulling up his trouser zip.

'We're out of cleaner.'

Berzan turned back and returned with a key in his hand. He unlocked the side door and went out, closing it behind him. Then his phone rang and he answered it. From inside Farood listened to Berzan's voice bleed into the traffic. Two beats later he tried the handle. It opened onto a sunlit yard with steps up to a road in one corner. Farood stopped himself from running to the steps and ran to Misha instead, tugging his sleeve. 'He's left the door open.'

Misha walked over, no further than the threshold. The yard was in front of him. 'It could be a trap,' he warned.

'We're living in a trap,' said Farood urgently. 'Let's run.'

'Go get the treasure.'

'No.'

'We'll need it. The watch will buy us some food.'

Farood jumped down most of the stairs and was back at the door with his tin in a matter of seconds. Misha was gone. The door was wide open. Farood looked into the disco area, calling his name. Then he ran to the steps in the far corner of the yard, mounted the first step and saw Misha standing across the road. He hesitated for a second or two, gazing at the sudden abnormality of the outside world with its onslaught of space and light. Misha called, 'Hurry,' from across the road; Farood reached the top step when the flat of Berzan's boot pushed him down again out of sight. Misha saw Berzan pause, look down to the bottom of his sunken yard. Misha ran.

He ran away from the main road down a narrow street between high houses, under washing lines, crossing alleys, along gutters. A Jack Russell chased him, the echoes of its bark overtaking him. The stone buildings turned wooden as he reached a hill and leaned into the gradient to the summit. It was early in the year and early in the day, but it was humid. He stopped, doubled up, then turned to face the long, downhill slope. There was no sign of Berzan, no one at all behind him. The grey of houses was cut off by the Bosphorus. He spat, straightened up and filled his lungs. As he breathed in, he could smell fish being fried in olive oil.

He continued up the hill and where it began to ease into a level there was a park with pine trees, a bandstand and clay surface football pitches. On one a group of men surrounded a commotion, a noise he had heard before, in Mazar – a camel fight. Two looming animals were heavily saddled under ropes and sacking. A man lashed out with a length of bamboo, and one camel snored, trotted towards the other, and brought its neck down across its opponent. The other camel tried to pull away, but its front legs had buckled. The ring of men cheered, waving money above their heads. Misha spectated silently from beyond the touchline. There would be no point asking anything of these men. His father used to do this every weekend, gamble on camel-wrestling. He even spent a months' income to part-buy a camel with two other men. Its neck was broken in its first match. They were all selfish men, all in the same shabby, dark grey suits. A younger man in a tracksuit looked over at Misha and smiled.

Misha approached him, placing his palm on his elbow. 'You speak Kurdish?'

The man nodded, held his hand.

'My name is Misha. I'm in a bit of a situation here. I'm lost, and I've lost my friend and I've lost my phone.'

The young man obliged without saying a word, handing Misha his phone and a lit cigarette.

Misha recited the agent's number to himself as he pressed the keys. 'Listen, Mohammed, don't fucking hang up and don't fucking say you don't know me. We paid you in Baghlan. Misha from Mazar and Farood. Yeah, now we're in Istanbul and I've just got away from some butcher Berzan, who's still got Farood... wait...'

He handed the phone back to the young man, who explained exactly where they were in Istanbul. Misha was told to stay where he was, so he sat down with the young man next to him. They sat there until dusk, when Misha asked him to go. He lit a last cigarette for Misha, stroked his head and walked away.

After dusk there was no street lighting in the park and very little light from the houses nearby. He went to a grass verge, resting his head upon his arms. He remembered his father in his dark grey suit, much younger than when he had left him. His father had a football – red and white – which he bounced too high for him to catch, laughing as he jumped. His mother shouted, 'Give it to him, what are you doing? Don't tease my son.' His father said to him, 'You want it, you want it? Jump, boy, jump.'

Then his shoulder shook under a hand and another Kurdish

voice was speaking. 'Did you telephone Mohammed in Baghlan? Was that you?'

'That was me. Who are you?'

'I'm an agent, I can get you to Greece.'

Misha was on his feet. 'First you need to get someone for me, someone I came from Baghlan with. He's in the cellar of a nightclub down there.'

'Berzan?'

'You know him?'

'All the agents round here know him. He wants to control Istanbul, Turkey if he can. But he can't, so he gets ugly.'

'Yeah, well, my friend's going to be very ugly if we don't get him out of there.'

They walked together down the hill and back to the club. In the end the extraction was routine. The club was open to the public, so the agent paid to go in, went down to the cellar forced the door and left with Farood the same way he came in.

Misha ran across the road towards them, his eyes on his friend's face. 'Are you okay?'

In reply Farood launched his tin of treasure at Misha's head.

SEVENTEEN

Lancashire, January 2012

It was their first date and it was painful to recall. He was with Sabana at Khalid's restaurant waiting to order. They had been sitting at a table in the corner by the door waiting to order for thirty minutes. The wait had killed the conversation. A conversation he had planned. It was a week since they'd cancelled the previous date because Khalid had made Farood work in the evening, yet still Farood insisted they eat at Khalid's restaurant. Khalid had promised him he would take special care of them this time, but Khalid was in his office.

'We should go. It's not like we haven't got a choice,' suggested Sabana.

'I could always take our order myself. I am a waiter,' he said, smiling.

Sabana was angry, at his humiliation not hers.

Khalid emerged from his office, seemingly in a rush, and he spoke directly to Sabana about problems with a supplier. He was wearing an expensive silk shirt. Farood was wearing his white work shirt from the market. Khalid moved around to Sabana's side of the table, leaned in to her shoulder, his eyes following her forefinger on the menu. He told her he thought he might need glasses, and smiled. 'Farood came in the other day and I didn't recognise him from just over there. Isn't that right, Farood?'

Farood smiled and agreed with his boss.

'I'll come and see you for an eye test, leave Farood in charge here.'

He smiled for him again, even though he had just realised that it was Khalid not him who appeared to be on a date with Sabana. Khalid told him to show some new guests to a table and take their order while he took Sabana's order.

During the meal Sabana told him she had found another job for him. A friend was opening a shop, a fashion shop, but he didn't want to work for a woman, and anyway, where would he live? Then Khalid came over and told him he could help himself to coffee. While he was at the coffee machine, Khalid told him he would be taking money from his wages for the meal.

Farood's anger at the memory was still raw. He walked out of his cell and onto the balcony. It was almost time for him and Barker to fetch the dinner trolley. To be outside for ten minutes, to be with Barker, who listened. Directly below him Atherton was at a table, pretending to play solitaire with a pack of cards. Standing opposite, with one foot on the seat, was Atif. Atherton and Farood technically at least had jobs on the wing; Atif wasn't a cleaner and he wasn't in education, but he was allowed out of his cell to wander at will doing the odd errand for Officer Scully.

Atherton spoke with his eyes fixed on the cards. 'You got to be careful on here now. You know why? Because there's a grass, Atif. On this wing.'

'So, who is this grass?' said Atif. 'No one would grass on me. The consequences for them would be too high.'

'Course, bro, but some of these rioters they've brought in, they can't do prison, they don't know prison, so they're always helping the officers, aren't they? So, Atif, you into picking up girls at kids' homes? Bitches from kids' homes. Do you do that?'

'I'm not a fucking paedo, Atherton, and you see those girls, yeah, they claim they were raped, but they weren't. They were paid to have sex and they enjoyed it.'

'You saying they're not nonces then. That lot on D wing?'

'I'm saying it's not how the media tell it.'

As Farood came down the stairs, Atherton looked up from his cards. 'What yer sayin', Roodie?'

He stood, hands down his jogging bottoms, nodding politely, just like the day he arrived from court.

Atif put a hand on his shoulder. 'I was just saying to Atherton, he doesn't understand Muslims and he doesn't understand the current situation.'

'I know what you're up to,' said Atherton.

'No, what you don't understand, white boy, is that the Jews control the media. Everything that comes out of that screen is thought up by Jews.'

Scully poked his head around the door of the wing office. 'Atif! Put these away for me, will yer!' He dropped a pile of towels and Atif went to do his errand.

Farood sat down at the table opposite Atherton.

'He knows everything, dunt he, your mate?' said Atherton, cards spilling out from his cack-handed shuffling.

'He thinks he does,' replied Farood.

Atherton bowed his head and said quietly, 'So, go find what else he thinks he knows.'

Atherton and Farood had become pals – as much as prisoners trusted each other. Atherton appeared genuinely interested in Farood's story, the details of his journey across two continents. He asked questions, and Farood welcomed the unburdening.

Atif could leave his cell door open and wander around the wing in the knowledge that no other prisoners would enter; in fact, that other prisoners and officers would keep an eye on his premises. It was a cell with more than signs of long-term habitation, furnished with lamps, mats, a Playstation, a stack of computer games, photographs and certificates across the walls, his prayer mat, and several different-coloured keffiyeh scarves. Technically prisoners were not allowed into each other's cells; it encouraged bullying. Scully at least was prepared to let it go, since bullying wasn't always bullying it was just another way of keeping order. Indeed, sometimes it was justice. On occasions he and other officers slid newspaper cuttings under the doors of prisoners like Atherton – cuttings about newly arrived sex offenders.

Farood was sat on the visitor's chair, Atif his bed. 'Do you want a coffee?' he asked.

'I'm okay.'

'Farood, I can help you in here. Make your time easier. I want to help you, but as a Muslim you have to play your part.'

'How?'

'You're an Afghan, which makes you a leading Muslim in the jail. There's too many brothers in here who don't take their religion seriously, who take part in things that are haram.'

'Like what?'

'They watch television. Let the propaganda fill their heads.'

'You've got a television.'

'That's just for games. And they associate with kaffirs. If you're going to convert someone that's fine. But people like Atherton and his crew. You know what, I think he's part Jew. He probably doesn't know, but I can tell.'

'Kaffirs don't know who they are, what they believe,' said Farood.

'They don't believe in anything. Only what they can buy.'

'In my country we don't have much more than our belief, but it has been enough to beat the British, the Russians and the Americans.'

'Exactly. This is what people need to hear, Farood. We need to turn Muslims into fighters.'

Farood nodded. 'You're not a Muslim unless you fight.'

Atif offered out his fist; Farood touched it with his. Then, from under the hand towel folded around his Qur'an, Atif produced an iPhone and offered it to his new brother.

'Here, take it. My solicitor's number's in there. He's good. When the time is right, I'll move to another wing. And this will be your wing.'

'Sharia wing,' said Farood, smiling.

'Like I say.'

'How do you get the phones?'

'Money. Some officers are easy to buy. Scully's no problem. But let me deal with him.'

*

Sabana didn't recognise the number when she took the call at the optician's reception.

'It's me,' whispered Farood.

'And how may I help you, sir?'

'Listen, is Khalid still in hospital?'

'Actually, I think that's no longer the case?'

'I need you to do something. I need you to speak to him, get him to admit it was him that shot Samir in the amusement arcade and *record* the conversation.'

'I'm not sure, may I ring you back on that?'

'No, no, no.'

He paced his cell, pointing a finger at the ceiling, the radio beating in the background. 'Listen to me, listen to me.'

She killed the call. He stared at the phone, suddenly a useless object. Nearly all the clandestine dialogue in the jail was about acquiring a phone, the influence this bestowed, yet at that moment with a phone in his palm, he had never felt weaker.

Later in the day, Atherton was grinning as he cupped it in his hand in Farood's cell. 'Could've done with something a bit smaller. What did he want for it?'

Farood shrugged. 'Nothing. He wants me to be one of his boys. One of his radicals.'

'A terrorist, yeah?'

Another shrug. 'Cos I'm an Afghan.'

Atherton smiled. 'You're nobody's boy, are yer, Roodie? Where's he getting them from?'

'Scully. You know what, I think he'd bring them in for us.'

'Course he would,' confirmed Atherton.

'Except I haven't got any money.'

'It's lucky I have then,' said Atherton, cleaning the phone's screen with his cuff. 'Have you spoke to your missus?'

'Yeah. Khalid's out of hospital. When are we gonna do this?'

'I've got a legal visit tomorrow. I'll know more then. Soon, I reckon. You need to be ready, Roodie.'

EIGHTEEN

Lancashire

He was back in the one room he lived in, provided by Khalid. Sunlight was there as well for once. On the days it made an appearance in the grey skies of England there was a forty-minute spell when it cut down the alley between the paint shop and his window. He was reading Surah four of his Qur'an in between a popular lads' magazine which featured the industrious sex life of a footballer. On the letters page, a communication from someone's girlfriend about the changing taste of her boyfriend's semen. The Qur'an spoke about the need for a dowry, a gift upon marriage. He remembered a family in Baghlan refused their daughter because the dowry wasn't good enough. He was waiting for his shirt to dry, draped over the back of a chair. His door opened, his living-room door which was also his front door.

Khalid entered shoulder first and put a box on his bed. 'Microwave. Means you can eat here.' Khalid looked around the room and sniffed. 'You know how to use it?'

'Sure,' said Farood, 'I use one at the restaurant.'

Khalid picked up the Qur'an, brandished it. 'Where did you get this?'

'Mosque.'

'I don't want you getting into any shit with those people. Bringing it to my door.'

'It's just my Qur'an.'

'You think I haven't got one? I don't read it on my day off, though. And what's this magazine?'

'I don't know.'

'Eh? Who do you think you are? One thing you need to know about women: they're not interested in you. They're only interested in what you can provide for them. In life, everyone has a price, and that's all women think about. And the first thing you need to know about a woman is her price. And I'm telling you, Sabana's price is too high for you. You're going to have to settle for less.'

'Sabana isn't interested in money.'

Khalid laughed, shaking his head. 'You think her father will agree to her marrying *you*? An Afghan with no money? Farood, you'll only upset yourself if you carry on like this.' Khalid sat down next to him, took a breath and lowered his voice. 'I've been hurt by women myself, Farood, so I know. I'm only trying to help.' He placed his hand gently on Farood's shoulder. 'And you know something, I need your help. Will you help me?'

'How?'

'I've never asked for it before, have I? But there's this man. He wants to buy my restaurant. He wants to take it from me: my livelihood, your job, this place you live. He's saying I have to sell it to him and he thinks I'm weak. So, I'm going to have to show him that I'm not. And for that I need my people to support me. Can I count on you?'

'Yes.'

'You know what, he calls himself a Muslim and he sells drugs.'

Farood shook his head, demonstrated his disgust. Khalid left without saying a word, leaving Farood feeling anxiously optimistic. He opened the box and looked at the microwave and saw that it wasn't new.

'You waiting for someone else to dig that hole for you?'

The prison officer's shout snatched Farood from his daydream. Barker smiled across at him, pushing his foot down on the shoulder of the spade, slicing down into the saturated earth. They were working on 'Farms and Gardens', except there wasn't a farm at the prison anymore. Not after the donkey lost an eye. They were planting trees on the central concourse, where the pond used to be before someone's head was held under for too long and the pond had to be filled in. A vegetable patch had also surrendered under the fear of food hygiene litigation and currently, in the interests of health, all vegetables consumed were now tinned. Farms and Gardens was a sought-after job, for lads who wanted to keep themselves to themselves or who needed to be kept off the wings. Working, or even walking, on the central concourse meant you were abused from the windows by lads who had to be kept away from other prisoners because they were so viciously and pointlessly belligerent. 'You down there, you fucking victim, go fucking hang yourself. Is your ma on the game? I'm gonna shag yer ma, lad.' Mothers were handy ammunition, and sometimes a target. A mother escorted by the governor, walked past the well-kept flower beds and the cut grass, under the seagulls to collect her son's belongings and view the cell in which he had hanged himself. 'Hey, missus, your lad string himself up, did he? String himself up because you were such a shite mother, did he? Is that right?'

Farood and Barker were waiting for a tree. The trailer reversed towards them as they received instructions on digging a hole and how to bend correctly. The willow stood delicate and pert; the supervisor remarked, 'That'll be a lovely tree in about ten years.'

Back in his cell Farood fetched his phone from behind a pipe and rang Sabana. Making a phone call from a cell was tricky, even at night. Staff were known to patrol close to doors with their shoes off. Some lads even put cornflakes under the door that would alert them to the presence of an officer. Phones were passports, leverage and they were weapons. Atherton understood their potential better than most. When he'd arrived for his current stretch, he was warned by an officer not to put his Paul Scholes poster up anywhere but on the noticeboard. Then, when he ignored this, Miss Nicholls threatened to take his television away, at least until she came home to find four of Atherton's boys in her living room. With a mobile phone it wasn't hard to find out an officer's address, it wasn't impossible to take a photograph of someone, or, indeed, a key. Farood had no such ambitions, no boys on the out – just Sabana.

'I've got an idea,' he whispered. 'I know what we can do. Get your sister to talk to him. And she wears a hidden microphone.'

'She'll wet herself.'

'Just ask her – it's the only chance we have.'

'You said you had another lawyer.'

'That could take years. Are you coming to visit next week?'

'I can't. I can hardly hear you. Are you on a mobile? Farood, Khalid came to our house, met my father and he knows I visit you.'

He killed the call, just in time. Senior Officer Robertson was at the door. 'Farood, trolley time.'

'Can't be arsed, boss.'

Farood ate alone in his cell, thinking how someone like Khalid would be dealt with back home by his brother or his father.

After dinner he was summoned to the wing office. Robertson was waiting for him, sleeves rolled up, hands behind his head in the prisoner of war position. He swivelled in his chair, took a sip of coffee.

'Sit down, Farood.'

Behind him Scully punched a keyboard from height with his forefingers. Farood wondered if Atif had paid for Scully's bracelet watch.

'I understand you must be struggling a bit,' Robertson began. 'With your appeal being turned down, and you've got a long time ahead of you. You need to settle down, Farood, accept your time and start serving your sentence.'

'I still have another lawyer to contact. And I'm going to write to the ombudsman.'

'Who told you about that?'

The reply was a shrug.

'Why don't you become a wing representative?'

'What's that?'

'Each month you represent the views of other lads at meetings. Put forward suggestions to improve things...' Farood was nodding. 'Atif's moving to another wing, so there's a vacancy coming up.'

As Robertson turned to Scully for a form to fill in, Farood slipped the teaspoon from his cup up his sleeve. 'Think that'll be a good thing for me, sir. Where do I sign?'

The following morning Atherton entered the arena of the visits hall. It was cold and it echoed, which was convenient. On a platform, above the ranks of bolted-down desks and chairs, sat two officers whose job it was to observe every visit, to watch for something moved from sleeve to sleeve, for trainers to be swapped under the desk, for something to be conjured from out of a girlfriend's hair, from under a baby's nappy. But today was a legal visits day and the only illicit exchanges were spoken ones. Atherton was patted down and handed a high-vis jacket. Across the hall, jabbing coins into a drinks machine, was his legal representative, Martin Walker. 'Mart' had been a brief for two decades, and for most of those years the Athertons had been his bread and butter. Two generations of Athertons had filled interview rooms and filing cabinets, and both parties had served each other well. No case was ever shut so tightly that Martin couldn't prise it open to the light of doubt and improbability. 'Just because my client's DNA was on the ammunition doesn't mean he fired it.' His client could extemporise from the witness box on how he was always picking up spent cartridge cases as a child. 'They were everywhere.' Juries were gullible, which they mistook for open-mindedness.

Martin smiled across the hall, choosing a table away from the officers. Atherton slapped his lawyer's palm briskly and tugged his arm. They talked about Paul Scholes' recent retirement and United's chances without him. Atherton enquired about his lawyer's wife and daughter, and his legal representative moved the discussion on to the case.

'The CPS has found a witness. Out of nowhere. Any ideas?'

'What are they saying?'

'They can put you in the car as it left the house.'

'Doesn't mean I was still in it when we hit the van.'

Martin breathed in and summoned his patience. 'Then we'll need a law-abiding citizen to say you were with them when it did.'

Atherton's eyes were baffled. Then they stared hard at Martin. 'That witness will be the old cunt from across the road. From behind a curtain. He's responsible for my ASBO. Fucker.'

'We're going for an ID parade. So, we'll see if he turns up for it.'

Atherton's voice slowed. 'When?'

'Next Monday.'

'Sweet. It's a day out of here. Where?'

'Longsight.'

Atherton bumped his fist against Mart's and was on his feet with purpose.

Whatever the weather, the protocol was to walk back to

one's wing in perfected slowness, yet Atherton made his way with some energy. He was cheerful and helpful throughout his servery duties during dinner. He worded-up Mr Scully. 'Some of these new lads, they never say thanks. A little bit of manners, Mr Scully – that's all we ask.' When everyone was locked up, he helped Scully empty the food bins into the waste buckets.

'Eh, Mr Scully. How much for a phone then?'

Scully's ladle missed a stroke. 'No good asking me, lad.'

'It's a good income for you, boss. People pay a lot of money for phones. Atif's leaving the wing, I'll help you get rid of that shitty Honda you got. Get an Audi or something.'

'It's a Saab I'm after. Leather seats, walnut dash.'

Atherton wiped his hand and dipped it into his whites' pocket and then offered it to Scully. Shaking it, he took the cigarette paper from Atherton's palm with a phone number on.

NINETEEN

Lancashire

Khalid had brought Farood to an amusement arcade. Outside
the door, close against the glass, was a twenty-year-old man
in a sagging overcoat shifting his weight from trainer to
trainer, chewing severely – Khalid looked at him twice before
he realised he was a doorman. The arcade was an empty room
of winking machines apart from two school boys at the back
punching buttons and arguing. Khalid sent Farood over to evict
them. One snarled, 'Fuck off, terrorist.' He grabbed the boy's
throat with one hand and pulled him up on his toes. The other
boy ran for the door. The eyes of the boy in his hand began to
close. He put him down and dragged him by his hood to the
door. Behind him, silently, a fifty-year-old man appeared. He
was wiry, wearing a moustache, reminding Farood of his uncle
in Pol-e-Khomri. *Except*, he thought, *because he is a Punjabi, he
will hide what he is thinking.* The man opened his arms, and his
eyes were a question. Khalid pushed out his chest and widened
his stance like a cowboy. The old man's gestures indicated he
wasn't ready for a fight. He was not a man who fights with
people; this was not his way.

'What do you want, Khalid?'

'I have an answer for you.'

'Who is this?'

'The Afghan I told you about.'

'This is your insurance? The boy from Baghlan?'

The old man swung an arm behind his back and withdrew a machete. His expression didn't change. Khalid took a step back. He looked to Farood for a lead, but Farood was motionless. Then Khalid turned to him purposefully, withdrawing from inside Farood's jacket pocket a handgun. Khalid gripped it with both hands, taking aim as if the old man was standing at the end of a shooting range. He kept the old man in his sights for so long Farood wondered if it was just a threat. The old man shook his head and smiled; Khalid fired into the old man's shoulder, then lowered the gun slowly and left the arcade with Farood behind him.

In the car nothing was said for a while until Khalid said calmly, 'I gave you the gun for a reason. If you had just pointed it at him – he might have dropped the weapon.'

'What did you tell him about me?' replied Farood.

'Quiet. And never speak of that man again.'

*

All kinds of objects were weapons in the prison. Even a pencil was useful, but a biro would do for an eyeball. Take the tap off your sink, place it in a sock. Empty as many sugar sachets as you could muster into the boiling kettle to tip on someone special from the balcony. Use your own bodily functions saved up in a milk carton for an officer's face – a female officer with lovely long hair. A metal spoon is a prize, an extension of your hand. The blade is a miniature scimitar carving a curved wound to leave an altogether better scar. First it has to be sharpened, and Farood had been grinding his up and down the bars of his window. If an officer looked in through the flap, his back was guarding his work. He lashed with it at a pillowcase and it went clean through the cotton and into the foam. It was ready. He ran it under a tap.

He waited until it was almost dinnertime, until he was about to be summoned to fetch the food trolley with Barker, then he began drawing the edge of the spoon down the inside of his wrists. He made three cuts on each wrist, long and shallow and productive. He cut from his hands towards his elbows. He clenched his teeth around the neckline of his tunic. When he breathed in, he could smell his blood. The intensifying pain spread from his arms to his whole upper body. He remembered a whipping his brother had once given him.

Karam had been in Baghlan with their father. By a traffic light for a three-lane highway, they'd watched the Taliban's religious police cane a young man without a beard, long after he crumpled to his knees. When they got home, Karam had chased him through the village with a length of sapling. 'Why didn't you say your prayers today? You didn't, don't lie to me.' His brother had perfected the impervious blank stare. When he'd stopped running at the top of the village, arms folded over his face, Karam whipped at his arms until they bled.

The Farood in the prison cell smiled, lay down and closed his eyes.

He heard the movement of bolts begin to echo along the balcony. Standing up, he created a line of blood drops from the door to his bed and sat back down. His door swung open; it was Robertson, diligent enough to look in. First the radio call for assistance, then the tourniquets and the hand towels, then other prisoners locked up and the escort to the gate. Farood was taken to the local hospital in the back of a car. He was handcuffed to Robertson with Farood's bracelet compassionately loose on his request. The prison had a healthcare wing but it only prescribed paracetamol, and only when the agency nurse was there. Healthcare wasn't really for people who were unwell; it was for prisoners who would be injured if they were on the other wings –

sex offenders. Any time officers' or prisoners' blood was spilled, they went to the local hospital, where they were begrudgingly treated.

Farood was behind a curtain with Robertson in front of him.

'You could've spoken to me.'

'And said what? That I don't want to spend the next fifteen years in prison?'

'Lots of people go through what you're going through. And I've taken a few of them to this hospital.'

'What happened to them?'

'They found a way to live through the next however many years.'

A nurse entered the cubicle. There was no eye contact; she noticed the towels over his arms and put her head back between the curtains. 'Staff nurse – he's cut his wrists.' She hurriedly unwrapped the hand towels tugging the wounds. She adopted a cheery tone. 'He knows what he's doing, doesn't he? Along the arm rather than across. Except, these are not even deep enough to need stitches.'

Robertson smiled genuinely. 'He's a bit of an amateur, this one.'

The nurse shook a canister. 'This may sting a bit.' She sprayed one forearm yellow.

The curtain swished back and a male nurse handed Robertson a clipboard. With one arm still handcuffed to Farood, he put it on his lap and manoeuvred a biro. 'Farood, remind me of your date of birth again.'

'The one the Home Office gave me was January 1st '92. But I was born in the summer.'

'We better go with the official one.'

The nurse sprayed the other forearm and dabbed randomly with cotton wool. Robertson uncuffed himself from Farood and secured the bracelet round the frame of the bed.

'How many birthdays do you have?' she asked.

'Two. The Home Office one and the one when I was born. But I'm not sure exactly when that was.'

'Didn't your parents get you something every year?'

'No.'

The nurse left. He was alone and might not be again. With his free hand he produced a sachet of shower gel from inside his sock. He tore it open with his teeth and spread the gel around his loosely cuffed hand and wrist. He left some blood on the bracelet and the floor, but his hand was out. *Where is Robertson?*

The nurse came back with a tray and a sachet of dressings. She wasn't fazed that both of the prisoner's hands were uncuffed. 'Sit down,' she ordered.

He did. Robertson was heavyset. He rolled around on the ground with prisoners all the time. But Farood believed he was manageable, if he got the first blow in.

The nurse began to turn a bandage around one arm when he heard Robertson's voice approaching. A voice Farood was destined to hear every day until it retired. He stood up.

'Sit down, will you!'

Farood reached a hand around the nurse's mouth and turned her into his shoulder. Robertson's silhouette was the other side of the curtain; it hesitated. He leaned heavily on the nurse, tightening his grip on her as he swung round his left leg in the arc of a roundhouse kick, through the curtain at Robertson's head. Except it wasn't Robertson's head; it belonged to the male nurse on the floor – out cold under the curtain rail. Robertson was at a coffee machine fifty metres away, and closing. He looked unstoppable.

Farood showed him the scissors from the tray, showed them pointed at the nurse's throat. 'You want me to open up her neck like a goat?'

The possibility halted Robertson – he raised his palms in surrender. Farood began dragging the nurse back through the double doors to the exit. He released his grip when he saw daylight and ran. Robertson wasn't giving chase. That was not the protocol and he had mess to clean up, handcuffs to retrieve.

In the town centre it took Farood a few minutes to calm himself, to realise nobody was looking in his direction. He looked at his reflection in a bookmaker's window – trainers, jogging bottoms, a sweatshirt – no different to any other lad in town. Except soon the police would know who they were looking for and what he was wearing. Behind him was a museum. At reception he made a point of picking up a leaflet. The woman behind the desk, small and demure, smiled at him. He nodded. In a glass case – the uniform of a Victorian soldier, a blood-red jacket to hide wounds, a sword and a musket, and a sheepskin drum.

'Are you alright?' asked the receptionist.

Blood was dripping down his arm onto the tiled floor.

'Do you need a bandage?'

'No.'

'If you come with me, I have a first aid kit.'

He nodded and followed her to the kitchen.

'Roll up your sleeve… How did you do this…? Do you want me to ring someone?'

'No, I'm fine.'

'You should go to the hospital.'

She bandaged both arms, then held his hands and looked into his eyes.

'Someone sliced me. Miss, can I use your toilet?'

Inside the cubicle he pulled the cellophane-wrapped phone from within his anus. More blood. He washed his hands and left. From an alley behind the museum he rang Atherton's uncle Vinnie, the number stored in the phone.

'Vinnie?'

'Who's that?'

'It's Roodie.'

'You on the out, mate?'

'I'm in the town centre.'

'You need to sit tight, mate. See that park opposite the jail? I'll be there in an hour and a half or so.'

'By the jail? Are you fucking joking?'

'They're not looking for you yet. Not for a good while. Hide behind a fucking tree or summat.'

Farood walked the two miles back to the jail and took up the highest point in the park opposite. He then clambered into a rhododendron bush to wait for Vinnie, though he needn't have bothered to conceal himself. Robertson would have telephoned through the abscond, but it was doubtful whether the local police would open the email for a few hours. If he was seen by a passing officer, they might well wave, but they were unlikely to mention it after lunch. The town was familiar with escaped prisoners. The last one had been apprehended in McDonald's. Deprived of his daily intake for months, he too had fled A&E to straddle the counter for a Big Mac Meal but failed to get past the outlet's security guard. Vinnie knew that plod would not be looking for Roodie, but they would make the local plod aware of wherever they thought Roodie was going that night. He knew this because he had picked up umpteen escapees from the park and he had planned accordingly. He finished his tea and fishfinger sandwich before driving north at a leisurely pace for almost two hours.

'Yo, Roodie, where the fuck are yer?'

Roodie was still in his rhododendron, answering his phone with a bad smell clinging on to it. Sometimes when Vinnie picked people up there was a girl in the back of the car for the escapee to have sex with whilst they were on the outside lane of the M6. Or there'd be a case of alcohol and a pouch of powder. None of this was required in Farood's case.

TWENTY

Atherton got on his bell. Prisoners were only supposed to press their bells in an emergency. An emergency such as: they were going to kill themselves and had made a start with a wardrobe screw into the throat. Not an emergency such as, 'Why isn't *Top Gear* on?' or, 'Do you know when I'm out, boss?' The bells rang into the wing office and officers would immediately flick a switch to kill them, leaving a flashing light the size of a bunion. They'd always finish the banana, the pork pie or the football pages before they answered the bell, on one occasion to find a corpse, for which the governor was sacked and became suicidal himself. Atherton knew the officers, knew who had sex with whom on nightshift. If he got on his bell Robertson would arrive rather than Scully, but he would take his time, because Atherton didn't have emergencies.

'You called.'

'Do you know when I'm leaving for this ID parade, Mr Robbo?'

'I shouldn't think they'll start without you.'

Robertson started to close the door, but there was something else; there was always something else with Atherton.

'Eh, boss, what did the governor say about you losing Roodie in the hospital?'

'He's putting me forward for an award.'

Atherton laughed lazily. 'Fuck-up of the year. Do you know what, though, boss, I can make it right for you, make you look good.'

'Put in a word with the governor for me?'

'You'll be in *Prison Service News*, boss.'

'For what?' asked Robertson, stepping back into the cell, his voice now easier.

'Question is, Mr Robbo, what are you gonna give me… if I give you the name of the officer bringing phones into this jail? And who he's selling them to?'

Robertson shut the door behind him. 'Tell me how you know this?'

'Because Atif the terrorist tried to sell one to me for stupid money and when I told him to fuck off, he said it was Scully's fault for charging so much in the first place. That's how I know.'

Robertson looked around Atherton's cell. He picked up a library book. *Pablo Escobar, The world's most powerful criminal.* There was a twinge in his shoulder. He said nothing and left.

An hour later Atherton was in a sweatbox again. One of eight coffins with a seat and a wire grill inside a transit van. He'd been in and out of them since he was eleven and like a lot of places – cells, interview rooms – they seemed to be getting smaller. The windows were blacked out and he was in the care of two private security staff that were deaf to all toilet requests, or slurs regarding their mothers. Although he couldn't see out, Atherton knew the journey to Longsight police station and Manchester Crown Court like a dozing underground commuter. He knew the extent of time on the M6, the M61, the M602 and the slow, stuttering miles thereafter broken by traffic lights and cyclical roadworks. As soon as they were beyond the gates, Atherton lifted himself to a squat and pulled a clingfilm-wrapped Nokia from his anus. Some lads reputedly managed more than one phone but were never allowed to forget it. Atherton sent a text to Vinnie. *It's on today.* Then he typed *ok* but left it hanging in the outbox.

Back at the jail Robertson was 'spinning' Atif's pad wearing surgical gloves in the company of a frisky spaniel, whilst officer Scully was being led to his car by security officers. It was to be his first taste of custody. When they opened the boot of his Honda Civic, they found a box of chargers, phones and even labels on the phones with customer's names. He got his first taste of handcuffs. When Robertson found two phones inside the back of Atif's TV, a question began to unsettle him. Why would Atherton give up Scully and Atif, even if he had beef with them? The consequent reputation of being a snitch wouldn't make it worth his while. Maybe he was looking in the wrong place.

Vinnie was at the wheel of a recently stolen Astra in the car park of the Copper Kettle public house, a few hundred yards beyond the end of the M602. The engine was running. In the passenger seat was Farood, across Vinnie's lap a shotgun – a 'shotty'.

'It's not as hard as you think.'

'You've done it before?' asked Farood.

Vinnie looked up at the Salford sky as if his crops depended on it. 'I'm no virgin, son.'

The driver of Atherton's sweat-van was an ex-service man with tattoos to prove it. His number two for the journey was a short, middle-aged woman whom he suspected of being part-Japanese. He was midway through an account of last night's veterans' get-together when he looked at his watch and noticed they were well ahead of schedule.

In the back Atherton was disorientated. He wasn't sure if he was in a motorway queue or a traffic light queue. 'Yo! G4 people, where are we!'

The closer they got to the police station the more vans there would be on the roads. Whilst Vinnie was staring at his iPhone, Farood leaned forward, spotting a G4S van the other side of the pub. Neither of them wanted to give the word. The phone flashed *ok*, the ski masks came on and they were nose to nose with a prison escort van in seconds flat. Farood took a long-handled axe from the backseat and smashed every window, calling for Atherton. Vinnie pointed his shotty at the windscreen and coolly made his request.

'I'd like the keys for the back door.'

The driver dropped them down to Vinnie. He tossed them to Farood, who shook his head.

'Listen!' he commanded.

Women could be heard shouting, cussing, crying.

'We've got the wrong van.'

Farood pointed to a second white van with a white-shirted driver further up the sputtering queue. They ran, up the middle of the road, with the shotty and the axe. Other drivers looked straight ahead, fingering the steering wheel, retuning the radio, pushing the door locks. The veteran van driver did not need the motivation of the shotty and held out the keys for Vinnie as he approached.

But Vinnie had been rehearsing this moment during the preceding forty-eight hours and so he shouldered the weapon, adopted a slightly legs-apart stance, and with one eye closed, commanded down the barrel, 'Where's Michael Atherton? I want Atherton unlocked.'

The veteran pissed his pants, his cotton kecks, the seat and the foot-well.

De Niro clicked back one hammer and jerked the end of the barrel, nudging him towards the sweatboxes.

'Yo! Open this box, boss, I'm Atherton.'

'Yo, yo, this one, this box here, boss.'

'No, I'm Atherton...'

'I'm Atherton.'

The G4S woman scanned her clipboard. 'He's in number two, Sarge.'

Atherton was lying down on the floor of the Astra and he felt the vehicle dart into the swarm ahead, elbowing its way towards the city centre. They dipped down side roads and under arches through the Manchester that had survived regeneration, pulling up at a barrier, two topless ten-year-old boys sparring the other side.

Vinnie led Farood and Atherton to a gleaming caravan with an interior of white and silver surfaces and brass appendages. Light shone from porcelain figurines: their heads turned, their arms outstretched. There were a lot of cushions with roses on all of them. Beyond the net curtains were a disused mill and fighting dogs, children riding bikes across the tarmac. Farood looked at the photograph on the opposite wall. It was of a boxer, a boxer without gloves, pale and sinuous, eyes set upon an opponent beyond the frame.

Atherton closed the shower door behind him, rattling the whole caravan. Towel around his waist, he lit the gas for the kettle. On his left shoulder was the same tattoo as the man in the photograph: a green harp.

'Nice, innit?' said Atherton through a custard cream.

'It's like a home,' ventured Farood.

'Better than a house, really. Thing is, Roodie, people say things about travellers, like they're dirty and that, but most other people wouldn't live somewhere as clean as this.'

Farood nodded over his mug. 'That's true, I have been in some houses, our cave was cleaner. Have you always lived in a caravan?'

'Me? No. Dad's side of the family, they're the travellers. Proper travellers, they are. But he chose to marry my mum, who ain't a traveller, and had to leave. This is one of me uncle's caravans. Plod will be looking for us where me dad lives.'

'Does it ever move, this caravan?'

'Yeah. Been all over with me uncle. Appleby Fair. That's the place. Racing horses, selling horses. There's a river there. I took this horse in it once, and it had a swim; and I swam beside it. Travellers are free, Roodie. Go where we want, do what we want.'

Vinnie stepped into the caravan. He wore a vest and although he wasn't henched like prisoners, he still had much of the muscularity in the photograph. They drank tea and joked about the escape.

'That driver started pissing when I flicked the hammer back.'

'We should've brought some of those bitches back here, Vinnie.'

'Minging fucking dogs, by the sounds of it.'

Anyone could do it, anyone with bottle. Atherton and Vinnie recalled when they had held up the Spar and Atherton had made the staff lie down on the floor, *fucking slaves*. Plod, plod would be nowhere. They would be getting the run around on his dad's estate: 'I might have seen Michael in the back of a car… but it could have been his little brother John Jo.' And if plod came to the site they would never get past the dogs before they were gone. Atherton decided who he wanted to look up whilst he was out, before he got on his toes, because he would have to go. Atherton and Vinnie had decided this a while back and now it was settled.

Atherton pointed at Farood with a spliff in hand. 'We've had enough of this country. It's not ours, anyway. Travellers don't have a country and we're not wanted here anyway. Where you going, Roodie?' he asked. 'Not going back home, are yer? Took long enough to get here.'

'I want to stay in the UK.'

Atherton coughed and had to spit in the sink. 'What, go back to jail?'

'I'm going to try and sort things out. I shouldn't've gone to jail in the first place.'

'Fucksake,' said Vinnie, switching on the TV.

Atherton passed the spliff on to Farood. 'You were there, you were standing next to the guy who pulled the trigger. That's joint enterprise.'

'What's that?'

'You don't even know. What kind of brief have you got?'

'Khalid's cousin.'

'Stitched up, mate.' Atherton pounded a fist into a palm. 'Joint enterprise is you're guilty by being there, by association. I got seven years for being in a car behind another car that had a gun in it.'

'Yeah, and what did those people get for murdering that child?' added Vinnie, pointing at the TV. He continued, 'You see that muppet that got sent to jail for robbing a sausage roll from Greggs? He got sent to jail cos it was during a riot. It weren't the sausage roll they sent him down for – it was the rioting.'

'That ain't joint enterprise,' argued his nephew.

'It's not right either, though.'

'I'm not *saying* it's right.'

Interpretations were shoved back and forth while Farood stood at the window. Two women – mothers, no doubt, at their age – were face to face, shouting at each other. A small girl stopped skipping, one grabbed the hair of the other and they began to wrestle. The girl dropped her rope and ran to a caravan door, out of which came two men, both carrying beer cans. They stood with the child between them, watching the women, now on the ground, twisting, thrashing.

'Is it alright if I go out?' asked Farood.

'Where do you want to go?' shouted Atherton from a bedroom.

'I have to see Sabana.'

'I have to see my bird too. Does she know you're out?'

Farood said nothing. He only realised he hadn't asked himself what she would say.

'Is she going on the road with you?' asked Vinnie.

'That's what I need to find out.'

Outside a man in a combat jacket took quick, short steps towards the fighting women. Without hesitation he marched between the spectators, lifting up the woman on top of the other and waving the men back to their caravan. The girl returned to her skipping and began to sing.

Vinnie took a brief look at the commotion. 'Roodie, don't be standing at the window all day. You know what I'm saying? You look different to everyone else.' Vinnie pulled out a black box from under the TV, pulled up its aerial, switched it on. It sizzled between police radio calls.

Atherton pleaded Farood's case. 'He wants to go out, Vinnie.'

'Why do you want to go out? You're safe here. No one comes on here.'

'He wants to see his bird.'

'What do you want to see her for? You're a fugitive now. Whatever you started you can't finish with her.'

'I just want to say goodbye.'

Vinnie's eyes consulted his nephew, who conceded. 'He's not in jail no more, is he?'

'We'll need you back here tonight. We've things to arrange. And we're doing a nice curry. Okay?' Uncle Vinnie gave Farood twenty pounds and a new phone. 'Never switch it off.'

He was taken to the barrier at the site entrance and pointed in the direction of central Manchester. He went to Piccadilly and bought a ticket for Burnley. The town that took him in as a refugee, the place where he was fostered. A middle-class Indian couple had fed and clothed him, given him a room. They found him a school place and a kickboxing class; they took him to Khalid's restaurant and introduced him to the owner. Still drinking lassi, he was shown the kitchen and introduced to the waiters. At first, he was offered a few hours on a Saturday, then when he left school for college, some days during the week. He had his own money for the first time and he could make it last when other boys had squandered theirs on clothes. Then the bedsit nearer his workplace and whenever the social worker made visits to his foster parents, he went back to the house and pretended he still lived there. An arrangement that suited everyone. The last day he was there, it ended in a police cell.

The cell door in the police station was deep blue, as were the plastic cushions around the perimeter of the cell. The floor, he thought, was like the sea off the coast of Greece. He recalled the lorry on the ferry from Greece to Italy. He tried to remember what the cargo was, who else was there and how many years ago that was. Until then he'd thought that his hours and days of waiting alone in rooms and containers were over. He was eleven when he had left Baghlan – it was autumn, that was nine autumns ago. He had also thought until that day, that he would take Sabana to Baghlan with him, to show her to his mother, but in spring time, when the rivers were rushing and the mountains were in flower.

The door unlocked and a man in a suit came in. He was thin, yet the suit was too small and worn to a shine. It was a moment or two before he made eye contact. 'Khalid has sent me. You're going to be interviewed, but you must say nothing. Do you understand me? Nothing.'

He reassured Farood that if the police were unable to prove anything, they would have to let him go. He said he could be trusted because he was experienced, that as long as he continued to work for Khalid he could stay in the country, and he begun or ended every sentence by saying 'believe me'. The door opened and he was taken to a room where a policeman in a superior suit smiled as if they were friends. The policeman, who didn't look at the lawyer, asked Farood if he wanted some water, which he didn't; asked if he had been given something to eat, which he hadn't. The policeman apologised. He was old, happily overweight and fatherly.

'Farood, you're being interviewed in relation to the shooting of a man in an amusement arcade. Do you understand?'

'I didn't shoot him.'

The policeman was surprised, gratified, by Farood's frankness; the lawyer was rattled and he flicked out a kick to Farood's ankle.

'I mean, no comment. No comment is what I meant to say.'

Thereafter that was all he said in interviews, before and after he was charged with attempted murder. His lawyer kept advising him he was confident that the case would *evaporate* once they got to court.

TWENTY-ONE

Lancashire

The afternoon was almost over when Farood's train pulled into Burnley. Market traders were dismantling their stalls; the precinct echoed with the sombre clunk of steel poles on van floors. Asian stallholders worked one side of the precinct, white traders the other. It was strange how it reminded him of the market in Baghlan: socks and plain tee shirts, batteries and baklava. Back home they were luxuries; here they were for the poor. And in England, the poor were sometimes fat and the rich always thin. A burger van chose its pitch for the evening; young men gathered at pub doors renewing allegiances; cigarette smoke merged with the smell of onions. It was match night, not a good night to be passing time on the streets.

He stood waiting in the corner of a shop front opposite the opticians. There was a vacant bandstand between him and the windows that glowed with a buttery light. Then he saw her, between the displays, standing at a desk, writing something down. She went to a rack, bringing back a pair of frames carrying them like they were jewels. A member of staff left the shop and Sabana smiled in her direction, in his direction. He felt fearful, eager and lonely. His phone chirped a text. It was from Atherton: *U ok?*

Sabana was the last to leave the shop, pulling down the shutter and locking the doors. Perhaps she was the manager there now. Her outfit was more expensive than anything he had seen her wearing at visits. In her tailored blue suit, she was very much the woman – a married woman, even. Her hair was cut short, and even from where he was stranding, he could see that it was tinted red. He didn't like this; he felt it was something they should have talked about, even if he was in prison. He sensed something had changed. What if she had done this for someone else? Two road workers in grubby high-vis jackets stared at her long after she had passed by. One seemed to say something to the other, which only made him angry at her. He kept pace with her some distance behind to the car park a few streets away. Once they were away from the precinct his pace quickened until he caught up with her on a quiet side road.

'Sabana.'

'My God, what are you doing here?'

'I got out.'

'How?'

'It doesn't matter.'

'For fucksake, Farood.'

'There's no need to worry.'

'Yes, there is. They'll come straight to my house because they know I've been visiting you. My father will find out and the rest of my family and there'll be hell to pay.'

'It doesn't matter about that anymore. We can't stay here, there's no point. I thought we could prove my innocence, but maybe I can't. I'm with some people, people I can trust.'

'You once said that about Khalid.'

'Sabana, listen. They can get me out of the country. They have connections.'

'You're going?'

'I want you to come with me.'

She took a step back, a breath in, her mouth opened in

silence. He took a step towards her, placed his hands upon her shoulders; she lifted them away.

'Where? Come where?'

'I'm not sure yet. But I want to visit my family. With you.'

'And meet your mother?'

'So, I can show her that I've achieved something.'

'Wow, thanks for the invitation, but you know what, I'm not a prize for an Afghan family.'

She turned from him and strode into the car park. She unzipped a shoulder bag and began to delve for her car keys.

'Where are you going?'

'You'll have to find something else to bring back with you.'

He grabbed an upper arm, fingers pinching on her jacket. 'Sabana, pack your things, we can go in a couple of days.'

'Get off me.' She broke away. 'Farood, I'm not going anywhere with you. I never was. I knew what Khalid was like – he was always going to use you and I tried to tell you but you wouldn't listen. Wouldn't listen to me because I'm only a woman. You should never have come.'

'You stopped visiting me.'

'To this country, I mean.'

The driver's door gave a gentle thud; the car hurried her away. He wished he had hit her. Slapped her to the ground, rubbed her face in the gravel. The phone rang, but he ignored it.

He headed back to the precinct, went into a café and ordered a coffee and water. He felt as betrayed now as he had done on the last day of his trial, looking up at Khalid in the gallery, sitting a few places away from Sabana. After being told to say nothing through a dozen police interviews, he was suddenly advised to plead guilty, but he refused. Even after the man whom Khalid had shot stood in a witness box and pointed at Farood – 'That is the man who pointed the gun at me and fired' – he pleaded not guilty, knowing he would be found guilty.

When he was sentenced, the judge talked about all the

things that this country had done for him – giving him a home, an education, a job, hope – only for him to shoot a man over a dispute about a slot machine. Farood looked across at the woman standing in a robe, the court usher. Her eyes had been on him all week. She reminded him of his foster mother, and her face was asking questions of him as the sentence was read out. 'The maximum of life imprisonment with a minimum term of thirty years.' He did not drop his head, for everyone was watching him. Sabana stood with everyone else, Khalid a moment or two after, straightening his jacket and pulling down his cuffs as if he had just finished a business meeting.

Farood cut through the bus station to the other end of town, brushing past two policemen. From over his shoulder he saw them halt. One of them spoke into a breast pocket radio. Farood darted off to his destination, near the council offices, next to the Super Pound Plus Store: to the Karachi King Restaurant. He sat on a raised flower bed nearby, noticing the new frontage, the neon signage above the walls of plate glass. It was 6pm. A family group wearing football scarves were flicking through menus. The waiters had matching waistcoats now. Behind the door, watching the street, smiling at passers-by, was a schoolboy waiter, an Afghan, maybe. Farood surmised if he walked in the front door and asked for Khalid, the police would eventually arrive. If he sat down and ordered a meal, it was unlikely that Khalid was going to bring him a plate of poppadoms. He went into the pound store and bought a knife with a short blade. Then he made his way round the back of the shops to where he used to take the bins out and once or twice tried smoking with the other waiters. The back door, a grubby white fire door, could not be opened from the outside. He waited close by, listening to faraway football chanting, his phone announcing another urgent message from Atherton. A dog trotted between rubbish skips. It looked thin and greasy. He considered he would miss England, but he would not miss the dogs. English people regarded dogs as something more than animals, as children, almost. They gave them seats and kisses, gave them fresh meat from the butchers, food that many people back in Baghlan were unlikely ever to eat. The animal trotted towards him and circled the restaurant skip. It looked up at Farood and its eyes pleaded for a charity that he had never acquired. The back door crashed open, a burly chef in stained whites carrying black bags shouted at the dog to 'do one'. Before he had turned around, the door was closed with Farood on the inside.

On his immediate left was the kitchen. To his right the stairs that led to the toilets and Khalid's office. He tiptoed to the top of the stairs and set his phone on record. Out of habit he knocked on the door, but there was no answer. He entered. The office was empty. On the wall to his right was a television with a film on pause. Two wealthy people frozen in a Bollywood courtship. Below the chef was thumping the back door. Farood sensed a trace of aftershave in the air and noticed a jacket over the back of the chair. He stood behind the open door and waited until Khalid walked in, closing it after him.

'What the fuck?! How did you get in here?'

'That was the easy part.'

Khalid switched off the television and turned his astonishment over to a smile, then a laugh. He opened his arms for an embrace. 'They let you out?' asked Khalid.

'I let myself out.'

'You escaped?' Khalid laughed.

Farood found himself laughing along.

'You fucking escaped. That's really something. My God. Sit down.'

His old boss, his former master, was elated and wanted details. He lit a cigarette mid-narrative. 'Show me your wrists... my God.'

Farood was the junior waiter again, the Saturday boy reporting for duty.

'What about Sabana, where is she in all of this?'

Farood's head dropped; he talked to his shoes. 'We're not in touch anymore.'

'That's for the best. I said that, didn't I? She's not right for you. So, what are your plans?'

'I haven't really got any.'

'I can get you out of the country. Set you up. Put you in a business.'

'Where?'

'Karachi. I've got people going back there all the time. I'm not the Karachi King for nothing. Listen, I'm going to order us both something to eat and I'll get you a first aid kit so you can change the bandages.'

Farood stared at the door after Khalid left the room. He felt as he had felt when left alone in police interview rooms. He turned around the framed photograph on the desk: Khalid in a white suit, on his wedding day, next to his bejewelled bride. He needed to steer the conversation his way.

'Here.' Khalid handed him a first aid box. 'Keep it.'

'You know, Khalid. That day at the arcade, I didn't know you was going to shoot him. I was really surprised.'

Khalid, though silent, was suddenly no longer his paternal friend.

'It might have been better if you had killed him. Better for me, don't you think?'

Khalid nodded and smiled in reply to the question. He stood, ending the interview. 'Let's eat.'

Farood was invited down the stairs ahead of Khalid. Waiting at the bottom was the burley chef, a carving knife in his embrace. Khalid's shove in the back further clarified the situation. They took him out back; Khalid forced him up against the wall. The chef put all his weight on a wrist and rested the carving knife on the thumb. Khalid went through Farood's pockets until he found the phone he was looking for, recording every word.

'What's this? You think this would do you any good? Anyone would believe this?'

He stamped on the phone. The chef's eyes let it be known they were awaiting instruction.

'Do you know how much it cost me to pay Samir off? To get him to stand up in court and point at you? Hardly anything. Know why? We don't want your kind in this country. You shouldn't have come here. You should have stayed in that stupid country of yours, the begging bowl of the world.'

A dubious-looking VW glided past the skips, chasing the dog in their direction and sounding its horn by way of a greeting. Atherton and Vinnie revealed themselves from behind its blacked-out windows. The crotch of his denims sagging towards his knees, Atherton approached and put one foot on the kerb. 'What yer doing?'

Khalid emphasised with polite menace, 'This is not your business.'

'You don't know what my business is, mate,' replied Atherton.

Vinnie splayed out his palms in surrender. 'Look, Khalid, we're peaceful people, us, and we need our friend to have all his fingers.'

'How do you know me?'

Vinnie half smiled then swallowed it as the chef broke his silence. 'You wanna keep your balls, old man, get back in the car.'

It was on. Almost, except Atherton's eyes were on Khalid's feet. 'Oi, is that your phone, Vinnie?'

'Where…?'

'Down there—'

'That better not be my fucking phone.'

'It is, yer know.'

The Bible-sized Nokia was crumpled, its grey innards strewn by a back-alley breeze.

'He smashed it, stamped on it,' volunteered Farood.

'Fucking Paki bastard, ye,' with which Vinnie reached to

the top of his arse crack and withdrew a nine-millimetre pistol. The casing was gold and for a moment looked like a cigarette lighter – until it was pressed against Khalid's temple. Atherton unbuttoned his snub seven millimetre from a leather ankle holster and pushed it into the chef's face. The stray dog began chasing its greasy tail as Atherton asked,

'What d'ya reckon? Shall we kneecap 'em, Vinnie?'

The loosened grip was enough for Farood to take the carving knife and draw it slowly across the chef's backside to laughter from Atherton.

'Fuckin' stitch that, mate.'

Vinnie pushed Khalid's head to the ground as Farood, one hand on Khalid's lower back, stabbed the blade into his buttocks like a plated turkey, umpteen times.

*

The carving knife was thrown into a coppice by a slip road off the M65. The two firearms taped behind the front-door panels.

'How did you know where I was?'

'There was a tracker setting on the phone. It's useful if you have a child who might go missing.'

The vehicle was thick with cigarette smoke and commercial radio.

Vinnie put his arm around Farood and left it there. 'We didn't want to lose you, Farood. We've got work for you, boy.'

PART TWO

TWENTY-TWO

Rotterdam, April 2012

Farood hoisted himself from the sleeping bag with the determined thought of opening a window. His tongue itched with cigarette smoke and his nostrils clenched against the odour of stale, heavy-sweet alcohol. He stood, coughed, then drew the curtains that tinted with April light. A willow tree was poised across the road, its skirts puffed out as if to present a better view of itself. He had been in the Rotterdam apartment for three weeks, but he hadn't noticed the tree before, not like this. It glowed, as if storing up light for this particular morning, projecting across the road towards him. He pulled up the window, letting birdsong enter the room. No traffic could be heard, just the quiet pattering of a ball off a pavement. Leaning out of the window into the Sunday of an unbending road with its queues of apartment blocks, with thousands of people living around him, he believed he would never be found. He walked over to the kitchen area to make some coffee, inhaling its aroma. Vinnie entered the room in his boxer shorts, revealing more of his blurred tattoos.

'I'll make some coffee,' volunteered Farood.

'Good lad.'

'You want me to make breakfast?'

'No need, son. We're going out for breakfast. And we're gonna start working.'

Vinnie spoke about starting work most days without ever saying what the work was.

'Vinnie, why don't we decorate this room? Brighten it up a little. What do you say?'

'It's not ours, is it?'

'Will he mind. Your friend?'

'I don't know. But it's not worth the trouble, is it?'

Every day for the last few weeks had been filled with TV, films, shopping, drinking, prison stories, traveller stories and the occasional bout of *sean-nós* singing from Vinnie. Neither Atherton nor Vinnie had attempted to persuade Farood to drink. He was left to watch their voices slow and swerve, their tempers soften and fray, their eyes widen and moisten with every swig. Some nights would culminate in Vinnie stripping to his boxers, bouncing off his toes and challenging either of them to spar with him. Farood would swing kicks against Vinnie's forearm blocks and needle jabs. When the lightbulb broke, they sat in the darkness concurring that prison was a joke, too soft, and as such had let them down. On the ferry they had played cards riotously, inviting other passengers to join them until they were required to leave the bar area because of their choice language. It was an overnight journey and Vinnie interrogated Farood about his journey from Baghlan to England.

'Did you know, Farood, that same route was used thousands of years ago? It was called the silk road back then.'

'I heard that. An agent told me that, I think.'

'They're clever people, these agents.'

Before leaving England, the brothers stated they needed to be 'cashed up' for the trip. For Atherton and Vinnie, this meant 'an armed' on a brothel: these were cash-only establishments that tended not to ring the police. Inspecting the back pages of the mid-week *Evening News* they circled some south Manchester parlours before heading out on the Friday afternoon. They were back by tea time with fish and chips, and anecdotes of how Atherton had to 'slap a bitch' to open a locked drawer. It seemed no more trouble than returning a Christmas jumper without a receipt. The cash had been kept in a bin-liner and by now smelled heavily of aftershave.

Vinnie sipped his coffee then flexed himself in the mirror. 'Let's go, boy.'

Having left his lorry in a lorry park they caught a tram back to the docks. The water was a board of grey, sometimes corrugated, sometimes reflecting the towers of containers waiting under the clutches of cranes. Leading Farood to a ballroom-sized cafeteria where departing drivers chewed away the hours, Vinnie ordered falafel specials and eased into a booth with English newspapers. An American soldier had gone door to door in Afghanistan shooting people – women, children, any Afghans would do.

Farood stabbed the paper with his forefinger, spinning the newspaper towards Vinnie. 'If I was there now, I'd fight. I'd join the Taliban and fight.'

'Those mad bastards?'

'I know who they are; they stole my country and they stole my religion, but someone has to make America pay.'

'Or you can think about how you're going to be paid,' replied Vinnie.

After the feature-length breakfast, they swapped newspapers. Drivers glumly came and went; the radio station was switched from Dutch to English and Vinnie tapped the table impatiently. Farood looked at the girls behind the counter. They looked like English girls, like they lived without God.

A cup was placed on their table; a short man in a grey overcoat and scarf sat down, enquiring of Vinnie, 'I take it he's with you?'

'He is,' replied Vinnie. 'He's sound.'

'How was your trip?'

'It was long enough.'

'We all have to work, Vincent.'

'Do you like this country? I don't like this country. Flat as fuck everywhere you drive. Canals all over the place. No wonder everyone's on drugs.'

Leaving the café, they walked along the quay. Vinnie's classic blue and white stripe Adidas trainers, symbolic of his eternal youth, flashed bright against the cobbles. The other man, Farood considered, was not a lorry driver; he was too slim, too refined. He dropped behind yet remained in earshot.

'I couldn't control the last consignment. They nearly got me bubbled and I can't be having that.' Vinnie sounded insistent.

'It won't happen again. The guests I have are well behaved. I'll speak to them.'

'You can speak their language?' Vinnie asked.

'I can always make myself understood.'

Vinnie halted, did an about-turn, pointing at Farood. 'My lad here. Afghan. He's done the route, from as far back as it goes. Can speak all manner of languages. He can explain to them.'

'He can do that when I bring them to you.'

'No, no, Mustapha. We'll go to the house and talk to them there.'

'We've been through this before, Vinnie. No one goes to the house.'

'It's too late when they get in the lorry. There can't be no talking then.'

Mustapha gazed out to the horizon for a moment. 'I need to make a call,' he said.

Farood watched Mustapha, conscious of whom he was ringing, of what was probably being asked and granted at the other end.

Mustapha drove them in his faded Mercedes with full ashtrays back towards the suburbs they had come from. They glided along Steenwijklaan until it became something else and crossed a line onto streets with graffiti and furniture on grass verges, children playing on the roads. The Mercedes made a succession of turns into a cul-de-sac where people were sitting on living-room furniture in front garden spaces. The vehicle glided to a halt and a teenage girl waved from a balcony.

'What's this?' asked Vinnie.

'This is the house and that is one of your passengers,' answered Mustapha. 'Aren't you lucky?'

'Who are you? Captain fucking obvious?'

'Calm yourself. Nobody minds round here. Nobody's watching,' said Mustapha.

The girl opened the patched-up front door and greeted Mustapha like an uncle.

He stopped on the stairs, delving into his pocket for some chocolate. 'These are the people you'll be travelling with. They'll take good care of you.'

'Hi.' She smiled shyly before springing up the stairs ahead of everyone.

The apartment at the top was a blank space crammed with people, sitting on mattresses and sleeping bags. Mustapha made apple tea whilst a husband and wife explained to Farood how they had all helped knock through to the apartment next door.

Vinnie stepped over people, counting from room to room. 'Is this everyone?' he asked.

'There's a few not back.'

Vinnie cursed.

'You know your problem, Vinnie?' cautioned Mustapha. 'You need to relax. Being on edge will only put them on edge. How many can you take?'

'Five, maybe six.'

'I need you to take more; as you can see, I've got a house-full here.'

'Two houses, apparently. I don't work for you, Mustapha; I just provide a service.'

A man clumped up the stairs with two bags of shopping. Farood took a guess and greeted him in Pashtu, relieving him of a bag. They exchanged introductions and accounts of their journeys. The man had spent a night at sea; the memory of his approaching death wouldn't leave him alone, he said. The agent here lacked connections, made promises that no one believed. He had people working in a food factory, making sandwiches day and night to pay for the apartment. Back home in Herat he had a wife and children who he wanted to join him in the UK, but not in Holland. And he had paid for the UK.

In the room next door Vinnie was explaining the travel itinerary to the next five passengers. The thermal blankets, fifteen hours in a coffin-sized box, plenty of air but bring your own water.

Farood interrupted, 'Vinnie, we need to take this man. He's been here too long.'

'It's not his turn,' dismissed Mustapha.

Farood put his new-found friendship to the test. 'We decide, right, Vinnie?'

'That's not how the money works,' explained Mustapha, patience in his voice.

'I know how the money works,' said Farood. 'I was the money once, just like him. You get paid when we take them. You want to get paid, then we take this man along.'

Mustapha swallowed indignantly; he led Vinnie by the elbow onto the landing. 'Vinnie, there are rules here. I allowed you to come here. That is unofficial. Then you bring this boy, I don't know who he is and now he wants to call the shots.'

Vinnie played calm. 'Okay, I hear you, Mustapha. I'll have a word with him and I'll come back tomorrow – I need to show these people something.'

'What you gonna show them?'

'I'm going to bring them the box they'll be lying in. With the polystyrene. I don't want them screaming in the back of the lorry. They need to practise.'

'Okay, just you.'

'Just me.'

It ended with a handshake, but before their backs were turned Mustapha began dialling his superior.

Walking back to their apartment Farood was apologetic but adamant that the contractor and traveller alike were getting a bad service from this so-called agent. Vinnie stopped every few hundred metres to pensively roll cigarettes that he didn't smoke. Outside the block Atherton was facing the elevated bonnet of a recently purchased, long-ago manufactured, blue transit van.

'A Vauxhall, eh?' stated Vinnie.

'It won't let you down, Vinnie. I knew a transit once that had four hundred K on the clock. Four hundred! And it wasn't even the right clock.'

Atherton twisted in a new spark plug then tenderly applied some grease to the battery terminals. He nodded Vinnie over to a carrier bag containing a few sets of number plates.

Inside the barren apartment Vinnie slumped into the embrace of an armchair, airing his doubts about the partnership with Mustapha. 'He's too casual by far. Too matey with the cargo. He's not in control of the property or the people in it.'

Farood testified as an expert witness. 'In my opinion he is unprofessional. A good agent never gets overcrowded with travellers. Not at this late stage in the journey.'

'So, why do you think he's so overcrowded?' asked Vinnie.

'It's obvious. Because drivers don't trust him. How much is Mustapha paying you?'

Vinnie wiped his brow, scratched his nose. 'Not enough.' He rose to his feet, looked out at Atherton revving the transit van and tried to join some dots. 'Roodie, tell me, who pays Mustapha, is it the border-jumpers in his flat?'

'No. Not always, not directly. The first agent, the main agent who the travellers pay one thousand, two thousand dollars to at the beginning of their journey, takes their cut and passes the money on, a piece at a time. Down the line. Into bank accounts, as agents move the people. Except some agents, most agents, always want more money. So, they keep the people, make them work for them, make more money. Sometimes the people never leave Istanbul or wherever. In the end, if families don't hear from people, that they have made it to France or wherever – they have to be compensated and bad agents get cut out of the chain.'

'We could do with Mustapha being cut out, couldn't we?' suggested Vinnie.

'I could do a much better job.'

'How?' asked Vinnie.

'I just need one phone number out of him. That's all.'

'Tomorrow then. We take Mustapha out of the picture. What do you say, Farood?'

'It's why you brought me here, isn't it?'

TWENTY-THREE

Rotterdam

T he van was reluctant on ignition and shuddered between two minds at traffic lights. Vinnie's tennis elbow was giving him jip on the shivering gear stick. Farood and Atherton were steadying themselves in the murk of the back. Between them lay a six-foot-long, two-foot-wide cardboard box.

'This van has a nasty smell to it, boys.'

'It's back here, Vinnie, it's bad,' agreed Atherton, squatting with one hand, steadying himself mid-ship.

Vinnie wound down his window and threw a question into the back. 'Who did you buy it from?'

'Some random Asian,' replied Atherton.

Farood smelled the brown stains that had stuck to his fingers and suppressed a retch.

'What is it?' Vinnie wanted to know.

He pulled over, ramped the van up on the pavement and tore open the back. Atherton stepped out, examined his trainer soles. He looked baffled; Farood did not.

'It's blood.'

Atherton felt faint enough to sit on the kerb. 'How do you know?' he asked.

'I've seen enough of it. It'll be animal blood. He's been

slaughtering animals in there.'

'Vinnie, can I sit in the front, please?' asked Atherton. 'And I don't think those border-jumpers are gonna like it in there one bit.'

Vinnie punched a dent into the bodywork. His eyes switched onto his nephew. 'Jesus, it's like a fuckin' abattoir. Did you not look at this?'

'I was looking at the engine, wasn't I?'

'Right, you looked at that and thought, *It's pissing oil so I'll buy it.*'

'It wasn't when I looked at it.'

'Because it wasn't running when you looked at it, was it?'

Michael Atherton's eyes were an admission.

Vinnie promptly composed himself before continuing. 'I need to have these people feel at ease. How am I going to do that in these kinds of conditions? We're involved in a business here and we do things professionally. Understand? I want it cleaned out this afternoon.'

They drove on to Mustapha's apartment where Vinnie got out and shouldered a coffin-sized box.

'Right, you two wait twenty minutes before you go in.'

He made his entrance, Mustapha watching the box nudge up the stairs.

'Are you ready, Mustapha?'

'I was born ready. Ready for what, Vinnie?'

'My demonstration. It's all in the box. Lead me to my intrepid travellers.'

Inside the stale departure lounge, Mustapha clapped his hands and a number of people rose from their sleeping bags. Vinnie stood next to him, one arm curled around the waist of the box. People lying on the floor studied his face from within their diminishing dreams, their memories of the past and the future. He appeared to be a magician of sorts or a low-budget undertaker. One or two greeted him with a delicate wave.

Mustapha compered. 'I want to introduce the man who is going to take you to the UK. To a new life. To plenty of work and a place of your own. Welcome, Vinnie!'

Vinnie carefully laid out his prized box. 'You're going to get there in my lorry. I'm a good driver, by the way, the best. But while we're getting on and off the ferry, I'm going to have to hide you. You'll be well used to that by now.'

Someone volunteered that they had once hidden in a lorry full of onions and now they can't eat onions anymore when they used to be keen on them. The interruption was acknowledged before Vinnie progressed on to point two.

'The security people going over vehicles have wands, and these wands detect body heat. So, I have...'

He prised open the flaps of his box to reveal a shining silver cloak that he encouraged members of the audience to touch.

'This will make you invisible. Pass it amongst you. When you wrap that around you, they won't be able to pick up your body heat. You lie in this box with this nice warm blanket around you and you wake up in England. Would somebody like to give it a try?'

The onion girl rose to her feet; Vinnie welcomed her into his thermal blanket and then the box. She dipped down and sprung up and insisted on a selfie that he wanted no part of. Once inside the box Vinnie closed the flaps and, for a finale, lifted it onto his shoulder and did a 360-degree turn whilst the girl inside screamed with laughter.

'Anyone got any questions?'

Farood's Afghan friend raised his hand cautiously.

'Yes, my friend.'

'How do we breathe?'

Vinnie was unfazed, was right back at him. 'Good question. Pass the scissors, please, Mustapha.'

'I have no scissors.'

Forced to improvise, Vinnie reached for a fork from a

deserted Pot Noodle to stab the box a few times. 'See these holes? There'll be plenty of these wee holes.'

Atherton and Farood were stood at next door's front door, unable to mount the surprise attack. Atherton knocked politely, twice, and no one came. He thumped, first with his fist then with his blood-stained heel. A child on his toes opened the door. They pressed him against the wall and ran up to the knock-through apartment. In the living room two boys kicked a ball about. Atherton confiscated the ball under his arm. He whispered to the boys, 'Go get Mustapha, say someone wants to see him – in here.'

The boys ran through the comic strip-style hole to the next apartment. A chair was placed centre stage; Farood pressed his back flat against the wall next to the hole. Atherton bounced the ball and Mustapha appeared at the hole, filling it out like a man at the entrance to a cave.

'Who are you?'

'I'm your new gaffer,' announced Atherton.

Seizing Mustapha by the collar, Farood hauled him to the chair. Atherton swung his instep into his groin, following it up with a thrust punch to the ribs, after which Mustapha settled into his chair.

Farood flapped his hands. 'Empty your pockets,' he said.

Their prisoner was breathless and submissive.

Farood snatched his phone. 'You do this job and you don't carry a weapon? What's the pin number?'

Mustapha grimaced as he recited the numbers.

Farood rolled the screen. 'This is the agent in Istanbul, right? Ring him. Tell him you have a new partner now. And know that I understand your mongrel language.'

Atherton produced a pistol from an ankle holster and ejected the magazine into his palm. He showed it to Mustapha. 'Full to the brim, mate.'

He clipped it back in, pressed the barrel onto Mustapha's right kneecap, which began to twitch a little. He wasn't very long on the phone, his voice frayed and breaking.

Atherton kept the gun where it was whilst Farood took the phone and introduced himself to the agent in Istanbul. 'The situation here is basically out of control... He can't move anyone on to the UK, he has two apartments full, attracting too much attention... He needs help... I've been up and down the line more than once... speak many languages... Yeah, I went through Istanbul... There's a lot of agents there... I'm called Karam... Okay... this is my number now... I've got a driver who can move some tomorrow...'

Vinnie shimmied through from next door. 'Everything okay in here?' That his nephew was scowling down the barrel of a firearm pointed at his Turkish associate confirmed all was in order.

Mustapha rose to his feet, protesting like a child. 'You think you can come in here and take over my operation?!'

Atherton booted his shins. 'We know we can, mate.'

'That's enough now,' ordered Vinnie. 'Mustapha, you'll still continue to be part of this. You're going to make a good living – we all are. We'll be back tomorrow, early, to pick these up. If anyone else comes here to doss down, show them the door.'

The van was jet-washed and scrubbed with bleach. That evening, whilst Atherton and Farood tried a medley of Dutch cannabis over a post-mortem on the day's insurrection, Vinnie made notes in his journal on the forthcoming voyage. Vinnie held an admiration for the Vikings, their singular brutality, their great endurance and obvious organisation. Historians, it seems, were always discovering new evidence of their arrival on assorted points of the globe leaving university types scratching their heads. These Norsemen had been underestimated by the clever clogs and by Kirk Douglas. They'd been portrayed as savage dimwits, yet Vinnie sensed they were the great thinkers of the Dark Ages, masters of what Eddie Stoddard called 'logistics'. And whilst they might not have written on a lot of stone pillars like the Greeks and Romans, they would at least have made a list. Vinnie broke his responsibilities down into 'packing them', 'keeping them quiet', 'keeping them alive', 'unpacking them'.

Five o' clock the following morning. Vinnie and Farood loaded up the transit with five boxes plus an economy bag of polystyrene pellets. At Mustapha's apartment Farood saw to it that the man from Herat was on board and that everyone had sandwiches that hadn't made it past quality control at the food factory. As they rumbled off towards the docklands area, Farood provided the five rear passengers with a heads-up on life in the UK.

'If you work hard in the UK you can make something. They won't pretend to be your friend when they're not.'

The teenager that had greeted them from the balcony took out her earphones. 'First day in London, I'm going to take a look at Buckingham Palace.'

Farood spoke in Pashtun to the Afghan alone. 'You won't be killed in a war over there, and you won't starve. But people will want to buy and sell you. The place will make you greedy and careless. Never forget the times when you were hungry. Don't get fat and lazy.'

They pulled up next to Vinnie's larger white delivery lorry in a cluttered lorry park to casually move some boxes from one vehicle to another.

Farood clambered into the back of the transit and crouched on the tarp. 'One at a time, wrap yourself in thermal blanket and lay in a box.'

Everyone was perfectly cooperative, enthusiastic, amused, even. Farood sprinkled in polystyrene pellets and one by one they were carried into the back of the lorry.

'From now on, no talking, understand?' whispered Vinnie.

He rolled down the shutter and shook Farood's hand. 'I'll see you in a couple of days. Get that house in order, understand.'

*

Back at Vinnie's apartment Atherton was squaring up to a mirror in a medium blue suit. 'Michael van Hurst – pleased to meet you, mate.' He shook a hand, leaned his head, listened attentively, nodded and smiled. The mirror said he was ready. Cool as a Budweiser. He strutted to the end of Farood's beached mattress. 'What d'ya reckon?'

'You're wearing too much aftershave.'

'Reckon?'

'You smell like a woman in a department store.'

'I'll wash some off then.'

'And have a shave while yer at it,' added Farood, turning back to sleep.

An hour later Farood and Atherton rode the blue van back to Mustapha's to pick up the work party. Mustapha hadn't fed or watered anyone, and this was noted. The workforce was bundled into the back of the van, stopping shortly after at a garage where Farood bought everyone cereal bars and coffee.

Atherton paced the forecourt, clutching his clipboard and fiddling with his tie. He signalled everyone over to the jet-wash area. 'Who knows the boss at this place?'

A Moroccan overwhelmed in an anorak raised his hand.

'What's he like?'

'He's a pig. A fuckin' pig.'

'What's he do?' enquired Atherton.

'He thinks we're slaves. And he touches the women.'

Just before 8am they were delivered to the middle door in a row of factory units, each with its own singular parking space and discreet window. Inside the stench of raw meat and mayonnaise wrestled one another. Beneath the strip lighting, lagged piping

193

and girders, line after line of stainless steel: conveyor belts, tables, vats, cages and steps. The work party pushed their arms into white coats, put on blue cellophane aprons and hats, and headed for their positions. Atherton tapped a biro on his clipboard, waiting for the gaffer. A phone rang, everywhere. A bald, ginger-bearded character, wheelie-bin wide, slammed an office door behind him and the ringing stopped. Atherton watched his work party mechanically fill and stack sandwiches that headed up rollers to be packaged. He watched a man stuffing a carcass into a super funnel throw a scrap of meat at them.

Atherton knocked respectfully on the manager's door and let himself in. Before the receiver was down, before the telephone conversation was over.

'Michael van Hurst, pleased to meet you.'

The ginger wheelie bin refused to take Atherton's handshake. 'Who are you?'

'I run the Van Hurst Employment Agency, I brought eight workers here this morning.'

'The Turk, Mustapha, he usually brings them.'

'There's a new arrangement now. That's why I'm here.' Atherton withdrew a glossy business card. 'Any you're not happy with, ring this number.'

The manager examined the card; it was reassuringly amateur. 'This is still a cash arrangement?' he asked.

'Best way,' confirmed Atherton. 'Friday alright?'

The manager nodded. 'So, Mustapha, he won't be coming back here?'

'No. You'll be dealing with me from now on,' concluded Atherton.

*

A few minutes off the N57, a few kilometres from the docks, Vinnie turned his lorry into a forecourt dignified by roses and hawthorn. He slid open a hatch behind him and faced down to the boxes below.

'Everybody okay?'

He took a roll of silver gaffer tape from the glove compartment and strolled round to the back of the lorry. He sealed all five of the boxes then stood above his row of buried passengers.

'We're going to be loading up here now. So, everyone stays quiet. As far as everyone else is concerned, you're all sunflowers.'

He went across to the low-rise glass-walled building where a receptionist with a flawless complexion phoned through to the warehouse.

Vinnie got back to the van ahead of the forklift and climbed in. 'It's only me. Here he comes, here he comes now. No noise.'

More long, narrow boxes advanced towards him then halted, jerked up a notch and advanced another stride.

'I got them from here, mate,' shouted Vinnie to the driver.

They were all heavily scented by their contents: tulips, daffodils, bouquets, lilies and wreathes. Between each load Vinnie chatted away cheerily to his passengers. He got his paperwork signed off and headed for the ferry.

It was a snug passenger ferry and aside from the odd caravan, his plain white delivery vehicle was the biggest thing shuffling towards the lip of the boat. He surveyed the queue, clocking the security team. They were a lethargic couple in high-vis jackets, one with a lollipop wand, the other with a scatty dog. When it came to his turn, he grinned down at them, hesitating whilst they looked over the formality of his paperwork.

'Pull over.'

'What?'

'Pull over. Open the back.'

Vinnie wrenched his steering wheel, jumped down from the seat, playing irritated, playing 'we've done this a thousand times' with his submissive arms.

'Open the back.'

He shrugged; the dog wagged its tail. He would put his ingenuity and professionalism to his test. He would not be rattled. He hoisted up the back. 'Look in my lorry all you like,' he shouted. 'Have yer dog sniff around and wave your magic wand, there's no asylum seekers in here.'

The spaniel was lifted onto boxes and a torch was shone from his cabin through the hatch.

'Satisfied?'

They drifted off to a Land Rover three vehicles behind.

Vinnie rejoined the queue and nudged his way onto the fume-filled car deck, bumper to bumper with holiday-makers and weekend stoners. He poked his head through the hatch, looking like a man in the stocks.

'We passed the test. Told you, didn't I? I'm leaving for a bit now, but when I get back, you can all get out and take a stretch.'

Vinnie had an illicit fag on deck before heading for the restaurant. He was very partial to Dutch food; even the spuds had meat mashed up in them. He went for the 'flying chicken wings' and sat down to scrutinise his newspaper and the other passengers, wondering if border control had plainclothed people mingling on the decks. It's what he would do if he were running the show. Things were certainly getting heavy with the old migrants. It was kicking off bit by bit in the Middle East; people were rolling up their blankets and their pipes and joining queues everywhere. Supply-wise, it was a good time to get into the business. Demand-wise too. He was going to get a good price for the five down below from a cabbage farm in Lincolnshire, but things were getting jittery at departure and arrival. Dover was a write-off these days, which was a shame – the country needed these people because the English worker was no longer a grafter. He'd gone soft, unlike the row under cardboard below deck. Lean and hungry. As Vinnie had promised the farm manager, 'they'd work all day on two slices of fresh air'.

He had another roll-up and went back to his lorry. He put

on a Chris Rea CD to mask the voices then went to the back. He was about to climb in but did a double take because the security officer from Rotterdam was edging herself between vehicles.

She smiled, waved at him, and made her way over. 'You have a lorry full of flowers, no? I could smell it as soon as you opened up on the quay. I can smell it from here. Nice to drive with, no?'

'Oh, it's a lovely drive alright. Makes me dream of beautiful women.'

He watched her go on her way, poking her torch at car windows. He pulled up the back of the lorry and switched on his own. He kneeled down at the end of the row, whispering, 'Can you hear me? Oi, can any of you hear me?'

The flaps on the box nearest him were being pushed up. He pulled back the gaffer; fingers emerged, then a wrist. Vinnie dragged the Afghan up by the collar – he spat out a polystyrene pellet. 'Are you okay, fella?'

The Afghan stared into nowhere, slowly gulping what air there was, his face waxen. 'I need some water.'

Vinnie fetched a bottle from the glove compartment. The security woman, a few aisles ahead, had asked someone to open a boot. Vinnie turned up the Chris Rea.

When he got back to the Afghan he was sitting up, legs still under the cardboard, the rest of him frozen.

'I have to get out,' he said, as if they might be his final words.

Vinnie pushed the bottle into his hand. 'And I'd like nothing more than for you to get out and come upstairs and have a chicken dinner, but you can't, fella. There's security everywhere, roaming around, and believe me, these people have eyes in the back of their heads. I need everyone to lie low a bit longer.'

The Afghan raised his knees and tried to push down with his arms, but Vinnie rested his hands on his shoulders. 'Shush now.'

'Open the other boxes, let the others out for a bit.'

'I will, I will. Have a drink, lie down. You'll be fine.'

The Afghan relented. The hours of claustrophobic inertia had exhausted him.

Vinnie watched him sink away into his bed of polystyrene, then he gently tucked the thermal blanket round his shoulders.

'Don't close the box yet, please.'

'I won't.'

Vinnie rested the palm of his hand on the Afghan's head. He waited with him until Chris Rea began to loop, then he closed the flaps of the box and taped it up again. He looked at the other four boxes and knew there'd be no getting them back in.

'I'll be back, back in a wee while. Have a sleep for now.'

The ferry had begun to take up a persistent roll and passengers were popping antihistamines. Vinnie went to the bar for a couple of Jamesons, to take off the edge, telling the barman all about the curse of 'border-jumpers crawling over his caravan' back in Rotterdam. He engaged a lorry driver, who once had a knife to his throat in Calais. Vinnie shook his head in solidarity. 'And who gets the fuckin' blame, who has to take the fall when the bastards are found?'

The lament of last orders sent him to his cabin. His cargo would take care of themselves. For now, he needed to give himself some attention.

He woke late and tremulous. Most vehicles had already alighted by the time he made it to the lorry, which stood marooned and overtaken. A crew member, waving vehicles down the ramp, shouted some encouragement his way to which Vinnie would've normally offered a choice reply had his tongue not been glued to the roof of his mouth. He clanged onto the ramp then into the brightness of Immingham without a word to his passengers. They were home now. They were about to step out into a new life, all the long journey behind them. He headed north into Lincolnshire farmland, along level roads between thickening hedges before pulling into a pub car park.

He drew back the hatch, no longer whispering. 'We're here, we've done it, guys.'

He unloaded enough flowers to flood the back with light then pulled back the gaffer tape on the Afghan's box. His face was as before, as it was the previous night when he had sealed the box. His mouth was open and so were his eyes. His forehead and cheeks were damp. Vinnie lowered his face to the man's mouth. There was no breath, just the smell of human dirt. He opened another three but didn't see the point in opening the last one. He was nearly three grand down. Vinnie had had bodies on his hands before, but never five. Disposing of previous bodies had involved car breakers, quarries or incinerators; once even a fishing trawler. The sea was only down the road, it would deal with the DNA issue, but it was busy with traffic. The flowers were for Hull, the migrants for a farm just south of the Humber. He went back to his driver's seat and rolled a fag. He lowered the window, inhaling deeply. He could still smell the Afghan. It would all have to be rethought, the whole operation. In the meantime, he would continue his schedule as if there were no border-jumpers to deliver. He headed for the river, for the majestic bridge, wrapped this day in fog.

Arriving at the delivery depot, there was an argument because Vinnie hadn't time to wait for 'some gormless bastard with a forklift' and set about leaving the flowers on the forecourt and the paperwork to the wind and hail. From there he found a Travelodge, took a shower and a meal and kept his eye on the lorry below. He stood in a towelling robe, sipping tea, knowing that any unease he felt with the situation was his foe. He concluded that it could only have been the ventilation. Taping the boxes was non-negotiable, but from now on, so was air. He was waiting for dusk and although he napped most days at this time, he avoided the uncertain pleasure, deciding instead to walk into town to buy a pair of wellingtons.

Seven o'clock and he was heading back over the bridge, taking it steady. On the other side, he took a steep left and made for the hamlet of Barrow Haven, past the fisheries, the sailing club. He began to run out of road on the riverside; the water had turned its back on him and was lost to the darkness. He was pushing through the floodplain and considered blundering through a hedge and driving through fields when a farm track presented itself. Beyond it the sky lay pinned down by lights on the opposite shore. Dipping his lights, he strolled his lorry until there was grass under the wheels and he could smell the river above the Afghan. He turned the vehicle and opened the gaping back to face the water, silent under the wind. One by one he slid his boxes onto the pebbles and heaved them out into the water. At the end he paused before he returned to the lorry, as if to say something, but the words did not come.

TWENTY-FOUR

Rotterdam

Farood was at the wheel of the transit van in the food factory car park. The migrant workers were always the last to leave, and the most tired. Half of them would immediately lie down in the back of the van and sleep. Some openly talked about 'never going back', which Farood decreed wasn't allowed. He described the work he had done in Iran: how people lay down and died in ditches that were filled in with concrete and wooden posts.

'You are lucky. You don't know how lucky you are.'

But every day they asked him, 'When are we going to the UK?'

He didn't know.

Vinnie had been gone for two weeks now – he'd said it would be two days and they had heard nothing. Atherton had two theories – either he was on a bender with his long-term on-and-off girlfriend, 'the lush of his life'; or he had gone to Corfu with the cash to get a tan. 'It's what I would do.' In his uncle's absence, Atherton had taken to calling the shots. He had Farood ferrying migrants back and forth from work as well as doing the shopping for Vinnie's apartment. Atherton had also put himself in charge of Mustapha and Mustapha's apartment.

'You better get this place sorted out, mate. It's a fucking pigsty. People coming here from some shithole of a country to lie on the floor. Today, right, when the others get back, we're gonna get some proper mattresses, you're gonna get some food and clean up. And you ain't in charge of the rent no more. We're gonna be having a meeting here to tell everyone how it's all gonna be run. You hear me, Musty?'

When he wasn't giving orders, he went to look for work for those that had no work. When Farood returned, Atherton was in a shouting match with the Moroccan who'd quit sandwich-making at the factory.

'You want us to work for almost nothing? Where do you think we are? This is not a prison. Where is the driver gone? Why isn't he back here? We know your game – you're keeping us here to make us work.'

With each reply, Atherton raised the volume. 'You're joking, mate, we want rid. Can't fucking wait. Sick of looking at the lot of you. And I'll tell you something else, point that finger at me again and I'll break it off and shove it up your arse.'

Farood observed casually, clutching the van keys, stroking his evolving beard. His coolness touched Atherton, who retreated to the kitchen. Farood glared at the Moroccan until he turned his back and rejoined his card game. Then he smiled at Atherton, giving him the go-ahead to protest.

'Tell me this, Roodie, why am I walking round this flat all day with a binliner whilst they're sat on their arses?'

'I agree, they need to be working, otherwise they're just costing us money.'

'Exactly,' confirmed Atherton.

'What's Mustapha doing about it?'

Atherton slammed the draining board. 'I'll tell you what he's doing. He's sitting on his arse, smoking. And the money the others bring in ain't enough.'

There was a slow thud up the stairs, out of which came a

double mattress with Mustapha beneath it. 'I got two others out there, I need a hand.'

'No, you don't,' replied Atherton.

Farood and Atherton headed down town for an all-day brunch in a café of oak floors and yellow lights. Atherton put both feet on the low brass rail and was leaning over the bar at the fridges, a habit amongst Brits that the barman found maddening.

'I'll have one of those Belgium beers, the one with the red label. Roodie, what you having?'

'Tomato juice.'

They sat beneath the glow of a televised football match.

Atherton shook his head at a missed penalty. 'I'm sick of them North Africans. They lie around all day waiting to be fed.' He ordered a meatloaf and reset his eyes to the TV. 'I spoke to Ginger Bollocks at the sandwich factory and he don't like 'em.'

Farood tapped the table for attention. 'You know what I found out today? Our people are paid half what the Dutch workers are paid. One of the Dutch guys told me.'

'Doesn't surprise me. We're having the piss taken out of us all ways. The Dutch, the fucking Africans, and where's Vinnie, eh?'

*

Vinnie was in Manchester doing sit-ups in his caravan, warming up for a bare-knuckle fight – a fight for his kingdom. Someone else wanted their initials on the asphalt at the site entrance; they wanted Vinnie's gone. During his absence a new family had been allowed on, even though all newcomers had to be run past Vinnie. Vinnie's first and last rule was 'no newcomers'. But Sammy had rented out a caravan, not to travellers, not even to New Age soap-dodgers, but to *settled* people: homeless tykes that other landlords wouldn't entertain. It was happening at sites across the country: people from the other side of the barrier were pleading to rent caravans to escape the confinement of hostels and bedsits. This could never be allowed. They were people not bred from the same stock – no matter their name, no matter what they claimed. Sammy had asked before and Sammy had been told; now, whilst Vinnie was working in Rotterdam, he had played his hand, so Vinnie had called Sammy out, to publicly put him back in his box.

Fights or bouts were regular events on the site, mainly for gambling. Men fought from age sixteen onwards. That was sport, this was kingship; there would be more of a crowd. Fights were not without rules; there was a referee who said little but was generally respected. The appointed place was between the garages, inside a shifting ring of barracking men. Compared to Vinnie, Sammy was flabby, fleshy and pale. Sure, he was heavy and he could dish it out but Vinnie knew, having looked into his eyes, he couldn't take it.

They were waiting for Vinnie. Sammy was in matching grey vest and joggers, stomping the damp ground, breathing like a horse, punching the wind. The referee was a man testing the seams of a black tracksuit, chewing vigorously. There was a crowd of around twenty men and boys and women at caravan windows. Vinnie strolled over to the ring in his Lonsdale shorts, no vest, no socks.

The referee held out an arm between the two. 'You know the rules. If it's one-way traffic I'll put a stop to it.'

The referee lifted his arm; Sammy began to prance clockwise. He shuffled and stooped, slowly, predictably, rotating his fists as if he were turning a handle. He flexed his shoulders repeatedly while Vinnie was without motion. His hands were on his hips. Older men in the crowd shouted their allegiance. 'He's yours, Sammy, lay into him, boy.' Sammy rushed in with a jab that burst his opponent's lip, then he hopped back jubilantly. Blood rolled off Vinnie's chin, but still his arms hung loose. The chorus in the crowd raised its voice: 'Lay the fucker out, Sammy.' They bunched and circled with Sammy: 'Again... again.' The referee commanded Vinnie, 'Fight!' But he didn't. He stood as a sentry whilst Sammy ducked his head against the blows that never came his way. Vinnie's eyes beseeched him to come again. When he did Vinnie swayed his head back but still the blow made contact with the cut. A small boy at the back asked, 'Why don't you fight, yer cunt? Fight, yer fuckin' coward.'

The referee got nose to nose with Vinnie. 'Start throwing punches or I'll end this.'

And so, he gave the referee a sweet left which sent him toppling into Sammy's boys. He then advanced on Sammy like a fencer. Long, even strides, knees bent. Two double jabs and an uppercut, and he was able to stamp on Sammy's head half a dozen times. Not in the rules, but with an unconscious referee he felt obliged.

'None of you bastards dare question my authority. I'm the boyo who calls the shots, because I takes the chances, I don't back down. I do what has to be done. To look after my people. The rest of you are gutless.'

He looked down on Sammy and spat on him.

'You can give it out, but you can't take it.'

Vinnie put on his crown.

*

Michael Atherton had gone to see Ginger Bollocks, to collect his resident's weekly wage and to insist on a pay rise. In the way the world of business makes its magic, the 'border-jumpers' were turned into 'residents', Mustapha's apartment into 'the hostel', the process of carting people in boxes into Immingham was now 'a shipment'. The Dutchman counted out the barely credible-looking Euros. Atherton declined to pick them up.

'Was there something else?' asked the Dutchman.

Atherton sighed, shamming confidence. 'I hear you're paying my people half what you pay other people.'

'That's the point of them, isn't it?'

'The point is, mate; I've got a hostel to run, and this here doesn't even cover the rent.'

The big man leaned back, straightening his legs. 'Okay, you can have another ten per cent, but I haven't got the cash right now. How's next week?'

'Sweet.'

Atherton pocketed the money, winked. He hadn't even had to sit down. The businessman strode out, patting his breast pocket, back to the blue transit, back to the Bier Café for a couple of hours.

Vinnie rounded the final corner back onto Dwingelostraat and kicked into a sprint to AC/DC. By the time he'd got to the front door the tank was empty; he was bent double and his eyes burned with perspiration. He'd knocked the fags on the head, for good this time. What had happened, what he'd had to do at the banks of that river, had made him stronger – it had to.

He barged into the apartment and knocked on the lad's doors. 'Business meeting, ten minutes.'

Back at the helm, he felt renewed. The team met in the living room, in three different shades of white boxer shorts.

'Item one,' announced Atherton. 'Where the fuck have *you* been?'

'I had a matter to sort out on the site.'

'Told yer, didn't I?' bragged Atherton to Farood.

'You said he'd gone to Corfu.'

'Why would I go to fucking Corfu?' Vinnie was genuinely perplexed.

For the next ten minutes they argued over the possibility of this hypothetical reason for Vinnie's absence and, not for the first time, Farood felt he was back on the wing. He clapped his hands to be heard. 'Look, we need to assess the present situation and plan our next move.'

Atherton reported first, grinning. 'Well, as of yesterday, I got us a pay rise from the sandwich factory.'

'Yeah, well, you need to get working on jobs for the others,' Farood reminded him.

'I am, I already said I am. How did the first shipment go?'

Vinnie took a moment to ponder, nodding to himself. 'Okay. It went okay.'

'What's that mean?' asked Atherton.

'What do you think it means? I got them there.'

Atherton pressed on. 'You got the money from the farm?'

'Too bloody right I did.'

Atherton let the next question brew for a moment. '...That's a grand each, right?'

It sent Vinnie to his feet, resenting the implication. 'I don't rip people off. People I'm working with. Never.' He went to the window, pulled back the porous curtains, craved a cigarette.

Farood moved on to the next item. 'The agent in Istanbul. He rang me. He wants to know when you're taking the rest. He has people he needs to send us.'

'Soon,' said Vinnie. 'I need to do some work on packaging. A few days.'

Over the following week they were all industrious. Vinnie gave Atherton permission to purchase 'a little runner', a Vauxhall Astra with a hundred K on the clock. He would need it. The business was alive; they had created something, and as much as they bickered, they were proud of what they had achieved. Vinnie went in search of the right-sized boxes, giving ventilation serious thought. He looked upon the first shipment as merely a prototype. There were definite advantages with the long, narrow box – it prevented the cargo from moving – the disadvantage was that the cargo had died. The farm in Lincolnshire had been on the blower asking about the whereabouts of their free, live-in labour.

Atherton scurried from one Rotterdam industrial park to

another and hustled down town at anywhere that might not ask for a CV and a passport – cafés, bars or fast-food orifices that looked like they were already hiring no-questions-asked labour. Another angle had also occurred to him, one that wouldn't have purchase with the likes of Ginger Bollocks but might amongst the less ugly. Perhaps the hostel was really a 'refugee centre'. *Hi, Michael van Hurst. I'm working on behalf of refugees. People escaping shithole countries in search of a better life, starting with you.* He would need to get the chat nailed, plus a new business card, but he knew how to identify the kind of prey that would offer refugees assistance from a hundred yards. The maternal women in flat shoes and the forgiving men who preferred wine to beer. His cheap suit would work better in that end of the market. *I went to that camp in Calais. It's not easy to describe.*

By the end of the week he had found a few companies prepared to welcome 'multi-cultural interns' for a small fee.

He was halfway through reporting on the results when Farood returned from the food factory pick up. 'The Dutch guy. He says they're all sacked. And he won't pay them this week.'

Vinnie ruled out any immediate retribution, even after a liquid brunch he was against it. They couldn't win this one. No matter how many times they hit Ginger Bollocks, he wasn't going to take the border-jumpers back, and if they hit him hard enough, he would go to the cops. Atherton would just have to dig deeper for some new openings.

A few days later Vinnie was on his way with a second shipment. This time his cargo lay inside wooden crates under thermal blankets, with loose straw behind *air holes galore*. The lids were nailed down rather than taped.

At the florist's depot he slapped his order on the reception desk like a domino and was told to go find his forklift driver in the order department who, when he got there, was in close conversation with a female employee. Vinnie waved the despatch note; the driver waved back.

Vinnie pointed out, 'Listen, son, on your toes, I've a ferry to catch.'

The production line of twenty flower packers, most of whom were plugged into iPods, were oblivious. All except one: a newly appointed Moroccan intern from a nearby refugee hostel run by a Michael van Hurst. The Moroccan had seen Vinnie before – demonstrating how he packed people into boxes.

*

Sunrise is the time to take photographs along the Humber. The photographer had shot hundreds of sunrises, but there was always something different about each photograph, each moment. Despite the Met Office putting a time on it, she knew that dawn was a sequence, not an instant, and the temptation was always to overshoot. So, she imposed a limit on herself of three shots. This would force her to locate the height of the drama. She walked the three miles out to the tip of Spurn Point following the beam from her headlamp along the sandy track. When the track drained into the flattened sands there was enough faint light creeping above the horizon to dispense with the lamp. She looked at her watch, looked over her shoulder to where the estuary lapped on the Point. She had no more than thirty minutes before she needed to head back. Beached and swollen at the river's very mouth, hanging off its lower lip, was a seal. She raised her camera and zoomed towards it. The seal was wearing a denim jacket.

TWENTY-FIVE

Humberside

It was the first occasion that the young policeman had been the initial officer at a crime scene with a body. *Luckily*, he thought, *it all looks simple enough.* There was only one cooperative witness – no other members of the public, no traffic and no Sherlock Holmes neighbours. He could've taped off a perimeter for a mile square if he wanted. He'd rung it through and was waiting with the photographer, their collars turned up against the sea breeze. *She is*, he thought, *without a doubt single. Also, potentially grumpy, overweight and probably a serial attendee of evening classes. He is*, she thought, *a policeman, and consequently someone who makes snap judgements about people.* Before he had arrived at the scene, she had taken a score or more photographs of the corpse. With each shot she became less afraid, moving closer until she was kneeling in the water, exploring the subject. Now in the full light of morning, watching the dead man bob and tug on the tide, she realised she much preferred looking at him through a lens. From a few metres away the body looked like he had fallen over and might get up at any minute. She had no conversation for the policeman, who repeatedly looked at his watch, turning to search for approaching headlights.

She touched his shoulder with her palm, pointed to the dead man. 'Tide's coming in,' she announced.

The current had picked up the body, the left arm pointing in the direction he was heading, upriver back to Hull. The young constable waded into the milky tan water. He was conscious that he wasn't supposed to touch a body, but it would be no use pointing SOCO in the direction that it had drifted to. Grabbing a foot, he dragged it onto the sand. Once on the beach, the dead man showed his face to the sky. It was swollen and paler than the other exposed areas. A white crab crawled from his mouth.

DS Gavin O'Grady and DI Esther Katz had left Spurn Road and were bumping along the rutted track, Katz with one hand on the dashboard, the other holding an electronic cigarette. They came to a 'No Vehicles Beyond This Point' sign, at which O'Grady braked.

'That doesn't mean us,' clarified Katz.

The young constable met them at the perimeter tape.

Katz, who was taller than either of the men, strode ahead down to the beach. Noticing the tracks in the sand, she halted. 'This is where you found the body?'

The young constable drew level with her. 'No, ma'am, the body was in the water—'

'And you dragged it out, did you?'

'The thing is, ma'am...'

The constable tendered his explanation, but Katz walked away from him and took out her phone.

He went on, '...it was beginning to float away.'

She raised a palm in his direction, began talking urgently to the screen. 'I do know what time it is... I've got a body, which a very keen first attending officer pulled out of the water... Hold on.' She turned to the constable. 'How long has he been out of the water?'

'Ten minutes?'

'I'm after an answer, not a question, Constable.' She flagged her palm at him again to resume the phone call. 'Must I? Hold on, I'll have a look.' She bent down towards the body's face. 'Yes, I can see... as soon as you like.' She put the phone back into her waterproof. 'Constable, seeing as you dragged him out, you can help me drag him back in.'

Taking the tall Afghan by the feet, they dragged him back into the estuary until Katz and the constable were both knee deep.

'Now, Constable, I need you to keep him there until the pathologist arrives. She's probably in the shower by now. Advice for you as an FAO: never move a body out of the water – it starts to decompose. Just anchor it if you need to.'

As she waded out, DS O'Grady wanted to tell the constable not to take it personally.

Katz put on a generous smile and approached the photographer. 'So, what were you doing out here, so bright and early?'

'Photographing the sunrise.'

'Any good, was it?'

'I got a bit distracted.'

'Bet you couldn't believe your luck.' Katz held out her hand, nodding to the camera. The photographer put on a face of blank resistance. Katz persisted, 'I need to see the photos you took of the body.'

The photographer handed it over; Katz began to click through the digital images of the Afghan: close-ups of a hand, an eye, his bloated lips. 'We're going to need to hang on to your artwork.'

She strode back to the car with O'Grady following. They passed the SOCO at the perimeter tape, replete with white jumpsuit and green wellingtons.

'All yours,' she announced, then added, 'The pathologist is on his way.'

The SOCO smiled sarcastically. In the vehicle Katz took off

her shoes and socks, rubbed her toes. O'Grady turned on the heater, spawning condensation.

'We'll need to do a pit stop at Debenhams, Sergeant.'

'Sure.'

'I know my feet are still there, but I can't feel them. So, Detective, what's your line of thought?'

'From where I was standing, ma'am, I couldn't see any wounds.'

'No, I didn't see any holes in him either.'

'Assuming he drowned then, a suicide? If you wanted to murder someone, would you throw them in the Humber?'

'You might. It's very awkward keeping a body in one's bath. You reckon he jumped from the bridge and made his way to the point?'

'From the Hull side, ma'am.'

'How so?'

'If it was the other side, he'd be taken out to sea.'

As they reached the end of the track, Katz looked at the ferry inching towards Immingham. She watched it shrink in the wing mirror, sounding its horn as it disappeared from view.

*

On the ferry's lower parking deck Vinnie tapped his fingers on the steering wheel. The engine ticking over, itching for disembarkation.

'Almost home and dry, guys,' he announced to his cargo.

'My legs, Vinnie, my legs,' someone cried.

He closed the hatch behind the driver's cabin.

At the hostel Berzan, the agent in Istanbul, had been on the phone to Farood more than once, wanting to know how soon people could be shifted. He had more for Rotterdam, more for everywhere. Among the latest arrivals at the hostel were a family from Syria, including two toddlers. 'Syria,' Berzan said, 'was going to be a goldmine.' The increasing turnover was the last straw for Mustapha, who had fled the scene for good. Atherton too was uneasy about the situation and told Farood that Vinnie would refuse to ship the kiddies.

'We come out here to run our own business and now we're being told how to run it by someone we've never met.'

The children's father was a Syrian doctor whose English was good and his Dutch non-existent. He told Atherton about how he had been imprisoned and tortured in Damascus for attending a demonstration. When he was eventually released, he was unable to walk for months, his passport was seized and the house was watched by the secret police.

'That'll teach you not to kick off, won't it?' said Atherton to it all.

That evening in the Bier Café, he impressed on Farood the importance of having the right cargo.

'Vinnie has a deal with a farm and they ain't looking for no doctors and kids. Roodie, man, you need to get on the phone to the guy in Istanbul. Tell him exactly who we want here: people who can sit in a box for a day and people who can graft picking carrots.'

'I know this man, he doesn't care. If people pay him, he'll move them down the line. It's up to the next agent to move them on.'

'Obviously,' Atherton stabbed the table with his forefinger, 'but *he* needs *us.*'

'And we need him.'

Farood made the call. He asked Berzan politely about moving children. His answer was that there would be more children, and sometimes children without their parents. Things were opening up, there was a lot of money to be made, but there were also a lot of new agents on the scene now. Demand was increasing, so was competition, plus the free movement nonsense in the EU had destroyed a lot of opportunities. But people still needed to get to the EU and a lot wanted to get to the UK.

'I'm calling a meeting, here, all my agents, from Afghan, Pakistan, France, UK. I want you to come.'

Farood took a pause. 'I don't have a passport.'

'Just send me a headshot – I can get you one.'

Atherton advised against him going. 'You're going to leave me to look after this lot?'

'They can look after themselves,' replied Farood. 'They got here on their own, they got out of Syria. I have to go.'

'Why?'

'For the business.'

It was not money that compelled him, he knew this. It was honour. This was his path; God had made it for him and he had to follow it – God willed it. He would return to Berzan, no longer a boy.

*

Vinnie was in a layby in Lincolnshire unloading his cargo, inviting them to stretch their legs, their fizzing, burning limbs. They crawled on their elbows, dipping their heads out of the rear of the lorry like seals sliding off pack ice. Vinnie looked uneasily up and down the A1173. He wanted to help them to the gate, into the field, behind the hedge, but they had all slumped down stock-still on the kerb.

Vinnie handed out some water and massaged a calf or two. 'That wasn't so bad now, was it?'

They'd been in the crates for eleven hours. They were not tall or stocky men, but then they were not big crates. It had been a cosy ride with knees raised, heads bowed. One man was crying; another held his hand.

Vinnie clapped his hands. 'Let's all have a walk now, in the field… Get up… Come on, move!'

The five casualties pushed themselves to their knees, Vinnie hoisted them to their feet; they hobbled through the gate. They stood on the brown clods of the field's verge, facing row after row of cauliflower crowns. One of the five looked up at the sky and laughed.

'Everyone, walk with me for five minutes. We don't want you falling over when you get there, do we?'

The farm was fifteen minutes away off the Grimsby Road. The entrance was a medley of automobile husks and caravans leading to a corrugated barn where Vinnie was greeted at the barn door by the farm manager and his Doberman. The five Algerians stood near the rear of the lorry; some were shivering, yet it wasn't a cold day.

The manager called across at them, 'Everyone want to work?'

'Yes, boss, yes,' two or three shouted, their voices stronger than their legs.

He waved them over and brought everyone into the hanger-sized barn. He showed his workforce to a tea urn and a loaf of bread; he led Vinnie into a glass-partitioned office. 'What happened to the last lot?'

Vinnie stumbled into a reply. 'They didn't want to work, didn't want to waste your time.'

The farm manager counted out the cash. Pushed it over the table to Vinnie.

'Grand. How many more will you be needing?'

'Depends how long these lot last. I'd say a dozen at most.'

Vinnie got back in the lorry and thought on his end of the business. With the cut from Istanbul, some extras they'd taken off the Algerians, plus the cash, he was several grand up. A few more trips during the summer and they could take a break, or call it a day, maybe. Come late autumn the farms wouldn't want them anyway – they'd be emptying the caravans. There was also two to three grand a month coming out of the hostel. It was a living, alright, but not an easy one.

Detective Inspector Katz was across town in the pathology lab. The report had thrown up some interesting news, topmost being that the man had been dead for at least a day before he entered the water. The cause of death was asphyxiation; polystyrene had been found in the gut and oesophagus, and cardboard under the nails. It was a useful report, but what Katz wanted to know was what the pathologist wouldn't commit to in print, his hunches and guesses that might not stand up in court.

Katz held up a bag with four polystyrene pellets in. They were smaller than marbles. 'Any indication that he was forced to swallow them?'

'None that I can see,' replied the pathologist, scrubbing his hands.

'So, he was packaged, so to speak, suffocated and was then thrown in the river?'

'That's up to you to decide, Detective. But there are labels on his clothing with washing instructions in Dutch. It could be that was where he was put in a box.'

'What, and was shoved off a ferry?' Katz couldn't see it. She aired an alternative. 'Or maybe it was a fishing boat?' Then replied to herself, 'Then why conceal him in a box?'

She went back to the office, 'the factory', as it was called, and made a phone call in the most courteous tone she could muster, requesting a favour. Then she shouted for O'Grady to follow her.

'Where are we going, ma'am?'

'Back to the river. Don't look surprised, it was your idea.'

They were looking at a chart of the Humber estuary on the wall of the lifeboat station.

The captain, who was wearing a raucous orange jumpsuit, drew his forefinger between two locations on the chart. 'Anyone who knows that Spurn Point exists would know if they put a body in the water around here it was bound to be washed up on the Point.'

'Okay. Let's assume they're not stupid,' said Katz. 'Let's say they've thought about it, they know about the Point and they want the body washed out to sea – where would you launch it into the river from?'

'From the south shore.'

'Sure, but they didn't, did they? Or we wouldn't have a body,' she continued, taking a closer look at the chart. 'Where's a good spot on the north shore, where you can't be seen and you'd have an even chance of getting the body washed out to sea?'

The lifeboat captain ran his finger in a circle and then plumped for somewhere. 'Here. That would be my choice. The old coastal artillery site. It's a good way out of Hull and its nose pushes into the estuary. Plus, there's a track to the water which is concealed by woodland.'

'Can you take me there?'

'Only if I get to see you in an orange suit.' The captain smiled.

The craft slid gracefully up the beach and the captain, Katz and O'Grady disembarked. The two detectives walked awkwardly up the beach, moving like armoured knights in their jumpsuits, lifejackets and helmets. After a few paces they were amongst an acre of thinned-out woodland that screened the gun emplacement. The bark and stone were layered with a film of moss to head height, giving it the feel of a cemetery.

'You could get a large vehicle in here, unseen. Unload your body and carry it to the water in broad daylight. Are there any traffic cams this far out?' she asked O'Grady.

He shook his head. 'No, ma'am.'

She lowered her voice, softened her tone for the lifeboat captain. 'Can we take a slow ride along the north shore all the way to the bridge?'

'Certainly can.'

Her phone rang. 'Yes… Where… What are they… I mean,

white or...? ...Right.' She poked the screen. 'Change of plan. Two more bodies have washed up at the Point. Maybe we *are* looking for a fool.'

TWENTY-SIX

Istanbul

It had been eight years since he'd escaped from Berzan's club. When the taxi delivered him, Farood believed he could remember the front doors, even though he had come and gone through a side entrance. He looked at the sign above the smoked glass, 'Meryem's'. Across the street, where there were once breeze block flats, there was now an Islamic bank with a strident façade.

Behind Berzan's doors a woman in a silk hijab reached out her hand over the marble reception desk. 'Your passport, please, Mr Karam.' She glanced at it, filed it under the counter and smiled at him. 'Right to the end of the corridor, Mr Karam.'

Farood made his way down the corridor; music and conversation approached him. Outside the club-room door there were two men, both in black, legs apart, hands clasped. One took his bag; the other conducted a rub-down search. Behind them the room was busy, his entrance unnoticed. Girls danced listlessly in the centre of the dance floor while on a raised perimeter were some nine men, at tables and booths, drinking tea, drinking beer. There was food on every table and there were more girls, by their sides, upon their laps.

Farood eased along the back wall and sat down at a table

on his own, scanning the room for Berzan. Eight years ago, he had been frightened to look at the man's face – its hollowness when once it loomed down on him, after he had been kicked to the floor. He remembered Berzan's eyes as round and grey, his frame short and wide. Even back then, climbing the cellar stairs appeared an effort for him. He heard a voice from across the room: the voice on his phone from a week ago. It came from a small, fat man in a light blue suit and greying beard. He was holding the hands of a girl on the dance floor, shouting to another man at a table. The girl swayed gently as he shuffled his weight out of time to the machine-made music. He turned her around with an upright hand then clapped and stamped his feet as she rotated in front of him. He implored others to join in the dancing. This was Berzan, older and wider, a Russian doll, soft enough to knock over with a push on the nose.

Farood dipped some bread in a potato salad and wondered if he would be recognised. He considered there were ways of pretending you'd never met someone before, the first of which was not to walk up to Berzan and introduce himself. If this was a room full of agents, there might be others whose path he had crossed. The Baloch man was there too, unmistakeably familiar. He had retained his lean intensity. And the Iranian from the Makran border was there, without his pistol and his dog. He was grey now too, pounding his fist down on a table in conversation with another agent. Would he still be walking the mountains?

The girl that had been dancing with Berzan came over to Farood's table. Her walk was obedient, as if he had summoned her. She waited for an instruction.

He nodded and told her, 'Take a seat.'

She placed herself on his lap and began to stroke the back of his neck; he continued eating, his only response to look down into her purple silk top and trousers.

'Would you like a drink?' she asked.

He shook his head. Her eyes were deep brown and dewy. She caught him looking and smiled.

Then Berzan shouted across the room, 'Karam! You need to tell me all about Rotterdam. I have plans for you. A lot of money for us both.' Berzan tossed a sugared almond into his mouth. 'If you two want some privacy, there's a door just out there.'

The cellar. Berzan had invited him into the cellar. With its black brick walls and the bucket in the corner. The girl continued to stroke his hairline; he reached up to hold her hand and she immediately kissed his cheek. He turned his face and met her lips. She kissed more softly than he, being more accomplished. They kissed in the corner for the duration of three or four songs, then the music was cut.

Berzan clapped his hands, hurried around the room, shooing out the girls. 'Time for business. Out you go.'

The rest of the room made their way to the largest booth at the end of the room. Farood followed and found himself sitting next to another Afghan, who asked, 'Where are you from?'

'Baghlan.'

'Baghlan town?'

'The hills, an hour away, by car.'

'Thought so. I can see the farmer in you. Where are you working?'

'Little operation in Rotterdam. One vehicle, an apartment to hold people in, work for them to do. Problem is, we can't shift that many people.'

'Getting into the UK isn't easy, is it?'

'What about you?' enquired Farood.

'I work out of Mazar, Kunduz sometimes, there's more and more people every week. The war goes on, so there's money to be made.'

Berzan faced the semicircle of traffickers. There were men there from Turkmenistan, Tajikistan, Pakistan, Afghanistan, Iran and two others from Turkey. Berzan spoke in English.

'Thank you all for coming once again. Before I take reports, I want to introduce someone new: Karam.'

Farood raised his hand in acknowledgement.

Berzan went on. 'He's been working out of Rotterdam. Moving people to the east of England. That Calais-Dover run is too risky, so he's opened up a new route. Karam is a young man with imagination – what this organisation needs.'

Farood feigned a smile; people either side of him leaned forward and nodded favourably.

Berzan then asked for reports and problems all along the chain.

The Afghan raised an index finger. 'I have a new contact in Iran now. The north-east border. I can go straight across. I don't need to take people through Pakistan.'

'Have you tried the route?' asked Berzan.

'Only once, but everyone made it.'

One of the other Turks nodded in confirmation. 'They all made it to Van. Though a few of them looked like shit,' he said.

Berzan sighed. 'Whenever we shorten the route, someone loses money.'

The Baloch agent raised a finger. He leaned forward and looked down the line at the Afghan. 'You and I,' he said. 'We have worked this route together for years. You bring people to me, I look after them and we are both paid for this. We make money by working together. We have talked about each other's families and now you do this. This cutting me out.'

He showed the Afghan his palms as if to catch a reply. 'What can I do?' declared the Afghan. 'The border is there. The road is there. People don't want a sightseeing tour. Why move through a country when you don't have to?'

Berzan closed the discussion. 'This is what we will do. You will use both routes. We say to some it's okay. We say to others, it's not safe. We will use both routes, fifty-fifty. Agreed? Before that, I want to speak to this new agent. I want him here.

Otherwise I'll close him down. We must remain an organisation. Professional, working together. I formed this group to stop the free-for-all and I won't let it start up again. No more using new agents without running it through me.'

The Baloch and the Afghan reached across and shook hands.

The Iranian agent present offered some conciliation. 'It's a good idea there's another route. Not everyone can walk the Makran. I lose people every time and then families demand money back, but they should never have set out. I can tell who won't make it. I feel like saying, if you want, I can shoot you now, save all the walking.'

He looked directly at the Baloch.

'But don't worry my friend, the London Road will always be busy.'

There were reports from elsewhere. The Turkmen had bought some caravans because people were backing up through the winter. Farood followed with an account of the operation in Rotterdam. He did so without obvious disloyalty to Atherton and Vinnie, but the description was of comparative amateurs.

When someone asked about Mustapha in Rotterdam, Berzan interrupted them to say he had retired, then he took a laptop from its case and pulled up the screen. 'I have a new contact. Couldn't be here with us today. But I must introduce him to you all.'

At the other end of the screen call was what looked like a student or a journalist in his early twenties.

'Now, tell everyone where you're speaking from,' said Berzan.

The young man waved merrily to the room in Istanbul. 'Hi, everyone. Right now, I'm in Kilis, close to the border with Syria. I can tell you it's a pretty hectic place right now. Assad is using artillery – he's not fucking around. He's shelling rebel areas and people are coming out of there in their thousands, many into this town.'

Berzan interrupted, 'Who's leading them across the border?'

'No one. There's no money to be made there. Nothing is going to stop them coming to Turkey. The money is to be made from here to the EU. Not all of them have money, but some of them do for sure.'

'Okay,' said Berzan. 'What do you suggest?'

'The place to start your business up is in the camps. There are two camps so far, but there'll be more. People are moving on from there to Greece, elsewhere in the Schengen area. The people who run the camps are happy to let them go. You can negotiate a price under their nose. You could do it in two stages: from the camp to the coast and then the boat to Greece, or maybe through Enez.'

Berzan thanked his contact and ended the call.

'This war in Syria is a goldmine for us. I need people to work with me down there and the coast across from the Greek islands.' He pointed at Farood. 'Rotterdam sounds like a waste of time. Small change for your gypsy friends. Syria needs an organisation. All of you have a think if you want to make serious money. Then come and talk to me.'

Then he shouted in Turkish down the corridor, pressed a button behind the bar and the Europop began bouncing across the room again. Farood headed back to his table. He observed the other men. They had done things he was yet to do, that he could not do. Some were sitting with more than one girl; some he knew had taken lives. They were people who exercised power over others whilst he was only acting the part of an agent, and under a false name at that.

Berzan came to his table. 'You know how to sail a boat, eh?'

'I'm an Afghan, I only know how to walk.'

'Then I'll teach you. Look, here she is. She's back for you.'

Berzan gestured the girl over and gave Farood a little nudge on the back as he departed.

The girl stood close to him. She was no more than five feet. He looked down at the underwear lines beneath her clothes, then at her eyes, that unnerved him with their expectation.

'Get me a drink,' he demanded.

He watched her elegant walk to the bar, watched her arm reach up to the beer tap. She brought his drink on a tray. He swept it up and drank too much too quickly so had to wipe his nose and his mouth.

She smiled at the spillage down his shirt; he thrust the glass towards her. 'Drink it.' She took a cautious sip; she was the more experienced drinker. 'The rest,' he commanded.

She drank half of it and handed him back the glass. He downed what was left. Across the room, he could see Berzan and the Afghan in discussion, watching him. Farood swayed; he grabbed the girl's shoulder to steady himself. She reached for his hand; he took it, glanced at Berzan and began to drag her towards the cellar door. She tried to break free, but he tightened his hold on her until the door was open. She stood stock-still at the top of the stairs, so he picked her up and carried her under one arm to the bottom. The strip lights flickered on with their presence. It was a different room to the one that had imprisoned him. Now there was a sink and cabinets, a table and chairs, bunk beds along the wall.

The girl asked him quietly, 'What's your name?'

'Never mind my name.'

He pushed her into a corner, held her neck between his index finger and thumb. Her mouth opened and he tried to press his lips upon hers, but they were clenched tight. He forced his other hand into her underwear. She withdrew his hand slowly, stroking his palm with her finger. He watched this and his breathing slowed. He kissed her again, with some tenderness this time. Then his hands forced their way across her and up to her neck once more. He dragged her to the table in the centre of the room and pushed her down across it. She pushed back at him, but it made no difference. She kicked back, so he placed his legs inside hers and lifted her feet off the ground, holding her firmly on the table. He pulled down her clothes and raped her.

Just before he finished the cellar door opened; Berzan descended a few steps and stooped slightly. 'Where are you staying?'

'Er...'

'Your hotel?'

Farood slammed himself into her one last time, breathed out and pulled up his zip.

'You can stay with me, at my house.' Berzan tapped the ceiling and left.

The girl fell to her knees, holding on to the table edge. Farood walked away from her up the stairs. After he closed the door behind him, she lay motionless on the floor; the lights flicked off.

*

Berzan lived on the hill that Misha had run up eight years before. He had three floors, a balcony and a carefully mannered wife, as well as a daughter called Meryem. Meryem was a grade A student who played the flute and piano – there were photos of her in various outfits and locations on every wall. She ran downstairs, wagging her ponytail, shook Farood's hand, and then returned to her room and to Mozart.

During the evening meal of baked fish, her mother asked Farood about England's palaces and castles, to which he confirmed that he had heard great things from friends, though had not had the time to visit personally. Meryem asked him about school in England, to which he told her, 'Education is totally free. The teachers want to help, but it's the students, the children in England don't want to learn. They don't respect the teachers, so they don't learn. And the girls in England don't respect their parents, like you do. Too many of them are out of control.'

Berzan nodded in approval and Meryem asked to be excused. After the meal Berzan invited Farood onto the balcony. He looked down on the spots of light in the harbour. Across the Bosporus, Europe glowed more brightly.

'My boat is down there. Tell me, are you afraid of water? Course you are. Maybe that will help you stay afloat. I want to show you something. Sit down.'

Berzan left the balcony and returned with a sealed glass jar, full to the brim with greyish brown fragments and clumps. He placed it on Farood's lap. 'Have a look. Open it if you want.'

Farood held it up to the outside light. At first he thought the jar contained figs, but then he saw, looking out at him, pressed against the inside, was an ear. Turning the jar, he recognised the contents as fingers, thumbs and other unidentified portions of human flesh floating in an overcast liquid.

'Pieces of people who wouldn't pay me, so I made them leave something behind. I'd let them choose what part of them I was going to cut off.' Berzan sniffed; he was about to broach a more delicate moment. 'Back then, you and that other kid, you were too young, too fast, eh? What was the name of that Turkmen?'

Farood could only shrug, his mouth agape.

'I know who you are. My memory's not so good these days, but I remember your eye. I asked my Afghan and he made a call. You came from a cave. Maybe that's why you didn't mind the cellar so much.'

'He was called Misha. My name is Farood.'

Berzan sighed. 'There's too many names for me in this work. You're prepared to take risks, aren't you? Maybe you like to do that. Tomorrow we're going on a boat journey. Yes, it will be risky – but that's why I chose you.'

Berzan showed Farood to his room.

Sleep came easy to him until his phone shuddered in his pocket. It was Atherton. 'What yer saying, Roodie?'

'Alright, Michael. What's happening?'

'Vinnie's back. Delivery went alright, I've got some money for yer. Vinnie's only going to make one more run, he reckons. Reckons the money's to be made here. Farming them out to factories. What are they saying over there?'

'Nothing much. There was a meeting of all the agents. I knew some of them from when I was a kid. It felt funny, yer know.'

'Sounds like a right laugh,' replied Atherton. 'When you coming back?'

'I don't know.'

'What do you mean, you don't know? Need you back here. Those Syrians are fucking cheeky. The doctor won't work anywhere.'

'I'll ring you tomorrow.'

Farood switched off his phone. Atherton was sound, he was strong, but he lived in a different world. He knew he wouldn't be returning to Rotterdam, to Atherton and Vinnie. He had helped him escape from the jail – but then he had broken *him* out of the prison van. And besides, Atherton was only interested in him because he knew about agents and migrants and Vinnie didn't. Vinnie was clueless. He had repaid them and was free to go, to work for Berzan – his former torturer. Berzan could no longer hurt him, though; he would take what he could from Berzan in return for the pain he had caused him. And then, he would cause Berzan some pain of his own.

*

The boat was a single-deck, two-berth affair named *Paloma*; the cabin was cluttered with fishing tackle, lifejackets and blankets.

'We need to clear this out – this is where we sleep. I'm going to buy some fuel and some food.'

'How far are we going?'

'A day or so. To Dikili. She doesn't move too fast, but she's sturdy.'

Farood looked out across the velvet blue of the Bosporus to where it was rolling, churning. The day his brother had handed over the money to the Afghan, he made it clear that water wasn't to be part of the journey. Stories of migrant drownings regularly made their way as far back to Baghlan province and such tales kept boys and men at home through the starving winters. It was the reason he had walked knee deep in snow for two days into Bulgaria from Turkey then spent a week hiding in a forest, waiting for his turn to cross the Greek border. He had lived outside in the mountains for months at a time with his father, and when other migrants sat down, he had remained standing. When they lay down and gave up, he sat down for a few minutes. He could endure more than most, but the world of the sea scared him.

They sailed south to where the Bosporus met the Sea of Marmara and the currents clashed. Up to then Farood had positioned himself at the stern, and with increasing confidence for a short while, he stood at the fore of the vessel. When the land to their left gave way to nothing but the chaos of water, he confined himself to the cabin, lying down on a berth.

Berzan looked over his shoulder from the wheel. 'You don't look at home. Bad memories of the boat to Greece?'

'I walked. Through Bulgaria.' Farood's voice was weakening.

'I know the way, know the agents. I have land crossings, sea crossings, just along the coast, no risk. I don't need the Bulgarians. I have my own people, so I cut them out.'

'Where will we take these people?'

'We'll take the Syrians to Lesbos. Thirty at a time, maybe more.'

Farood swung his feet down, stared out ahead for a moment before running to the side of the boat to vomit.

Berzan gave him some water before telling him to take the wheel. 'Best place for seasickness. Hold the wheel, look to the horizon. See how far the coast is from us now? Keep it like that.

I'm going to catch some fish. Eat fish?'

He fished off the stern and was frying sea bass within the hour. They anchored whilst they ate; a seagull steadied itself on the cabin roof.

'What happens when it gets dark?' asked Farood.

'You can't see. Sleep if you want, but we keep going.'

The sun rose over the Turkish coast, eventually revealing the Greek island of Lesbos to the west. By midday they were at Dikili, some seventy kilometres away from Lesbos. Farood tossed the rope onto the jetty, jumping after it. He looped the rope over an iron post and looked up at the white and terracotta houses and flats rising from the scrub hills. He was cured of seasickness and he felt ready to start work for Berzan.

TWENTY-SEVEN

Humberside

Katz leaned towards the mirror to examine the lines around her eyes, the complexion that was flattening in tone. She took a step back from herself, smoothed down her grey jacket. *Forty next month. What is the point of looking at yourself? By now you should be fulfilled; the mirror is telling you something you already know. Be resigned.* She wondered if she was in the region of O'Grady's sexual interest. If, indeed, such a locality existed. He was eight years younger than her and, she suspected, cossetting an OCD affliction. Much of what he said sounded pre-planned, his body language rehearsed. You could smell the spray starch off him. How tidy and ordered must his flat be, how disappointed, repulsed he would be by her shambolic house. She applied peach lip gloss. He would not be interested in sleeping with her, not even between his freshly pressed sheets. She didn't really want to sleep with him. He was sufficiently feminine, but he was conceited. She imagined him walking into her bedroom and noticing the pile of dirty laundry next to the swollen laundry basket, having to listen to his religious convictions in the aftermath of it all. She just *wanted* him to want to sleep with her; or at least give the matter some consideration.

She hurried out of the staff toilets and into the main office with a pronounced sense of purpose. O'Grady glanced up from his screen, but she declined to look in his direction. Entering her own glass cage, she patted her lips with a tissue and signalled him in.

'Morning, ma'am,' he said crisply.

'I stopped off at the path lab. The estimated time of death and entry to the water of the other two bodies matches the first. And they both have a Rotterdam connection.'

From the depths of her handbag she withdrew two plastic snap bags that she tossed over to her sergeant. O'Grady held them up to the light as if they were antiquities.

'A library ticket and a bus pass,' she said.

'Fingerprints?' asked O'Grady.

'Too long in the water, and I'm not sure people smugglers tend to borrow migrant's library tickets, however...'

'You never know.'

'Say we assume the three bodies came from the same vehicle. What kind of vehicle are we looking for?'

'How many people do you need to smuggle to make it worth your while?'

'No idea, Gavin.'

He always savoured the rare occasions she used his Christian name. He continued, 'They can't have much money, can they, the immigrants? You'd need to maximise the return for such a risk, I'd say—'

'It's not Cluedo, Sergeant. Stick to what we know rather than our imaginations. An articulated lorry could not have got that close to the water.'

'Or maybe they transferred the bodies.'

'Three? Maybe more, into a Fiesta? Someone's panicked. We're looking for something between a people carrier and a container.' She turned to her screen and began to ask questions of the internet instead.

He suddenly felt unwanted and, after a deferential delay,

sought her attention. 'Ma'am, have we definitely ruled out the immigrants being tossed from a boat?'

'They were in boxes. Why put people in boxes if it's a small boat? Why put them in boxes inside containers? Whoever moved them expected the boxes to be seen. The lifeboat man said he reckoned they went into the water from the north shore – that's why they ended up at Spurn Point.'

Katz walked over to the laser jet and handed the sergeant a piece of paper that was a lorryload of work. She opened her door for him in case he was in any doubt it was time to get on with it.

'There's two ferries a day. Go a day either side of the estimated day of death, ask the ferry company for records of all vehicles of the sizes on there, coming this way. Then run the number plates against the traffic cams and PNC the owners. Let me know what you find.'

He took the instructions to his desk. He would find something; he would make sure of it. Not for the sake of the immigrants, but for her.

*

Not that far from the port of Rotterdam, Vincent and his nephew Michael Atherton were waiting pensively on two all-day Mediterranean breakfasts when it occurred to Vinnie that there was something he had taken as a given these past two months. A given which he should have questioned.

'Can you smoke in this fuckin' country?'

Atherton looked around the humid café and identified several suspects in black garb with shrapnel in their faces who were without roll-ups. 'Not in here, you can't.'

Vinnie shook his head in astonishment. 'Takes the living piss. They're selling drugs at corner shops and I can't have a fag with my cup of tea?'

'But that's because weed isn't as bad for yer.'

'Don't be starting that again.'

Vinnie and his nephew held widely contrasting views on drugs. Vinnie strongly disapproved of cannabis and the piss-boiling bores it attracted and spawned. Michael, he noticed, increasingly talked like one.

'Thing is, Vinnie, cannabis, is completely natural. It's hemp. It grows, yeah? I can't see how a government can say to someone, "You can't put that in your body." And they understand that here.'

'What they understand here is how to get a few quid out of hippies and hookers.'

The breakfasts arrived. Vinnie looked at the assortment of olives alongside his bacon and breathed in despondently; Michael rolled some falafel into a fried egg.

'You know what?' said Vinnie. 'The sooner we leave this EU the better.'

'You reckon?'

'There's people coming into the country and we don't know who the fuck they are.'

Michael nodded as his uncle spoke.

'The jail was full of them. And some of those Poles, they'd already done time in Poland. Bad shit. They don't do no licence, they come straight over here, do the same shit.' He paused, looked above him, nibbled at his forkful.

'Thing is, though, Vinnie, we are bringing in a load of border-jumpers ourselves, aren't we?'

Vinnie raised his voice down the aisle to enquire on the whereabouts of his extra toast; he didn't lower it thereafter. 'You know why we have to do what we do? Because the work I done, the work my people have always done – which is building that country of ours, the roads, the bridges, canals, the fucking houses – is now being done by the Eastern Europeans for half the money. An Englishman, an Irishman couldn't live on it. Which is exactly what those fuckers in Brussels want. Everything done for a pittance by foreigners. Since I was being fucked over, I decided

I might as well make a few bob bringing in the foreigners for them.'

Michael let it be known he understood.

With breakfast conquered, they headed back to the car.

Vinnie lit a cigarette. 'Have you heard from Roodie?' he asked.

'The other day.'

'So, what's he saying? When's he back?'

'He didn't say.'

Vinnie took a drag, exhaled through his nose. 'He's gone for good, Michael. I'm telling you – he's gone, boy.'

Michael was suddenly gloomy at the notion that his friend, his best boy on the wing, had forsaken him. 'No way. Roodie is sound.'

'He's an Afghan, Michael. I met someone who was out there, said half the Afghan Army was Taliban. Told me he must have shot fifty ragheads and they still kept coming. Whatever he said to you, he knew he was never going to stay with us.'

'We could do with him at the hostel. They're kicking off, yer know.'

'That's up to you now. I'm doing one last run and then I'm shutting up shop.' Vinnie tossed his cigarette.

They drove out to an expansive supermarket to buy overdue food supplies for their tenants. At the hostel food had become as much a cause of conflict as any of the situations the people had fled from. People who worked came back to find the food they had bought from what little money Atherton doled out was gone. People who didn't work, whose travelling money was long spent, stole from shops and from each other.

On that particular Friday afternoon, the Moroccan who worked at the flower depot for some euros in hand, came home to find the lamb casserole he had prepared the night before eaten by persons unknown. The dish lay poised on the draining board, the remains of a label with his name on, refusing to leave the scene. He marched around with the dish, demanding, 'Who did this? Who ate the food that I worked for? I want to know!' No one said a word until asked directly: 'Was it you?' Except the doctor, who maintained his silence, gathering up his daughter who had gravy stains on her romper suit.

Vinnie looked round at the new faces. 'Where did all these come from?'

'I dunno. Every time I put my head in here, someone else has rocked up.'

'You need to put a lid on it.'

A man of six feet and more, wearing a black vest, black joggers and wiry body hair, stared out at Vinnie from the centre of the room. Vinnie's return stare signalled to him, 'You are in my house and this is more my country more than yours.'

Michael Atherton sidled up to his uncle. 'They're all asking when you're taking them over.'

Vinnie left his eyes where they were, locked on Black Vest Man. 'You choose, Michael, you know who's been waiting the longest.'

Atherton pointed at the chosen passengers around the room. 'That one, that one and… that one there… They're all next. It's up to you what you do about the doctor.'

'Michael, son, everything I do is up to me.'

'I know, just saying he has been here for a long time… but he's got a wife and kid tagging along.'

Everyone could tell that transit arrangements were being made, and who was and wasn't included. Two women sharing a bowl of noodles stood up and approached Vinnie, but he dismissed them. He was looking at the doctor, sat on a blanket under a window, writing something in a notebook. His wife and child were sleeping.

Vinnie squatted down beside them, whispered thickly to the doctor, 'I need a word with you, in private.'

The doctor wrote one last word and closed his book.

'What are you writing there?'

The doctor showed him a page of Arabic verse and Vinnie nodded, reassured by how unfathomable it looked. He led the doctor through to an empty room in the knock-through apartment.

'I'll be straight with you. I can take you, but I can't take your wife and child.'

'Why?'

'You know why. You know how I take people. Everyone needs to be silent in the lorry. Not a peep on the ferry. Can't do that with a child.'

Black Vest Man appeared in the doorway with an announcement. 'I want to speak to you, boss, about my journey.'

Vinnie shrouded his annoyance under mock courtesy. 'Yeah, well, I'm awfully sorry, but I'm with someone right now, as you can see, I'll be with you in a minute, fella.'

'I've been waiting for a week already.'

'Then you can wait a little longer.'

They looked at one another full square in the eye and neither blinked. Black Vest Man retreated to the hall.

The doctor had made his decision. 'I'll go to the UK alone. Get asylum and then my family can join me.'

'Sure? Be ready, we're going tomorrow.'

Vinnie took a few strides down the corridor when Black Vest Man grabbed his elbow. 'You're taking people to the UK tomorrow. You can take me.'

'Full up for tomorrow.'

'The next time. When's the next time?' He tightened his grip.

'There will be no next time.'

'What the fuck are you saying? What am I doing here? Why is anyone here?'

Vinnie looked down at the hand on his elbow as something alien. It was withdrawn; Vinnie went on his way.

Black Vest Man walked up to the doctor with the news.

'You shouldn't leave your wife here alone. I will have your place tomorrow. Understand?'

Next door in the kitchen, Michael Atherton was deflecting questions and accusations about arrangements to England, and Vinnie realised that if he didn't make a public announcement, Black Vest Man would. Best to deal with kick-offs at a time of your own choosing. He cleared his throat. 'Listen to me, everyone... Fucking listen! Those of you who are working, can stay here. Anyone else not coming with me tomorrow, I want you out. No more trips to the UK after that. Clear?'

'I paid,' shouted someone. 'From Iran to London.'

'I don't care what you paid. I want you out.'

Vinnie was out the door with Michael hurrying behind, dodging a salvo of insults in five languages. The young man who worked at the flower depot, still clutching his casserole dish, watched them from the kitchen window. He looked in the freezer then the fridge, at the food they had bought; he looked at others, sitting cross-legged peeling potatoes, dipping wilting slices of greyish bread in tinned soup; he decided he would buy himself a takeaway, and after that he would make a phone call.

*

Detective Gavin O'Grady was working his way east to west, meeting and greeting some of the vehicle owners from the ferry company records – for the third day running. DI Katz continued to endear herself to colleagues in Rotterdam via Skype. She had decided that it would be best for her sergeant to meet a number of candidates with the right-sized vehicle on the right ferry to see how his instincts responded. O'Grady thought it a time-consuming and unscientific exercise, and had said so. When Katz had said she wanted anyone who could feasibly have been smuggling illegal immigrants questioned and confronted, he had suggested that this would only spook the culprit, at which the inspector had laughed sardonically.

'When instead, Sergeant, we should allow another lorryload of people to suffocate to death, as part of a sting operation, where you catch the smugglers in the act of another multiple murder. Is that it?'

And so, he had set forth with a print-out of a dozen registration details, a sat-nav and the latest John Tavener CD. Astonishingly the ferry company didn't ask owners of small commercial vehicles about their cargo. He decided that he would ask that as an aside. His stated reason for making enquiries would be that their vehicle had been reported as being involved in an 'incident' in Rotterdam. He didn't like dealing with the public much, particularly in their own environment. In this he was no different from most officers, in or out of uniform. Anyone who claimed they loved 'policing their patch' was too pedestrian for the smallest of advancements. After a while everyone wanted away from the cast of reality TV, from the sportswear-clad Morlocks. O'Grady was aware how he had tired quicker than most. He had joined the force after a spell as a wildlife warden and had been much happier in the company of birds than the laddish constables at his first station. He got himself a transfer and found female superiors more to his liking. One in particular saw the problem-solver in him, how when most other officers preferred to kick a door in, he liked to unpick the lock. He was given fraud cases, invariably avoided by other officers. And he could always follow the money – when it went into hiding, when it was in disguise, when it divided itself into a thousand parts, like rain – he could tell where it landed. Within eighteen months he was doing it for CID and eighteen months later he passed his sergeant's exams. For the moment it was as much seniority as he wanted. Management meant grief from either side, no matter how high you climbed. And since he wasn't tucking anyone into bed at night, he didn't need the money either.

A third of the number plates he'd run had form, which was

par for the course. Some had been to Rotterdam in works vans, some had been bringing in booze, some had been carrying nothing, apparently, including one who'd been making the journey every month to visit a favoured sex worker. He was arriving at his most westerly enquiry, Manchester. The address was curious – a temporary dwelling of some sort. Then when the sat-nav showed him the railway arches he understood what the print-out meant.

He parked the pool car out of view of the yellow barrier at the site's perimeter. Word in the station canteen was that traveller's sites were enemy territory. They were 'off the reservation'. O'Grady wasn't in uniform and he wasn't even in his drab standard CID suit, but even in his speedos, he was unmistakably a copper, a 'peeler', 'plod'. On the other side of the barrier two boys, stripped to their shorts, were play-fighting. They were no older than five or six but already they had cute little biceps. They stopped brawling as he passed, everyone smiling under the June sunshine.

'Alright, fellas?' he said affably.

They began to march behind him, mimicking his purposeful walk. 'What do you want here, mister? Eh? Who are ye after?'

It struck him that he didn't actually know where he was heading. There were half a dozen rows of half a dozen caravans, no numbers, no names. It was Trumpton, an *anti*-Trumpton.

'Boys, do you know someone who lives here called Mr Gilheaney?'

'Who? No one of that name here, mister.'

'Never fuckin' heard of him.'

He started off down the first aisle, peering at windows for a friendly face. 'There's nothing down there, mate.'

Either side of him a window blind ruffled. Behind him a door jolted away from its frame and a man with a freckled torso sat down on his steps, pulling on his trainers, a cigarette clenched between his lips. When O'Grady looked in his direction the man displayed his back and tugged his door closed. O'Grady did a

U-turn at the bottom where some garages waited padlocked and chained. At the top of the second aisle he saw a silhouette, no more than that. Screening the sunshine from his eyes, he advanced. As he did, the silhouette emerged, wearing a black shirt and saggy jeans. The man halted midway down his own street; the two boys ran to him.

'Can I help you, mister?'

O'Grady recognised the tart quality in the accent. Belfast voices had been present in his upbringing, an anecdote that would have no cachet here.

'Are you Vincent Gilheaney?'

'No, I'm not.'

'Can you tell me where I can find him?'

'No, I can't.'

The sergeant ripped at a Velcro pocket on the side of his walking trousers; the boys cried, 'He's a peeler, a fuckin' pig.'

O'Grady confirmed as such with his ID. 'I just need to ask him a couple of questions, about his lorry. Nothing important.'

'Well, yer see, I can't tell you where he is because I don't know.'

The boys took this as an invitation for the peeler to exit. 'You need to fuck off, mister.'

Other than peelers all settled people had to ask permission to come on the site. They got no further than the barrier without an appointment. He was invading. As the sun relented under cloud, O'Grady saw the faded bruising around the man's eyes, plus a scab on a pulverised ear.

'Are you a friend of Mr Gilheaney?'

'A friend? Two weeks ago, I fought him, bare-knuckle, in front of those garages. When I see him, I'll tell him you're looking for him, no bother. Let me see your ID again.' The traveller grasped O'Grady's warrant card, reading it slowly. 'Come all the way from Humberside for a couple of questions about a lorry? You usually write letters about nonsense like that.'

'Can I have your name, sir?'

'No, and don't call me sir. On your way now.'

He turned on his heels; the boys ran after him and the sun re-emerged. On the way to the barrier he thought about how he could exact some revenge on these people. These cash-in-hand parasites. Why weren't those boys in school? The Mercedes vans over there, neither of them looked roadworthy. This was a publicly funded den of thieves that considered itself beyond the law and the law was glad to be rid of it.

Back on the motorway Katz came on via Bluetooth.

'How did it go?'

'In what sense, ma'am?'

'In the sense of you finding a people smuggler, Sergeant'

'It didn't.'

'Well, Rotterdam just rang. They've had a tip off that a lorry importing flowers is carrying illegal immigrants.'

'Have they got a registration?'

'No. But they're going to put someone on the ferry. It's due in tomorrow morning at eight. See you at the terminal at 7am.'

TWENTY-EIGHT

O'Grady's black gloss Audi skimmed into the ferry terminal car park and cosied up alongside Katz's Skoda. Katz's Spaceback hatchback was a tasteful wax-jacket green underneath a duffel coat of crud. Pausing on her electronic cigarette, she lowered the greyish smear of a passenger window. 'Get in, Gavin.'

They were both all smiles, as they always were when they hadn't seen each other for a spell. She was well aware that she looked forward to seeing him but also that she desired the days when he wasn't around.

'Do you want to get a coffee?' she asked.

'No, I'm fine.'

He'd been up since shortly after sunrise, around half five, taking breakfast on the balcony, telephoto lens on the table. He owned a first-floor flat out in Cottingham overlooking a walled garden that belonged to the aged lady below, which she allowed him to tend but hadn't expected him to install a pond. She had asked a few times about cutting back the bushes, the shrubs, the ivy and the waist-high grass, but he always replied that he was 'rewilding the space'. Still, she too enjoyed the birds on the feeders he'd placed by the pond.

He flicked through the photos to show Katz. 'Lesser spotted woodpecker. First bird most mornings this time of year.'

'Lovely.'

'It's on the red list, you know.'

'Is that because of its markings?' she enquired.

He paused, silently astonished. 'No, what that means is that it's endangered. It's currently rare.'

'Ah. I'm currently feeling a bit endangered myself and what I meant when I asked you if you wanted a coffee was, I'd really like one.'

She ordered a double espresso and a fried egg sandwich; he ordered a fruit tea then she told him about the phone call from her counterpart in Rotterdam. 'All we've been told is that a lorry or a van exporting flowers to the UK is also carrying illegal immigrants. We don't have the name of the driver or the registration.'

'Who's responsible for the tip-off?'

'Don't know. Probably a migrant worker in the flower depot.'

O'Grady dunked his tea bag up and down then produced the list of passengers he'd been following up for the last two days. 'Are any of these names on the ferry?' he asked.

'Unfortunately, we can't get a passenger list. The tip-off came in after the ferry offices closed and it's due in before it opens. The Dutch have an officer on board but unless they search every vehicle…'

She switched her attention to her egg sandwich.

*

On board the ferry, Hans van Duren, a Dutch plod, or *hoofdagent*, was moving observantly through every corridor, vestibule and the lounge of deck three for the second time. He was with the deckhand who was sure she had spoken to a man importing flowers several weeks ago. She said she couldn't describe the face but somehow would know it when she saw it.

'It wasn't so much his face I remember, it was... it was... it was his eyes. It sounds odd, but he sounded very emotional about the flowers in his lorry.'

She told Hans she needed time to look, but he refused to let her stand and gawp; presumably he didn't want the man to know they were looking for him. Probably a drug smuggler. After they had completed a survey of every passenger deck for the second time van Duren took her down to the car deck. 'This is where you saw him. Yes?'

'Over there.'

'Good.'

He asked her to walk to the exact spot. 'Now I want you to close your eyes, listen to the hum of the engines, breathe in the petrol residue, remember the image of this man, the vehicle he was standing next to.'

'I remember saying, "What a beautiful smell." He'd just shut his doors and he started going on how he never tired of it... I can't really remember his face, I think it was scarred, a hard face because it surprised me how polite he was.'

At that precise moment the face in question was pitted against the wind, watching the shoreline of Humberside materialise in the distance. Vinnie was on the top deck submerged in nostalgia. He remembered another ferry, the one that sailed from Larne to Stranraer when he was beside two other young men, watching the mainland free itself from the mist. It was 1981 and he was going over to work in England. Maggie Thatcher was getting rid of all the lazy bastards, so there was work for Irishmen who could leave English workers standing. Belfast was not a safe place for him. Of the two lads with him one eventually went home after too many fights and the other, as far as he knew, to this day hadn't got beyond cash in hand and digs. The seventeen-year-old Vinnie had gone to live with his elder sister Kathleen in Manchester. When cancer began to take her, her son Michael grew wild and his father had long given up any pretence of being a parent. In her last months Kathleen asked to be with her own people and a caravan was provided for her on the site. The husband never showed his face and Michael was put in a children's home. Vinnie wondered what more he should've done. Michael wasn't his son, as the boy kept reminding his uncle, but now, now at least, he was doing right by him. Setting him up, trying to teach him about people. Because Michael was soft; he didn't know when he was being taken for a ride, like with that Afghan. They would finish with the border-jumpers and get in to something else in Manchester. Open a shop, or a scrapyard. There was plenty to be had.

He pushed himself away from the rail and went to get some breakfast. He gambolled down the stairs, colliding with a deckhand, hauling herself up towards him. He skipped aside, muttering, 'Sorry, darlin.'

She took a breath, flushed and dizzy.

'That was him. Him. That man.'

Van Duren told her to stay put and began following Vinnie whilst casually admiring the sea and the sky. He tailed him to the restaurant and while the suspect was eating van Duren went to commandeer a deckhand's high-vis jacket and name badge.

Vinnie paced on the edge of the overcast car deck. Van Duren watched him from the other side of the exit-door glass. Then Vinnie advanced, walking, van Duren thought, as if for an audience, which was the way Vinnie always walked.

He shut himself in the driver's cabin and addressed those members of his cargo coming around from liberal portions of Rohypnol syringed into their water bottles. 'Everyone okay back there? We'll be landing in a wee while, then we'll have you all out of there.'

Someone was weeping.

'You'll be as right as rain in no time. Not long now.'

Van Duren nonchalantly patrolled the deck, memorising a number plate.

Back in Katz's Skoda, O'Grady was reading the debris around the interior the way a detective reads a crime scene. She had once said she needed a spacious four-door to lug her elderly mother around in, but there was no room for her. On the backseats he deduced a weekend with friends in Whitby: the waterproofs, walking boots and bright evening blouses, but what about the racket still tucked in its case?

'Do you play squash or badminton?'

'Neither, and it's a badminton racket. Do you play?'

'I play squash.'

'Course you do.'

The ferry was in view. One colossal white lorry on top of another approaching on a runway of water.

'Was there really no one over the last two days who struck you as a suspect?' she asked.

'I don't know what a people smuggler looks like, don't know the type.'

'They look like people you can trust.'

Her phone rang. She waved her free hand at O'Grady; he produced a pen and a pad; she recited the registration number.

'Thank you. And pass on my thanks to the officer on board, will you?' She turned to O'Grady. 'Is the registration on your list of visits?'

He already knew it was. 'Gilheaney... Vincent Gilheaney. Travellers' site in Manchester. I never got the pleasure.'

'Where's he taking them?' she wondered aloud.

'Bradford, Leeds. Maybe he drops them at the first roundabout.'

'They're money, Sergeant. Illegal immigrants are money. And we should follow it.'

'But when I suggested we shouldn't spook him, you said...'

Katz glared at him.

'Two cars?' he asked.

'Two cars,' she said. 'I'll start.'

Katz sent the uniformed officers away whilst O'Grady drove to the first exit of the nearest roundabout and parked up on a verge.

The scattered convoy of vehicles dragged along the Humber road, along Clive Sullivan Way. By the time they got to the bridge, O'Grady had overtaken Katz. Always they left a vehicle, sometimes two between themselves and their subject, and always a vehicle between one another. Both were keenly conscious of the twin dangers in tailing: the 'swamped environment' and the 'fallow environment'. Meaning either so many cars on the road that you lose your subject or so few he rumbles you. Both had completed the police training course; neither, though, had ever followed anyone in a car before outside of an exercise. So far Vinnie was a breeze: he was steady, he didn't stop for petrol, he even indicated well in advance. Once over the bridge onto the A1077, amidst the unvaried farmland of north Lincolnshire, the traffic thinned out, becoming so fallow there was nothing to leave between him and them. They both dropped back, but for all Vinnie was aware he could have been towing them. He wasn't looking at his wing mirrors; he was looking into the rear view at the crates behind him. They were beginning to move; they were beginning to cry out – they were, in fact, beginning to speak to one another.

'Masood... Masood! Are you okay? Hey!'

'I hear you... I'm okay... fuck... I pissed myself, you know.'

It was distressing, even for Vinnie, and his lorry would stink to almighty heaven, so he accelerated.

Then Katz lost O'Grady, who suddenly realised that the white lorry wasn't around the next shoulder of hedgerow; there was just empty road. He must have clocked them. O'Grady thumped the wheel. *Outsmarted by a fucking pikey.* He pressed the ball of his foot against the pedal. Hedges like walls, barn-sized houses jutting out from bends, and when the road straightened, nothing in front but a tractor. *Bastard must have taken a side track.* He hadn't been looking, but surely he would have noticed any side roads. He did a precarious U-turn with the aid of someone's front lawn and retraced at forty mile an hour. Entering the cup of the bend, he saw a white stone building that would have been a blur in the other direction. He slowed and picked up on a side entrance. A pub with a car park and there, making an appearance in his wing mirror, was the lorry. He parked up a hundred yards beyond.

*

Vinnie was unloading the lorry. Sunlight engulfed the crates and the people inside screened their eyes. He began to break the slats away with a claw hammer, throwing pieces into a corner of the car park. 'We're here, you're here now.'

For sure more than one had pissed themselves, and more besides. People flopped out like new-born calves. Vinnie collected their water bottles; most were empty, some had left an inch or two, perhaps realising the water was doped.

'Wakey, wakey, everyone. Get on your feet. Once you do that you'll be as right as rain.' He demonstrated what walking was by stomping as many paces as the crowded lorry would allow. No one managed to raise themselves. One or two kneeled awkwardly then toppled; others looked up, bewildered by his feat of motion. Vinnie began to massage the doctor's legs. His eyes were jellied, his mouth like that of a landed fish; he bent one knee then the other, appealing for sensation to return. Taking the doctor by the hand, Vinnie led him Lear-like to the lorry's edge. He lowered him by the armpits, then, with due warning, let go. Bingo – the doctor stood unaided. *That's one that can stand. Hopefully he'll be digging up spuds by tomorrow.*

Katz had arrived at O'Grady's Audi.

'I've just seen him in the pub car park down there.'

'So, what do we do now?' She was more afraid of losing the suspect than losing face.

'Not sure,' he said graciously, 'depends on what *he* does, but I think we need to be out of sight.'

Katz was fretful. This was all unplanned. She had gambled because she was with Gavin. The sergeant led his superior to a farm track beyond the pub; they parked a hundred yards up. Between them and the car park lay a field of flourishing leeks, a copse of birch trees, a mixed hedge. They wanted to be in the company of at least four gym fanatic officers in black boots, stab vests with radios and a dog or two, but it was just them. An hour ago, she had envisaged winding down a window from a safe distance before ordering in her troops, opening emails the following week that concluded, *Once again, congratulations on a real hands-on resolution.*

'I'm going to get two units here.' She made it sound like a question.

'Shall I go over and take a look?' He made it sound like a fait accompli.

O'Grady slung on his camera, ran along a row of leeks, before ducking down behind a birch. He crossed the fifty metres to the hedge on all fours. The suspect he could see, was shaking out his legs and arms, jogging on the spot, leading an exercise routine for people who could barely move, could barely see straight. O'Grady filmed the six men and women stumbling their way through Vinnie's moves as he shouted instructions, their necks too listless to lift their heads. Fifteen minutes later Vinnie had decided they were in reasonable shape for delivery. He clapped his hands and waved everyone back into the lorry.

O'Grady ran bent double back to Katz. 'He's on the move,' he said, scurrying into his Audi. Then, 'Wait there,' before mysteriously driving up the farm track. Two minutes later he returned inside the skeleton frame of a soft-top green Land Rover. 'We need something different behind him. The farmer was fine about it.'

Vinnie continued raising morale as he flashed along the road past the end of the track. 'Anyone know this one? *Moving on up...*'

They sang, hypnotised behind a haze of medication, believing themselves to be compelled, sounding fearful of further punishment.

The farmer's run-around could shift, and Katz gripped the roof strap as she summoned officers towards their location. Finally, the lorry turned under a sign: 'Tate's Farm'. O'Grady rattled to a stop well beyond and ran off to conduct more surveillance. He filmed the new arrivals as they were shuffled into caravans and he saw that Vincent Gilheaney wasn't hanging around. O'Grady fled in pursuit whilst Katz remained at the farm. It took an hour for a squad car and two vans to arrive, and then Katz had to summon a third van to accommodate all thirty migrant workers at the site, plus the farm manager and his wife. Immigration would come and pick them up from the station, but not before Katz had questioned them about the people who had brought them to the UK.

*

Vinnie led O'Grady to an industrial estate in Grimsby. The detective left the mud-bespattered Land Rover in the first bay of the first unit. *Right, let's arrest this fucker.* He rang it through and thought it best to locate the suspect on foot whilst he waited for boys with tasers and batons. He walked the cul-de-sacs of the estate, all thirty-seven units, and surprisingly there were several white lorries. When he'd gone full circle he saw one pull up opposite the first unit. The owner got out, looked about cautiously, walked over to the Land Rover, peered in through the windows, looked about some more. O'Grady was rooted to the spot behind a skip. He knew he'd been rumbled. Vinnie went back to his lorry and returned with his claw hammer and a Stanley knife. He slashed two tires, shattered a back window and left with O'Grady's camera. He sped off. Esther Katz had gone from having her people smuggler in the bag with all the necessary evidence to having lost both.

Vinnie's pulse told him he needed to put as much distance between him and anything else plod were driving. On the A180 he passed two blue lights coming the other way and saw it for the posse it was. Watching his tail, he headed for Scunthorpe. He remembered reading that Jesse James had once joined a posse in pursuit of himself, the last thing the Pinkertons had expected. Perhaps it was this unconscious literary memory that urged him to double back, continuously scrutinising the vehicles behind him, in front of him and on the opposite carriageway. Not a lawman in sight. He reached the Travelodge in Hull an hour before he could check in. He sat at the wheel for a good twenty minutes, flicking through the images on O'Grady's camera. They had him banged to rights at the pub and the farm. He kept going, impressed by the shots of the woodpecker, and who was this, on some beach taking a paddle? They would have his registration, so he would need to lose the lorry this side of the North Sea. This was not the first time he'd had to ditch transport. The same way Jesse had to change horses moving through Missouri.

Plotting Vinnie's odyssey and his manoeuvres from a mile and a half away on the second floor of Clough Road nick was O'Grady, muddied and chastened. He might have lost the suspect, his camera and the evidence, but he still had the registration number and a computer, so he could see how Vinnie had been up and down the A180 and the M180 hogging the traffic cams. O'Grady also had his rank and was barking out orders like a crew member at McDonald's. He had people ringing hotels and the ferry company before finally pinning Vincent down to a room at the Travelodge and a half eight ferry back to Rotterdam that same night.

Katz came up from the custody suite, calmed by her weariness. 'You lost him, didn't you? Christ.'

'And found him again,' he asserted.

'Then why isn't he locked up downstairs?'

'He's going back to Rotterdam tonight.'

She didn't ask, she didn't nod, but he was compelled to follow her into her office. Her voice was shrill, less contained. 'How did you lose him? I told you not to lose him.' She turned her back on him, looking out on a vast car park bordered by a disused gas works, arguably the worst view in Hull, so dismal she looked at O'Grady's reflection. 'I didn't invite you to sit down.'

He got back up; he was exhausted. 'He rumbled me.'

'He knows we're on to him? Bollocks.'

'I'm sorry. What are the illegals saying?'

'I think the correct term at present is *migrant*, Sergeant. Sounds like he's running a hostel of some kind and sending them out to work. He's got at least two others working with him, one of them an Afghan. The Dutch are very interested.'

'Anyone give you an address?'

'No. Either too scared or they may want to go back there, I guess. I'll keep trying. Most won't get asylum.'

She sat down, rubbed her eyes. 'I think I might have a name or two. Of the people who suffocated in boxes. But it's not enough to go on. I'm going to release some details to the media, if only to put the wind up him.'

She held out her palms; he sat down and made the suggestion she was waiting for. 'He's bound to lead us to the hostel. He's not that smart. He's all over the traffic cams and might not expect us to follow him to Rotterdam… He'll be part of a chain, reaching back…'

'I know, I know, Gavin. But, did he get a look at you?'

'No. He recognised the Land Rover. When it was parked up.'

'Sure? …Okay, put someone on him and on his lorry, and this time have a tracker put on it, and book yourself a room at the Travelodge, you're going to Rotterdam as well.'

TWENTY-NINE

The main attraction of the Travelodge for Vinnie was not its room rates; it was that it was always either under, or completely unstaffed. No one came knocking on your door, or asked you questions at reception when you checked in or out. No one except a computer screen. But neither was there anyone to inform O'Grady if Vincent Gilheaney was currently in his room, which he wasn't. He had bailed in a taxi, unnoticed by the surveillance officer outside lying flat on his back, placing a tracking device on his lorry, just as the taxi pulled up. Vinnie had abandoned both the lorry and the Travelodge for a public house in downtown Hull. This didn't stop O'Grady staring down at the vehicle for the entire afternoon from his top-floor room, cossetted in a towelling dressing gown. He had sponged off his muddy trousers, socks and jacket from the elfin bathtub, and they were drying on the storage heater. O'Grady radioed the officer on the ground and told him he was moving away from the window for a few minutes; he wanted to be informed if the suspect even approached the lorry. It occurred to him that he had better be dressed, even if his clothes were still damp. Katz had trusted his instincts for a second time, and this time the suspect would not give him the slip.

Vinnie wasn't keen on the pub. It was real ale at made-up prices, fish and chips handed to you on a slab of wood, the clientele wanting of men who worked with their hands, people with whom he might converse about scraping a living. He turned to his phone, his smartphone, and he saw there, under multiple layers of the news app, a headline: 'Bodies washed up in the Humber estuary'. There wasn't much else, a line or two about 'several bodies, several weeks ago, more to follow'. He felt like ringing it in: 'Listen, if anyone should fuckin' know'... His composure surprised him. Maybe it was the ale. Maybe it was because there was another occasion when he had been associated with a body that had made the news. He knew they would have a job on to connect him to the corpses in the water. Still, to be on the safe side he should've taken the lorry somewhere and torched it. Michael. He wasn't much for current affairs. If he happened to see something on the news, he wouldn't ask him outright, 'Was that you, are they ours?' But he would be wondering. If it came to it, if plod caught up with him, Vinnie would keep his nephew out of the picture, but he had no idea how he would explain it to him. He had at least given them a watery grave. The fuck-up was in the ventilation. It was a mistake, nothing more. Michael was soft-hearted, though. If he got wind, he would go his own way.

Vinnie looked at his phone, dialled the number and walked outside. 'Alright, son? ...I'm on the ferry in a few hours... Listen, my lorry, it's goosed... I don't know what it is, but I haven't got time to fix it... Yeah, you need to pick me up, but listen, son... Get hold of a decent car, something with a bit of poke... Yeah, we're gonna need it. Listen, son, we're getting out of that hostel, finished with all that now... We're gonna move on... Copper cables, that's the thing to get into...'

O'Grady was sitting on the storage heater in his damp trousers, clutching the radio. Seven o'clock – Gilheaney was cutting it fine.

He radioed the eyes on the ground. 'Are you sure you haven't missed him?'

'Well, the lorry's still here and I've barely seen anyone come and go.'

O'Grady turned around and pressed his crotch against the heater. Half an hour later he was ventilating himself when Katz rang. 'Gavin. How's the surveillance going?'

'Okay. The suspect hasn't moved.'

'Well, that's funny because he's just walked onto the ferry as a foot passenger.'

Vinnie had bought himself a trench coat and a fedora hat, but the disguise was made redundant by the ticket officer who signalled up to Katz on the deck as he crossed the ramp.

Forty minutes later O'Grady made it to the ferry and caught up with her in the onboard brasserie. Katz's eyes were on the menu.

'I thought he might ditch the lorry. Hopefully he thinks he's lost us now, but we need to be on our toes. And let's face it, we lost him when he wasn't trying. You look a state, Sergeant.'

He smelled like a damp rag. She was dressed as he'd never seen her before. A fern green dress, a necklace, a bracelet, the vicinity of evening wear and more make-up than in the day job.

'I didn't have time to go home and change,' he said, curling his toes gummed to their moist socks.

'Too busy watching a parked lorry?'

'Still, there'll be forensics all over it. And he wouldn't've left it if he hadn't rumbled us,' he said.

'True.'

They looked at their menus and both could've used a drink, but O'Grady didn't dare ask and Katz didn't dare suggest. For the inspector the long ferry journey was an opportunity to relax; she didn't always find it easy to be alone in her house, a silent place. Here there were people around, distractions to indulge in, she had Gavin to talk to and a premium cabin to withdraw to and emerge from. But this, this was not a social occasion, a date of some sort; it was a meeting, wasn't it? Except there wasn't that much on the agenda. The only item was also on the boat and would be disembarking at the same time as them. Twelve hours from now. It could only be a chance to *get to know one another.* She decided to find out whether this man was good company or not. 'Do you know what? I think I'm going to have a steak. I haven't had one for ages.' She closed the menu. 'What about you?'

'Er… well, I'm a veggie.'

'Oh, sorry, course you are. Well, there's a cheese and herb roulade.'

'Yep. I think I'm in the process of becoming a vegan.'

'How long do you think it'll take? Maybe you could squeeze in the roulade before it happens.'

She smiled, but he didn't. He was going to have to tell her sooner or later, and he judged the informal context to be the best one. 'There's something I need to tell you.'

'Is it about seasickness?' She smiled again.

'He's got the camera. My camera. He broke into the Land Rover.'

'The one the woodpecker on? …And all the evidence? …Bet he hasn't got it now.' She tried to think through the implications rather than dwelling on the severity of the disappointment. 'Then we're going to need to get some of the migrants to ID him. They'll ask for a deal on residency. And any decent defence lawyer would smell that a mile off. The farm manager better cooperate, or we don't have much.'

All of that tear-arsing around Lincolnshire, you crawl around in the mud to film him and then you leave the sodding camera in the Land Rover which you park under his nose. There're no traffic cams out there, no CCTV.

She leaned forward with a last complication. 'Here's another thing. He's on foot. He'll be looking to get off the boat pretty sharp. My car was almost first on, it'll be last off. What about you?'

'Almost last on, I'll be near the front when we dock.'

'We take your car. I'll have to speak to someone about leaving mine here. I've asked for the Dutch to have a car in the locale.'

They didn't say a great deal during the meal. Katz watched O'Grady dissect a courgette. He was so methodical about his food he could have been wearing a white coat. She wondered if how a man ate a meal was an indication of how he performed as a lover. Afterwards O'Grady bought a change of clothes from the ferry mall; she went to the on-board cinema to watch the latest *Jason Bourne* movie.

He was at Katz's cabin door early the next morning in a new beige fleece, checked shirt and hard-wearing trousers. She invited him in while she finished packing. He looked at the bed she had slept in and sat on the corner, his back to the pillows.

She patted down her white blouse and faced him. 'The camera. Don't beat yourself up about it. It was your camera; I didn't expect you to have it. Following him was something I decided on the spur of the moment.'

He stared at his shoes, still blemished with dry dirt, uneased by her kindness. 'I keep thinking about what he's done and how we could've nailed him with the footage. But I gave the game away... lost the evidence.'

She held the cabin door open. 'We'll get him. You drive. I need to liaise with the Dutch.'

Vinnie was on starting blocks, nose pointed at the foot passenger door. As soon as the footbridge grabbed on to the side of the ferry like the docking of a spacecraft, he hurried across to the terminal building where folk stood waiting for you, car keys hanging off their thumbs. He looked at the assembled who looked back and beyond. No Michael. *Too clueless to find this place.* He skittered down the stairs and fled into the July sunshine. It was eight forty-five and it felt like noon on a first-rate day. His gaze got to work on the car park then he realised he had asked his nephew to arrive in an unfamiliar car. Behind him the bow doors were already unveiling the car deck. Vinnie jogged up and down past the parked cars on dry land, peering at windscreens, his phone at his ear. He threw down his day-bag and sat on it. He should've told him. If he had told him that plod were on their case Michael would've stepped up, would've relished the fight, the game. But then he would want to know how come the fuckers found out and if he saw the washed-up border-jumpers on the news he'd run off on his own somewhere.

Katz managed to ID Vinnie as they drove away from the terminal and phoned Hans van Duren.

'I've just passed him on the way out, we're in front of him.'

'Yeah, I've got him, Esther. There's only one road he can take. You park up a couple of kilometres ahead, I'll be behind him.'

Tyres squealed from within the sun's rays. Vinnie tried to make himself visible. It was impossible to make out the driver from that distance, but he could tell by the reckless speed that it was his nephew behind the wheel. A silver VW Scirocco hurtled round the last row of bays and came straight for him.

'Yo, Vinnie.' Michael stepped out and patted the roof. 'What d'ya reckon?'

Vinnie got in, slammed the door and snatched at the seat belt. 'You're late.'

'Yeah, well, I'm having a nightmare with the hostel, aren't I?'

'Just drive.'

Atherton spun the dodgem-sized steering wheel with one hand and headed for the front of the exit queue to bully his way in. 'That's what I'm saying. They won't leave the hostel. That big fucker in the vest, wherever he's from, he won't shift and he won't work neither.'

'It's not our problem anymore, son. We're moving on. I don't like this town.'

'I don't mind it… Where we going?'

Michael had leap-frogged, cut up, asked permission and took permission all along Moezelweg and was about to unwittingly give Hans the slip on the N220. Vinnie looked over his shoulder, pleased with their progress whilst the *hoofdagent* was waiting for some lights to change colour.

'Brussels, that's where we're going, son.'

'Yeah? …How far's that?'

'Not fucking far enough,' hissed Vinnie.

'When yer thinking?'

'Tomorrow, today, maybe.'

'What the fuck, Vinnie?! We got wages coming the end of the week. Wait till Friday at fucking least. We could get off with everyone's pay then.'

O'Grady and Katz waited at the next set of lights. Van Duren had phoned to tell them to expect to be passed by a silver 'Scirocco, registration…' O'Grady hugged the right-hand lane and, just as van Duren had promised, a Scirocco enlarged itself in the rear-view mirror and then pulled up alongside them in the left-hand lane. O'Grady looked down at his lap; Katz looked in the glove compartment.

Vinnie looked across at a right-hand drive, at a couple that weren't well-matched, at… the fucker in the camera, the bastard peeler. 'Tell yer another thing, Michael. See, this car… yer going to have to get shot of it.'

Michael shook his head, revved up and kickstarted the car in third gear, under a new-born red light, taking out his fury on the clutch. In three and a half seconds he had vanished.

O'Grady jumped the light in his wake, the thoroughfare tightening to single lanes with the addition of roomy cycle paths either side. His way was clear until he approached a bend with a cyclist taking the long curve as slow and as wide as he liked. O'Grady gambled on straddling the white lines when a 4x4 coming the other way flinched him to the right. Katz heard a sound like a tambourine thrown onto the pavement. 'Stop!' She turned to see the white polyester figure lying star-shaped in the road.

'Gavin, forget the pursuit. We have to stop.'

O'Grady braked and went back, returning to the scene of the accident.

THIRTY

The casualty wasn't moving.

'You alright, sir?' enquired O'Grady.

The man lay on his front, head to one side, on the edge of the cycle lane. There was no blood and he had a helmet on. He wasn't stirring or groaning, and the sergeant was unsure of where to take it from there. Katz kneeled and took a hand to hold – the fingers were limp. From closer inspection he was somewhere in the pastures of mid-life. She located a pulse, but his eyes remained shut, though there was some dribble on his chin.

'Hello, can you hear me, sir?' she said slowly.

He remained oblivious.

'Ring an ambulance,' she said.

O'Grady reached for his phone, then hesitated, 'What's the number for that here?'

Katz shrugged; the casualty stirred and said, 'It's 112, and ask for the police as well.'

O'Grady walked up the road out of earshot to make the call. As the traffic glided past, he looked in the direction that Vincent Gilheaney had gone. When he returned to the scene the casualty, whose name he didn't want to know, was on his back with his knees raised and his head propped up on Katz's coat.

'Where does it hurt?' O'Grady asked him.

'My neck and my back,' he replied.

'But you can move your legs okay?'

The casualty whimpered, lowered his legs and placed a palm over his face.

'Try not to move,' cautioned Katz.

Van Duren arrived and started getting out traffic cones and a warning sign. Without a word to his English colleagues he went over to the casualty and began a conversation in Dutch. Although he didn't speak a word of the language, O'Grady was certain van Duren had asked him for an account of events and the cyclist described the driver as a dangerous grim reaper of the highway. He walked over to have a word in van Duren's multi-lingual ear.

'Fact is, Hans, he swung out of the cycle lane into the car. He was going too fast on the bend. Way too fast.'

'On a bike?'

O'Grady replied with a glare; van Duren responded loud and clear as if he were chairing a public meeting. 'Okay, I hear you, Sergeant, and you will have your chance to tell your story at the station.'

It was like that then.

The casualty smiled up at the heavens. The ambulance came and he was softly helped on to a stretcher, requesting a neck brace.

'Okay, you must follow me to the station now. Esther, you can drive.'

O'Grady slammed the passenger side door.

'For a moment I thought Hans was going to draw a chalk line around him.'

Katz reacted with a look that semaphored, *don't*.

Michael Atherton raged all the way from the jumped traffic lights to the flat on Dwingelostraat.

'What do you mean, sell the motor? Just fuckin' got hold

of it, you dick. Are you mad? I graft too, yer know, I have to deal day and night with those fuckin' pain in the arse border-jumpers, you asked me to get a car – well, this is it and it's no run-around – it's worth a lot of dough to people who appreciate cars...' He snatched up the handbrake and fell silent.

Vinnie allowed the hush to colonise before voicing his lines. 'Look, son. It's a nice car, a lovely car. But the peelers are here. And they have the number now. That was them next to us, back at the lights you left.'

'You're joking?'

'They must have been on the ferry,' surmised Vinnie.

'Why?'

'Why do you think? They're after you, son. Through me. They've followed me from Hull to find you. That's why I left the lorry, that's why the car has to go. I'm sorry, it's a nice car 'n' that. How much did it cost?'

Michael had calmed; his voice verged on apologetic. 'Nothing. I robbed it. But I like it.'

'A shame, right enough.'

'What do we do now?' asked Michael.

'We leave town, son. Get on our toes. Dump this car somewhere else. I'll pack the van and we just go.' Vinnie clicked his fingers. 'You remember what De Niro said in *Heat*?'

'Yeah, yeah.'

They recited in unison. '*Never have anything in your life you cannot walk away from... in thirty seconds if you feel the heat come around the corner.*'

Michael nodded. It was time to get professional.

*

Katz and O'Grady were in the main office of the *politie bureau*. Katz was introduced to someone of equal rank while her sergeant was invited to sit in a corner. Dutch bobbies weren't the laid-back types O'Grady had envisaged. Patrol officers marching through the building wore body armour and even the one nearby playing solitaire on her computer was packing a sidearm. Everyone, bar van Duren, was kitted to some degree in a black uniform. There was no background radio, no coffee or apple-based pastries on anyone's desks. One or two *politieagenten* looked in his direction and spoke in repetitive glottal stops.

The solitaire player clicked back into a document, turned and smiled; O'Grady smiled more.

'*Wacht je om iemand te zien?*' she asked.

'Not sure, I'm English. I think Hans van Duren is taking care of me.'

'Okay... I'm Brigitte.'

'Gavin.'

She was short, stocky, defined by hips and shoulders, by her blonde bob, but mostly by welcoming eyes. She swivelled back to her keyboard and he looked around for any sign of Katz or van Duren. He was being typecast as a suspect, as someone parked in a waiting area until after dinner. Officers glimpsed at him and he looked back until they looked elsewhere. He considered leaving the building for an elevenses but instead got up and strolled over to the eight-foot-high windows. He was eye level with the crown of a sycamore. The tree was not yet mature; its leaves were bright, splayed, shimmering with sap, and the time would come, probably within the next ten years, when it would have to be reined in with a chainsaw. Cyclists sped along under the canopy.

'Would you like a coffee?' asked a voice from behind.

'Indeed, why not, Brigitte,' he said.

'Want to come with me?'

He followed her down the length of the open-plan office into a small room of water coolers, microwaves and the tang of melted cheese.

'I hear you're a police officer from England.'

'Indeed,' he said once more. He went on, 'I'm here on an operation pursuing a murder suspect.'

'Really, well, let me know if there's anything I can do to help… I'm just trawling through files right now.'

She was, he estimated, about his age, and he thought for a moment how absurd it was that he had considered holding Katz in his arms. He filled Brigitte in on his case and asked about their traffic cam software, but before she could answer Hans van Duren thrust his head around the door.

'Okay, Sergeant, if you please.'

He thanked Brigitte with his most boyish of smiles and followed van Duren to a windowless interview room. Resting on the centre table was a black box tape recorder. O'Grady pulled up short.

Hans pointed to a chair. 'Okay, sit.'

O'Grady stood his ground. *We usually say please, even to the rapists.* 'Are you interviewing me under caution?' he asked.

Hans placed his first-choice biro down on his clipboard. 'Okay, you've been in a road traffic accident and the casualty is in hospital. We need to treat this like we would any other incident.'

O'Grady sipped his coffee and took a moment to swallow. 'Here's the thing, Hans, I'm a serving police officer and I was pursuing a suspect. He, Mister Casualty, didn't stay in his cycle lane. He hit me, with his pension plan bike.'

Van Duren ignored that. 'Do you want a lawyer?'

'No. Because there's not much more to it. He left the pink cycle lane as I was passing him and bounced off the rear of the car. There was nothing I could have done.'

'Okay, we'll see what Detective Katz has to say, but I should tell you something, Sergeant. The law in Holland is a little different from the UK. Where there is a collision between a cyclist and a motorist, the presumption of guilt is always with the motorist. Until proven otherwise. We feel it provides protection for the cyclist.'

'And I bet Mister Casualty knows all about the law.'

Van Duren got up and opened the interview room door for him, the way the police do for suspects.

He went back to his corner to wait for Katz. After another humiliating interval she was finally led back into the office by her opposite number, a woman so power-dressed in comparison to Katz, she made her look like a middle-aged intern. The Dutch detective half nodded to a few obsequious uniforms before being approached by van Duren who requested, in English, a few minutes with 'Esther'. O'Grady watched her enter van Duren's interview room and watched her intently thereafter, seeking signs of loyalty, signs of betrayal.

*

Vinnie swung his case into the back of the blue transit; the chosen wily getaway transport to Brussels. Michael had been sent to leave the VW Scirocco a few miles away from the flat. The transit might be in need of a service and a jet-wash, but a train journey would expose them to the scrutiny of cameras. Vinnie had spoken to cousin Kenny, and Kenny had a room for the two of them and six shifts behind the bar between them. He would know something was amiss but wouldn't ask any questions and wouldn't expect any asked of him. Vinnie had once thrown a fight for Kenny for a slice of the proceeds; like Vinnie, he was a survivor on his toes. He would be sure to have contacts in Brussels and beyond, in other countries, no doubt.

Michael had left the Scirocco on Geertruidenbergstraat with the keys in the ignition and was ambling back to the flat. The walk had given him time to think. Maybe it would be best for them to split up; there might be less chance of them both getting caught. Vinnie had helped him escape and would get some time for that. They could go their separate ways for a year or two, perhaps – plod wouldn't chase them forever; they'd leave a warrant outstanding and hope that the two of them would turn up somewhere. He'd known people who'd escaped from jails, from court, from transport, after twelve months they were back drinking in their local with their backs turned to the door. Plod must be pretty pissed off to have come all the way to Rotterdam. Pretty clued up as well. How did they know it was Vinnie that had sprung him and that they were in Rotterdam? Michael's slowing stroll came to a halt. *I'll tell you why, you stupid fucker, because they're on to his game with the border-jumpers. It's not you they're after – it's him.*

He arrived at the flat; before he could drop down into an armchair, Vinnie issued an order. 'Pack up everything up, every last trace of you, put it in the van.'

Michael stared at his uncle, incredulous at his cheek, at his own naivety. 'Plod haven't come all this way for me, have they? They've come for you, haven't they?'

Vinnie shrugged – his nephew spelled it out for him. 'They might not find this flat, but they will find the hostel. We need to stop off there and lose the evidence.'

'What evidence?' asked Vinnie in his 'chill your beans' voice.

'The fucking boxes and crates, the stuff you've been putting people in.'

Vinnie raised an eyebrow in a 'you might have a point' way.

In front of the apartment block, on a patch of grass bordered by a knee-high wall, Black Vest Guy was conducting a wrestling class for a group of children. He spat on his palms, waved them towards him, swaying on his haunches. Holding a boy on each shoulder while another tugged at his leg, he still managed to acknowledge the arrival of Michael and Vinnie. Michael headed into the hostel whilst Vinnie went around the back to the garages. He raised an aluminium door and took in the contents: a skip full of crates, cardboard, soft packaging and clusters of one-pint water bottles. Vinnie envisaged an out-of-control bonfire but settled instead on a familiar plan of a series of fly-tip stops along motorway slip roads.

'You making another trip to England?' Black Vest Man's voice was close behind.

'That's right,' answered Vinnie.

The shadow of Black Vest Guy spread into the garage, but Vinnie didn't turn.

'When are you going?'

'Soon, very soon.'

'You'll let me know?'

'You'll be the first to know.'

As the shadow retreated Vinnie breathed out. He had played him like a violin.

Except the instrument played one last phrase from the alley: 'Hey, Englishman, you better not be lying. You better not fuck with me.'

Vinnie looked sideways; he didn't even look in his opponent's direction, but the glance was enough.

'Because if you do, I'll come for you. Believe that.'

Vinnie's composed exterior fell away, keeled over and died, and his nose was suddenly flush against Black Vest Guy's chin. 'Listen, Tarzan, I owe you fuck all, understand? You can get yourself to fuckin' England.'

Vinnie left a pause for the guy to make his play; he didn't. But as Vinnie returned to the garage it sunk in that this man wasn't going to take him anywhere now, was nothing but an arrogant and ultimately weak English piece of trash. He paced over and shoved Vinnie from behind. It was on; it had to be.

*

O'Grady studied the table tennis of questions and answers between van Duren and Katz, writing the subtitles for himself. He read the meaning behind every question and answer, the pauses before Katz's answers; he could tell that her posture of clasped hands upon her lap, elbows to her sides, was an admission of guilt, but not hers, *his*. He could tell when the interview was coming to an end. Hans laughed at some droll remark from Katz as he stood to hold the interview door open for her.

'Constable!' ordered Hans.

O'Grady didn't sit and didn't close the door behind him.

'Have you reached a verdict?'

'Not quite. I have to go to see the casualty now, to get a statement. Best if you guys hang around for a couple of days until I can make a decision on this – you never know, you might even find your suspect.'

'Well, that's the plan, Hans. Brigitte over there tells me you have traffic cam software, just like us. We could have run Gilheaney's number plate an hour ago.'

'I'll see to it, later,' said van Duren.

O'Grady raised his voice a quarter-turn of a dial. 'Later, Hans, our people smugglers might be in Poland or somewhere.'

Katz raised her head a few degrees, signalling her disapproval to O'Grady. 'Gavin, why don't you go and arrange a hotel for us? I've got a few things to sort out here.'

Back in his corner Brigitte was occupied on a call. It was twenty minutes to the end of her shift, but now two officers were urgently required to a location, putting paid to the gym and the spa. O'Grady watched her interrogate her caller. She was on her feet before the receiver was down.

O'Grady raised his hand for attention. 'You don't know a half-decent hotel, do you, a few stops away?'

'I'm going towards town now. I can drop you at a tram stop on the way. Come.'

O'Grady waited in the underground car park whilst Brigitte and her partner got kitted up in a locker room. They were larger when they emerged, something protruding from every pouch.

The vehicle was dark and menacing inside, the sat-nav a little smaller than an ATM screen, its voice militaristic in tone.

'What's the job?' asked O'Grady.

'Reports of a disturbance,' said Brigitte, imitative of the sat-nav. 'Routine for the locality.'

From the backseat O'Grady looked out into the sunshine, at the coffee drinkers under awnings and parasols. He remembered a student holiday with his first girlfriend, how she had saved every train and bus ticket, and then put them in their photograph album. He found himself asking Brigitte about places to eat, drink and visit.

'I thought you were here on a case,' she said.

'I am, and now I'm a suspect in another.'

He failed to elaborate.

The sat-nav led them through an expanse of suburbs that had the character of an exclusive caravan park. Perhaps it was the sunshine, but the streets looked clean and ordered and safe. This was social housing, but not like merry England. The shops propping up the apartment blocks were almost elegant; there were no iron grills to be seen and no devil dogs. Citizens were better dressed – they had a better body mass index and superior sunglasses.

Brigitte pulled over and peered into the rear-view mirror. 'I'm sorry, we're off the tram route here. But it's in that direction,' she said, pointing.

'Right.' O'Grady paused on the door handle. 'Or I could tag along… to the disturbance…?'

A question crackled out of her partner's radio. She spun the steering wheel; a siren began to wail and all three tensed to the G-force.

'Alright, but stay in the vehicle.'

As they rounded the corner, the melee ahead began thinning at the edges, but no one was heading indoors; instead they backed off to observe the forthcoming scene. A bunch of around ten still huddled around whatever it was in their midst. They rolled back and forth like a scrum whilst someone bawled encouragement from a balcony above. It was a scrap alright. Brigitte strode purposefully towards the crowd, cleaving a passage right through to the source. O'Grady watched her lodge herself between the two combatants whilst her colleague unsuccessfully tried to shoo the gathering away as if it consisted of pigeons. Brigitte knew that anything less than maximum assertion was only encouragement to the mob. She was good. A solid bobby, sound in a bundle. Her partner led his heavyweight contender a good ten paces away from his opponent who remained rigid, bloodied.

What are they fighting about? Money, no doubt, or some imaginary slight on their masculinity. *Who is he? He looks like... he is... fuck me... it is him.* Gilheaney. Who had given him the slip twice, who had made him look a fool, made him run over a pain-in-the-arse cyclist, who had robbed his camera and, *also*, who had killed at least four people. Brigitte began to tell spectators to *move along*; you don't do that if you're going to cuff someone, if you're going to make a collar. O'Grady sensed she was going to give him a caution, possibly an invite, to report at his convenience. He gave it two beats for a second thought, for a breath, before O'Grady walked, then charged, head bowed at his suspect, taking him to the ground from below the hip. Vinnie swung his fists as the O'Grady hung on to him at the knees. He was twisted and dragged like crocodile prey, but still he hung on.

Brigitte shouted, 'Let go of him, let go!'

'Cuff him! Cuff him,' replied O'Grady from under Vinnie's backside.

'We're not arresting him!'

'He's my people smuggler.'

'What did you say?'

Atherton rushed over and attempted to wrench O'Grady away from Vinnie, but he only succeeded in tugging the two of them across the grass. Atherton kicked O'Grady's ribs, three, four times in succession, swinging hard from the knee. O'Grady cried out. Brigitte and partner got busy, with the batons, the boots and the cuffs on Vincent Gilheaney and his nephew Michael Atherton.

*

Vinnie wouldn't say a word to plod. He did, though, put together the bones of a story for his glum brief, along the lines of…

'I was at the shop around the corner, and he, the big guy, is asking me for money, like a beggar, an aggressive beggar, and I just said, "No," but then he gets angry and puts his hand on me, gets a little pushy, like…'

His brief wrote it all down, keeping pace with Vinnie's speech, and then when it came to interview, recited it all to O'Grady and the tape recorder. O'Grady wasn't exactly listening. He smiled at his prey and at the satisfaction of having collared him. Brigitte had agreed to overlook his unofficial part in the arrest in her report in exchange for her credit in the collar of the people smuggler. It meant that Atherton wouldn't be charged for the salvo on his ribcage, but that was the least of his crimes.

Vinnie's lawyer finished his tale. '…my client didn't want to fight… he absolutely didn't, but had no choice…' He clicked the top of his pen for a full stop.

For once O'Grady spoke softly to a suspect. 'I believe you, Vincent, I honestly do.' He paused as if he had just said, 'Now are you sitting comfortably?'

Vinnie finally spoke to plod. 'So, what am I doing here?' he asked.

'Because, Vincent, I can link you to the people watching the fight, the flats they live in, to your lorry back in Hull, the ferry journeys and… the bodies in the Humber. And I can do all that without asking you a single question.' O'Grady paused. 'This isn't going to end in a manslaughter charge, Vincent – it's going to be murder.'

Michael Atherton had been in more police interviews than his uncle. When required he could do silent, for days at a time if needed. He had done silent all the way through court proceedings – he was a soldier. But this time there seemed no point, he was wanted for being 'on his toes' and he had been caught. They had his name and his prison number, and a photo to match. He hadn't asked for a lawyer; there was only one question bothering him.

'Am I going back to the same jail?'

Katz was turning the pages of his pre-convictions print-out. 'No, you're not, Michael.'

'Why's that?'

She put her answer to one side for a moment, lifting her head to look at him. She squinted as if the concentration of her eyes might probe what was going on behind his. They were blue and distracted; when he turned to one side it was as if he was sitting on a bus, raking over a memory from his childhood.

He broke into a half-smile. 'I didn't exactly break out of that van, did I? Someone else broke in.'

Katz nodded as if to say, 'I'm listening...'

Michael prodded the table with his index finger. 'I didn't even know who they were... They just offered to give me a lift... Not what you'd call an escape...'

Katz tilted her head back slightly. 'What part did you play, Michael?'

'In the escape? Hardly any.'

'In the murders, Michael?'

'What are you talking about?'

'I'm talking about the murder of four migrants. Stuffed into boxes where they couldn't breathe and then dumped in the Humber.'

Michael's neck tensed. He took a breath. 'No idea what you're chatting about.'

'A search of the property you were outside this afternoon found packaging identical to the type found in the victim's stomachs...' She was about to say something else then switched to, 'Do you know where Farood Abdali is?'

'Who?'

'Roodie.'

He shook his head, clenched his fists. 'I want a brief. Now. Go get me one.'

Katz left the interview room to observe him through the one-way glass. She knew the chances of him cooperating against his uncle were currently less than even, but that would change. She had, however, secured one interesting immediate result. She had texted the other wanted escapee, 'Roodie', from Atherton's phone. *What u up 2 Roodie?* A reply pinged back with the name of a town on the western edge of Turkey.

THIRTY-ONE

Dikili, Eastern Turkey, July 2012

A tourist town by the sea, with a harbour mid-way, jetties at either end and hillsides behind; a town with fixed borders against land and sea. The small hills provide a cushion against winters that sometimes bring snow. The hills are low but steep enough to deter developers advancing up the slopes. A town of sunsets. In July the sun shines down so abundantly you can feel its warmth on the soles of your feet as you walk along the front, looking out towards the brushstroke in the distance that is the Greek island of Lesbos: an island that has been conquered and reconquered by armies from Greece and Turkey since the days of Homer. The tourist town appeared affluent; polished shop fronts sold stylish jewellery and scarves; there were marble verandas and new cars outside houses with west-facing glass walls. In the harbour and around the jetties were yachts, pleasure cruisers and a ferry offering daily return trips.

Between the hills is a valley that holds a road that runs straight east. At this time, it was bordered by fields of vegetable crops and meadows and in places lined by willow trees that embraced one another. Since the previous spring the road had carried thousands of people from Syria: families and fragments of families, escaping one army or another, one religious doctrine or another. People had clambered out of the ruins of their houses, wiping the dust from the faces of their dead children, the same grey dust that had turned black under their fingernails by the time they picked the unready knee-high kale to eat on the roadside. Some walked the road to town, knowing they would have to hand over what they had to pay for the boat to Greece, others could afford to pay for a bus or had been put on a bus by the police in towns to the east. They gathered near the harbour, on the beach and the pavement either side. Some erected tents, most sat upon blankets and coats. For such an assembly they were quiet, scores of them were silent, they lay or they wandered between sleep and wakefulness. The dozen old men from the town that met on the benches that surrounded the town square made more noise. Few begged. Some stole from a supermarket but were caught and kicked by security staff. After that the supermarket put collection boxes at the end of each checkout and most mornings a group of school students handed out fruit, bread and water, starting at either end of the line along the seafront.

On their first morning, Farood tailed Berzan from one gift shop to the next as he searched for something for his daughter. He asked Farood's opinion, holding up scarves, brooches and necklaces, to which Farood gave his positive approval every time. Farood looked at the postcards. He picked out one with a silhouette of a couple holding hands, in front of a sunset. He would send it to Sabana, to show her that his life was going on, in some place better than where she was. She was never going to be his wife; she only ever pitied him. He understood that now. There would be no message, only his name. Maybe he should send one to Atherton, who would be wondering when he would be back, but then he would have to write that he didn't know.

Berzan bought his teenage daughter a scarf and nodded Farood out of the shop. They headed along the front in search of a café. Berzan did not give the group of people assembled by his feet a second look; Farood looked down at every face, observing what they wore, what they carried. He saw how some were wearing too much, carrying too much. But they had left behind homes where they had possessions, whereas he had left behind nothing much beyond a cave. They passed by a squabble over a blanket. An old man had one end and an old woman the other: she was shouting at him whilst a young man put his forearm around the old man's throat. As he squeezed tighter, she pulled harder and the old man released the blanket. Two strolling police officers crossed over from the other side of the road and politely acknowledged Berzan. At the other end of the harbour he chose a café, and they sat outside in the cool of its awning's shadow.

They ordered coffees and water, cheese and salami sandwiches. Berzan showed the waitress the scarf he had bought; she smiled in approval, asking who it was for. The bread, dry and crusty, flaked over the tablecloth. To be in the shade, even at this hour, was reviving.

Across the road a mother and two sons were dragging themselves towards the assembly at the harbour. The woman carried bloated bags whilst holding the hand of a small child and a little ahead of them, her elder boy: maybe ten or eleven years old. They stopped to sit on the wall at the top of the beach; the ten-year-old's feet dangled off the ground – one of his shoes split. Covering his face with his palms, he peered through a crack between his fingers, and noticed the two men opposite with their sandwiches, looking in his direction. He dropped down, walked into the road, looking straight at Farood, whose chewing slowed. The boy took from his pocket a bay leaf and began to shred it between his fingers. Then another. Berzan stared back and swallowed; Farood went into the café, bought more water and sandwiches, and took them to the boy and his mother. She clasped her hands together in gratitude.

Berzan laughed. 'You're going to feed them all?' he shouted. 'Just them,' replied Farood.

'You shouldn't start something you can't finish. They need to find their own food. Like you did. The boy must learn to steal. Better to steal than to beg.'

They walked around the rest of the little town, the square with the statue of Kemal Ataturk, the narrow back streets of bars, barbers and metal workshops. A car mechanic emerged from shadow, wiping his hands, wanting to know who they were.

'Business people,' said Berzan.

They returned to the front, with Berzan now leaning on a rail, studying the Syrians. In the last hour, more had come, but none as yet were leaving on boats. They watched tourists board the ferry, the ticket collector asking occasional questions and pointing to seats.

'Okay,' said Berzan, 'let's take a trip to Lesbos. Your job is to fetch me the cargo.'

'How many?' asked Farood.

'Twenty. But we need the right cargo at the right price.'

'What's the right cargo?'

Berzan spat onto the gritty sand. 'The right cargo pays a hundred lira and doesn't take up much room.'

'What about children?'

Berzan scratched his head as he negotiated with himself. 'If they're carried, that's okay. If they take up a seat, it's a hundred like everyone else. Same as an aeroplane. And only lira. No Syrian money. It'll be worthless soon.'

Farood was given an hour to bring them to the boat at the northern end of the harbour. He set about being as business-like as he could, directing some to the bank to exchange money and refusing those who offered him watches and jewellery as part payment. Many were unfriendly to him, talking to him as if he was a criminal. A woman who was handing out food told him he ought to take people across to Greece for nothing. 'They're refugees, for God's sake, they're escaping war.' But most had the money and agreed to pay. He longed to tell all about *his* journey, how far he travelled as a boy. He came across an English teacher from Aleppo and told him how his father was killed and how his mother had to sell their sheep for him to get to Greece.

The Syrian told him, 'A father is not a son. Would he be happy with what you've become?'

Farood went up and down the line telling people to follow him and to have their money ready.

At his boat Berzan helped them aboard with one hand and took their money with another. 'I told you twenty,' he said to Farood.

'Twenty was all I asked, I counted.'

Farood looked behind him and saw that others had joined the queue or were jockeying their way in with elbows and threats while others protested. At Berzan's instruction he blocked any more trying to board, and when a group of three teenagers tried to side-step him he grabbed one by the collar and threw him back, shouting, 'Later, later.'

Berzan switched on the engine and Farood stepped back on the boat. The teenager ran forward, leaping on board, clattering into a woman holding a child. There was some shouting, but not much. The boat backed away from the quay and Farood joined Berzan beside the wheel.

'Ever sailed to Lesbos before?'

'No, but I can see it. And there's no traffic lights.'

Berzan slapped the takings onto the console. 'Count it.'

Farood counted it twice, which Berzan noticed.

'We're two hundred lira short.'

'Okay, throw two people overboard.'

Farood looked back at him blankly; Berzan looked straight ahead, then filled the silence with hearty laughter. He steered the boat directly ahead for around half an hour, then when he was sure he could see the white of buildings, he veered straight towards them. Although there was little wind, the bow lifted and spray hissed as it washed the deck.

'Soon be there,' said Farood to the passengers, 'and once you're in Greece you can go anywhere.'

A small boy in front of him pushed his face into his mother's arm and cried as if he understood every word as well as the implications.

Farood went on. 'I lived in Greece for a couple of years. They were good to me.'

He knew some could understand, but overall they appeared uninterested. The English teacher seemed to pity him. Farood could see this was no adventure, could recognise his own remoteness. The boat abruptly listed to the side where most had gathered; Farood clapped his hands and ordered a group shuffle across the deck. Within an hour the sea quietened in the arms of a bay.

Berzan pointed, called over his shoulder, 'Mytilene.'

The town looked twice the size of the place they had sailed from. As they approached, most of the town's people seemed to be right in front of them, on the shore, around the harbour, all looking out to the boat. It occurred to the crew that they were now embarking on the most awkward part of the operation. Over the last few weeks tourists and locals had seen boats like this arrive every few days, attracting more curiosity than concern. The Syrians were being housed in a shelter on a football pitch and some had been able to pay for ferries to Athens. They had not gathered, not yet sat down in their hundreds on the beaches, by the hotels and bars and supermarkets. But anyone who flicked to a news channel knew in time they would.

The boat's hull bounced off a wooden jetty; Farood hopped off and hooked the rope end over a post. A man in shorts with a small dog advanced, shouting in Greek, but was overwhelmed by disembarking passengers rushing against each other, like people leaving a tube train on their way home. Farood lifted people ashore while the dog barked and a policeman marched up the quay, all boots and shades.

Berzan hurried up the ten or so remaining, telling them as they went, 'Go see the policeman, he's there to help you.'

The policeman cut a swathe through the rush, relaying information into his radio; he addressed Berzan in Turkish. 'You have to have a licence to ferry people here. And you can't just bring anyone on a lousy little boat like that.'

'Really?' asked Berzan.

Farood flung the rope back, but before he could board, the Greek policeman jumped across, propelling himself onto Berzan's boat.

Berzan squared up to the invader, pushing out his chest, lifting a foot onto a rail. 'I have a licence.'

'Show me,' ordered the policeman.

Berzan walked into the control cabin; the engine revved. 'I left it over there, in Turkey.'

The boat reversed away from the jetty just as Farood landed on the deck. Berzan then pushed the policeman into the sea. For a few seconds he was underwater, then Farood saw him ascend an iron ladder onto the quay as if he'd taken a uniformed dip.

'Do you think that was a good idea?' he asked.

Berzan considered Farood's right to ask such a question of him. 'You want to spend some time in a Greek jail as well?'

When they arrived back in Turkey, a small group of would-be passengers were waiting and edged towards the boat the moment Farood secured the rope. Berzan shoved them back, announcing, 'One hour, one hour!'

He'd decided they needed a map of the island, to give themselves some other landing options, now that he'd almost drowned a Greek policeman. Ten to twenty metres behind them, following them across to the gift shop, walked a man, maybe five years older than Farood, carrying a motorcycle helmet. They came out and walked up the shaded side of the street towards the morning's café – and so did he.

After fifty metres Berzan sighed and effected a casual about-turn with both hands in his pockets. 'What the fuck do you want with us?'

The hanger-on was around Farood's height: a pink tee shirt, a beard and moustache trimmed short, hair waxed back, no sunglasses, a smile.

'That's no way to talk to someone.'

He wasn't feigning coolness. If there was any threat, it hadn't ruffled him.

He looked at Farood. 'You don't even recognise me, do you?'

Recognition seeped its way across Farood's face as the man moved closer to him and confirmed, 'Have you gone blind, you bastard? It's Misha.'

Farood repeated his name back to him in two halves; his smile swelled to a grin. They squeezed each other's hands as Misha pulled Farood into an embrace. Though the Afghan was initially the less demonstrative, the same joy flowed between the boys that had dared and endured together from Baghlan to Athens.

Farood took Misha's hand again and clasped it inside his other hand. 'What are you doing here?' asked Farood.

'I'm doing the same as you.'

'I remember you, Turkmen,' said Berzan.

Misha was no longer the teenager in his cellar. He was now in his early twenties, barrel-chested and the tallest of the three. He and Farood were still holding hands. 'And I remember you, Berzan.'

'You have a boat, Turkmen?'

Farood interjected. 'Berzan, it's *Mi-sha.*'

'Yeah, I'm working on a boat, a bit bigger than yours.'

Berzan spat on the ground and asked, 'You taking any Syrians over today?'

'No. We're doing some cleaning today, but there's plenty more on their way.'

Farood led him by the arm to a café; Berzan ordered coffees and offered food that Misha refused. Though Berzan probed Misha about, 'How many Syrians?', 'How much money?', 'How long have you been here?', Misha evaded all details, directing the conversation towards Farood's last few years, in particular this unexpected relationship.

'How did you two end up together?' he asked.

Farood was suddenly shamed. He wanted to say that he wasn't anyone's prisoner anymore, that he'd been making a lot of money, was with Berzan because he had taken control of things over in Rotterdam, but he knew what it looked like. It looked like his life had gone backwards.

Berzan answered for him. 'I found him moving people into England from Holland. My people. Can you believe it?' Berzan laughed and the other two smiled. 'You two, you got some fucking nerve. You run away, cheating me out of money, then you have the balls to set up your own business.'

The other two laughed this time.

'But I always knew you had something – you weren't as scared as everyone else, or as stupid, and you had each other.'

Misha leaned forward. 'Actually, we *were* scared of you. *Terrified.* That's why we ran. Hey, Farood, did you ever make it to England?'

'I'll tell you later.'

Cordiality was thawing; Misha rose and extended an invitation. 'Thanks for the coffee. Why don't you come with me and I'll show you my boat? My boss would like to meet you.'

Misha fetched his motorbike and wheeled it ahead. The bike gleamed and bulged black and chrome, and despite heaving its bulk, he pulled away by several lengths as Berzan sullenly lagged behind. They passed through the town square, bordered on three sides by elderly men on benches, rolling beads through their hands and smoking, watching young women pass by. A group of Syrian men were sitting on a plastic sheet playing cards beneath Ataturk's plinth. Out the other side of the square was the southern end of the harbour and a fishing trawler with a bleached blue hull.

Misha kicked down his bike rest and introduced them. 'So, this is her. Guys, meet *Zerrin*.'

Compared to Berzan's vessel she was high in the water with a gangplank at thirty degrees. Two men were washing the cloudy yellow deck and as they walked past the gaping entrance to the hold, they could hear another man singing to himself in the hollow below.

'Guys, this is the captain.'

The captain lifted his head slightly by way of a greeting. 'Berzan?' He held out his hand, streaked with oil, which Berzan smothered with his. The bigger man tried to make the most of his size, rolling back his shoulders, taking a slow breath and half a step in, but the captain was oblivious. 'You want to run Syrians over to Greece?' he asked.

'We're already taking them.'

Berzan glanced back at the men cleaning the deck – they were both watching him. The captain threw down the cloth. Misha led Farood back down the deck to provide some privacy.

'Okay. It is important that we cooperate. We were the first here, my boat has taken a lot of people to many islands and I look after my passengers. That's important. How much are you charging?'

'That's my business,' replied Berzan.

'No, it's mine as well. You charged a hundred lira, and that's too much. It will drive people to other towns, other boats will come and charge less. Put us both out of business.'

Berzan pointed behind him. 'They're already queueing at my boat now.'

The captain looked away, out to the sea, to Lesbos. His tone softened. 'Misha says you haven't any lifejackets.'

'It's only over there,' said Berzan.

The captain remained patient. 'The water can change. The wind too. Something goes wrong, they'll say we murdered people. Then the TV people will come, because they will like that. Then there will be no more business for anyone. Not one person must drown, understand?'

'Of course,' Berzan concurred.

'Then you'll take some lifejackets from me?'

Berzan nodded, and the captain called for Misha to collect the jackets from the hold and take them to Berzan's boat.

'I appreciate this,' said Berzan.

'No problem,' said the captain. 'I'm only asking twenty lira a jacket.'

It was now confirmed what Berzan had assumed from the moment of Misha's invitation, so he turned and addressed everyone. 'Supposing I don't want to buy them?'

The crew member from the hold ascended and all three looked at Berzan as the captain casually gave his reply. 'I'll sink your boat for you. Misha will collect the money for the jackets.'

Farood helped with the lifejackets as Berzan left the captain's boat, his heavy steps echoing across the steel deck. When it came to the exchange at Berzan's boat he slapped the notes against Misha's chest. 'Turkmen bastard.'

Misha looked directly back at him then counted the money. 'You know what, Mr Berzan. Things are different now. We're both older, aren't we? And my boss, he has a crew behind him who do what he says. And if he says we have to sink your boat, we will.'

Misha left in a strut, left Farood still working for Berzan, as he had worked for Vinnie, for Khalid. He left Farood feeling like a boy, and feeling too, some sense of loyalty to Berzan, even when the old man yelled at him, 'Go get me a boatload. Get more this time.'

By way of defiance he found the family he had bought the

sandwiches for and gave them the money to give to Berzan. When he led the passengers to the boat, he carried the mother's belongings down to the quay and put a lifejacket on the ten-year-old. By the time Berzan was satisfied there were around thirty-five crowded onto the boat, half of them without lifejackets. He took another look at the map then shrugged and started the engine. It was now early evening; they were sailing into a sunset but there was still ample light ahead.

Farood smiled at the children; he spoke to his passengers in English in the hope that some would understand. 'Anyone not been on a boat before? It's nothing to worry about. And if you can't swim, don't worry, you won't need to.'

The ten-year-old boy returned the smile on the rebound of Farood's cheery tone.

As Mytilene began to present itself, Berzan commanded Farood to take the wheel whilst he peered through a telescope at the coast from the bow. His eye hovered over something. 'Bastards!' He ran to the wheel, ousting Farood; the boat veered, its stern overcompensating. People held the sides, shouting and screaming. Farood steadied himself on someone's shoulder; a child began to cry.

Berzan yelled over his own shoulder, 'There's a police van at the harbour. We'll go around the island a bit.'

The boat picked up speed against the current that tugged between the mainland and the island; a wave or two began to spill over the bow.

'Where are we going to land?' called out Farood against the raised pitch of the engine.

Berzan seemed to be racing a phantom. They cleared the headland and crossed into a shallow bay with fragments of the town lying beyond the beach. They taxied straight at it, stopped to a bobbing drift as Berzan scanned the beach with his telescope. Everyone looked at the shore. Farood's ten-year-old stood and pointed at a petrel skimming the water, moving his arm along its line. The boat lurched away again, beyond the next headland, closer to the rocks than before. The bay beyond was narrow, the beach shingly. There were fewer bathers, no buildings behind, but they approached cautiously. Berzan gave the wheel to Farood and looked down over the side of the boat, shielding his eyes to find the bottom. He raised his hand as a signal for Farood to cut the engine. As they edged in with each wave, Berzan ordered everyone off the boat and into the sea. Children apart, he took their lifejackets first. Some refused to disembark; the teacher protested, 'We paid to be taken to the island. We're not there yet.'

Berzan dropped himself over the side of the boat; the water passed above his waist. 'See. Come, come.'

He ferried children to shallower water, but after the third journey he halted at knee depth, looking up the beach, beyond his stumbling cargo, at a police vehicle parked on the scrub and its former occupants who were heading his way. Berzan waded back to the boat. He hurried everyone off: the flailing mother, the submerged child, the half-swimming father. Then he turned on the engine, and when it kicked its heels, screams could be heard inside its wash.

'Wait, wait!' implored Farood.

'The sooner we are in Turkish water, the sooner the coastguard can't touch us.'

Farood looked back at the bobbing heads, floating garments. He thought about using the telescope but decided not to.

THIRTY-TWO

Dikili, Eastern Turkey

It was September, with cooler, shorter days and a breeze most mornings. Red-rumped swallows gathered on telegraph wires. It had been several weeks since Farood and Misha had last met and they were under the café awning looking out on a scene that had enlarged since then. The police were no longer observing groups of ten or twelve people; they were marshalling the crowds now living on the promenade, in the square and in side-street doorways. There were more police as well as private security personnel protecting shop-fronts and shop-behinds. Privately, the two men enjoyed the scene, taking some pride in its creation. They were eating baklava and drinking Turkish coffee behind new sunglasses. Farood's head was shaven and he was growing a beard and sporting a new tracksuit. Misha was in overalls and his longish hair was screwed into a ball on the top of his head. They sat in silence as the police searched two men across the road. They found a knife on one and when it was shown to him, he said, '*Taeam... taeam*' – food. The officer kept the knife and shunted the men down the promenade towards another bench.

Farood tilted his wrist to show Misha his new watch.

'It's fake,' said Misha, smiling.

Farood sniffed then asked, 'Where's your boat been?'

'We've been down the coast, running people to smaller islands. A few trips to a place and we move on.'

Farood spooned the bottom of his coffee. 'That boat of yours—'

'The captain's, you mean.'

'Yeah. It's big. Deep. How do you get people onto the beach?'

'We have a couple of dinghies.' Misha raised his sunglasses. 'We don't drop them in the water.' He pressed a cigarette out.

'Plenty of new boats here,' said Farood.

'Too many. Stupid little boats getting in the way.'

Farood nodded in the direction of Lesbos. 'There's a coastguard circling the island now.'

'Picking people out of the sea?' asked Misha. He stood, lowered his sunglasses. 'We're heading off, Farood. The captain has had enough of watching his back.'

'Where?' asked Farood.

Misha led Farood in the direction of Berzan's boat. 'The captain hasn't decided yet.' Misha stopped, raised his sunglasses and smirked. 'Look around you, brother. People are on the move everywhere. It's like some nature thing and people can't stop themselves. Like the moon is in a one-in-a-thousand-year phase and everyone knows it's time to head off. Like those geese we saw in Iran. And not just Syrians now. Africans, Asians, all migrating. One big flock of people as fast as they can, all moving north, whatever the risk, whatever the cost, and we have tickets to sell them. I've heard that people are willing to give you their wives for a place on a boat. You should come along with us and quit working for Berzan.'

Farood looked at the crowd on the beach. They were not tourists. 'I'll have a think. There is plenty of money to be made here.'

'Berzan. I don't know how you can stand to look at him. I can smell that cellar off him. And my own blood. He still owns you, doesn't he?'

'He thinks he does.'

Farood's reply couldn't take the edge off his shame. They walked to the boat and to some relief Berzan wasn't there.

'Expect he's at the laundry,' said Farood.

'How much you making a day?' asked Misha.

'Nine or ten thousand lira,' said Farood.

'And you get half?'

Farood made a 'round about that' gesture with his hand.

'Are you two living on this boat?' enquired Misha.

'Yeah.'

'You sleep there every night?'

'Yeah.'

'Like being on the road again.'

As they stood on the quay by Berzan's boat a mother tugged at Farood's arm and asked of him in English, 'Please... please... a place on your boat.'

He swept the woman's arm away without looking at her. Two police officers strolled in their direction; Farood and Misha ignored them. The older, more senior-looking officer took a sheet of paper from his breast pocket, held it out in front, looked at the image before him.

Farood told the officer, 'This woman, I don't know her, okay?'

'You're Farood Abdali, right?' said the officer.

Farood shook his head as they took his wrists and handcuffed him. He was led to a parked van and neither he nor Misha asked why. Misha charged out of town on his motorcycle.

Only when Farood arrived at the century-old police station did he begin to protest his innocence. 'Why have you arrested me? I'm just here on holiday.'

'Sure, because Afghans are always coming here on holiday, staying in hotels, buying gifts and drinking beer. We don't know what you've done – we were told to bring you in, so we're hoping you might tell us.'

*

The cell that contained Farood wasn't really a cell; it was an area under the stairs that had been barred off, with standing room in about a third of it. There was no air-conditioning and Farood had been left a bucket in one corner. The two officers went out, came back with food for themselves and a bottle of water for Farood. Flies congregated in his cage for the shade and the stench. He wondered why Misha hadn't followed him down and whether he had told Berzan. Either way, what did he owe Berzan? Not even the last few hours.

'Okay, okay, I'll tell you. I'm taking people over to Greece. I'll tell you all about it.'

The arresting officer moved listlessly down the corridor, holding a chicken sandwich.

Farood lowered his voice. 'I'm helping a man who owns a boat. We take the Syrians to Greece.'

'Really, is that right? You're one of those people traffickers, aren't you? My God.'

Farood continued, 'They pay us for the trouble. And it's not even my boat.'

'And you think that makes it alright, do you?' asked the officer.

'No. The man that owns it, he's from Istanbul. I know where he lives.'

'Okay, so what's his name?'

Farood hesitated. His father would never betray, not even an enemy. It was against his honour.

The officer took a bite from his sandwich and spoke through the food. 'I'll tell you, shall I? If you can't say it yourself. His name is Berzan. Ber... zan.'

'Yeah, that's right,' admitted Farood.

'And he smells worse than the fucking migrants. Isn't that right?'

Farood took a step back from the bars.

The officer swallowed the last of the sandwich. 'You're not here because you're a trafficker who dumps people in the sea. You're here because you are wanted in the UK. But we're wondering what you did over there. You're an Afghan, right?'

Farood bowed his head.

'Are you a rapist?'

Farood withdrew, crouching in the lowest part of the cell.

The officer shouted down the corridor to his colleague. 'He's a rapist! Was she English? I bet she was, wasn't she?'

Soon after they locked up and left him behind. The knowledge, the familiarity of being in a cell had never really left him. A warrant from England. How had they found him? Sabana. She was the one person who could trace him to this town. She would prefer to see him in a cell, so she could feel sorry for him, laugh at him. *Dumb Afghan.* Sitting under some stairs, stinking of urine and disinfectant. She hated his freedom; it frightened her.

On the veranda of a rented house, on a hill above the harbour, Misha had just finished reporting back to the captain.

'Does Berzan know?' asked the captain.

'He wasn't there,' replied Misha.

'Go watch him, see what he does.'

Misha watched Berzan ferry paying passengers to Lesbos, remonstrating with some, offering assistance to others. Maybe he thought Farood had joined the captain's crew. His pride would prevent him from going to find out. Berzan considered he had done his best for the Afghan. The Turkmen was a thief, as all of them were.

At night in the police station a rat ran through a slither of moonlight; the phone rang. In the morning the same two officers arrived with coffee and a pastry for the prisoner who was unlocked from his barred cupboard.

'Showtime, Farood.'

'What's happening, boss?'

'Izmir,' said the officer.

'I want a lawyer.'

'Plenty of lawyers in England.'

Izmir was a long way. All this just for him. He was uncuffed and the motion of the vehicle rocked him into the sleep he had been denied the night before. He dreamed that he was sitting at the back of a room full of people, strangers to him, and that he knew he had been sentenced to hang. Sabana emerges from the crowd, kneels before him. She tells him that his appeal has been unsuccessful. Behind her, in the opposite wall, there is an open window. The crowd part as if to make way. There is nothing stopping him running and diving away. He asks himself where he will go and he doesn't know. There is no home and no friends with homes. He cannot run; he will have to hang.

The rear doors of the van opened; a light surge awoke him.

'Out!' shouted the officer.

Farood stepped out and looked around. There was just the road. Scrub ether side.

The officer grabbed his shoulders and turned him to face the van. 'Go, Afghan, don't come back.'

The van pulled away to reveal a motorbike glimmering in the sun. The rider raised his visor.

'What are you doing here?' asked Farood.

'I was just passing,' said Misha.

Whilst the van headed back down the hill to town, Misha glided his bike higher up the road. Swaying behind him, Farood couldn't feel the engine, couldn't feel the ground beneath the wheels, until they turned onto a track that led to a pale blue house on the summit of the hill. The bike pulled up and two goats bleated.

Inside the captain was watching coffee come to the boil on a stove. 'How are you, Farood?'

'Good, thank you.'

'Tired, I would imagine. You can't sleep in a police station. The only people who sleep there are the police.' He poured Farood a coffee. 'They let you go then, that's good.'

'They were going to send me to the UK. Back to prison. Could I have some water, please?'

Misha obliged with a jug from the fridge.

'Misha insisted I get you released.'

Farood smiled, but the captain didn't.

'How?' asked Farood.

'I told the sergeant that if they didn't release you, we wouldn't take any more migrants away, and neither would anyone else. At first, he laughed at me. But then he changed his mind. Possibly it's the rate they're arriving.'

The captain led them outside. They looked down on the brochure-blue Aegean. He went on, 'But the police don't want you here either. You're going to have to leave. I promised him that. You should come with us. I didn't tell him about that part.'

'Where are you going?'

'It is the "why" that is important, Farood. Some of the people you took to Lesbos drowned. Berzan will drown some more today, no doubt. The coastguard is on the lookout. Hopefully they'll shoot him. We're leaving tomorrow.'

'You're coming, right?' asked Misha.

'Yeah. Sure. But there's something I want to ask Berzan before we go.'

'So, phone him.'

'No. I want to see him.'

The captain sighed and said, 'If the police get either of you, I'm not getting you out a second time.'

*

They went down at dusk. Berzan's boat wasn't in; people were bedding down on the beach.

Misha handed Farood his motorcycle helmet. 'Put it on. If the cops show up, we're straight on the bike. After I left Berzan's cellar I promised myself I'd never be locked up again.'

Eventually the boat came trundling out of the darkness. Farood took a couple of steps to the edge of the quay.

Misha cautioned him, 'Whatever you're going to do, do it on the boat.'

Before the engine was off Farood shouted to Berzan, 'Throw me the rope.'

He held out a hand and smiled, tied off the rope and boarded the boat.

Berzan looked past Farood at Misha and said loudly, 'Be careful of him. The Turkmen is a snake in the grass.'

Misha jumped down on to the boat. 'You need to go home, Berzan.'

Berzan lit a cigarette. 'You're telling me what to do? I made you, Turkmen. Made you both. You need to thank me that you have the balls to do what you're doing. You were like mice when I found you.'

Misha sighed, affected a tone of weariness. 'Berzan, you only teach people about cruelty. It's all you know.' He turned to Farood. 'You wanted to ask him something. Do it and let's get out of here.'

'How did you know I was in prison?' asked Farood.

'What?' replied Berzan.

Farood raised one foot onto a bench seat. 'You said I'd been sent to jail in England. But I never told you that. How did you know that?'

'Someone told me.'

'Who?'

'Khalid,' answered Berzan.

'Khalid? How do you know Khalid?'

Berzan flicked his cigarette overboard. 'I know plenty of people in the UK. People who take people like you. Khalid I've known a long time, since he was in London. He told me about you, nothing special, just how he had stitched you up and we laughed, we both laughed. sounded like a work of art. He said you told him all about me, how you cried when you told the story. He said you spoke to him like he was your fucking mother.'

With which Berzan laughed, until Farood swung Misha's crash helmet down onto the crown of his head, the blood dribbling from his ears and mouth. Misha started the engine and steered the boat out into the darkness.

PART THREE

PART THREE

THIRTY-THREE

Coast of Libya, October 2012

I t had first assumed a place of significance in the seventh century BC when the Greeks arrived.The surrounding province became one of the greatest intellectual and artistic centres of the Greek world, famous for its medical school, its learned academies, its Hellenistic architecture. It even produced a school of thinkers: the Cyrenaics, hedonists who believed that pleasure, especially physical pleasure, is a supreme good in life. The Greeks bequeathed it to the Romans, and the remnants of their villas, their subterranean cisterns and baths were photographed by the few bold tourists who continued to visit, against consular advice. There were pillars and statues, most without faces, reaching back into the desert for miles, some with daises growing at their feet. There were the remains too, of the later Christian era that survived the Cretan earthquake of 365 AD but could not withstand the Muslim conquest of the Maghreb. To the south beyond the desert, are mountains, green in the North African sense of the term.

At the southern end of the town, a group of men and boys were crashing hammers into statues and plinths. Two men with automatic rifles circled them, urging on their work. A boy, sore-shouldered, let his hammer drop to his side for a moment's rest, looked out across the open ground littered with artefacts and sighed. A rifle shot cracked into the sky; the guard shouted at him to get back to work.

Although there was a headland and a jetty, the captain anchored his trawler a quarter of a mile out – he wanted advance warning of anyone approaching. The town was built on trade, beginning two millennia ago with olive oil, wine and slaves. Recently people traffickers had built a squat lighthouse to watch out for naval vessels, or competition. Their destination was Crete, 230 miles north-east. It was where the captain planned to take his cargo, the cargo being a mass of people fleeing behind the government army that was fleeing faster by land and sea. The captain had been informed that the town was in no man's land, and those people who had missed the last government boat were prepared to pay handsomely for someone to take them to Europe's most southern landfall, anywhere at all if it was away from the approaching militias. As soon as the captain and his party were ashore it was clear that their intelligence was wrong, was stupid, in fact. They were questioned by militiamen as soon as they crossed the road, the captain forced to hand over money for anchoring his boat nearby – the caliphate extended into the sea.

The captain, Farood and Misha walked through the streets of the little town, some of ancient stone, some of broken tarmac. On a street corner, a militiaman thrust a Qur'an into Misha's hands. He took it and walked on, shrugging his shoulders.

A few yards on, the captain looked behind and saw that the militiaman was watching them. Without glancing at Misha, he said, 'Turn around and thank him. Graciously.'

Misha walked backwards for half a yard, grinning and bowing.

'That's too much,' said Farood. 'You're not his slave, just yet.'

'You know what, boss,' said Misha quietly, 'we should be packing something ourselves.'

'That would only make me all the more nervous.'

Turning left off the strand they delved into the innards of the town. There were a handful of market stalls on cobbled stone, selling socks, mobile phone cases, pieces of goat. There were parked cars and cars being driven with bullet holes in, you could pass an egg through. There were new ruins to join the ancient ones; there were mothers and children peeping from doorways, but few walked the streets. Black flags fluttered from white apartment blocks built for tourists. A dog, shot multiple times, rotted on the street.

'So where are our migrants?' asked Farood.

'They're here somewhere. The bandits aren't here for the good of their souls alone,' said the captain. 'Anyone thirsty?' he asked.

They passed through three blocks of rolled-down shutters and closed doors. Women, veiled and shrouded, scurried away from them. They found a teashop and sat in the darkness at the back. The owner bowed to them, mistaking them for militia. When he brought the tea, Farood offered him some money but he wouldn't accept.

'I'm going to grow one of those beards, man,' said Misha.

'It will take a bit more than a disguise to fit in.' The captain smiled.

A procession moved past the front of the shop. Leading it was a man no more than twenty, with a gangster roll of a walk, an automatic rifle slung lazily over his shoulder, the backside of his jeans halfway down his backside and a matchstick in his mouth. His beard was long and combed. Behind him staggered people who bore the faces of prisoners more so than migrants. The three came to the door of the shop to observe.

An African man, the soles of his shoes flapping, holding a child above his head, went to the head of the line, to the side of militia homeboy. 'Hey, hey. I want to know, where is my daughter?'

'I don't know who she is.'

'You do, you do. You took her to your boss.'

'Ah yes. They have gone. Gone on ahead,' said the homeboy, pointing out to the sea.

The man carrying the child continued to keep pace with him.

'But how did they pay? They don't have any money – I have their money.'

The father came to a halt as the answer occurred to him. The homeboy left him behind; the captain walked to him and offered him some tea.

'Where have you come from?' asked the captain.

'From Derna, in the east, some way.'

'Do you know where they're taking you?'

'Some camp, they say,' he said, pointing.

They returned inside. Misha smoked, something he had taken up recently, after Lesbos.

'You said farewell to Berzan then?' asked the captain.

Farood folded his hands together. 'It was necessary.'

'And you feel okay about this?' probed the captain.

The other two nodded.

The captain leaned in like a coach in a dressing room. 'Some say killing a man is no big deal. People die all the time, they say, which is true. But killing someone is a responsibility; it sets you apart from other men, not only because most people don't kill. It's a responsibility because nothing changes the world so much as death. Not even a birth. When you kill a man, it changes the world, in ways we cannot comprehend.' He got to his feet. 'Come. Let's follow and go find that camp.'

They walked in the direction of the line, the captain estimating the number of boatloads ahead of him.

Misha asked, 'Is Libyan money any good?'

'We can take it to the government side. American dollars always best, anywhere.'

Farood wondered why everyone had agreed to be herded, why they hadn't paid proper agents and gone their own way.

Along the touchline of the football pitch goats nibbled the grass, then a mass of makeshift bivouacs made of cardboard and plastic sheeting – and men, lying on their backs and their elbows. Women sitting with children in their arms, older children standing and waiting for some event, some conclusion. At each corner flag of the pitch there were soft-top jeeps serving as low-level lookout towers. The procession of fifty or more that walked ahead of them were looking for a space to settle down, the African man with the child in his arms still arguing with his escort.

The captain picked out a senior-looking militiaman from the half dozen surrounding the camp. Before he approached, he ruminated to Misha and Farood. 'I saw a couple of boats at the jetty. And I didn't see any people waiting on the beach. So, what do they want all these people for?'

'Maybe they exchange them for prisoners. Do a swap,' said Misha.

'Does either side here take prisoners? Taliban never took any,' said Farood.

The captain put on his sunglasses and the three walked over to a jeep, slowly, the captain showing the two men leaning against the dusty vehicle his open palms. The taller militiaman raised his head slightly by way of interrogation.

'I have a boat,' said the captain.

'Congratulations. You should go for a sail, it's a nice day.'

Farood took a step forward. 'We've just sailed all the way here. We want to pick up some passengers from you,' he said.

The militiaman levered himself off the jeep, clasped his rifle. 'Then you'll need to buy them from me.'

The captain only had to turn his head towards Misha, enough to prompt him to drag Farood back two steps. Misha's tone was hushed. 'You don't talk for the captain. You should know that.'

Behind the guards, a squabble over water was taking place.

An old couple had some, a younger family didn't. A child was crying and two men had their hands on the same two-litre bottle. Both were shouting.

'You buy each one from us, American dollars,' said the militiaman plainly.

'But how do I know they'll have any money left to pay me?' replied the captain.

'You don't.'

'Why don't I give you a cut of what I take from them instead? There's plenty more from where they came.' He needed a deal.

In the background, the younger man grabbed a knife out from his boot and stabbed the old man. His wife began screaming. The militiaman turned and took a few seconds to read the plot behind him. 'You see that?' he turned to ask Misha.

'That one there, stabbed the old guy.' Misha pointed.

The militiaman nodded in gratitude before walking over and firing two rounds into the chest of the younger man. He returned, examining the knife taken from the corpse. 'So how many do you want?' he asked coolly.

'Fifty,' said the captain.

'You must give me five hundred dollars up front.'

The captain sighed demonstrably. 'Let me think about this, maybe come back tomorrow.'

The militiaman shrugged and spat on the ground.

On the way back to the town, they crossed another escorted procession on its way to the camp. The captain noticed the suitcases, the polish on the shoes under the dust. The three of them stopped and observed the scene like a film unravelling.

'They look like they've just left a hotel. They haven't come far, maybe we should get beyond the reach of the militia.'

'The government side of the war?' asked Misha. 'Isn't it further away, longer to sail to Crete?'

'But we might not have to pay for our own passengers,' was the captain's answer.

When they got back to the tearoom there was a small crowd outside. A group of men gathered around a table. A game of draughts, perhaps, with spectators. Through a gap in the huddle, a grey-haired old man could be seen sobbing, his head heavy with grief. Another man was standing, reading aloud from the Qur'an, beside him another pressed record on his phone, moved to one side, zooming in on the two men pressing down on a forearm above a tourniquet. The old man stood and wept, pulling his son's head into his breast as a cleaver was raised and plunged down. Farood and Misha rapidly walked away, crossing the road; the captain remained. Someone brought a bucket to the table. The man reciting the Qur'an walked off down the street, yelling, 'Allahu Akbar.' The teenage amputee was carried into the tearoom.

It was dusk when the three of them got to the jetty; there were twenty to thirty migrants waiting on the beach under guard, all men.

'You two okay?' asked the captain.

'We should get out of here, boss, we really should,' said Misha.

'We will. But I don't want to be driven out by these savages. Let's see if we can't get a boatload to Crete. Then we should move the hell away from here.'

He rang for the launch to collect them. Farood climbed down from the jetty onto the other side of the beach, made his way to the incoming surf, crouched, and washed his face and arms in the sea.

'I'm going for a walk, I think,' he shouted up.

Misha was incredulous, embarrassed by Farood's behaviour in front of the captain. 'Where? We're not in Paris. This ain't no tourist town, bro.'

'Well, I don't feel so good, and I don't fancy returning to the boat just yet.'

The launch tilted towards the jetty and drifted to a halt.

'Stay away from the teashop,' shouted the captain.

Farood set off along the beach then up onto the strand until the end of the town. He was shivering; the sunset was blood and bone. He closed his eyes and he could still see the boy carried into the tearoom – his stump wrapped in a towel. There was a checkpoint ahead, so he turned left down a side street. The captain had watched the butchery like a tooth was being pulled. *What else must he have seen?* The street he was in had only shadow; he could taste blood in his mouth. He spat. He thought about returning to the beach, bathing in the sea.

His phone rang; it was Misha. 'Farood, come back here, I'll fetch you. We're having a drink, helps clear the mind.'

Farood hung up; his own voice wasn't under his command. He carried on walking. A raptor's wings, black, beat above, sailing in the same direction.

'Hey, mister… Hey, what you doing today?'

The question echoed. A woman's voice, from a rooftop, maybe.

'Hey, hey, up here.'

He spun around, looking upwards – an orange and black scarf drifted down. It passed his eyes and he saw a dark-haired woman leaning from a window. He caught the scarf; he could smell its musk, he wanted to press it to his face.

'Bring it up to me.'

She spoke as though he knew her. A buzzer sounded on a door nearby. He went in, trod slowly up concrete stairs. On a wall beyond a window frame, there was a spray of pockmarks, gouged by gunfire. As he turned for the second flight of stairs, he saw her waiting for him at the top. Her hair was thick, coal black, down to her shoulders; her face was warm and strong, and she had one hand on a door and another on her hip. She wore an orange floral skirt and a purple blouse, and he wondered how she was allowed to dress that way, that maybe he was in a place that the militia did not know about, some kind of a sanctuary.

He took the second flight more slowly, stomping a little, all the time watching her half-smile that broadened when he reached the landing. He presented her scarf to her as a gift. 'Come,' she said, holding the door for him behind her.

They walked down a darkened corridor, his eyes following her shoulders as they ruffled her blouse, the rocking of her hips. He smelled her scent again, walked its path. There was music behind the doors they passed, Arabic and English pop music. They turned right along the black and gold carpet, to a rust-coloured door with dried drip marks. She looked over her shoulder to make sure he was still there. When she opened the door, a man in a black leather jacket rose to his feet. He was bald with a closely cropped beard. He was waved away.

'Have a seat,' she said to him.

He sunk into a wicker armchair. There was shelving with books and CDs, a cactus and a lava lamp changing from green to purple. The light from the ceiling didn't reach the walls, barely made it to the floor. There was a permanent coldness in the room.

'You want a cigarette?' He shook his head. 'What's your name?'

'Farood.'

'You're an Afghan?'

'How did you know?' He presumed an accusation.

'We have a few in town,' she said, sitting down on the bed, her back against the headboard, her shoes kicked off. 'They're very religious. Except when they come here.'

He picked up a magazine, flicked past the photographs of cruise ships, banquets, and dancing.

'Where did you learn your English?' Then she exhaled cigarette smoke, silvering the light.

'England. Where did you learn yours?'

'University. Come and sit next to me. I'm not going to jump on you.'

He dropped the magazine, stood by the bed and waited for her to make room for him. She raised her eyes to him instead. He shuffled himself next to her, with one leg dangling to the side, his hands resting on his other knee, his eyes upon the rug on the floor, the mattress bowed under them.

'Are you tired?' she asked. 'I'm tired. You look tired to me.'

She lowered her head to a pillow beside his lap, her eyes gazing up at him.

'Where's your gun? You don't have a gun.'

'I don't carry it all the time.'

She put a hand on his thigh. He didn't move, but her fingers felt his muscles tense. He wanted to go, but he would not run away. He was a man now, moving people from one part of the world to the other. He stretched out, folded his hands behind his head.

She began to stroke the back of his neck. 'Nothing to be uptight about, is there?' she said quietly.

Her leg overlapped his; her lips came to his. He let her kiss him, half responding, waiting for it to stop, but it didn't. Then her hand reached for his waist; he swung away and stood up, spoke angrily. 'Why have you brought me here, what do you want from me?'

He left the room, closed his eyes and took a breath. He wanted to walk away silently, but she was behind him, reaching for his hand.

'Do you want a shower? You should have a shower.'

'I have to get back, people are waiting for me.' His voice was formal, strange to him.

'There is someone I want you to meet. Someone nearer your age, younger than you.'

'Who is she?'

'The daughter of a friend of mine. She plans to go to England. I wondered if you'd speak to her, tell her what it's like.'

She led him to a door around the corner, knocked softly.

'Salma?' she queried, opening the door. 'This is Farood. He's been to England, a long time. He can tell you all about it.'

The room was smaller than the last, little more than the length of the bed upon which she sat neatly. She was black, like the American soldiers he had seen back home, fourteen, maybe, her hair a small afro. She wore jeans and a black singlet.

The woman with the scarf left; he faltered next to the door. 'She says you want to go to England.'

'Have you been to England?'

He nodded. 'I lived there a long time. It's not how you think it is.'

'How is it?' She was eager, yet respectful.

'It is a hard place. People pretend that they will help you, but they don't.' He let her think on that and added, 'How will you get there?'

'I don't know. I was with my father and brother, but the soldiers brought me here. I need to find my family first.'

As she spoke Farood could hear remnants of youthful optimism. He sat down on the bed next to her. She was a captive there, he knew, from having been one himself. He knew also that she couldn't have been there long, for she hadn't realised yet that she would not be allowed to leave the apartment and would never see England.

'How long have you been here?' he asked.

'Few days,' she said, the words weighted with shame. 'They said I can leave, day after tomorrow.'

'I don't know what I can do for you. I work on a boat, but I don't think we'll be going to England.' He got to his feet.

'It's too soon to go. If you go now, they might be angry with me. You have to say you enjoyed your time with me.'

She took his hand and he sat back down.

'Okay, I'll say I had a good time, if you like.' Then he smiled, moving his mouth in to kiss her. She stiffened a little, leaving her lips tight, but she did not oppose him. He pushed her shoulders down and straddled her. He pulled up her singlet, feeling her elfin breasts in his palms. His forbidding eyes saw a redness about her throat he hadn't noticed before; this momentarily interrupted his strokes. He pulled off her singlet; he laid himself down next to her.

'Can you do something for me?' she asked him softly.

He smiled. 'Course.'

She took a photograph from her jean pocket and showed it to him. 'If you see my father, will you tell him where I am?'

He took the photograph from her – a family of four having dinner. He saw something in it. It was the man and the boy being taken to the camp, outside the teashop, who asked about his daughter. She was there too, with shorter hair, a broad smile.

'This is your father?'

His incredulity gave her hope. 'Yes, why? Have you seen him?'

'I haven't seen him. You all look so happy, that's all I was thinking.'

He lay back and stretched out his arms; she fell inside them.

'It was taken when we were on holiday, in Tunisia. We stayed in a hotel, a man there took it for us.'

'What happened to your mother?'

'She stayed behind.'

He looked at her blankly for a moment then dragged her jeans off her. He entered her roughly, but not violently. Before, in the basement of Berzan's club, when he had raped, it had been so brief an act – an attack on a stranger. Fights in prison had lasted longer. On this occasion, he deferred his climax, but not for long. He slept until his phone rang. He didn't answer it but accepted that he had to return to the boat.

'I have to go; I hope you find your father.'

'Please, may I use your phone? To ring my father?'

Her plea embarrassed him. They would have taken her

phone. He gave her his phone; she turned her back to Farood and waited for a reply.

She shook her head. 'His battery must be dead. He wouldn't have switched it off.'

'I have to go.'

He nodded and left the room. At the main door to the apartment stood the woman who had invited him in and the man in the leather jacket, who held out his hand.

'Twenty dollars.'

'She could be a good friend to you,' said the woman.

THIRTY-FOUR

Libya

I t was almost dark; there were no streetlights outside the
apartment block. He heard a scream, a man shouting in
Arabic, a gunshot from somewhere else. He headed back to
the jetty, the way he had come, up the street, then along the
strand. They would be angry with him. He rang Misha to let
him know to send the launch. There was a new checkpoint. Two
men, one in gangster apparel, another inside a shalwar kameez,
a *pakol* balanced on his head. It reminded him of the gift he had
left home with. They saw Farood approach and stepped apart
but then turned as a moped rattled from the other direction.
They waved it down with torches. Farood was close enough
to see that the passenger riding on the back was a woman, in
jeans and jumper, a scarf around her neck rather than her head.
The taller man under the *pakol* pulled her off by the hair onto
the ground. She got to her feet; he kicked her legs and pointed
her away. The moped snarled on past Farood, who advanced,
undeterred, towards the checkpoint. He had less fear of the
militia than Misha or the captain, the Taliban being part of his
childhood, and being an Afghan would almost make him above
suspicion. He would talk to them, wish them well. Of the two,
the Westerner in jeans would be the more dangerous, for he

would have made his way from Europe to know what it felt like to kill someone.

As he got within twenty yards they shone their torches in his direction.

'*As-salāmu* ʿalaykum,' said one.

'*Wa ʿalaykumu as-salām,*' said Farood, guarding his eyes.

A torch still fixed on him; he was questioned by shadows, in Arabic first. 'Where is your beard, brother?'

He shrugged at this, replying in Pashtu. 'I had to shave it off to get a job.'

'You won't need to do that anymore, make sure you grow it back,' said the Afghan militiaman.

'Okay, boss.'

The torch was switched off; he was in the clear. Heading past them into the gloom, the Afghan militiaman called after him. 'Hey, Pashtun, what's your name?'

Even before Farood could utter his name, some recognition began to surface. 'Farood.'

'And you don't recognise your own brother?'

The militiaman lit up his face with his torch. It was yellowish, severe, but familiar. 'I know you, brother,' he said. 'It's been ten years, but I know you.'

Then he laughed and opened his arms, and Farood realised it wasn't a trap; he entered the welcome embrace of Karam, his older brother, breathing in the scent of him, remembering the forgotten power of his grip, his laughter.

'You were supposed to be a rich man in England by now, and I find you wandering through a battlefield.'

'And I come across you, armed to the teeth. You were supposed to be looking after our mother, what the fuck, Karam?'

'The Most High called me. I was with the Taliban and then I understood the struggle was greater than just our home.'

'Fight them until there is no more, fitnah,' called out the other militiaman.

'Are you here to fight?' probed Karam.

'No, I'm not,' said Farood, not hiding his distaste.

'So why are you here – holiday?'

'I'm working on a boat, taking people to where they want to go.'

'Really? For money?'

Farood heard the launch in the distance and saw the glow of a headlamp close in on the jetty. 'I have to go, Karam, to my boat.'

'There's a curfew, you know,' said the older brother.

'What? On the sea?'

'I have to see to it.'

'Why?' asked Farood. 'It's just a boat.'

Karam bid goodnight to his comrade and followed Farood, who was running ahead, shouting Misha's name.

'Your brother? What the fuck is he doing here?' asked Misha.

'He's in the militia. We haven't seen each other in ten years. I can't believe it.'

Neither did Misha, who was so incredulous that when they got in the launch he wouldn't start it. He believed the coincidence to be part of some scheme. Farood too must be with the militia. An Afghan fanatic all along, or maybe he became one in that English jail.

Karam held out his hand, smiling. 'Karam, pleased to meet you.'

'Misha... You're bringing him aboard the boat?' he asked of Farood.

'Yes!'

The launch kicked into motion.

'The captain's gonna like you even more,' said Misha.

'It's useful to know someone with a rifle.'

'Just as long as he doesn't want to cut some poor bastard's hand off.'

'Misha and me, we were on the road together. All the way

from Baghlan. Now we're agents, like the people who took us. Except we're a bit fucking nicer than they were. You spoke to Mother recently?'

Karam shook his head ruefully. 'She's living with her brother in Khomri,' said Farood, observing his brother's expression. 'You didn't know that?' Karam didn't have to shake his head. 'When did you leave home?'

'Not long after you,' confessed Karam.

'You were supposed to look after her. And your sister. All this time I thought you were at home, caring for them, after our father was killed.'

'All this time, we thought you were working in England. We didn't hear from you, your mother praying every day that you were still alive. I left to avenge our father's murder, to kill infidels. Is this as far as you got?'

'I got to England. And ended up in jail.'

They were sent down to see the captain, who at first glance thought Karam was part of a militia boarding party.

'Boss, you'll never guess who this is.' Farood grinned.

The captain's face remained blank, as if he wondered whether the bearded man in his cabin, with an automatic rifle, was a celebrity jihadist. 'No, Farood, I don't know who he is.'

'This is my brother, Karam.'

Karam put his rifle on the table and reached out his hand. The captain didn't consider the likelihood of this coincidence but saw instead, someone who might be able to help with business. He made everyone some tea while Farood acted as interpreter.

'You're with the militia?'

'I'm the commander of an Afghan brigade.'

'Seasoned fighters.' A compliment Farood passed on with pride.

'You take people to Europe in this boat?' asked the commander.

'That's right.'

Karam held something under consideration for a moment. 'Where to – Italy, Greece?'

'From here to Crete, which is Greece, it's in the EU, so you can go anywhere. All the way to London.'

'You don't have to sneak across the border at night, you can just drop people off there?'

'More or less.'

There passed an exchange between the two brothers, a rehearsal for what was about to be said, though the captain already knew the script.

'Can you take me?' said Farood, translating for Karam.

'Of course I can,' said the captain, 'but not just you. I want to take fifty people from the camp, but when I went there, they wanted five hundred dollars, before I had taken any money for myself.'

Farood and Karam argued in Pashtu, not about money the captain believed, but about Karam's travel plans.

Farood got to his feet; for him the meeting was over. 'He says he can help us at the camp. That we won't have to pay much at all if we agree to take some fighters across to Crete. We'll go with him tomorrow.'

'Good. And what do you think of that, Farood?' enquired the captain.

'I think it's just business. And if we don't take them, someone else will.'

Karam lay on the floor next to his brother's bed, Misha in the bunk above, trying to sleep. Farood and his brother argued through the night.

'You should be heading the other way. Instead you're going to Europe to start a war. Everyone we take on this boat, they're risking their lives on the road to escape war. You want to bring it with you.'

Karam's voice was calmer, having come to terms with his new direction. 'Farood, you must go back to Mother, for both of us. Take the money you make from this work and give some to her and our crazy uncle. I will avenge our father.'

'How many times have you avenged him already? I saw what your people did to someone today, outside a teashop. They cut off his fucking hand. Made me sick to my stomach. You were never going to stay and look after Mother, were you? You just wanted me out of the way before you left.'

'Alright, alright,' shouted Misha in English. 'You know what, at first, I didn't believe he was your brother – now I do. My God.'

Misha lit a cigarette and, in the light of the flame, saw the disapproval in Karam's eyes.

*

In the morning the three went along with the captain back to the camp on the football pitch. Karam spoke with the militiamen in the truck, whose demeanour, the captain noticed, was a lot more cooperative than the day before. Farood relayed Karam's negotiations to Misha and the captain.

'We pay a hundred dollars and we pick the fifty ourselves. Also, we have to take some more militia with us. That's the deal.'

'Thank your brother for me,' said the captain, preferring not to shake hands with Karam himself.

Farood and Misha went through the crowd with carrier bags and moneybags, hawking a passage to a better life. Misha shook his bag in the breeze, remembering his market-stall days in Mazar.

'We are taking people to Greece – do you want to go? Come on now, what will you give for your last journey? How much is too much for freedom?'

He sought out the eyes of younger, single men. When they couldn't speak English, he called over one of the militiamen. 'Tell them they won't need money anymore. They're going to the EU. They will be looked after there. When they land in Greece, there will be people to meet them. It's how it works.'

Misha took cash in any currency, plus watches and necklaces; he even helped women get their rings off. When people had paid, they were directed to the captain, who sat them in rows. Farood saw the black man with the boy, the man who had asked the militia about his daughter, the father of Salma. He wasn't stepping forward to buy a place on the boat, he was sitting on the ground, stroking his son's head and watching others haggle with Misha.

Farood approached him respectfully. 'You want to go to Greece? We're taking passengers.'

Salma's father waved a palm up at Farood.

'You understand me, you speak English?'

The man looked ahead, not up, waiting for Farood's shadow to move away.

'Your son would have a future there.'

The man looked up, shielding his eyes from the sun. 'I have lost my daughter – she's too young to be here alone. I can't leave here until I find her.'

Farood swept a few plastic bottles aside with his foot and sat on the ground beside him. 'You know, I think she is already in Greece.'

'How can you know this?'

'Because we took a black girl across the other day.'

Salma's father bowed his head and seemed to be weeping. As happened before, his boy began to cry. 'No one knows where she is – one man says this, another says that.'

'She was wearing a black singlet, jeans, about this high. Her hair, quite big, like this, no?'

Salma's father showed Farood his face. 'She would not have gone without me. Or her brother.'

'Maybe she thought you had gone without her.'

Her father sobbed now.

Farood placed an arm around his shoulder. 'Look, you don't

322

have to pay. You can go on the boat for free. Come with me.' Farood tried to lift him to his feet.

'You're sure, you're sure it was her?'

'I spoke to her, that's why I remember. Hang on, she told me her name. It was... it was, her name was Salma. Is that right?'

He grabbed at Farood's shirt, pushing his face towards him. 'That's her, that's her. You spoke to her. How was she?'

'She seemed fine; she was okay. You'll see her soon, I think. Wait by that man.'

It was almost a day to Crete. Farood and Karam barely spoke during the journey, Karam occupied in conference with other militiamen. Farood asked himself if he had ever really known his brother, even when he was a child in Baghlan. The captain waited off shore until light began to break, and then Misha and Farood took up to twenty at a time in the launch to a beach. When it was Karam's time, he sat next to his younger brother, who raised his voice above the buzz of the motor.

'I don't understand why you want to do this. Why can't you just join a mosque, become an imam?'

'You think that's enough?' replied Karam. 'They insult the prophet every day. Their television, their music, their sodomy. The way they let their women live. They can change or they can die.'

The launch rushed up onto the Cretan shore. Beyond the shingle, through splinters of orange grey light, they could see landed refugees. Karam hurried out of the launch and didn't look back. Salma's father followed him, Farood passing his son into his arms. He shook Farood's hand, turned and began to wade through the pebbles, looking up at the road above the beach.

THIRTY-FIVE

Libya

They returned before dawn the next day, mooring at the jetty this time.

The captain brought everyone to the galley. 'We get some sleep, then we get some fuel, then we leave this place.'

Farood and Misha had become used to the smell of oil in their cabin but not the headaches. The pipes that ran over the walls, that were either cream or dirt white, coughed even when the ship was anchored and yet the cabin, which Farood considered was the size of a double cell at the prison, was always cold. They sat playing chess on the bottom bunk.

'Mish, you think we made much money today?'

'No. Not enough. That's why we're trying somewhere else. We did a lot better in Greece. You know what, Farood? I don't think we should have made a deal with those fuckers. I know he's your brother, but they're just going to bring a war to wherever they end up. I mean, did he say what he was planning?'

'No.' Farood rested his hand on a knight. 'You know where I was the other night? I was with a girl.'

'I didn't know there were any left alive.'

Farood slid his piece into no man's land. 'When we were in Berzan's cellar, did you ever think, *I'm not going to get out of here?*'

'Once or twice, maybe, but not for long.'

'Same here, and you know why?'

'Because we're soldiers, Farood.'

'Because you were not alone. We had each other's backs. This girl, they've got her, they're using her, and she's all alone out there.'

Misha dropped his head into his hands. 'Don't tell me,' he said, 'you're planning to help her escape? And all because you feel bad about your brother?'

'No, because they'll kill her in the end. Come on, Mish, it'll be easy.'

Misha nudged a pawn and opened up a space for Farood's knight. 'It's not why we're here, bro. We're here to make money. Unless we're being paid to move people, we don't. Nobody looked after us on the road. Not for free.'

Farood leapfrogged his knight onto a square facing Misha's castle. 'Can I borrow your gun?'

'I don't have it, the captain has it,' replied Misha.

'It's under your mattress,' said Farood quietly.

Misha picked up his castle and stamped it back down on the same square. 'You know what, Farood, I reckoned I owed you after Berzan, so I got you on this boat, but I'm not going with you on this one.'

'No?'

'No. You're on your own,' reiterated Misha. He went on, 'The captain will kick my arse off the boat if he finds out you held up a brothel. And if I lose this job, what do I have?' Misha fetched the pistol from under his mattress. He released the clip. 'There's three men in the clip, the captain will know that. If you have to shoot anyone out there, best kill them. They'll cut your fucking head off on TV if you're caught. This is the safety catch, on and off. That's all you need to know.'

A few hours later, Farood crept off the boat, hurrying into the chill of the dawn. Reaching the road, he looked both ways. There was no one in sight, no checkpoint, only sea birds wheeling in the assembling light. To his left in the distance, a funnel of smoke spiralled into the heavens. He turned right and walked west up the strand. On the beach beneath was a body; blood soaked into the sand under the head. Whatever the man had done, he figured he was guilty of the same. A fighter jet appeared in his eyeline, a ubiquitous rumble left in its wake. He turned left down the street where Salma was being kept. So narrow the street, so high the buildings, dawn was struggling to squeeze itself in. He buzzed the door, but there was no answer. He buzzed again, long and angrily.

The woman in charge appeared at the top window, her eyes opening and closing. 'It's early, what do you want?'

'Salma.'

'You need to come back.' Her head pulled away and the window began to come down.

'I'll pay double,' shouted up Farood.

The door buzzed; she was waiting at the top of the stairs like before, but this time she was older. She placed her bulk in front of the entrance door. 'Money first.'

He handed over the money willingly, believing his exit with Salma would now be easier.

She counted it and made way for him. 'Don't you sleep?' she sighed.

'Things on my mind.'

He watched her return to her room before entering Salma's. He woke Salma softly. 'Salma, it's Farood. Get up, get yourself ready, we're leaving.'

She looked up as if he were part of a dream.

He needed her collusion and whispered into her ear, 'Quickly. She won't be expecting it so soon.'

'Can I wash?'

'No time.'

She dressed behind him, facing the wall.

'Get a scarf for your head. Have you got a passport?'

'No, she took it, the manager.'

'The woman?'

He opened the door and checked the corridor. He led Salma out the front door onto the landing, a forefinger across his lips. Then, half silently, 'There's a side street opposite. Hide down there. I'll be right there.'

He wondered about the man in the black leather jacket. It didn't look like he lived there, but he might be in the manager's room. If he was, he would kill him first. One bullet to the head. She would hand over the passport without hesitation. He clicked the safety catch off and on and tucked the gun down the back of his trousers. He rushed her door, went in and closed it behind him.

She was alone, awake and smoking. 'Everything alright, Farood?'

'I want Salma's passport.'

She was on her feet directly but took a moment to reply guardedly. 'I don't have it – I have to hand them over.'

Farood snatched out his gun, shoved her down on the bed, pressed a pillow over her face, speaking calmly down into it. 'A bullet would be quicker, but it will wake the neighbours, so it's going to have to be like this.'

Her arms waved about wildly, her legs kicked and there was a baritone humming from behind the pillow. When her back arched he lifted the pillow. Her eyes were bulbous; she grabbed at his shirt as if he were oxygen itself.

He suspended the pillow above her. 'Passport,' he commanded.

She breathed in heavily. 'Take me with you, I come as well. Please.'

'Only if you give me her passport.'

She waved a finger in the air; he looked over his shoulder

to the wall behind, at a chest of drawers. He dragged her off the bed and from her knees she placed a palm on the middle drawer. He pocketed Salma's passport and took a moment to collect himself before his exit. The woman at his feet was not about to shout the house down. As he stepped over her, she tugged at his ankle; he shook her away and the door swung open and there he was – the man with the black leather jacket stood before him in white underwear. Farood raised his gun. The man stood his ground, just shifting his weight a little. There was a smell off him, vinegary and pungent. He said something in Arabic, a sentence that included a curse. It sounded like an invitation. The man watched Farood take the safety catch off with his thumb; his eyes expanded in disbelief. Farood waited for the man to move out of the way, for a reason not to shoot, but nothing changed, so he shot the man in the chest before pushing his stumbling body down onto its back.

Salma came out from behind a skip in the alley. 'Did you get my passport?'

'I have it. I'll look after it for you. No one will ever own you again. Come with me.'

She held his hand as they ran up the street. A war waggon sped past the junction ahead of them. The sky to the east was stained with smoke. When they got to the boat, Farood was relieved that no one had risen from their bunks. He shushed Salma and led her to his cabin, waking Misha from an anxious sleep.

'Fuck, you brought her *here*?'

'You want me to leave her out there? They'd just take her back or put a bullet in her.'

Farood's words left Salma shaking for a moment.

'The captain ain't going to be pleased, bro,' added Misha.

He jumped down from the top bunk; Salma turned her face away to the wall. He went to urinate; Farood closed the closet door behind him.

He told Salma to sit on his bunk and sat beside her. 'He'll be fine. I've known him for a long time. The captain will be fine. He's a nice man.'

Misha pulled on his clothes. 'Best that you go and tell him, Farood, before he finds out. We have to go and buy some fuel, are you coming?'

'No. Take someone else, I'll stay here, mind the boat.'

Misha laughed at Farood's pretence at loyalty. 'Then you better keep the gun,' he said, and left.

Farood and Salma laid side by side. He only realised he'd been shaking when he stopped. He knew that what he had done was wrong – all of it – the killing and the smuggling. But how else could he return to help his mother and sister? He had been wrongly imprisoned in England, tricked by Khalid and by Sabana. He had escaped and could never go back there, yet he had to repay and protect his family. Karam had left them, long ago; they needed him more than ever. What he had done was also right.

Sleep enclosed him, held him fast. His teeth were clenched, his breathing shallow. He dreamed of his father, sitting in a darkened corner of their hovel home, scowling at him. He was a boy again, his father tossing crusts across the room at him, before lifting himself up with a stick and leaving. He was alone in the shadow of the room, waiting – no one came. Where was his brother, his mother and sister? He went outside – the village was empty; in the distance, for the first time in his life, he could see the sea, swirling like a whirlpool.

The pounding of the engine woke him. He shielded his eyes from the light he had left on, and saw that Salma was gone. The boat was heaving forward. He opened his cabin door and listened; there were voices from the galley. He knew that if she had been put ashore his anger would not be tolerated by the others, that he was little more than a migrant passenger himself. But he was beginning to seethe all the same. He called out her name. Then he opened the galley door and saw her laughing, sitting between Misha and the cook.

'Salma, I told you to stay in the cabin.'

His tone could not dampen the room's cheerfulness. Misha, his arm resting on the back of her chair, admonished him with a smile.

'She was hungry. You rescue someone, but you don't feed them. What kind of hero are you?' And Salma laughed again. 'They are looking after me. Alex is a good cook. If you don't mind what the food tastes like.'

Alex let out an exaggerated laugh and put his arm around Salma from the other side. Farood despised the pretence of her innocence.

'You spoken to the captain yet?' asked Misha. Farood shook his head. 'Well, you should.'

Farood walked round the table, held forth a hand. 'Salma, come back to the cabin, I have some things I need to explain.'

'But I was going to teach Alex how I cook rice.'

Alex put on a serious expression. 'Yeah, man. We've got a cooking lesson here. Go tell the captain what we're up to.'

Farood grabbed Salma by the wrist. As she stood and tried to squeeze past Misha, Alex moved round the table and clutched her other arm. Farood put the flat of his palm into his face and pushed. Alex rocked back and rushed forward. They were head to head.

'Hey, hey!' shouted Salma.

The galley door opened; it was the captain. Farood and Alex stepped away from each other; Salma looked nervously at the man in the doorway.

'Welcome aboard,' said the captain to Salma. 'Best keep out of everyone's way. Misha, go to the wheel room. Farood, come with me.'

The captain's cabin was noisier than Farood's. He had a desk with a laptop and two crud-covered windows. There was a row of books on one of the windowsills. The room smelled of feet and antiperspirant. Beneath his bed was a swollen rucksack.

The captain pushed off his boots and dumped his feet on the table, toes twitching inside his socks. 'Farood, you rescued this girl, brought her on board. You wanted to do a good thing. They were keeping her in some house?'

'They were using her. I'm trying to help her find her father.'

'Good job we've moved on, they would've come after her and cut us to pieces. And you're trying to keep her for yourself, Farood, which is okay, but I don't want a girl on this boat. She's already trouble. We're going over to the government side. They will look after her.'

Salma was standing at the sink in his cabin, gazing at the mirror. 'What did he say?' she asked meekly.

'We're going to the government side. It'll be safer there. You should be careful of that cook, Alex. He seems friendly, but he can switch. Best if you don't leave the cabin.'

THIRTY-SIX

T hey journeyed for another day and a half, close enough
to the coast to view the features – the faces of towns, the
condition of the buildings. Often the plumes of smoke gave
it away. Their course took them past Benghazi into the Gulf of
Sidra. A mile off from Benghazi, the captain could pick out a
tank on fire and a crowd of people on the beaches. At Sirte, he
could see coloured fishing boats lined up on the quay and cargo
ships in the harbour. There were some gutted buildings, but
none burning. There were government soldiers at the harbour,
one with binoculars looking back at him. The captain steered a
course.

When they moored an officer with a pistol drawn boarded
the boat, accompanied by two young privates. They went
through the boat, speaking Arabic, and the captain ordered
Farood to summon Salma to interpret.

'He says it doesn't look like you're doing much fishing.'

'Tell him we've come to take people to safety,' said the
captain.

Salma explained, and the army officer shared a joke with the
other soldiers.

Salma smiled. 'He says you don't look like the Red Cross.'

'You can tell him we rescued you.'

The officer's face toughened; he had Salma explain that he could provide the captain with passengers for his boat.

'He wants us to come with him.'

They crossed a deserted dual carriageway. It was midday and cloudy. They were led down a street of whitewashed apartments and shuttered shops. Everything closed, but not scarred like the last town. New balconies gleamed desolate as show homes. They crossed another main road and before them lay the carcass of a street, a disembowelled bus obstructing its junction. Where the street before was whitened, this was all ash, as if volcanic lava had passed through. Halfway up, a bombed water main had flooded the street. The soldiers splashed onward through the middle; the others clung to the sides. The patter of distant small arms fire could be heard, which had been out of earshot off shore. At the other end of the street, the edge of the scorched ground was oddly abrupt – within yards they were in a park between some young trees dignifying a path. A child's coat was draped over a climbing frame; a pair of sandals waited on a bench. Across the park, a line of palm trees in front of a three-storey building which betrayed the frenetic quality of a hospital.

Farood, Misha and Salma were ordered to wait in the foyer with the two soldiers, the captain to follow the officer down the bustling corridor. The foyer was a procession of men on crutches, levering themselves back and forth, watching the haemorrhaging arrivals wheeled through the front doors. A man was hurriedly scooped out of an ambulance and placed centre stage, the two bloodied ambulance workers jogging back to their impatient vehicle. The man's shirt had been pulled up to his chest, showing a lower torso that was only blood, as if all his lower body had been peeled. Farood's eyes moved to the football shirt and wondered if it was any English team. Nurses plugged lines into his arms. The man was conscious yet silent, repeatedly trying to lift his head and failing.

Misha would not look and pulled at Farood's arm. 'Fuck this, bro. Being an agent in a warzone. I didn't sign up for this. Waste of time.' He hurried outside and started kicking the wall with his heels.

A group of three women medics came into the foyer from behind fire doors, women with headscarves, speaking English, like English people. They ferried the butchered man away.

'Maybe I should offer to help here,' said Salma.

Farood looked at her, annoyed; she read it as disbelief. 'I could clean up or something.'

He shook his head.

'Can I have my passport now?' she asked.

'Later.'

The deeper the army officer and the captain went into the hospital, the greater the density of patients. All rooms, all enclaves, were places for the burned and the mutilated, on beds, stretchers and mats. Opposite an empty room with a blood-soaked floor, the captain and the officer entered a children's ward. Two small boys, five or six years old, shared a bed. One had both eyes bandaged, the other held his hand while they shared a chewy stick. The captain listened to the officer consult with a nurse. She pointed out three children; the officer marched into a room next door, quickly counted out some others. In a third room, a room of leg injuries, a senior doctor, in age and status, reached out to shake the captain's hand, who hesitantly gave his.

'How many can you fit on your boat?'

'People like this?' asked the captain.

'Yes, I'm expecting you to take the injured, not the medical staff. '

'Not many.'

A flash of disapproval crossed the doctor's face. 'You will be paid,' he said.

'Maybe thirty,' negotiated the captain.

'How much do you want?'

'A thousand dinar.'

The doctor winced in resignation. 'Very well,' he said. 'The officer will have them taken to your boat and see you are paid. You're taking them to Italy, yes?'

The captain nodded; the officer smiled, understanding he had brokered the deal.

'Doctor, could you explain to the officer here, that the girl I left out front is not travelling with us? Is there a refugee centre somewhere?'

'Try the university.'

The captain and the army officer moved quickly back through the hospital; when the captain reached the entrance, he kept walking, signalling Farood and Misha to follow him. When Salma began to hurry after them, the officer held her back.

'Farooood!' Her cry did not turn his head.

He walked back to the boat with Misha and the captain, the captain putting them in the picture. 'We're taking the sick to Italy. Not so much the sick as the maimed. Children as well.'

'How much they paying us, boss?' asked Farood.

'Not enough, I can tell you.'

'Boss,' said Misha. 'If we're bringing injured people, no one in Italy will give us any trouble. We'll be heroes, won't we?'

At which the captain suddenly halted, looked hard at them both, in what they weren't sure was praise or disapproval.

'Boys, when we get back, we clean the boat. When they bring us the half-dead, I want them to see us swabbing the deck and sterilising the galley. We're the Red Cross from now on.'

The patients arrived on the back of an army lorry. The captain and the officer carried them down; the quay became a ward. The officer said in Arabic he would fetch some more and it was understood. The captain touched the officer's sleeve and said in English he wanted his money and was also understood. Alex the cook and Misha began carefully leading and carrying the patients aboard, Misha taking the hand of the small boy who held the hand of the other with both eyes bandaged. With the second lorryload the officer brought along an English nurse, who paraphrased the officer's remarks.

'He says to take them to a harbour, not to put them on some beach from the dinghy. And he wants the children below, not on the deck overnight.'

'Does he? Ask him if wants to come with me,' said the captain politely.

Farood had been assigned to clean below decks. He had finished the galley which, like everywhere else, smelled of engine oil, but also vegetable oil, and was mopping around the narrow passage outside the captain's cabin, when, without much forethought, he tried the door handle and found it open. He went in, not to clean but to go through the side pockets of the rucksack under the captain's bed. In each pocket, there were rolls of notes in different currencies: euros, US dollars, Libyan dinar, Turkish lira. He took it all – the US dollars and the euros in each shoe, the rest in his pockets – then he went up top.

'Finished cleaning down below, boss. What do you want me to do now?'

'I want you to go back to the hospital in the lorry and make sure they don't bring back more than another ten. If he thinks I won't leave sick children behind, he's wrong.'

Farood jumped in the front passenger seat next to the nurse, smiled and asked her, 'A friend of mine, a girl, was at the hospital this morning, and the soldiers sent her away. She wasn't sick.'

'To the university, probably, behind the hospital.'

*

The horizon was leaden. He could smell the fuel, feel it in his eyes even when he looked at the ground. He went to the university's main hall. It was like so many halls he had lived in himself, from

Pakistan to Paris; a terminal, a place where people's lives had been delayed, with no clues given for departure. There were several hundred in the main hall; Farood took to the stage, and although he did not notice Salma, she made her way to the front.

'What are you doing here?' she asked.

He sat down, legs off the edge of the stage, and lifted her up beside him. 'I've come to give you this.' He presented her passport to her.

For a moment, she expected him to leave.

'There is a bad fire outside,' he said, merely for the sake of conversation.

'The soldiers are saying the rebels have set fire to an oil field.'

'Then they can't be far.' He was unsure of what to suggest.

'They're saying that a French ship is on its way here, from Benghazi – maybe we could get on it,' she said, like a proposal.

When the lorry returned to the boat with the last patients and no Farood, Misha questioned the nurse.

'He has gone to find the girl from this morning. At the university,' she said, waving her hand behind herself.

The captain shouted to his crew, 'We're not waiting for him,' before shaking his head at Misha, as if to say, 'You did everything you could.'

THIRTY-SEVEN

Baghlan Province, 2013

It was a meal for five, but they had neither the pans nor the bowls to feed that many. Farood had given his mother five thousand Afghanis and promised there would be more, but she was not about to waste it on pots when there hadn't always been food to put in them. This was her brother's house near Pol-e-Khomri. She had taken Yashfa there after Karam had left to join the Taliban. Her brother had been a coalminer since Soviet times. The Russians had dug the mine, built the houses and the shower block. After they were driven out, the mine collapsed, the showers became a dribble and the empty houses were plundered for their breeze blocks. Her brother came home one day to find part of one of his walls had been scavenged. He had patched it with mud bricks but was wary of leaning against it. The uncle threw the remaining handful of coal grit onto the fire, which flickered rather than burned. He was a man without teeth and his skin was grey like a wolf's. They were eating steamed dumplings, filled with garlic and chives, in a lentil gravy. Farood and Salma shared a bowl, as did Yashfa and her mother.

Farood and Salma had been in Baghlan province for the past ten days. They had driven in from Pakistan, having flown there from Italy, where they'd spent December in a refugee camp in the Sicilian port of Catania. When Farood asked to be released to go to Pakistan, the authorities were confused but eventually agreed. Before they left, Farood bought a ring off another refugee, a little large for Salma's finger. He told her it was a gift; he told his mother they were married. Salma resisted the burka and often even the headscarf. The uncle glowered through the dark at her, occasionally cursing, occasionally lowering his eyes to his bowl. Farood was tired of berating the old man.

'Leave her alone,' he sighed.

It was January; there was a dusting of soft snow but no drifts or ice. A goat came into the house, scratching its head on the bricks near the fire. They sat on blankets, laid upon a mat, which was laid upon concrete. It had been ten years since her son had left in an agent's car; when she saw him, she sang and then they all prayed, facing the raging winter sun.

'She is a bad influence on Yashfa,' said the uncle before spitting into the fire. 'This African you have married—'

'Yashfa likes her. She can be a friend to her. They're close in age,' replied Farood.

The uncle had seen Yashfa stroking Salma's hair and had struck her for it. Salma believed they were talking about her all the time.

'Farood, can you ask your mother if I can cook a meal tomorrow? If you give me some money, I'll go to the market with Yashfa.'

He nodded. 'Make sure you cover yourself.'

'When are we leaving?' she asked, as she did each day. The reply troubled her.

'I'm going to see someone about some work.'

'You said we were leaving, leaving in a day or two.' She slapped her hand on her knee.

'I have to get some more money. I know an easy way. It won't take long.'

Salma began to shout – the goat fled the house. 'You lied to me, lied to me again. I'm sick of your lying!'

The uncle pointed his finger at Farood and gave him some advice in a steady voice. 'You need to beat this wife, every day for now. Someone will cut off her nose if she carries on like this.'

*

It wasn't hard to find an agent, someone for whom people sold all that they had to get away. Mobile phones had spawned the profession, and after a few conversations he was speaking to the man who had come to his cave ten years ago.

'You've come back? Why?'

'To visit my mother. To show her my wife.'

'You got to Europe?'

'I got to England. I did well. I've got a place back there and everything. I rang you because I wanted to thank you.'

The agent wanted to hear more; he asked to meet. 'Farood, do you have a car here?'

'Of course.'

'I have to go to Kokan today. Can you meet me on the main road, at the turn-off?'

Farood drove north through the town and out the other side, past the scorched tarmac of a roadside bomb, to where the valley widened with low, mushroom-cap hills to the east and yellow grasslands to the west. The agent was wearing an oversized bodywarmer, leaning against his 4x4. In the front passenger seat sat an older, poorer man. Farood remembered the agent, the Tajik who promised much for all his family's sheep. He had filled out since then and there was some greyness in his hair. Farood put on his broadest smile; they shook hands.

'How is your mother, Farood? I remember her.'

'She's okay. She's living with her brother now. I was able to come back and give her some money, thanks to you.'

'Tell me about your life in England. What are you working at?'

'I have a burger place. I started out working there as a kid, and now I run it.'

'What about the journey? Did the agents treat you well?'

'Fine. It was hard – I was so young. But people looked after me.'

Farood was the grateful veteran, philosophical about his past trials, successful in his mission – like a general returning triumphant from a campaign at the far reaches of an empire.

'Farood, I have a request of you. I'm going to talk to some men in Kokan. They're thinking of making the trip, but they're not sure. Would you talk to them for me?'

'Sure.'

They drove into a village of irrigation ditches, faded grass, cherry orchards and barefoot children. Four men were waiting, stamping out the chill on faded scrub beside a bridge.

The agent took off his dark glasses. 'Some of you are not sure you want to leave here. Your families have run out of land to share, of sheep to pass on. You can see how you will live and die here, but still you are not sure whether you want to leave or not. I have brought someone to talk to you – if you don't believe me, listen to *him*. He has been to where I am offering to send you. Farood took the highway, the London Road, all the way. He has come back to tell the story, to look after his mother with the money he has made in England. He made something of himself there. I'll let him tell you.'

Farood stepped forward and shook the agent's hand. Then he spread his arms, presenting his largesse. 'These days I live in England but have come back to visit my family, to give them the money I made. I went across many countries – it took me a few years, I met a lot of people, but I was in good hands. I was never hungry. I was hungrier here than I was on the road. When I got to England, someone gave me a place to live, a place at school, work. I am married now, running a business. I have this.' Farood held up his passport.

The agent stepped forward. 'Those of you who want to make the journey, be here, Friday, first thing, with your money. This will be your driver to Kabul.'

The older, poorer man bowed.

Salma and Yashfa set out along the track from the mine to the highway. They walked slowly, behind burkas, the world partitioned. For Salma it felt she like she was undertaking a test, taking part in a game that would end at the destination, with the removal of the hood. At the top of the track, by the junction with the highway, a concealed woman sat begging. Salma stopped, tried to construct an image of her, but Yashfa pulled her away. They walked down the side of the highway towards the oncoming traffic for a mile and a half. It was a day when it would scarcely get light, it was as the hour before dusk, all day. Men walked the market in shawls, stalls were lit by lamps, the light intensifying rose-red pomegranates. Salma gazed through her burka at birds in cages and the ancient-looking men selling them. Everyone, she felt, looked older in Afghanistan. Everyone, that is, whose faces she could see.

She had planned a rice dish with apricots, almonds and turmeric. They got to a spice stall with pyramids of coloured powders and seeds. Salma could see pine nuts, chickpeas and dried fruits she couldn't quite make out. She pulled up her burka and stooped to smell the turmeric, paprika, the cardamom. She breathed in, remembering her mother's kitchen in Benghazi. She stood up straight in the aisle, rubbed her face and looked around her. A crate of parsley, a cart full of melons and another of pumpkins of astonishing size. A breeze crept down the aisle; she closed her eyes to feel it on her face and thought about freeing her hair. She heard Yashfa say a few anxious words, then she felt a blow to the back of her head. She turned to face the market trader, smelling of hashish and stale clothes. He waved her away from his stall.

Salma told Farood about this, but he only admonished her.

'It's not safe here, for a woman. I don't like it – I can't live here,' she remonstrated.

'We won't have to live here; we're just staying here a little while longer.'

She had bought enough for a meal, but not the one she wanted to cook. While they were still eating in small mouthfuls, a man came to the door. A man with sharp features, accentuated by a stoop. His hair, his close-cropped beard, was not yet entirely grey, but that was soon to come. His eyes were humble, his skin dyed by coal, for he was a working miner. Despite the hardness of his life, his voice was soft as he spoke to the uncle outside. Farood had greeted the man, and as money was handed over to the uncle, he asked its value. Farood spoke to his mother, who spoke to her daughter patiently. Salma tried to decipher the conversation.

'Farood, what is everyone talking about? Who's that man?'

'Yashfa is going to marry him,' he said, leaving the house for the twilight.

Salma was on her feet and shouting after him, pointing at the visitor. '*Him*? She is too young to marry anyone. And he… he is like your father.'

'His wife died and his sons have gone. He needs someone. He can't be on his own.'

'And he has paid for her. This is disgusting. Give me my passport. Do you hear me!'

Farood ignored her; he walked off up the track to the highway to phone the agent he had met that morning. 'I have some more people who want to meet you. Want to make the journey.'

'Where are they?'

'Near my uncle's. I'd have to show you. I've known them years. Two brothers.'

'Can't it wait till tomorrow? It's almost dark.'

'They work all the way in Doshi; I'm on the main road south out of Pol-e. I'll wait for you here.'

Farood ended the call. *Will he come?* He had left his audience smiling and hungry that morning. Now he had new passengers for the agent.

He took his time, but eventually the headlights flashed and the 4x4 slowed to one side.

'So, tell me about these men?'

Farood paused before he began, wondering how to describe his old friends. 'Two brothers. Their uncles have put up the money. One I know, used to work in the mine, the other I don't know.' Farood climbed in beside him.

'Which way?'

'Down the track.' Farood pointed. 'Who is your driver to Kabul?' he asked.

'Abdi. You met him. He's sound. He only works for me. Which way now?'

Farood directed him to the left, to the deserted houses away from his uncle's. The furthest one, with no lights burning inside. They pulled up.

'Are you sure they're there?' asked the agent.

'Sure.'

Farood followed behind the agent as he approached the door. Just as the agent was about to knock, Farood reached inside his jacket pocket for his handgun. There was none of the hesitation of before.

Salma shuddered and squeezed Yashfa's hand when she heard the single gunshot. They both held their breaths for a moment and returned to the rhythm of Yashfa's sobbing, and the stroke of Salma's thumb across her palm. Like partly lit by embers, the uncle's eyes were locked upon the two.

THIRTY-EIGHT

The next morning Farood took Salma to Pol-e with him. He needed to get the agent's phone unblocked and he wanted words with her.

'It will not be so hard for Yashfa to marry him. She has no need to be frightened and you are making it worse, not better.'

'She's not old enough to be married and neither am I.'

She was more self-confident than he thought. Farood's tone tried to make the match sound reasonable. 'It is the way here. Look, nothing will happen. He won't touch her for a long time.'

'How do you know?'

'I just know.'

When the phone had been unblocked, he scrolled through the contacts and found Abdi, the agent's driver to Kabul. Then he rang him from his own mobile, asking for a meeting.

Abdi was standing by a green Skoda. Salma watched him deferentially shake Farood's hand.

'There's been a change of plan,' announced Farood. 'The agent has asked me to be there for him in Kokan – make sure it goes okay and take payment for him. He has to be somewhere else.'

'Where?'

'He has gone to Mazar, for a meeting. Have you heard about agents from Mazar working down here?'

Abdi shook his head defensively.

'Well, they are, and it could get nasty. See you tomorrow.'

It was a given that Farood was lying, but it was customary that Abdi played along.

On the way back to his uncle's, Salma asked, 'This village where the people are leaving...'

'Kokan.'

'Where is it?'

'To the north, why?'

'Why are they leaving? Is there war there?'

'No. But the land is not great, so it can't support everyone.'

He looked at her again in anticipation of another question, in search of her purpose, but none came.

It was still dark when Farood left for Kokan the following morning. He rehearsed his lines in the car, telling each man to put his phone number in theirs. Abdi would be paid when the next agent in Kabul sent him a photograph of the three men at his house.

Salma woke Yashfa with tea and flatbread, saying, 'Today – market, market.'

The uncle went to scavenge coal and returned with a half-full bag, talking angrily to himself and the girls. Mother offered them some fresh goat's milk, but Salma held Yashfa by the hand, saying, 'Come, market... market, Pol-e.'

At this, the uncle waved his arms across himself like a line judge and began to shout, his voice hoarse and high, and for the first time Yashfa turned and screamed at him from behind her burka. When they got to the top of the track, Salma led them down the highway, in the opposite direction to Pol-e. Yashfa tugged back; Salma crossed her arms like the uncle, shaking her head and shouting, 'Marriage no... no marriage... Come...'

Salma tried to drag Yashfa, but she threw her weight onto her back foot. Salma lifted Yashfa's burka, pressed her face towards hers. Yashfa held her eyes closed for a moment or two. When they opened, Salma's widened.

'Ka bul… Ka bul, Yashfa.'

Salma smiled, almost laughed, at the prospect. Yashfa switched her stare to one side. Salma read the fear in her eyes and took her hand, gently leading her down the road. After a few kilometres they stopped at a bend, Salma taking Yashfa to sit on a boulder at the bottom of the rockface. Salma watched the cars come and go for an hour. They slowed before the bend and she looked out for a dark green shape, low and box-like. A green vehicle approached, putting her on tiptoes, squinting, but the car was too high, the colour too washed out. Yashfa was crying. Salma wanted to tell her the plan, but even if there was an interpreter to hand, there was no plan, other than escape. She went over to her, lifted her burka, held her cheeks this time. Then Salma folded the burka down over her shoulders and stroked Yashfa's hair. A breeze off the rocks raised some matted strands.

Finally, it came. Salma saw the car she was looking for, the green Skoda, Abdi's car, Farood's driver. She set herself as a statue, standing in the road, looking straight down the tarmac as it closed upon her. A hundred and fifty yards away it slowed but didn't stop. She waved her headscarf above her head. A lorry's horn burst behind her; Abdi thumped his three times. *What is she doing? She is mad, drive round her.* Salma widened her stance and closed her eyes; she heard the tyres howl as they gripped the road and she heard a car door slam. Abdi stood before her, dumbfounded.

She took off her ring, shook it in front of him. 'Kabul?'

He took the ring, tossed it in his palm. Its weight was worth the ride. He gave the merest of nods before Salma fetched Yashfa and stood her before him. He walked round to the back of his car and opened the boot. Salma pushed Yashfa into the edge of the backseat and climbed into the boot. She lay on her back and prayed. The acceleration and the bend's pull forced her forward, lodging her up against the backseats. She tried to push herself away, but even when gravity swung her way, she could not. After a few minutes, less than a few miles, the car stopped hard, pushing her face into the roof.

Farood had been going through the agent's phone, ringing contacts all the way to London, the agent conveniently having put the city as the contact's surname. He explained how he was now running the route and would want a photograph of all travellers having arrived safely at each stop before money was transferred. If there were any complaints of mistreatment, couriers would be replaced. A few more carloads would provide enough money to buy his mother a house outright. His uncle would probably want to stay where he was. He was about to go to Pol-e, to bank the cash, fill the boot with food, when the green Skoda came jogging down the track. Abdi was at the wheel, but in the front passenger seat was the man who had paid for Yashfa with a rifle across his lap. Salma and Yashfa were in the backseat alongside his uncle.

'This whore you brought back – she was stealing my bride. You will have to punish her or I will,' said the old miner.

Farood stooped into the rear of the car and tugged at Salma. She swung out at him; he saw a weeping wound below one eye. He lifted his sister's burka – she hadn't been beaten, but she was crying.

'He beat Salma, badly.'

The uncle and the miner were in conversation about the price paid for Yashfa when Farood pushed his pistol into the back of the miner's head, reaching around for the rifle. Farood pushed his pistol hard against his skull, marching the miner up the track. He slipped the pistol down his waist and crashed the rifle butt into the back of the miner's head. The miner fell to his knees; Farood walked around him like a warrior walks around the wounded on a battlefield. The miner peered up at him; his eyes were meek. He held the back of his head with both hands, preparing himself to be returned to God.

Farood looked down on him as a butcher looks down upon livestock. Then he threw a roll of notes in his face. 'You're not marrying Yashfa, do you hear? Don't ever come back here.'

He swung the rifle round and offered him the bloodied butt by way of a conclusion. The uncle followed his friend down the track.

*

Farood's mother washed Salma's face and made her some tea. After the evening meal Farood asked Salma to walk with him under the blood-red moon. She leaned on him across the stubble grass behind the house to where the ground became full of tussocks near the river.

'What were you doing?' he asked her.

'Escaping.'

'You're not in a prison.'

She leaned her head in against his upper arm; he pulled away, threw a stone into the river.

'There's no need to take Yashfa now,' he said, dusting his hands. 'She's not marrying him.'

'If it's not him, it will be someone else who wants to buy her. Life here is hopeless for women. There is no school for her; she can't even walk around without a burka. Nothing for us in this country.'

'So where will you take her?'

'To Italy with me. We'll find my father, live with him.'

He sat down on the ground and patted the ground for her to join him. The grass was cold and dewy, but they both knew they must sit until it was talked out. She rested her head on his lap and took his hand, laying his palm on her cheek where she had been punched.

'Are you in charge of the route now? From here to London?'

He nodded. 'I take the money and pass it along.'

'And you could arrange for us to be looked after on the way.' Lifting her head, she raised herself onto her knees. 'You buy your mother a nice house and come and join us.'

They kissed.

The following day Abdi was summoned and told to bring the men from Kokan. Some supplies were bought for them: a little food, jackets and shoes, rucksacks to carry them in, all by way of compensation. The two girls were given phones and introduced to the men, who were told to be sure to look after them along the way. If anything happened to either of them, he would have them both killed, no matter who was to blame. Then he told Salma to look after his sister as Yashfa said goodbye to her mother, who thumped the ground as she wept.

Farood took his mother and uncle to Pol-e; he bought them clothes and bought food and fuel. On the way back Farood talked about buying a house in town; it would happen by the spring. Outside of town, they came across an American army checkpoint. Farood joked with a soldier, asking for some of his gum, which he was given and for which he slapped the soldier's palm, his uncle cursing from the front passenger seat. Farood considered he had kept his word to his family as best he could. He did not have the money as yet, but he had the means to acquire it, then he would be able to buy a house that was better than the one destroyed by a drone ten years before. He had tried to find the money in England and failed, but was succeeding in the business that his brother had sent him to be part of when he was a child. It was his path now and he had a right to be proud of it.

The four miners came for him just before dawn, Yashfa's former groom at the head of the group. They walked along in a line, fitfully, like startled sheep. The uncle was awake for their arrival, lifting a creaking latch on the door. His friend went straight into the door-less bedroom, his rifle pointed towards Farood from waist height. The smell, the heat off the miners woke Farood. He sat up, stretching out his arms in a pretence of waking, reaching for his pistol under the pillow. The miner brought his foot down on Farood's arm; two other miners ran into the room swinging their rifles. He was dragged out into curdling light, his arms held tightly behind his back; he bent forward, facing the ground. His mother awoke and began to scream.

'He has taken my honour,' the miner shouted. 'Your family's too, you know that.'

He placed the end of the rifle barrel at the top of Farood's neck. Farood's mother ran as best she could to throw herself on her son, but her brother grappled her to the ground. Farood looked across at her. He was leaving her again, looking at her for the last time, once more, and she was weeping again. The trigger was pulled; his body jolted forward before rolling to one side.

*

Salma and Yashfa, plus two men from Kokan, had been in Kabul for three days, waiting for someone to take them over the border. They were happy to wait, for the house in Kabul was a joyful place. There were two older women in the house, and Salma and Yashfa played contentedly with their children. It was a detached building with a steel gate surrounding it, leaving a yard at the back and a parking port at the front. It was a bright winter's morning. From behind a window it looked like spring, but outside, in the cold truth, it felt like snow might come.

They were playing *sangchil*: throwing a pebble in the air and picking up another from the ground before catching the first pebble; then picking up two, then three. Yashfa was on a four-pebble throw. She steadied herself, then leaped a little, throwing a white piece of flint up towards the blue; she dipped to her knees and scooped up pebbles with each hand before opening a palm to catch the falling circle of light, but it bounced off her hand onto the ground. The others laughed; Yashfa kicked the stone away. She had switched her burka for a headscarf and would often stand outside alone in the morning with her head bare.

Salma asked one of the Kokan men about Quetta.

'We shouldn't have any trouble,' he said. 'People go through there all the time. It's a normal thing. Iran, they say, is harder.'

The owner of the house watched the four from an upstairs window. He checked his phone again, took another photo from the window and sent it to Farood's number. *This*, he thought, *will be my last year in the business.* There were so many unreliable, unprofessional people muscling in these days.

Snowflakes tumbled onto the window; below Yashfa clapped her hands around them as they fell. She and Salma were in winter coats, the two men under shawls. The owner went outside, smiling. The four gathered round him, anticipating, but it was he who had the question.

'Have you heard from Farood?'

Salma shook her head. 'Have you?'

'No,' he said, still smiling. 'You need to go back and find him. I can't send you on to Quetta without the money. And the next agent will need to be paid too, and the one after that. It won't take long. There's a car going back tomorrow.'

The following morning, they waited at the other side of the building. The driver emerged from a side door of the house, yawning and limping. He unlocked the car for them and then slid the steel gates apart. He drove out, leaving the engine running as he closed the gates behind. Salma looked across to Yashfa while silently opening the back door – the older girl's eyes beckoned. Yashfa glanced away for a moment – when she turned back, Salma was gone. The driver shouted after her and slammed the door. He got back behind the wheel and looked in his wing mirror to see Yashfa running down the street after her.

ACKNOWLEDGEMENTS

During the research for this book I spoke to many people who had made their way to the UK as asylum seekers, refugees or simply as migrants, but all of them through unofficial means. I am grateful to them and hope wherever they are now, they have somewhere they can think of as home. I would like to thank Clive and Eleanor Worley for their feedback on an early draft of the manuscript, and Mary Ellen for editorial work on later drafts.